Humanity
and
Humility

A sequel to
A Grandmother Named Desire

John David

authorHOUSE®

AuthorHouse™ UK
1663 Liberty Drive
Bloomington, IN 47403 USA
www.authorhouse.co.uk
Phone: 0800.197.4150

Published by AuthorHouse 03/23/2015

ISBN: 978-1-5049-3922-5 (sc)
ISBN: 978-1-5049-3923-2 (e)

Dedicated to
Maurice Richard Burwood
6 November 1902 - 19 December 1969

'But all our worries were in vain
We had no need to fret
The "maestro" with complete disdain
Was always there to "vet".'

Save me, O God,
for the waters have come up, even to my neck.
I sink in deep mire where there is no foothold;
I have come into deep waters and the flood sweeps over me.
I have grown weary with crying; my throat is raw;
my eyes have failed from looking so long for my God.
Those who hate me without any cause
are more than the hairs of my head;
Those who would destroy me are mighty;
my enemies accuse me falsely:
must I now give back what I never stole?
Psalm 69

PROLOGUE

The reception officer at the Southside Juvenile Female Detention Centre had good reason to be tired – it was nearly midnight on Friday evening.

As a result she almost welcomed admissions as helping to keep her awake. It was not unusual for girls arrested on Friday nights to be remanded to Southside. Local precincts disliked keeping kids in their cells overnight, especially sixteen year old girls over weekends when there were drunks and worse and much worse to detain while trying to maintain some semblance of order in current days of global religious conflict, relentless alien attacks and encroaching colonisation (correction: that should be 'visitor' attacks and colonisation as all staff had recently been instructed that 'alien' was an offensive word never to be uttered). If local police precincts were unable to bail a girl they would often shunt her over.

The reception officer had even received a warning that this one was coming. A rich brat from the alien (correction: visitor) enclave way to the north of the city – maliciously known as the Quisling Quarter and for judicial purposes technically outside the city, though the brat had been arrested inside the city. This brat's father was one of the big alien (okay so she still thought 'alien' not 'visitor') associate business tycoons, and recent acquirer of an actual 'alien trophy wife', as they were snarkily entitled. The reception officer had no idea whether 'alien trophy wife' was now officially an offensive term but had never heard anyone say 'visitor trophy wife'.

The reception officer was prey to seriously mixed feelings about the Quisling Quarter, and about aliens in general - mixed feelings shared by most Americans. At first the arrival of that gigantic spacecraft *Freedom*, three years earlier, had produced both excitement and terror until the aliens had shown their faces and turned out to look human. Bewilderment and fascination had joined the excitement when it had turned out that all alien girls were small and white-skinned and all alien men big and black-skinned. Even more stunning had been the revelation that all aliens were born female, and that only a select few were medically 'ascended' to men by genetic modification at puberty, but so select that there were eight females for every male and the species were very polygamistic – generally assumed to be why alien girls were marrying human men – mostly wealthy men - and the menace of so-called 'alien trophy wives' began to antagonize human females the world over.

The reception officer was much happier about alien men indulging the hobby that they called 'hunting', because most targets of alien hunters were terrorists or religious fanatics so usually enemies of America. She remembered exhilaration on first hearing about the simultaneous nuking of several 'hostile' bases around the world, but shock when alien soldiers had, minutes later and on live television, ruthlessly gunned down some UN delegates in the middle of a General Assembly with no more comment than that the targets had been identified as 'hostiles'.

The aliens clearly did not intend to stop eliminating anyone they designated as 'hostile'. It was fortunate that America had not acquired that designation - especially now that there were three gigantic alien spaceships orbiting Earth. All three were made of some sparklingly reflective material that made them clearly visible from Earth as often the largest stars in the night sky – 'beacons of light' some called them, but others called them 'death stars', and everybody knew how deadly were the weapons that those stars could unleash on Earth. Besides the tactical nukes they routinely carried aliens had already resorted to attacking 'hostiles' with genetically targeted pandemic germ warfare.

There were constant official assurances that no alien diseases were loose in America, but it was no coincidence that a serial killer recently arrested in Arizona for murdering three white girls had claimed that his victims were aliens trying to infect him with alien diseases. His on-line rantings about aliens, and on-line campaigns by other trolls, had contributed to provoking some authorities into decreeing that 'alien' was an offensive word to be suppressed.

The reception officer understood the authorities' desperation to avoid giving the aliens any offence. She would happily have become a so-called quisling herself – like her cousin who had a good job in the Quisling

Quarter, so while the reception officer feared aliens, she felt no hostility towards aliens.

Except of course for 'alien trophy wives'.

But this was no 'alien trophy wife' - just another rich brat named Tiara Maitland. The officer had never heard of Tiara before, but she had heard of Tiara's billionaire father Edward Maitland. It was strange that the brat had not been lawyered up and immediately bailed, but it was not the reception officer's job to reason why – just to do her job as some spoilt Daddy's girl got a sobering dose of cold reality.

The girl was not quite swaying as she was pushed in, but she was also not looking totally steady. In all fairness, that might not have been down to alcohol. Her very expensive white dress was a mess, and the reception officer studied it with amusement before looking at the face of its occupant.

And got the shock of her life.

———

"Is this a joke?"

The police escort was surprised by the surprise of the reception officer, and still more by the question.

"Fracking well is a joke," the teen whined. "This is my brother playing a joke on me. Or my sister. Taking advantage of Dad honeymooning round gas giants to humiliate me."

Both adults present were provoked with jealousy at the reminder that Edward Maitland, billionaire father of this brat, was at that moment touring the Solar System in an alien spaceship.

"They made you drunk," the policewoman retorted, "and put you in a stolen car with a drunken boyfriend?"

"I'm not drunk," the teen sulked, then brazenly added, "and it was only Tasha's car we took and Carl admitted not telling me there was alcohol in the punch."

As the policewoman remembered, the youth had seemed too paralytic to speak let alone drive, so it remained to be seen whether his admission would continue when coherent words replaced incoherent grunts as his means of communication.

Could the Maitlands really have deliberately fixed it to lock their girl up for the weekend? Possible. Edward Maitland was big in the enclave from whence came the incredibly cheap power on which the whole city was now running, and that was only the beginning of the technological and medical advances anticipated from doing business with aliens. The motor racing world was in turmoil as manufacturers introduced cars powered by alien batteries that would last for years without recharging yet deliver much more power. It was no accident that global energy prices were in free-fall – along with shares in energy companies and the power of oil-rich governments. Meanwhile alien medical treatments were quite literally making the lame walk and the blind see – at a price – not to mention selling more controversial medical procedures like gender change on demand.

But alien weapons technologies provided the steel fist behind the velvet glove of alien technologies – along with their ruthless ongoing deployment by hunters against any human they deemed 'hostile'. Not that the 'hostiles' were getting any less hostile – just more afraid to attack aliens directly – and readier to target everyone else.

"Okay," the reception officer still sounded disconcerted. "So you're not drunk. Just in for a reunion with your sister?"

———

Tiara Maitland was trying to convince herself that she was not *that* drunk.

But it had been seriously dumb to 'borrow' Tasha's car from Tasha's driveway at Tasha's own party. Running some red lights in it to pay Tasha back for that drunken sneer about Tiara only being adopted might have been clever had it only been street cameras recording the prank, but not noticing the police car had been dumb, and it had been seriously dumb to put her foot down when she heard the siren.

Lucky she had only gone through a fence into a flower bed instead of into another car and a shop window, but getting caught this time really sucked. To her credit when Carl had stopped to throw up she had not abandoned him and had been smart enough to warn him to say that he had been driving if he did not want her to mention their previous much nastier crash when Carl really had been driving.

No successful get-away this time, but Tiara naturally assumed that Daddy or Brett would fix it – like her boarding school had fixed both shoplifting 'incidents' before expelling her, and like Daddy had paid a store-owner not to prosecute six months back - without bawling her out any more than when she had been expelled or when he had caught her drunk – but how could a girl go to a real party and be taken seriously if she refused alcohol? Aliens imposed no age limit on alcohol consumption, and Daddy idolised alien customs – as she had once shouted at him, so he was just being hypocritical in telling her not to drink.

Okay, so it was a first being actually charged and fingerprinted and DNA swabbed and all that crap, but Daddy was big in the enclave, and everyone sucked up to aliens even though aliens in this enclave did not slaughter 'hostiles' in surrounding areas like they did elsewhere. Tiara took it as given that 'stuff' would get 'sorted'.

She was more concerned about the warders being so close to hysterics. Why did they keep asking if she had a sister? Why laugh more when told that she only had a half-sister who was not a real sister but an adopted sister and twelve years older and possibly the spiteful bitch who had put her in this dump. Tiara resentfully refused to mention her two new alien stepsisters, though one was due to arrive in the morning. Such intruders did not count in Tiara's world, and she was resentful enough about having to wear such crappy clothes and share a cell. What could the warders find so funny about the girl already in the cell?

"She already has nightmares," was a line that seemed to put her escort in stitches for some freako reason. "That is why she is alone. Another nightmare shouldn't make much difference."

Just you wait, Tiara thought, as a warder opened the cell door. Just wait until I get out of here. Even though 'only adopted' I am still a Maitland.

The first warder stepped into the cell as the second warder pushed Tiara in behind her.

"Corner not a good place to ..." the first warder was saying, before switching suddenly to a panicky – "Oh, crap!"

Next second the first warder was shouting something while the second pushed past Tiara, knocking her forward into the dismal little dump with its double bunk bed, little furniture, and no visible sign of occupation except the slumped figure in the corner.

John David

It was when the warder pulled the slumped figure away from the corner into the light that Tiara nearly went into shock herself, but not at the sight of blood streaming from the wrist of the trembling figure. It was the girl's face that shocked Tiara.

Because it was identical to Tiara's own face.

PART ONE

DOUBLES AND TROUBLES

Now as they went on their way, he entered a certain village, where a woman named Martha welcomed him into her home. She had a sister named Mary, who sat at the Lord's feet and listened to what he was saying. But Martha was distracted by her many tasks; so she came to him and asked, 'Lord, do you not care that my sister has left me to do all the work by myself? Tell her then to help me.' But the Lord answered her, 'Martha, Martha, you are worried and distracted by many things; there is need of only one thing. Mary has chosen the better part, which will not be taken away from her.'
Luke 10.38

For promptitude, vigour, success does he stand
Condemn'd to receive a severe reprimand!
To his foes I could wish a resemblance in fate:
That they, too, may suffer themselves, soon or late,
The injustice they warrant. But vain is my spite,
They cannot *so* suffer *who never do right.*

From 'Of a Ministry pitiful, angry, mean'
By Jane Austen

CHAPTER ONE

<u>*Sixteen years earlier*</u>

Twelve year old Brett Maitland ran furiously up the wide stairs of the Maitland Mansion and along to his sister's bedroom - barely waiting for an invitation before pushing the door open.

Normally Sara would have told her twin off for his abrupt entry, but after the text she had sent him she was only surprised that he had not stormed home sooner. His tardiness had given her the time to shuck her tennis dress and shower and agonize over her outfit to greet a less than welcome new addition to the family.

"They've done it!" was Brett's incredulous opening line. "Tell me it's a joke."

"Oh, it's a joke, all right," Sara bit back. "But they've done it for real. Just as I warned you. Our stepmother has got herself a living dress-up doll without having to risk her lingerie model figure by carrying it for nine months."

Her brother did nothing but stare for several seconds.

"Looking on the bright side," Sara felt impelled to carry on talking in response to his silence. "At least the Witless One might give up on trying to make me dress like Cinderella now she has another mannequin bought and purchased."

Brett snorted derisively – about as close as even his twin sister could ever get him to laughing.

"So," he moaned. "We've got an adopted half-sister. Bet you Astra demanded a blue-eyed blonde."

"Didn't say. But they're calling it Tiara."

"Seriously! God help us."

"God help Tiara. Last week Astra told me that she couldn't remember the last time she read a book!"

———

"You okay?"

Tiara forgot to maintain her carefully nurtured 'sarcastic teen' persona at the duty nurse's solicitations. Not only had Tiara barfed embarrassingly just ten minutes ago, but her freaky intended cellmate was in the next room of the medical office being checked out by a medic who seemed insanely cheerful for that hour.

Must be getting a good fee, Tiara guessed. A remark about needing to find 'something sharper than that' had been as condescending as the rhetoric about 'a really silly little girl'. As if nothing important had been at stake – just a girl's life – 'only a foster kid', Tiara had heard someone say.

That really upset Tiara. She uncharitably interpreted the staff as only caring because an attempted suicide had happened on their watch. Tiara's resentful guess was that none would have really cared if it been Tiara instead of Emily, but they would all have pretended to care just because she was a Maitland.

Yet Tiara Maitland was sufficiently honest with herself to know that she herself would not have cared about any Emily from foster care - were it not for that face!

That face. Crappy nails – worse hair – no rings on ears or fingers – apparently forgotten everything there was to know about make-up or maybe stopped caring – and those eyebrows! But that face!

"You okay?" the nurse repeated her question, looking at Tiara closely.

"Great!" Tiara reacted with not too much of an eye roll. "Lot better than my clone, anyway. Who is she?"

"You don't know?" the nurse sounded disbelieving.

"Never seen her before in my life," Tiara retorted with a shrug. "Except - I …"

She hesitated as the enormity of what she was about to say really sunk in.

"Except – what?"

For just a moment Tiara paused – not exactly their business. On the other hand, Tiara rarely curbed her tongue without extra special reason, and spilling might make Emily someone in their eyes – might motivate the bitches to keep her alive.

"Except," Tiara continued, defaulting to her deepest personal resentments, "that I was 'only adopted' - as Mum always put it - as a baby. No clue about my real parents. Mum hasn't spoken to me in six years, and Dad hardly speaks to me except to shout at me. Why'd they bother to tell me if I had an identical twin?"

———

Sixteen years earlier

Susannah carried her beautiful new baby through the front door of her wonderful new home, and had never been happier in her life.

After everything she had been through – all the misery and despair and loneliness and pain of living with her drug-taking mother until one of Mum's boyfriends raped and beat Susannah so badly that she could never have her own children. Then the lonely and unloved years of foster care, then struggling to survive on her own, yet now she was barely twenty and not only had a lovely home but also a wonderful husband – strong and masterful and caring and mature; and – ultimate icing on the cake – she had a beautiful little baby girl – her own darling little Emily – all hers to love and to care for and adore.

She hurried through to the idyllic little nursery that Matt had fixed up with such devotion, and laid her sleeping bundle of joy down in the perfectly prepared cot, and grabbed for one of Matt's cameras to take the very first pictures of her little angel in the beautiful 'manger' as Matt so romantically had christened it.

Susannah might have got carried away with her snapping had Matt not slipped quietly in behind, and performed his favourite trick of coming up behind and lifting her off the ground and hugging her tight into him.

"My little girl happy?" he whispered into her left ear, "with her very little girl."

Happy did not begin to cover it. Susannah was in seventh heaven, and all thanks to Matt. She did not care that he was nearly old enough to be her father. She justified the fact that he discouraged friendships with other girls her own age by deciding that it only proved his devotion to her and his loneliness at having no family of his own. She had no family either, but they would make a family together, and little Emily was proof of that.

"Yes, Daddy," she whispered gratefully up at her tall husband. Normally she was only supposed to call him that when she was in costume, but saying it now should hint at how she would reward him later. Susannah was in the mood to wear whatever costume he asked of her – catholic schoolgirl, cheerleader, girl-scout – whatever.

Whatever 'Daddy' asked of her.

———

Emily was wallowing in shame and despair as she stared down at her heavily bandaged wrist, while the doctor cheerfully scolded her for causing so much trouble.

The doctor was right. She had been horribly stupid. Why expect to be alone in her cell all night? How often did that happen? Why imagine the edged plastic was sharp enough to cut her wrist properly? Why would Juvie inmates have access to anything sharp enough? How dared she make such a mess of her cell?

'Cleanliness is next to Godliness' was a Ma Galley saying – but the kindly Ma Galley never meant it half as seriously as Emily took it - because Ma Galley never realized how obsessive Emily's Daddy had been about keeping his home in perfect order, nor how much he had drilled Emily into the habit of keeping it clean and tidy.

Maybe the Galleys were right about God punishing sinners – but wrong about such punishment only happening in the afterlife. Emily did not quite believe that God was punishing her for her sins, but nor she did quite disbelieve it. Ma Galley's well-meaning platitude had helped to embed Emily's early obsession with tidiness, and praise for keeping her room so clean and tidy further reinforced an over-eagerness to please which made her hard to love by other foster parents and seriously resented by foster siblings. Daddy never allowed Emily to make any friends before starting school, nor to bring any schoolfriends home to play 'in case they made a mess' nor let her visit their 'dirty' houses – and it was hard to make close friends even at school when they wanted to talk about television programmes that she was not allowed to watch or music that she was not allowed to hear.

She was further handicapped by being much smarter than most kids. Emily was so intelligent a little girl that she both observed and absorbed Mummy's obsessive desire to please Daddy – and Mummy's shame and Daddy's annoyance whenever anything was not done exactly as Daddy liked. Emily quickly learnt to feel all the distress that she saw Mummy feeling, and soon learnt to remind Mummy of things that Mummy was forgetting or doing wrong. Mummy was often forgetful and lacked energy a lot and often fell asleep when she was supposed to be looking after Emily so Emily had to play alone, except that Emily often could not play for worrying whether Mummy would wake up in time to get everything ready before Daddy got home as Daddy got so angry, and Emily was not allowed to watch television or go into the garden without Daddy to protect her so she often just sat beside Mummy and read everything she could get her hands on while waiting for Mummy to wake up. In time Emily learnt when to wake Mummy to get things clean and tidy and ready for when Daddy got home because Emily hated it when Daddy got angry at Mummy, and then Emily learnt to get everything clean before waking Mummy up because that way it was properly clean and Daddy was less likely to get angry.

Something was wrong with Mummy, Emily knew, so Daddy made Mummy drink special energy drink every morning - though Emily thought that Mummy seemed more alert when she forgot to drink it - but Emily got obsessive about helping Mummy stay out of trouble because Emily felt as bad if Daddy got angry with Mummy as when Daddy got angry with Emily - though Daddy only got angry with Emily if Emily did not keep everything clean and tidy or made noise or asked naughty questions – but Emily had no idea what questions were naughty so quickly learnt never to risk any. Her reminders earned Mummy's hugs when Mummy had the energy, which inspired Emily to try to make friends with other children by giving them helpful reminders to do stuff like be tidy and quiet - which the other children usually resented – often bitterly.

In Emily's first year with the Galleys she noticed that a ten year old girl - on a week of what they called 'respite' care – was going to the bathroom after every meal to be sick, then not cleaning the toilet basin very well. Emily was fulsomely praised for telling the Galleys, and ecstatically happy at such praise, and desperately eager for more - but the Galleys kindly decided not to attempt to explain eating disorders to a seven-year old, so Emily was unintentionally encouraged to tell them about what seemed, by her Daddy's standards, to be untidiness or laziness.

The Galleys were tolerant and appreciated her good intentions, but her foster siblings resented her and took every opportunity to humiliate her, and later foster parents usually supported their own progeny against Emily until it sunk in even to Emily that 'telling' was a serious crime and she resorted to merely offering help.

As a result she got accused of being bossy.

Emily became more and more friendless as she spiralled between cringing away from other children and trying too hard to help them - when relaxing and laughing with them could have made all the difference. Now she was cringing at the jocularly scolding words of the doctor and the balefully scolding gaze of the warder. She should have waited until she was released, she scolded herself viciously.

Then gone somewhere remote so that nobody would ever find her body.

––––––

Sixteen years earlier

Brett and Sara Maitland looked on in stony silence as the highly-qualified and expensive new nanny took the crying baby away from the arms of their pouting stepmother, and hurried away to change it. The Witless One seemed to be annoyed at Tiara for crying in her arms.

Sara decided that her father's mid-life crisis had a lot to answer for.

"That's the way, doll," their father reassured his twenty two year old second wife. "Leave her to it, and come to dinner. We've got two other children who are starting to feel neglected."

"We're fine, Dad," Brett retorted immediately. "We're old enough to look after ourselves."

"But we do appreciate it," Sara asserted icily, "when you manage to remember that we also live in this house."

"Never forget that, honey," Edward Maitland declared cheerfully, as his wife gave his obviously resentful daughter a less appreciative glare, "but you can't blame us for wanting to make a fuss of your gorgeous little step-sister. Don't you just want to hug the little beauty?"

"Too old to play with dolls, Daddy," Sara declared – trying unsuccessfully to sound as withering as her late mother. "I'll follow Astra's mature example and leave the joy of changing nappies on my mail order sister to Mary Poppins."

"The nanny will do it better, sweetie," Astra chimed in with her fake-girly voice that made Sara want to vomit. "But when a girl grows out of playing with dollies she usually starts wanting to play with real babies. Just you wait."

"She is right, Sally-girl," Daddy cut in, obtusely insisting on using the nickname which she had once loved but grown out of now that she had achieved the mature dignity of twelve years old. "I saw your face when you looked at little Tiara. All you wanted to do was cuddle her."

Crap – Sara nearly said aloud. Why did Daddy have to pick the most inconvenient time to put on his sensitive spectacles? Most of the time he was so unobservant but then – always just at the wrong moment – he could look at her, know exactly what she was thinking, and embarrass the hell out of her.

She did her best to maintain her dignity – ignored Brett's bemused stare, rolled her eyes impatiently, announced that she was going to change, and stalked out.

Trying not to look humiliated.

———

Tiara was incredulous at being taken back to the same cell.

"We cleaned it up," the warder dismissed. "Count yourself lucky to have a cell all to yourself tonight. Don't expect they'll let Lovelace back yet."

"My twin is called Love-less!" Tiara articulated in disbelief, then worked it out. "Or is that her surname?"

"Surname," the warder responded as if she considered Tiara stupid. "And it's Love*lace*, not Love*less*."

"So if you call her Lovelace you'll call me Maitland, won't you?" Tiara snarked back. "Just another faceless nobody you're locking up and not a real person."

The warder coldly pulled the cell door shut.

"Now you've got it," she said through the hatch. "Sleep tight, Maitland."

"Don't blame me if I try to cut my wrist!" Tiara called mischievously after her, but got no response so settled for rolling her eyes at the unresponsive walls of the cell.

———

Sixteen years earlier

Matthias Lovelace, as he now called himself, walked down to the end of his garden before making the call on his cellphone.

He did not have to wait long to be answered.

"Got the doll home?" an anxious male voice demanded. "No problems?"

"None," Matt confirmed. "Baby loves dolly to bits. Should get great pictures playing with it, bathing it. You'll love them."

"I'll get them all? No charge? I went to town for you big time, you know. Mother was in a coma for a month before they pulled the plug. Lucky the Feds weren't interested in the piglets – not once they identified dead Daddy as a rogue mercenary – well, not really Daddy because he was black - they just wanted to know who put a bomb in his car. Merc died instantly – no family - and Mummy had fake I.D. – probably illegal - and some millionaire wanted to buy a baby girl for his new trophy wife so I fixed it that he never knew there was a twin so spare was going begging. I earned those pics – and – when it's old enough?"

"You'll get your pics – and it one day. That was the deal. I keep my promises."

Matt cut the conversation before the Child Welfare official could say anything more compromising. Matt had not yet decided whether to fulfil his part of the bargain. The man had been essential to getting Matt and Baby accepted as suitable parents for adoption without proper background checks, but the man could hardly complain to the police. The pictures already sent - Baby in age-play costumes - would make the man immediately suspect if anyone found them on a hard drive, and Baby was over eighteen so those pictures were legal even if Baby only looked about fifteen.

But what really made Matt not want to help the man was that the man's tastes revolted him. Matt prided himself that he was not really a paedophile because he was not interested in pre-teen girls. Juliet had been fourteen, was *the defence that Matt proudly proclaimed in the privacy of his conscience, and nobody ever called Romeo a paedophile so it was unfair to call Matt one, whereas the official was what Matt called a <u>real</u> paedophile and Matt was reluctant to give such a man pictures of little Emily – quite apart from the risk if the man was arrested, though a guy in that job should be above suspicion unless very careless, and could surely pass off stuff on his computer as professional research.*

No rush to make a decision, Matt assessed, as he walked back into the house. Time now to make Baby happy with a little attention. Foster kids like Baby were so lonely and desperate for affection that it was easy to fake it enough to groom them – and Susannah had been an easy mark. She was now his property – body and soul, and he was deploying his most refined mixture of kindly indulgence and stern discipline – and drugs - to keep her that way. In time she would burn out, he knew, become too debilitated or raddled and he would have to dispose of her.

But by then he should have Emily groomed to take her place.

———

JassaVar was pulsating with excitement as she stepped off the spacecraft.

It was her first landfall on the new colony planet of Earth with its enormous oceans and unique possession of a native species who not only looked like aliens but were genetically close enough to interbreed. JassaVar was fortunate to be joining her mother DinzaVar to serve as housegirl at the house of DinzaVar's rich new human husband. After five years aboard the Dissociation spacecraft *Anarchy* she yearned to live on a planet again – to enjoy the sheer luxury of breathing free air.

It had been three Earth years since *Freedom* had been the first alien spacecraft to make overt contact with humans, though three childhoods since the first small venture vessel had identified the planet and its uniquely lookalike species, and set up a research base on Earth's moon and begun sending researchers down to study the humans secretly. Now five years of endurance had finally paid off, and JassaVar was going to reside in the household of Mister Edward Maitland.

The price would be changing her name to HumilityGirl, or just Humility – just as JassaVar's mother would be known by her translated

English name of ModestyGirl. 'Girl' was an inexact translation of 'var', since not all human vars were called girls - humans possessed so many alternative words like woman, lady, and lass – but 'girl' was assessed as the closest translation of 'var'.

Edward Maitland was what humans called a billionaire – a level of wealth barely imaginable to aliens aboard any of the three competing colony ships that had made the unprecedentedly long journey to Earth – so it was JassaVar's duty to become Humility. Her mother had taught her daughters to adjust to each new household to take best advantage of all opportunities, so JassaVar needed to start thinking of herself as Humility. She did not mind the name, and knew that her mother had made an extraordinary catch for a housegirl. Maybe DinzaVar would now forgive JassaVar for not qualifying for the choice?

Not that JassaVar had desired to qualify for the choice, having always wanted to pursue the path of motherhood, but she knew that DinzaVar always wanted a daughter to achieve ascension and become a son. DinzaVar had been a lifelong housegirl, never married and with two daughters from two different households from each of which - and others - she had been ejected after clashing with housewives.

For a girl with limited career skills on a colony planet suffering serious economic depression, environmental decline, and limited resources, possession of a son enhanced a mother's breeding value by proving that she could produce high intelligence progeny. JassaVar knew that she had bitterly disappointed her mother by not achieving ascension, and tried hard ever since to be obedient – though her mother ensured that anything less had painful consequences. JassaVar had copied her sister LaskaVar – PatienceGirl in English - by doing all she could to acquire translation skills, and helped out whenever commanded while DinzaVar was establishing a career as a freelance interpreter between *Anarchy*-based companies and Earth businessmen.

That was how her mother had first met Edward Maitland. Such men were prime targets for girls like DinzaVar – reputedly very susceptible to the charms of alien girls, and sometimes inexplicably single even when wealthy.

JassaVar had first seen EdwardYar when DinzaVar invited him back to her room for duvay. JassaVar had assumed that their tiny single room apartment on one of the poorest decks of *Anarchy* would have deterred a human, but DinzaVar explained that imaging poverty appealed to human sentimentality as well as lust, and helped persuade Edward Maitland to make her his regular interpreter not only on *Anarchy* and other alien spaceships but on Earth.

From that platform DinzaVar had ascended to marrying Edward Maitland – more as businesswife than housewife, but JassaVar comprehended that the quaint human tradition of monogamy meant that humans did not make distinctions between types of wife, and her mother had confided how much more vulnerable monogamy made human males – so much easier to control.

'Men command girls, but girls control men,' was the proverb that DinzaVar often quoted, but JassaVar possessed secret fantasies of her own. On the voyage to Earth she had watched many intercepted Earth broadcasts of human dramas – encouraged for girls desiring to learn Earth languages – and been enchanted by the strange Earth concept of romance.

JassaVar knew that her mother was hoping that JassaVar would acquire a wealthy human husband, and had dismissed JassaVar's romance fantasies as nonsensical. JassaVar remembered spending that first night on *Anarchy* waiting in the corridor in case EdwardYar desired a second girl to duvay that night. Humans generally preferred only one girl – but if he had desired a second then JassaVar took it for granted that she needed to be available to keep any rewards in the family.

Only later had her mother firmly pointed out that humans possessed religious-origin prejudices against duvaying both mother and daughter – especially when the daughter was defined by human laws as under-age. Such strange prejudices were linked to their religious-origin tradition of monogamy, so it might have caused offence to offer her body - so JassaVar could have slept on a more comfortable floor - a reminder that, despite looking like aliens, humans were a very different species. Male humans were actually *born* male instead of being born female and becoming male at puberty, and male births were normal for most species on the planet - an evolutionary variant very rare in the galaxy.

JassaVar had kept the room on *Anarchy* occupied while her mother was away acting as EdwardYar's personal translator - living alone since her elder sister LaskaVar had exercised Freedom of Departure to find work on *Freedom*, combining roles of housegirl and assistant gardener in the household of a garden-deck owner while seeking an opening down on Earth. JassaVar did not like garden decks – never forgetting their first night as stowaways on *Anarchy* when the three of them had hidden on a garden deck and been caught and painfully punished.

JassaVar missed her sister. They had not met since LaskaVar had departed the household. Neither could afford to travel between spaceships, and JassaVar was old enough that DinzaVar no longer needed to take JassaVar with her at all times – fortunate as human mothers possessed a disturbing tradition of imprisoning young children in schools instead of taking them to work.

JassaVar was even old enough to have chosen to depart her mother's household if she could support herself, but the prospect scared her, and DinzaVar still dutifully paid rent plus water, power, and oxygen, and when in residence put food on the table – though since JassaVar had failed the choice she had been expected to start earning for herself.

Anarchy possessed a shrinking population and reducing job opportunities, so it had been a struggle to find enough odd jobs to feed herself while DinzaVar was away, and it was also the first time in her life that JassaVar had been separated from her mother for more than a few hours. JassaVar had struggled through by doing dirtier chores of other neighbouring housegirls while they undertook more profitable employment, all in return for food – and she knew that most of those 'jobs' had been given her more as acts of kindness by neighbours than proper employment.

JassaVar had lacked contacts to get her body used to train new ascensions in duvay techniques, and her mother had advised against that until she possessed more experience, but it was hard for so young a var to gain experience when competing against so many older housegirls for the attentions of young yars who came from work to *Anarchy*'s social areas seeking girls to duvay – and JassaVar possessed only one remaining quality dress which she was reluctant to risk around young yars. It was even a struggle to pay door tolls, so when leaving *Anarchy* JassaVar had waited beside closed corridor hatches for other travellers to let her through.

If reports about households of rich humans were correct, a housegirl should enjoy a much better lifestyle – and possess opportunities to meet many human yars who were reputedly very susceptible to the pheromones of alien vars, maybe making it worth risking the one quality dress.

There were risks to living on Earth, as on most colony planets. On Earth hostile tribes were the primary risk – early hostiles mostly coming from aggressively tyrannical sects of a human cult which aliens named the Cult of Submission. The Freedom Consortium had anticipated the threat posed to aliens by such sects and formed early alliances to covertly assist local tribal gangs like the American government in combating them. When adherents of one such sect had attacked and killed aliens on Earth the Freedom Consortium finally unleashed hunters on extermination campaigns against the sects and their supporters. Standard colonisation policy: - do honest business with natives who collaborate, bypass natives who do not collaborate, exterminate natives who oppose.

If nothing else, the more hunting that young alien men enjoyed, the easier they were to control in domestic life. Most young men from all three colony ships eagerly volunteered the traditional one day in eight on hunter teams co-ordinated by the Freedom Consortium to locate and exterminate hostiles. Other young alien men already resided in colonial enclaves and defended them from hostile tribes while also providing sanctuaries for native girls from primitive barbarities practised by those local tribes, but there was no need for sanctuaries and little need for defences in the enclave where the Maitlands lived. It was in a territory possessing the name America, and its native tribes were mostly friendly, so JassaVar possessed more anxiety about the strangeness of her new residence than its dangers.

Her mother had promised that JassaVar would be met, but not said by whom. It was an effort to carry all the bags because she had brought all her mother's remaining possessions – JassaVar's own stock of clothes and personal possessions only took two shoulder bags.

She had devoured every last crumb of food before departing so only carried emergency survival tablets – gambling that there would be food at her new home, though unsure how she would earn it while her mother was still in space.

With an effort, JassaVar managed to pick up all the bags except the one carrying her own clothes as the one she could most risk losing. She had chosen to risk wearing her one remaining quality dress and did not want to risk losing any of her mother's possessions. She was about to follow the other passengers when she heard someone say "Humility", and saw a human approaching. She recognized him as Brett Maitland – her mother's husband's son. He looked different in the flesh – more masculine than JassaVar had expected but still inches shorter than any adult alien man, and not as broad-shouldered – and pale-skinned where all alien men possessed black skin.

JassaVar feared that it would be excessively optimistic to expect both mother and daughter to catch wealthy men, and that humans possessed prejudices against duvaying family connections, so it might be considered improper for her to duvay Brett Maitland. He probably would not be interested in her, though the way he looked at her suggested that her body pleased him. Maybe it was just her last quality dress – though she hoped that Brett was also enjoying her bare legs and shoulders.

She hastened to scold herself with the vanity of that thought. A rich human could surely possess as many girls as he desired and not even notice so young a girl - or if he did, it would surely only be for a single duvay – not that she would be unwilling. He was rich, so might reward generously if he enjoyed her body.

"It is Humility, isn't it?" he repeated with a smile, recalling JassaVar to the moment.

"Yes," JassaVar responded anxiously, and curtsied as per custom. "I am HumilityGirl. Humility. Sir. I hope my body pleases you."

"My name is Brett," he replied with a smile. "Not 'sir'. Technically you are my beautiful stepsister now, so you call me Brett and I call you Humility."

"Yes – Brett," JassaVar responded quickly. "Thank you."

Then paused in momentary consternation, and pulled her translator out of her bag to double-check. Did 'beautiful' really mean what she thought it did?

Nobody had ever called her that before! Success for her last quality dress!

She wished that she could have afforded a proper earpiece translator, like her mother possessed, so that she could have comprehended the full meaning of such human words in real time, and reacted more spontaneously.

If only her memory were less average.

CHAPTER TWO

Tiara Maitland was brusquely woken up by an impatient warder.

Only slowly did Tiara's achy brain register that the warder had called her 'Loveless', and Tiara was positive that the woman had said 'Loveless' not 'Lovelace'.

Screw that. More important that 'Maitland' had not been bailed out already. She knew that Brett was meeting Miss Humble-pie but that should not take forever, and Brett was a corporate lawyer with 'connections', and Tiara had seen many television shows where parents bailed kids out of custody every other week.

If Brett or Sara or Dad did not extract her soon she would get seriously annoyed. Okay so Dad was in space and Sara in another city with a young baby, but where the hell was Brett? It sucked to recall that they had dumped her in a prison before, though her first prison had called itself boarding school. No surprise that boarding school and Juvie had lots in common – starting with the inhuman waking up time and the 'shame' uniforms – though Juvie uniform was even more shaming than school uniform.

Third resemblance was the food. Having a hangover made it easy to refuse the offered pigswill. Instead of eating she surveyed the battlefield - deciding quickly that nobody looked worth talking to, but still irritated that nobody seemed interested in talking to her. Or was it her doppelganger getting cold-shouldered? If not all warders were clued in yet odds on nor were the dreggy horde, which seemed to be flocking much like in boarding school or High School canteens. Individual weaklings huddled alone in corners – barely bold enough to lift heads. Cliques congregated with their respective queens and minions - when not amusing themselves by intimidating weaklings. Okay - more like High School than Boarding School.

At Boarding School the cliques were all fashion plates or athletes or geeks or tomboys. At High School there were also cliques of trouble magnets with face piercings or tattoos or weird fashions. In Juvie obvious trouble magnets were plentiful – one group of which watched her depart for the washrooms - but she ignored them. Such morons were not worth Tiara Maitland's notice.

Which was why she never noticed the group following her.

————

Ten years earlier

Tiara was devastated - second again.

What had she done wrong? The dress Mommy had ordered for her was her cutest yet. Mommy had dyed Tiara's hair blonde again to hide all hint of the darkening hair that so annoyed Mommy, and Tiara had posed and danced and sung her heart out, desperate not to let Mommy down again, but still not won like Mommy had won as a child on the way to becoming a beauty queen! Mommy was so furious!

Tiara felt so bad about letting Mommy down again, and knew there would be no hugs from Mommy that night – just a scolding and having to wear horribly ugly stuff that Mommy called shame-clothes and not even a good night at bedtime like when Tiara was a really good girl and Mommy was really happy.

Maybe Sara would come to say good night. Sara gave Tiara more kisses and cuddles than Mommy now but Sara might be out again with the boyfriend she was always talking about. Tiara wanted a boyfriend to hug and kiss her like Sara's boyfriend hugged and kissed Sara.

Mommy told Tiara to sit in front beside the chauffeur so Mommy could talk to Mr Cecil in the back. Mommy only made Tiara sit in the front when she was mad at Tiara, so Tiara cried quietly all the way to Mr Cecil's house. Mommy had said that if Tiara had only been naturally blonde Tiara would have won.

Tiara was so ashamed to have failed Mommy by not being naturally blonde.

Lecture time.

Emily accepted that she deserved punishment. Taking your punishment, Pa Galley had said, was the best way to admit your faults and begin to make amends – not that the Galleys ever punished any child for anything.

Emily could never forget that people were dead because of her, so maybe it really was God's doing that she was being punished. Was that why the woman interviewing her was the prison chaplain and not some warder? If there was a God, that might explain a lot. Emily would neither protest nor argue - protesting and arguing had never gained Emily anything but more punishment. She was resigned to taking her punishment – like she had taken her last kicking from Sukie's gang.

Luckily the nurse had not checked her ribs. It had been hard to keep from wincing when she moved, but it had worked – nobody had caught her. The punishment for attempting suicide was likely to be bad enough without adding whatever punishment she could expect for being beaten up.

"I see from your child services file," the chaplain began, less harshly than Emily had expected, "that you're an excellent student – on all written work, anyway. Stellar grades - advanced classes – about to skip a grade in High School."

The chaplain paused as if expecting a response, but Emily refused to look up. Emily literally could not imagine that the chaplain might genuinely care about helping her. To Emily adults were just people who told her what to do or told her off - teachers especially. All Emily's life she had been academically excellent due to her exceptional memory and despite negligible parental encouragement. Most teachers were too busy with problematic students who provoked attention or confident students who sought attention and could spare little time to pay personal attention to quiet students who never dared to ask for help or advice. Most foster parents only cared that she kept out of trouble. So it was the rare times when teachers or foster parents told her off for anything that emotionally registered in her memory because only then did most adults emotionally engage her. Casual words of praise for good schoolwork were normal and commonplace but so formulaic that they had long ceased to mean anything to Emily. Such praise was just words – empty words which counted for nothing whenever she got in trouble. All her efforts, neatness, tidiness, grades had never earned a hearing for her defence from anyone - let alone leniency in punishment.

There was something seriously wrong with her, she knew. Nothing less could explain why other kids always disliked her and tormented her, or why she had been kicked out of home after home. Now only strong evidence to the contrary could overcome her prejudiced expectation that everyone must dislike or despise her.

So Emily did not respond. She did not even look up at the chaplain - Sylvia something – as if Emily cared about the name of the latest adult to have Emily skewered helplessly in her gunsights.

"Except for that first term in High School," the woman added in what Emily wrongly assumed to be contempt. "Suspended for fighting. How did that happen?"

'I tried to defend myself' Emily thought, but did not say.

"Were you being bullied?" came an unexpected next line. "Did you think you were defending yourself?"

'I *was* defending myself!' Emily would have protested had not bitter experience taught her that defending herself never earned her anything but more punishment.

"You did much better in your next school," her inquisitor continued – surprisingly making no mention of stolen computers. "Even doing eleventh grade classes instead of tenth grade. On course to graduate a year early – that is really special."

'For a delinquent' was the next line - Emily anticipated.

"For a girl in foster care," came instead. "Quite an achievement! Do you know that you can continue your education in here? I help with the programme – it is regarded as an important part of rehabilitation. If, God forbid, you stay with us, you can get your diploma – even start college level work – do you know that?"

But make herself even more of a target, Emily thought bitterly, if that were possible – and what use was a diploma to a girl with a criminal record?

"Of course, that option would not have been necessary if you had not stolen a car," came the inevitable next line. "Out of the blue: car theft! Though according to the file your boyfriend was driving."

Emily knew that it was no use saying anything. No-one would listen if she did.

"I see no mention of your boyfriend's name," the woman continued. "It says here that you refused to give it. I hope he deserves such a loyal girlfriend – ready to go to Juvie rather than give the police his name."

Emily had heard that line before. She no longer found it funny.

"If you want to get your life back together, Emily, being honest with yourself and everyone is a good place to start."

Emily no longer found that funny, either.

"Your life is far from over, Emily," the chaplain tried again. Was the woman standing in for the prison counsellor that Emily hated being forced to see? Emily had not asked – daring to ask questions was not among her abilities, partly because her Daddy always got annoyed when Emily or Mummy asked questions though Emily had never understood why and Mummy had never explained, just told Emily to be a good girl and *never* annoy Daddy. "You're an intelligent girl. Finish High School with your current G.P.A. and go to college. Stay out of trouble and in time your juvenile record can be sealed. Real opportunities exist for girls like you – more than for most girls in foster care. The sky could be your limit."

Emily did not even bother to roll her eyes at that crass piece of nonsense. Did adults live in another universe? Did they really think her stupid enough to fall for that 'sealed' fraud? What was the point of even listening, let alone talking? Her criminal record would cripple her for life - no escape - and she was guilty of much worse than the crime to which she had pleaded guilty.

"Don't you have any hopes, dreams, or ambitions?" the chaplain persisted irritatingly.

'Not any more' Emily thought, then wondered if she had spoken the thought aloud, but was pleased to decide not. The chaplain would just go back to that fresh start nonsense. She was only surprised that a chaplain had not yet mentioned Jesus. That would have made Emily even more uneasy over her nebulous fears that maybe God was really punishing her.

It was those fears that finally disintegrated Emily's determination to keep silent.

"Please," she begged bitterly. "Please just tell me what you're going to do to me."

The chaplain paused an unnervingly long time before continuing.

"Do to you?" came an eventual response so stupid that Emily almost looked up just so she could roll her eyes. "What do you mean do to you?"

"Punish me," Emily hissed – trying not to break down. "Please just tell me how you're going to punish me!"

————

Ten years earlier

Emily ran out of the house via the side door, and just kept running.

She ran frantically down the street, desperate to escape the horror behind her, taking the route to school by instinct because Emily was in a complete panic.

She found herself approaching the crossing – school was right across the crossing – school where teachers lived. Emily knew no other adults and nowhere else to go, even though she was nervous of the teachers despite easily coming top of the class at all written work.

Emily had recently got in what she thought of as serious trouble at school. To her teacher it had been a minor incident quickly forgotten, but to Emily it had been a traumatic event that still demoralised Emily every time she thought of it: she had been told off for talking in class!!! She had only opened her mouth to helpfully warn other children to stop talking before they got in trouble. Emily hated it when she saw other children get in trouble, empathising with how upset they must feel - even when they showed zero sign of caring. Emily felt the shame that she imagined they must be feeling, but that was nothing to her shame when she was actually told off. That one incident had haunted Emily ever since – making her feel ashamed every time she even saw that teacher, and reluctant to open her mouth anywhere at school.

It had not eased a difficulty in making friends created by her father forbidding her to meet any other children anywhere outside school. Her teachers had begun to worry that there must be something wrong with her because she never talked except to answer direct questions. It ended in one teacher impatiently telling Emily off for not speaking up more – inevitably only making Emily more afraid to speak up.

But now Emily knew nowhere else to go. As her initial panic subsided she did worry that her teachers might tell her off for going to school on Saturday, but it never occurred to her that teachers might not live there, so she was still worrying about angry teachers when she reached the crossing, jumped up and pressed the button like Mummy had told her, and started to run across.

A terrifying screech stopped her just in time before a big red car braked to a halt less than a foot in front of her. Next moment there was an almost equally terrifying crunching sound and the big red car jerked abruptly forward several feet, scaring Emily even more as a terrible thought sprung belatedly into her panicking brain.

She had not waited after pressing the button to check that the cars had stopped – like Mummy had told her.

———

The cubicles in Juvie were even crappier than in High School, Tiara decided as she went to wash her hands.

Several equally crappy-looking girls were hanging around the basins. Tiara ignored such dregs, being too pre-occupied between wondering where her clone was and when Brett would get her released. She only really noticed the dregs when one asked why 'loveless' had forgotten to crawl on the floor like a good little alien.

Alien-baiters, Tiara assumed with irritation. Not only nasty but so behind the times. There had been waves of so-called 'alien-baiting' after the aliens' arrival, and the realization that alien researchers had been secretly coming to Earth for decades had triggered paranoids around in the world into suspecting petite white girls or big black men of being aliens.

In some cultures foreigners matching those descriptions had been attacked in the street – even raped or murdered or both on occasion.

Such attacks multiplied after the aliens launched nuclear strikes and unleashed their hunters, while in America 'alien' had become *the* fashionable insult among teenage schoolgirls. Some school authorities had panicked and tried to suppress such 'alienophobia' by banning use of the word. When Tiara had first arrived in her current High School, a group had tried making fun of her, so she had simply recorded them throwing the world 'alien' at her and got them all suspended – the fascistic bigotry of political correctness had its uses – so her first thought was that this gang of idiots had set themselves up for her like those High School patsies. Tiara was in the mood for trouble - she loved watching adults imitate headless chickens because of her pranks and provocations. But then Tiara realized that the gang must be mistaking her for her doppelganger and that made her genuinely mad.

They were girls, for God's sake. Surely they should have noticed the subtle highlights in her hair, the manicured quality of her nails? Her eyebrows! How could they be so stupid as to mistake her for loveless Emily?

The insult so annoyed her that she failed to grasp the significance of the bit about crawling on the floor - until two of the girls tried to grab her.

Three minutes later warders were calling in all available support to break up a screaming fight which produced several nastily scratched faces, and more serious injuries to a girl who had eventually been forced to the floor and kicked repeatedly.

A girl whom the warders initially assumed to be Emily Lovelace.

———

Ten years earlier

"I found Tiara sobbing away on the stairs to her bedroom," Brett told his twin sister - as excited as when getting his acceptance from Harvard — as if that had been anything other than inevitable. "Astra could not be bothered to speak to her after the pageant — except to say Tiara would have won if she'd been blonde."

"Isn't that Standard Operational Bitch?" Sara retorted with frustration, wanting to go herself to check on Tiara, but not having the time before Mark arrived for her date. "Why get so excited? Tiara is always getting upset about something."

"Tiara also told me," Brett was not dialling down his excitement, "that they did not come straight home from the pageant. They went to Uncle Cecil's house instead."

Okay, now that was really interesting.

"Cecil Duvane?" Sara asked hopefully.

"I'd guess so. Best bit: Tiara had to 'wait in the car like forever' while Mommy went in with Cecil, and when Mommy came out Mommy was smiling again but still just told Tiara to shut up and keep quiet."

Okay, now Sara got why Brett was so excited. Sara had been sure there was someone, just from the way Astra was behaving — although Dad and Brett had noticed nothing due to being typical males incapable of noticing anything without subtitles enabled. If they now had a name?

"I could call Auntie Clarissa," Brett suggested. "She always hated Astra. She could call Macey's and instruct them on my behalf without Dad finding out. I'm sure she'd go for it this time — if we give her an actual name."

"Works for me," Sara agreed. "Just do it."

"We could get rid of Astra at last," Brett added superfluously. "Works for me."

Like a charm, Sara thought. But she could see one problem.

"But what about Tiara?" she asked.

Brett looked blank. Obviously that detail had not occurred to his obtuseness.

"If Astra goes, will she take Tiara?" Sara asked.

"Presumably," Brett pondered thoughtfully. "Tiara is her daughter."

"Adopted only. Do you really think Astra loves Tiara enough to take her? Do you think Astra loves anyone except herself? S.O.B."

"Maybe the kid will get lucky," Brett suggested — but before Sara could berate him for insensitivity he really surprised her with his next words. "Maybe Astra will leave Tiara behind. Of course, it may not come to anything. Astra might not have been doing what we think. Or it might have been a one-off."

"Or he might just be one of her customers."

"Maybe," Brett mused aloud. "Maybe we should take the trouble to talk to Tiara more often. Not a total brat. Not yet. Upset about Mommy neglecting her already. We could wean her away."

"She could be the perfect spy," Sara enthused. "She'll hear or see where Astra is going or who the bitch is seeing, and you know Tiara can remember and rattle off reams of stuff verbatim without trying. Good thinking, Spock. I like it."

───────

Sylvia Godwin was relieved to have finally breached the wall of silence that Emily Lovelace had built around herself.

Not an ideal start for the girl to ask about being punished, but Sylvia knew that she would get nowhere unless they could engage on some level, and Emily was refusing to even look up - a bad sign for any girl and especially for an intelligent girl.

Quite apart from the wrist-cutting, all reports were that the girl had been isolating herself since admission, not eating or sleeping well, having nightmares, and looking thin and twitchy. A girl like her - not charged with a violent crime - would normally have been bailed, but Emily's foster family had disowned her, accusing her of stealing from them – as had a previous foster family - suggesting a pattern. Even worse, Emily had not co-operated beyond simply pleading guilty – basically Emily was a girl that nobody loved or wanted so had been dumped in a secure facility until the court made its decision. Sylvia had not met the girl before, but the official counsellor was on holiday, which was why Sylvia had been requested to dust off her therapist qualifications and read the counsellor's previous reports and Emily's file – neither happy reading.

Yet it was clear that Emily Lovelace was smart. According to school reports on her social services file she was an obsessively good pupil with a remarkable memory but abysmal social skills. Great at written work, terrible at speaking up - shunning all social and community activities. One school had described her as almost living in their library. Possibly sexually abused when young - an early psychiatric report had strongly suggested but the girl refused to admit. But seriously smart, and surely meriting a special effort.

"Do you expect punishment?" Sylvia ventured cautiously, wondering if she would have done better not to wear her collar.

The girl twitched her shoulders in what Sylvia interpreted as a shrug, then shifted position on the chair yet again - with another slight grimace as if moving was painful. Sylvia quickly checked the report – just a slashed wrist, nothing more – maybe the girl had twisted something.

She gave the girl a bit longer to reply, before leaning forward in an attempt to widen the breach in the girl's wall of silence.

"I promise you, Emily," she said gently, "I'm not here to punish you. I'm here to help you."

The face shifted slightly – just enough for the eyes to turn suspiciously up at Sylvia – and the mouth twitched oddly.

"You all say that," a small voice hissed.

Sylvia tried to analyse that while she waited for the girl to amplify.

"We all say what, Emily?" she asked into the silence. "That we're here to help you? Why do you find that hard to believe?"

"Because I'm not stupid," was almost spat back.

"I promise you," Sylvia asserted, hoping that she sounded convincing. "I'm not here to punish or hurt you in any way. I'm here because you hurt yourself – because you tried to kill yourself."

"And you can't have that happening in Southside because it looks bad if any of its denizens commit suicide?"

Denizens? Had a teen actually used that word? Okay, a smart girl and an avid reader, but still! A least the girl was responding, though still stubbornly looking down.

"I don't want you killing yourself - period," Sylvia asserted. "That's why I'm here."

No point in pretending otherwise.

"Reflect badly on you if I do after you lecture me."

"Lecture? Do I sound like I'm lecturing you?"

Emily's eyes finally flicked up, and stayed up – at last – as she responded.

"Lecturing. Talking. Whatever."

Bleak eyes, Sylvia assessed. Eyes without hope.

"Talking," she selected – trying to lock gazes so as to listen to face as well as words. "Just want to understand what you're thinking and feeling."

"You mean whether I'll try to kill myself again?"

At last – an opening to ask a question.

"Will you?" Sylvia kept it simple.

"I apologize for making a mess of the cell," came a far from simple response. "I know I'll be punished for that and I promise not to do that again."

The eyes dropped sharply back down – switching off contact just when Sylvia least wanted it switched off. Did the girl really think they would punish her for that?

"Do you promise not to attempt suicide again?" Sylvia had to ask.

A hint of a shrug. Even a hint of an eye-roll. No verbal response.

"How do you see your future?" Sylvia tilted again.

"Constant punishment," snapped back instantly. "What else?"

"Do wrong you get punished." Clearly the issue of punishment looked large in Emily's mental territory. "I don't deny it."

Standard teenage eye-roll – but there was something familiar about the Emily version – something that Sylvia could not quite put her finger on.

"But," Sylvia pushed on anyway, "by the same token, good behaviour and hard work can earn real rewards."

"Since when?" came a hissed response as Emily's gaze returned to Sylvia's face. "Since when?"

Sylvia nearly said 'Wow!' aloud in reaction.

Okay – no question - Emily Lovelace's emotions were boiling over. Another eye-roll was delivered – and Sylvia was positive that she had seen it before – then Emily's eyes dropped back to her hands – hands that were visibly shaking.

But the girl was, at last, engaging.

"Have we met before?" Sylvia asked casually. "That eye-roll of yours is so very familiar. I know I've seen it somewhere."

Result. The girl looked up again – frowning and suspicious, but still a step in the right direction.

"I don't remember you," came a calmer response – though the hands still shook. "I don't remember seeing you before."

"I know we never talked before," Sylvia continued chattily – hoping to initiate a good old-fashioned girl chat. "But I'm sure I've seen you somewhere before. It'll come to me. Let me know if it comes to you first."

A completely blank response, but at least the eyes stayed up – looking back at Sylvia's face – for the first time like two women would normally look at each other's faces when in conversation. Real interpersonal engagement - essential to get the girl to view Sylvia as a real person - not just a faceless authority figure.

"Rewards can be real," Sylvia upped the ante. "With your grades you can get into a good college. Get a good degree – a great career. Another eye-roll? I've just said some very stupid adult thing proving I'm incapable of understanding what you're going through, haven't I? For my own education, could you tell me what?"

"In case you'd forgotten," came a sarcastic but emotional retort. "I'm a foster kid with a criminal record. What college would admit me even if I could afford to go? What good employer would want to employ me? Who would want to be my friend?"

"Oh, I'm sure plenty of boys would," Sylvia could not help interjecting. "That earns me another eye-roll?"

"Only the wrong sort of boys," Emily declared.

"Wrong sort?"

Yet another eye-roll as the girl leaned forward – at last fully engaged – though she winced a little and put a hand on her ribs as if they hurt.

"Foster girl," the girl declared fervently. "The only guys who want to get to know you are the wrong sort. Nice guys don't want to know - they want girls they can take home to their parents. Guys like that are the only way a foster girl can ever get a family of her own. Long shot, maybe, but a girl could hope. But I'm a convicted criminal now – no-hoper."

"I think you exaggerate," Sylvia replied easily, confident that if they were talking about boys they were really connecting, and that the girl would eventually grow out of her very teenage black-and-white analysis of life – if she only lived long enough to realize the grey realities of human life. "And underestimate many boys. I know for a fact that you're very wrong about colleges and employers too, and forgetting that juvenile records can be sealed so you don't have to declare them to employers."

"Of course I'll have to declare them," came a response almost dripping with teenage disdain for adult stupidity. "What does it matter what the Law says? I have to tell anyone I want to work for, or live with, or even be friends with, that I have a criminal record – if I don't I'll always live in fear of them finding out – and when they do find out they'll never trust me again. I'll always be a convicted criminal. The aliens are right about Laws not being reality. Laws are just words on paper. Just because I'm here doesn't mean I don't know the difference between right and wrong. Whether something is legal or illegal has nothing to do with it being right or wrong."

Okay, Sylvia thought, there is a strong moral core - even if manifesting as stubbornness.

"Is that it?" the girl added impatiently. "I promise not to kill myself today."

Hardly enough.

"What about tomorrow?"

"Can't think that far ahead."

Peremptory. Dismissive. Not good.

"Why not?" Sylvia asked cautiously.

At least the girl looked up before replying, but she also shifted uncomfortably, and Sylvia just knew that there was more hurting Emily than her wrist.

"If I survive today, I'll worry about surviving tomorrow," came a bleak reply. "Like going to school – no point in worrying about tomorrow until you've survived today."

The girl shifted her position again – definitely wincing slightly.

"Is it your back or your ribs that are hurting you?" Sylvia asked on impulse.

Why did that simple question induce such obvious panic on the face of Emily Lovelace?

———

Ten years earlier

Officer Barbara Spade and her partner Bill Cotton had been delegated the job of tracing where the little girl had come from – while traffic officers and EMS staff resolved the mess at the lights.

One car had rammed the back of another hard enough to injure both drivers, although neither looked seriously hurt. At first Barbara had thought that the crying little girl found sitting in the middle of the crossing had been in one of the vehicles, until an eyewitness told them that the kid had caused the accident by running onto the crossing. One girl in big trouble, but not as big as whoever should have been caring for her. There was a school across the road, so maybe that was where the kid had been trying to go, though it was Saturday.

The eyewitness pointed them up a side road along which Barbara carried the little girl hoping to find a searching parent, until a neighbour pointed them to number 227 - commenting that the girl's father had driven off in a hurry ten minutes earlier.

That statement, and the girl's whimpering as they approached 227, set alarm bells ringing in the minds of the two officers. Barbara stayed at the front door while Bill went round the back, and found the back door unlocked.

The strangled corpse of Susannah Lovelace lay on the kitchen floor.

Emily was taken by social workers. Initially they just told her that she could not go back to Mummy any more, and nobody ever got around to actually telling Emily that Mummy was dead – because nobody wanted that job and everybody assumed that somebody else had bitten the bullet and Emily had been too terrified to ask.

She overheard people talking about someone being dead and about an accident. She sort of knew that Mummy was dead – which she knew was something very bad – but that fear had been overlaid by the panicky fear that someone had died in the crash and that Emily was being taken away because she had been naughty. Daddy had often warned her that naughty children could be taken away from their parents when telling her that it was naughty to ask questions or tell things to teachers or other children. That was why Emily had not asked what he did on the computer in his study that neither Emily nor Mummy were allowed near, but Emily did see him once typing in a dozen key strokes which she easily memorized and copied when curiosity made her naughty enough to switch it on while Daddy was out.

Mummy had told Emily how naughty it was when Mummy had caught her looking at Daddy's computer, but then Mummy had looked at the girls on the screen and got scarily upset, and when Daddy had come home ten minutes later Mummy had started screaming and Daddy had grabbed Mummy by the throat.

Emily had seen them in the kitchen – had seen Mummy's distorted face – had run towards the only place where Emily knew anyone.

Emily did not dare ask anything, and nobody asked her anything. They had enough evidence without having to upset her. Or so they kindly thought.

It was two weeks later when arriving at her first foster family – the Galleys – that Emily overheard someone say that Daddy had killed Mummy. She did not dare ask anything in case they said it was her fault for being naughty and switching on Daddy's computer. She also overheard the social worker telling the Galleys that she had been adopted.

The social worker had not realized that Emily would overhear him because they had left Emily in the next room, and he did not give a thought to his supplementary remark that Emily's biological parents had been killed in a car crash. Emily had been so busy puzzling over what 'adopted' meant that she entirely missed the mention of her biological parents, and barely caught the mention of a crash. She was almost sure that she had heard the word 'killed'.

Emily had to look up what 'adopted' meant. She did not dare ask any more in case she was told that the crash which she had caused had killed someone. As long as she did not ask she could hope that she had not heard what she knew that she should not have overheard. She remembered Daddy being very angry once when he had caught her listening to him and Mummy in their bedroom, so she knew that overhearing adults talking was very naughty. Once she understood that she had been adopted, she could not help wondering why her real parents had not wanted her. Her guess was that there must be something wrong with her – a fear already drummed bitterly home in the taunt first thrown at her by schoolgirls who ganged up to sneer at the nasty little know-all who was only a nothing foster-kid.

'Loveless Lovelace –

Always gonna be loveless.'

Everyone knew that Galley kids were foster kids, and few stayed long – many for only a week or two as respite care - so Galley kids rarely made friends outside their own number. Emily could have overcome that social handicap had she not been so expert at annoying other girls. Not only did she routinely offend girl-codes by being top of almost every class, but she kept trying to tell them to be as tidy and quiet and well-behaved as she was herself. Emily was just trying to be helpful because she still got upset when she saw others in trouble, but she earned herself a reputation for being bossy and priggish - not least among foster siblings who reacted with almost unvarying hostility to her anxious efforts to help them.

Emily was not a normal girl, she knew, and other children never let her forget it. Whenever snow fell she ran frequent gauntlets of snowballs, but it never occurred to her to throw any back because her instinct was to assume that others shared her dislike for being pelted with snowballs, so her fear of making enemies by throwing them destroyed an opportunity to make friends by joining in the game.

Instead she learnt to hate snow and fear other children.

Nobody ever talked to Emily about her parents or her adoptive parents. The Galleys were unaware that Emily knew about being adopted and kindly thought that it might upset her if they told her before she was old enough to properly understand. If she had ever asked, they would have done their best to answer her, but she never dared to ask, so they said nothing.

That was why nobody ever told her that Daddy's fingerprints had been matched to a convicted paedophile who had assumed a false identity. Nobody ever told her when he was arrested three years later, and a year after that convicted of strangling his wife along with many other offences – thus finally clearing the way for Emily to be found a permanent home – in very belated theory.

Nor was the crash ever mentioned, and Emily never dared ask about it. Her nebulous fear that she might have caused a fatal accident intensified as she grew older and more able to understand the ramifications - especially when the quietly religious Galleys talked about the importance of admitting guilt and accepting due punishment as atonement for sin. Emily was way too ashamed to mention her fears to them or anyone – instead becoming increasingly terrified of doing anything wrong, and more and more afraid of taking risks. Being so quiet and restrained meant that neither the Galleys nor her social workers imagined that she might need any form of therapy even as she sank deeper into the emotionally isolating conviction that people had died because of her.

Until the guilt gnawing away at her soul began to manifest itself in nightmares.

————

Brett was pleasantly surprised by the prettiness of the girl at the enclave's alien landing field – literally just a large field because alien spacecraft could land anywhere without even scorching the grass and no Customs or Immigration officials dared to obstruct alien arrivals or departures. Aliens got entry visas immediately on request - if they even bothered to apply. Nobody dared to obstruct aliens.

No surprise for an alien girl in a gorgeous alien dress to be pretty, but Brett judged Humility prettier than he remembered as she curtsied and used that standard alien girl line about hoping her body pleased him – easily the sexiest greeting ever. Alien ages on official American documents were effectively guesstimates, since they did not measure anything by Earth years, and further complicated by the fact that alien girls aged much slower than human girls. Brett's new stepmother claimed an age officially guesstimated as forty-four, but could have passed for half that age. Humility was guesstimated to be sixteen – the same age as Tiara, but Brett would have guessed about fourteen. At just over five feet, the alien was also about the same height as Tiara.

The only alien spaceship that Brett had ever visited had been *Freedom,* and Humility had never left *Anarchy* so Brett had only seen her on screen. Aliens did not treat weddings as social events, let alone large ones, as they were little more than contract signings. Brett and Sara had been the only human witnesses at the alien wedding protocol – you could not call it a ceremony - on *Freedom.* Sara's husband had stayed home with their new baby son and Modesty's elder daughter Patience had been Modesty's only guest - as the only daughter resident on *Freedom* where Patience was a housegirl and assistant gardener while studying to become a translator.

Brett had been surprised to be told that Humility had not been there because she could not afford to travel between spaceships. It had been Brett's first insight into the fact that Modesty's background was, by Earth standards, practically indigent. Humility had only been able to land on Earth because Brett's father had paid her fare on an alien transport delivering materials to their enclave, but it still surprised that the few bags she carried could be the sum total of not only her possessions but Modesty's remaining belongings.

He found it no chore to drive Humility back to the Maitland mansion, nor get uncharacteristically voluble pointing out objects of interest and introducing her to the family grounds and mansion. Humility's awe at the size of the mansion enchanted, yet paled against her reaction to the size of her bedroom suite. She even asked how many other girls would be sharing it with her, bewitching him into going so far beyond the call of duty as to offer to take her shopping for clothes – after explaining the concept of a dressing room.

He even decided to maximise his masochism by suggesting that they take his sister Tiara along – knowing that what for him would be torture would for Tiara be ecstasy – but it would be a pretext to spend more time with Tiara - on the reasoning that his adopted sister's constant shenanigans were the cry for attention that everyone said they were. He was just wondering whether he could now politely leave Humility and get Tiara bailed out when he received a call from a friend in the District Attorney's office, and discovered that Tiara would be facing extra charges on top of the initial car theft which Brett had confidently anticipated being able to make go completely away because the car had belonged to one of Tiara's friends.

Tiara also faced the serious charge of lying to police officers about who was driving the car as well as driving a stolen car while under the influence.

CHAPTER THREE

Same nurse's office.

Different nurse.

Tiara Maitland naturally saw the upside to every situation, and even managed to enjoy herself while nursing a split lip, a bloody nose, bruised ribs, and some broken fingernails – because she was watching warders and officials milling around like headless chickens.

Score one: – her nails would need serious manicuring but they had scored some satisfying scratches, serving the bitches right for assuming that she was Emily. They had clearly expected no resistance – which did not speak well for Emily's courage but spoke even less well for the observational abilities of the gang. They were girls, for God's sake! How could they possibly not have noticed Tiara's nails! Her hair! Her eyebrows! Had they been sniffing testosterone?

It was not only the gang. The warders had all assumed that Tiara was Emily, and openly mocked her claim to be Tiara Maitland - even leaving her in the same room as her attackers while telling them all without distinction that they were in deepest trouble for fighting. Even the evidence of her remaining fingernails and remnants of her hairdo failed to clue in the morons until evidently more senior officials burst in and escorted 'Miss Maitland' to a separate room.

The bewildered faces of the other warders and gormless gapes of the gang almost made getting locked up and beaten up worthwhile, and Tiara had to stifle her glee that they would have to report this - meaning that it must get to Brett.

And the fun kept coming. She embellished the story of her assault to now credulous officials by maliciously mentioning that one girl had used the word 'alien', then added that the gang had mistaken her for Emily and referred to giving Emily 'a kicking' only two days ago.

Inevitably the word 'alien' provoked even more entertaining paroxysms of panic among the authorities who suddenly had to take the assaults on both Emily and Tiara really seriously as possible 'hate crimes'. Tiara could not resist winding them even further, by asking – in her most innocent voice – if they had heard that school authorities were suppressing 'alien-baiting', and surely they must be doing the same! Being Tiara Maitland they were forced to listen, yet Tiara just knew that Emily Lovelace could have been beaten to a pulp and still been accused of fighting - and that added a touch of venom to her pleasure at their squirming discomfiture.

But their responses did not get beyond stuttering before all Tiara's attention was taken by Emily being brought in by a woman wearing a clerical collar. Both Emily and the cleric stared at Tiara in shock – confirming Tiara's suspicion that Emily had failed to notice Tiara when they first met, and Emily had always been in the inner room during the previous night in the nursing station.

Tiara had wondered how Emily would react on discovering that she had a twin, and been disappointed not to see it, but evidently nobody had bothered to tell her, nor even the chaplain. That really annoyed Tiara.

Emily just stood and stared back at Tiara, allowing the chaplain to grab a nurse and ease Emily's top up several inches to display Emily's ribs. The nurse then carefully eased the top up several more inches, producing winces of pain from Emily. Tiara was feet away, but she needed no medical training to recognize that no ribcage should be that colour. Clearly the jerks had no idea that Emily had been beaten up in their detention centre. Probably they would not have cared about a girl like Emily even if they had known – unless maybe someone had called Emily an alien and turned it into a 'hate crime'.

A minute later and Emily was led into another room, while Tiara was approached by the chaplain who asked if she was really Tiara Maitland.

Tiara treated the stupid woman to an ultra-elaborate eye-roll by way of response.

"Oh, yes," the stupid woman smiled. "You're Tiara! I'd remember that eye-roll anywhere. It was you I met, not Emily, though I'm sure you won't remember me."

That actually got Tiara's attention. Had she met the woman before?

"It's ten years since I visited your house," the woman added. "No reason you should remember. I'm Sylvia Godwin – I knew your sister Sara at school – I was at your house for her eighteenth birthday party. Does she know you're here?"

———

Six years earlier

Tiara was alone again on another birthday – this time her tenth.

Sara and Brett were in the middle of college finals. Both had big exams that day. They had sent their presents with recorded messages – a super cute birthday dress and a fun box set from Sara and an incredibly boring set of 'interesting and informative' history discs from Brett.

Tiara could not quite decide whether Brett was simply being his normal obtuse self or whether he was subtly paying her back for once pretending to be up past her bedtime watching a historical documentary. Even Tiara could never quite tell with Brett. Meanwhile Daddy was in China for the week and had sent a message promising to take her out when he got back – though she knew that he would probably end up paying someone else to take her out and only if she persistently reminded him.

The chauffeur had collected her from school as normal, and Daddy's housekeeper, Mrs Henderson, had promised that Tiara's favourite meal would be served for dinner, but otherwise Tiara was abandoned to her own devices with no party till Saturday when Sara and Brett could squeeze in a flying visit to supervise - since Mrs Henderson had refused point blank to sup from that poisoned chalice, though happy to organize the food and decorations and all that.

Fortunately Tiara had wangled a free pass to invite whoever she wanted – with Daddy's non-travelling P.A. Laura delegated to identify the addresses of the parents and sending all invites to parents as Tiara had insisted – claiming that was how it was done nowadays, gambling that nobody would question that statement any more than they would question the huge number of invites.

At least Tiara was getting a party this year. Mommy had never bothered herself with throwing parties for Tiara, and after Mommy had gone Tiara had not had one on her ninth birthday due to having a broken leg from falling off a horse.

Never being able to give parties had cost Tiara invitations to other parties, and contributed to Tiara getting surrounded by a set who were less friends than sycophants leeching off the girl with the richest Daddy, and even some of them had turned nasty on discovering that her excellent memory always made her top of her class without really trying. It had steadily been borne in on Tiara that refusing to 'dumb herself down' to fit in with her friends got her seriously resented for 'getting above herself' – and being adopted magnified tenfold that resentment into 'thinking herself a somebody when she was really a nobody because she was <u>only</u> adopted'.

Innate stubbornness made Tiara refuse to knuckle under merely to make friends, but on days like today she had her doubts, and her resentments – hence her determination to have a big birthday party and invite as many as possible, and the point had been accepted by Daddy and Brett and even Sara.

But that party was not until Saturday. Today she would eat in normal depressing solitude. She could use social media to communicate with friends but the ones worth talking to were too busy revising for their exams and that the ones not too busy revising were all boring or stupid. She had got a routine card from the staff, but none of them were being paid enough to pretend to care about her. But they might regret that after Saturday – or so Tiara hoped. It was not just among the guests that Tiara had scores to settle.

Fifty kids were coming – she had sneaked that number by protesting to Dad that she had not been allowed a party for years so deserved a large party – anticipating that he would take the option of least hassle: - Agree. Spend. Delegate. It had even been her 'helpful suggestion' that the party be delayed to Saturday. She had tricked her Dad into delegating Laura to send the invites to the parents because she knew that few parents in the area would turn down the chance to drive their kids to the Maitland Mansion, regardless of whether the kids wanted to go.

What she was careful not to clue anybody in about was how she had selected her guests. Her usual gang of sycophants who loved to boast that the Maitland heiress was their friend would all be there – but so would all said sycophants' deadliest enemies, and all the known troublemakers she could squeeze in – especially boys with a reputation for fighting (and their enemies).

There was every chance that chaos would ensue. If all the boys turned up food fights — and maybe real fights — should be easy to provoke with a few carefully placed taunts, and if all the girls turned up a few well-placed reminders of past insults should soon have several girls at each other's throats metaphorically if not literally. Tiara only need pretend to be distraught at the wrecking of her party and she could have everybody scurrying around to make it up to her — hopefully for days. The trick might be to keep herself from laughing and giving the game away.

Not a word from Mommy, of course. Tiara had heard not a word from Mommy since the day Mommy had disappeared with her multi-million dollar pay-off. Mommy's last words to Tiara had been to call her a nasty little sneak and a useless daughter who would never be good for anything and had not deserved to be adopted. Tiara not only never expected to hear from Mommy again, she never wanted to — or so Tiara told herself - insistently.

It was Mommy who had been useless, Tiara had kept stubbornly insisting to herself but, on lonely days like this, a whisper of paranoia kept digging at Tiara's soul.

Had Mommy been right that Tiara had not deserved to be adopted?

———

Emily lay on the bed scarcely noticing the nurse gently pressing her ribs.

She had even forgotten to worry about the extra punishments she was expecting – nor even about the nurse saying that she might have a cracked rib and needed an X-ray. All Emily could think about was that girl. Either Emily was going insane, or there was another girl nearby who was her identical twin.

That would mean that the impossible was now possible.

Warders were asking who had attacked her. She was not stupid enough to tell them, but she was determined not to lie. Pa Galley had always said it was better to remain silent than to tell lies, and she had already told too many lies. Besides which she did not want to get Sukie in more trouble – she could not blame poor Sukie for hating her or attacking her. No way would Emily ever do anything more to hurt Sukie if she could possibly help it, whatever Sukie did.

"No point in hiding it, sis," a voice so like her own came out of nowhere.

Despite her pain she thrust herself sharply away and up against the wall.

"Crap!" the voice came from a face even more like her own than the voice. "Never scared anyone that easily before!"

"Who the hell are you?" Emily squealed, ignoring the nurse's attempt to get her to sit back down.

"Emily Lovelace," Sylvia spoke up crisply. "Meet Tiara Maitland. Your records say that you were both born on the same day and were both adopted at birth. I don't think we need a DNA test to deduce that you're identical twins."

———

Six years earlier

On her tenth birthday Emily Lovelace was removed from her third foster home in fourteen months.

Nobody even noticed that it was her birthday, but she barely remembered it herself. Daddy never let her celebrate her birthdays with anyone but him and Mummy, and her 'parties' had merely involved her putting on a selection of birthday clothes including nightwear and swimsuits as well as cute frocks that Daddy had bought so that he could film her wearing them in mini fashion shows. Even the Galleys had not realized at the time that it was their new arrival's seventh birthday, and their plans for her eighth birthday foundered on the Galleys' inability to cope with a foster son who had severe behavioural problems.

Nobody had remembered her ninth birthday, either. Her most vivid memory of her ninth birthday had been when her pleas to be allowed to clean the kitchen provoked an impatient remark that if Emily was so desperate to clean something then she could go clean the dog kennel. When she surprised her foster mother by taking the suggestion seriously the dog had horribly messed up and torn Emily's clothing during its valiant efforts to lick her to death.

Her foster siblings had promptly mocked her for looking a mess – deliberately teasing because she was always urging them to be tidier so they had no mercy in enjoying payback and taunted her so mercilessly that she cried herself to sleep wishing that she was back with Ma and Pa Galley.

The Galleys had been her first foster home. She had liked it from the start, after hating the group home where she had spent the previous weeks afraid of all the other kids running around and being scarily noisy and horrifically untidy all the time.

Ma and Pa Galley were a kindly but ageing couple who had spent two decades fostering up to half a dozen kids at a time on a rolling basis, mainly respite care kids or temporary care kids. The Galleys were not tactile, nor trained to parent problem kids. Emily behaved too well to be treated as having problems but her legal status was uncertain while her father was on the run and then awaiting trial, so she ended up staying longer than any other child. In truth the Galleys' parenting style was more like grandparenting than parenting, and though kindly they were not organized which was why they were late noticing the date of Emily's seventh birthday, but they gave Emily two and a half years which provided most of Emily's few good memories of childhood.

Those years also inculcated the Galleys' personal beliefs more strongly into Emily than they had into any other children. The couple were not aggressively evangelist, but they took their kids to Sunday School when they went to Church. At home they talked about right and wrong through sayings and proverbs and stories – only mentioning religion when repeating parables like the Good Samaritan - and their numerous aphorisms extolled the virtues of thrift and tidiness and prudence with regards to money, and of working hard at school and the wonderful careers possible with a good education.

Emily called them Ma and Pa Galley like everyone else, but became very attached to them. She could never get enough of the small hugs that Ma Galley would occasionally use to reward good behaviour, so was always trying to earn them by high grades at school, keeping her shared room impeccably tidy at all times, doing many extra chores unasked, and absorbing their aphorisms deeply into her soul - far more obsessively than anyone ever suspected of the quiet girl who never argued, never complained, never asked for help, but was always asking to help.

Emily had not understood that the Galleys had never kept a child as long as they kept her, so had hoped to stay for good, but then Pa Galley was diagnosed with terminal cancer. The Galleys made what they considered to be the kindest decision for the children and never told them about the cancer.

Unfortunately that had left Emily in complete shock when told by a social worker that they had found a new home for her. As no explanation was given Emily automatically assumed that she must have done something very wrong to make the Galleys not want her any more, but she did not dare ask what.

That night Emily had a nightmare that the crash which she had caused had killed people. It recurred and got worse after her move to a new family – who found themselves with a girl who kept disrupting the sleep of the whole family. Even worse, she wet her bed during some nightmares – humiliating herself and stressing foster parents who had busy lives and struggled to cope not only with her nightmares but with her frantic attempts to compensate by constantly pestering to clean things whether they needed cleaning or not.

It might have been different if she made friends with the other children – but she was still helpfully telling other children how to be tidier or cleaner, provoking them into taunting her for being a dirty bed-wetter. Two weeks after her ninth birthday, she eavesdropped on an irritated foster dad suggesting that they make her sleep in the dog kennel 'since she loved cleaning it so much', so they could all get a good night's sleep. She had not been meant to overhear, and it had not been meant seriously, but Emily had taken it seriously and hardly dared go to sleep at all for fear of having a nightmare and being sent to the dog kennel.

It was three weeks later that Emily was removed from her second home in three months. Her next foster family, the Frasers, had been willing to consider keeping Emily long term, but found her obsessively tidy, unsmiling, over-controlled personality hard to love – especially when she tried to tidy up their happily chaotic household.

Even so, the Frasers worried deeply about the occasional nightmares and bed-wetting, and genuinely tried to do their best for their troubled foster daughter by seeking social services help – and attempting to discourage the other children from mocking her. The social workers made the disastrous but natural mistake of referring her to a child psychologist.

The psychologist who took the case was young and eager and fresh from training in recognizing cases of child sexual abuse. Looking through Emily's file she had pounced on Matt Lovelace's criminal record of paedophilia – even downplaying his murder of Emily's mother, and totally missing the mention of a road accident.

Early on Emily mentioned the mini-fashion shows on her birthdays. The psychologist seized on this and tried to get Emily to admit that she had felt degraded by the experience, but succeeded only in making Emily think that she had been very naughty to have enjoyed dressing up and posing for pictures. It made it worse that Emily was smart enough to sense that the psychologist was hinting at Emily doing something very wicked but unspecified with her Daddy, and Emily started feeling guilty that she could not remember whatever it was. If it had not been for the Galley axiom that it was better to say nothing than to tell lies Emily might have tried to please the psychologist by telling the woman what she wanted to hear, and even ended up manufacturing false memories that would have genuinely traumatised her.

Instead she started obstinately refusing to even talk to the psychologist, while mentions of 'bad adults touching her in ways that were unpleasant' had confused her about all physical contacts with adults. She started pulling away from attempts by her foster parents to give her the hugs for which she had once been eager. Instead of the counselling helping her it had only made Emily's internal turmoil worse. Fortunately her nightmares quietened and the bed-wetting ceased purely due to her increasing physical maturity, so social services concluded that the therapy had worked well enough that it was not worth forcing her to attend against her will.

But it was too late for Emily to fit in with the Frasers, as she pulled away from the parents and failed entirely to make friends with the children, and Emily was removed from another family on her tenth birthday. It had not been deliberate neglect on the Fraser's part – neither they nor the social worker who collected her had realized that it was her birthday and Emily had never mentioned it.

Emily overheard the social worker being told that the family had tried and been very patient, but all agreed that it just was not working. Emily blamed herself totally, and cried with shame and guilt – but silently so as not to upset anyone. As they were leaving the social worker had sounded downright annoyed with her, and driven Emily deeper into despair. She had really wanted to stay with them despite the constant teasing by other children both at home and school. The Frasers had never been less than kind, and tried their best to be tolerant - had given a very nice room, a more than adequate supply of nice clothes, had seen her through her bed-wetting and done their level best to tolerate her obsessiveness – had been so generous with Christmas presents that Emily had been miserable with embarrassment at the inadequacy of the presents she had given them in return and promised herself to do much better the next year – except that she never got the chance.

Emily had felt safe with them, if not exactly happy, and she was convinced that they had not loved her because she had not worked hard enough. Being moved yet again convinced Emily that there must be something seriously wrong with her – and her guilt feelings about her mother's death and the car accident embedded themselves deeper into her soul. She started to seriously fear that God might be punishing her for real, but never dared voice her fears. Tears streamed quietly down her face for the entire car journey with the social worker, but as she kept her eyes averted the whole time, and made no sound, the social worker just thought that she was sulking.

He told her that they had found a family willing to take her in, but it was miles away so she would have to change schools again and be passed to a different child services office. Emily rightly interpreted that the man was glad about the latter fact. She was miserable about leaving a school where she had finally started to make friends with a couple of girls – social outsiders like Emily – but she had hoped that they might in time become real friends like normal girls had friends.

As they drove Emily decided that there was no point trying to make friends at her new school, as she was sure to have to leave them soon.

But, unknown to her, luck had come to her aid. Emily finally found a family where she fitted in - a family who were happy to let her take on all the chores and not interested in her thoughts and feelings.

So Emily was able to enjoy the safety of emotional solitude.

––––––

It might not have been strictly correct policy to leave the twins alone together, but Sylvia Godwin took advantage of the general confusion while they were awaiting transport to hospital for precautionary x-rays.

Left alone, they stared at each other - Tiara all excitement, Emily all confusion. Tiara had been violently assaulted in mistake for Emily, so Tiara's injuries were all Emily's fault, yet Tiara was not blaming Emily for it. Tiara was even talking of being assaulted as fun! Emily found that awesome. How could Tiara be so forgiving? It stopped Emily from wanting to challenge Tiara about anything.

All Emily wanted was to know who Tiara was, and all Tiara wanted was to know who Emily was, so straight out asked her why she was here. Tiara meant Juvie, but Emily assumed that she meant the nurse's office and felt raw with guilt.

"I'm sorry," was all the response Emily initially whispered.

"Sorry for what, little sis?" Tiara replied – completely puzzled.

"It should have been me," Emily burst out. "I was the one who failed her. I was the one she hated. They thought they were attacking me!"

Tiara felt bemused as Emily sank down into the safety of the corner to let tears silently flow. Had Emily been hostile or friendly, Tiara would have reacted on instinct, but weaklings she was used to ignoring or mocking – and she wanted to do neither to her twin. She wanted to – Tiara was not sure what. Very rarely for Tiara, she was at a loss for words, and her usual default of sarcastic teen backchat was hardly an option.

On impulse she stepped forward to hug the girl, but Emily flinched at her approach, and that *really* shook Tiara. Comforting people in distress was way outside Tiara's comfort zone, and she had never seen a sister upset like this before. She had seen Sara upset as in annoyed on many occasions – once annoyed enough to turn Tiara over her knee - but not upset as in distressed.

But Tiara did remember times long ago when Sara had comforted Tiara, when Sara had still been around. But Tiara remembered how Sara had comforted her, so just sat beside her twin sister and gently placed one hand on the girl's arm.

That face looked up – strained, afraid, and streaked with tears.

Tiara considered offering to help to repair that make-up.

And definitely to do something about those eyebrows.

———

JassaVar ventured cautiously onto the main staircase of the mansion.

It had been years since she had used a toll-free staircase or corridor or elevator, so it felt strange to walk down this sweeping curve of steps without having to pay or seek permission.

An unnerving thought struck — maybe she should not be using this staircase? Maybe she should be using a more modest stairway? But Brett had invited her to wander the house and grounds so she could always plead misunderstanding. Her mother would never excuse a social error out of ignorance, but humans might.

The room at the base of the staircase was huge. JassaVar had never seen a room so large inside a private residence, and this — if she comprehended correctly — was merely a transit area called a hallway, though there were many chairs and tables in it. There were also several doors off it, and JassaVar possessed no idea which led where, nor whether she was permitted to enter any or all of them.

At the foot of the stairs she dithered over where to go, hesitantly inspecting doors for any way to request entry. Seeing nothing she moved towards the front entrance to the mansion - the one door where she knew what was on the other side, but she did not know how to get back in if she went out.

If only Brett had not rushed off.

A door opened and a smartly dressed human woman came out. As the woman saw JassaVar, and turned towards her, the petite alien felt an instinctive fear that she was about to get into trouble.

"Miss Humility, is it?" the woman approached with a reassuring smile. "Welcome to Maitland House. I was just coming to find you. I'm Mrs Henderson. I hope your bedroom was to your liking."

"Liking!" if JassaVar translated correctly that was not an adequate word. "It is giant, Mrs Henderson. I possess no memory of so large a bedroom. I possess difficulty comprehending that I do not share."

Mrs Henderson looked surprised, and JassaVar wondered what age the woman might possess. Had the woman been alien, JassaVar might guess a hundred and fifty. As the woman was human, if JassaVar remembered her mother's guidelines properly, the woman might be about fifty years old.

JassaVar wondered if the woman was past childbearing age, and how many daughters the woman might possess.

"If there is any way I can help you," Mrs Henderson declared politely, "please do not be afraid to ask."

"Thank you, Mrs Henderson," JassaVar obeyed her mother's advice and carefully tried to match the manners of the human. "Do I comprehend correct that your employment is named housekeeper, and you manage household on behalf of Mister Maitland because large household? Apology if my comprehending incorrect."

"On behalf of the Maitland family," Mrs Henderson replied with an encouraging smile.

"Should I be assigned my housegirl duties by you?" JassaVar asked, anxious to make a good impression. "Our normality it is housewife who commands and disciplines housegirls in managing household, but if management of household is your duty should I submit to your command and discipline?"

Mrs Henderson looked completely stunned by that question, which threw JassaVar into something of a panic.

Had she already committed some terrible indiscretion?

She had only been on the planet three hours. Surely she could not be in trouble already? Her mother had commanded best behaviour.

And warned of very painful consequences if not.

CHAPTER FOUR

Brett Maitland finally arrived at the hospital at just after two in the afternoon that Saturday.

It had been a frustrating day. He had cancelled other commitments for the tedious chore of introducing his new stepsister to the family home. On meeting Humility he found her company anything but tedious and could have cheerfully spent hours with her before Tiara interrupted his plans in epic style. Then he got called to collect his twin from the airport on the way to the hospital. It had delayed him another hour, but he knew better than to provoke Sara in argumentative mood. Sara had been furious about his decision not to bail Tiara out the previous night, so it had taken most of the journey to calm her down.

"We've got to do something," he asserted again, as they pulled into the hospital car park. "Unless we find some way to rein her in she'll end up in really serious trouble. I thought that a night or two in Juvie might give her a bit of a shock and knock some sense into her."

"Some gang of girls did the knocking for you, did they?" Sara retorted acidly. "My bet is Tiara enjoyed every minute, and will be really juiced now that we're running after her like groupies."

"You didn't have to fly in, you know. I could have managed."

"Yes I did, and neither you nor Dad can manage Tiara. You never have and you never will."

"Feel free to take over," Brett offered without hesitation, "but I don't think giving her another spanking or sending her off to boarding school will work better than they did six years ago."

Sara slammed the car door without responding to that humiliating reminder. Brett had to hurry to catch up. Within minutes they were following directions to where 'the Southside girls' were being treated.

Girls plural, Brett noted – assuming that one or more of the gang who had attacked Tiara must also be there.

Sara hurried on ahead, reaching the row of cubicles described to them, saw a warder in standing in front of one of the cubicles, and aimed straight at it. The warder stepped in front of her at first, then stepped nervously backwards as Sara imperiously announced that she was there to see her sister.

Brett approached more slowly, letting Sara do the heavy lifting of intimidating the warder. Brett could handle lawyers and bureaucrats almost as well as his father, but uniforms were harder to pressurize in his experience – but not harder for Sara, who swept past the woman and pulled aside the curtain of the cubicle, then called her sister's name and stepped inside.

Only then did Brett happen to glance to the left and see his adopted sister in an entirely different cubicle against the opposite wall – smirking as though pulling off one of her practical jokes – and with plain evidence of having been in a fight.

"Tiara," Sara's voice came from behind the curtain. "What is wrong? My God, what happened to you?"

The warder turned around in confusion, clearly unsure what to do, while Tiara looked ready to kill herself laughing. Brett wondered what Sara was doing, and headed after his twin to retrieve her when another voice spoke from behind the curtain.

"This isn't Tiara, Sara," the voice announced hurriedly. "This is Emily Lovelace – Tiara's twin. Tiara is over there."

The curtain between Sara and Brett was pulled firmly back by an attractive woman wearing a clerical collar, as Tiara skipped off her bed and walked across to join them. The curtain revealed a confused looking Sara, and a girl who seemed to be cowering against the wall in near panic. A girl who looked exactly like Tiara except for lacking an injured lip.

Sara looked across and saw Tiara, and stared in sheer disbelief, as Brett himself stared at the girl against the wall in comparable confusion.

"I don't expect that you remember me, Sara," the cleric continued. "I'm Sylvia Godwin – we were at school …"

"Shame on you, Sara," Tiara interrupted loudly. "Call yourself a girl! How could you possibly think Emily was me? Since when did I let my hair or my nails get into that state? How could you think those are my eyebrows?"

———

Three years earlier

Tiara marched straight back to the door of the Principal's office and knocked, determined to do it before she lost her nerve.

Her reception was unsurprisingly chilly – Tiara had been one of five girls in the same room, ten minutes earlier, being placed in detention and informed that their respective parents would be getting very stiff letters.

The punishment had not bothered Tiara half as much as the tears on the part of one of the other girls. The detention had sounded boring, but almost everything at boarding school was boring, which was why Tiara had pitched into the practical joke at the expense of Melissa Gordon.

Tiara did not normally join in jokes inspired by others, but Melissa Gordon had rather got under her skin as the one pupil who outshone Tiara academically, but Melissa achieved her results by working hard so was popularly despised so sabotaging her science project had seemed like fun. Unfortunately the sabotage had been rather more effective than hoped when Melissa was demonstrating it, resulting in a desperately upset Melissa turning on Tiara and her cabal and accusing them of sabotage.

The name-calling had been returned with compound interest - developing into a mini catfight before staff intervened and hauled all five girls off to the Principal's office for a withering telling-off and summary punishment.

Detention was boring, but not exactly an unusual punishment at that school, and not a new experience for Tiara. Tiara's father had received letters from Principals before, but Melissa's had not.

Melissa had never been in detention before, and was distraught at the humiliation. Tiara had not seen a girl so distraught since her Pageant days. When Tiara's friends mocked Melissa for taking it so seriously, Tiara did not join in the sneering. Instead, she went back to the Principal's office, calmly faced down the atmosphere of chilling disapproval, and confessed that they had set up Melissa, and that Melissa was only trying to defend herself and did not deserve to be in detention.

Tiara entered the room confident that she could work the system and save Melissa from the punishment. She was coldly asked if she was really stupid enough to think that the teaching staff did not already know all that. A girl, the Principal firmly asserted, had no business trying to take the law into her own hands. A girl who was bullied had only one legitimate course of action, and that was to take her complaint to the teaching staff who would resolve it.

Melissa was obviously getting no credit whatsoever even for past good behaviour. Tiara could scarcely believe that the teachers were punishing the girl just the same as the rest of them. Even Tiara's twisted concepts of justice were outraged by that, and she declared so very bluntly.

The only response was to order her out before she completely forfeited the small amount of credit she had earned by coming forward to speak for another girl.

Tiara had stormed out, and nearly slammed the too-heavy door behind her.

She went off to seek out Melissa to apologize or something, but was distracted by the shouting of other girls who dragged her into a television lounge, telling her excitedly that there was a gigantic alien spaceship threatening to attack a NASA spaceship in orbit!

By the time it had finally sunk in that the whole thing was no hoax, Tiara had forgotten about Melissa Gordon.

———

"You want to what?"

Brett spoke for Sara, and for once she did not mind him doing the talking for both of them, being completely dumbfounded at Tiara's latest demand.

"You heard," the princess of insouciance declared through her damaged lips. "I want to stay in Juvie with Emily until she is released. Then I want her to come and live with us. Well, why not? It's only fair. You've got each other. You've both got your twin. I want my twin!"

"There are some things even money can't buy, Tiara," Sara told her firmly.

"But this won't cost you any money. Think of it as dumping me in Juvie so that you can forget about me – you know, like you all forgot about me when you dumped me in boarding school – shouldn't be that difficult."

"Dad sent you to boarding school in an attempt to keep you out of trouble," Brett explained defensively.

"Futile attempt," Sara amended firmly. "Futile as everything we ever tried to stop you getting up to mischief."

"I can't get up to much mischief while I'm in Juvie," Tiara taunted her sister.

"You could get up to mischief while in a coma," Sara snapped back. "Look, Tiara, I'm sure we can arrange for you to see Emily, but her family may ..."

"She hasn't got a family," Tiara interrupted - sounding at her most petulant. "She is a foster kid. She has got nobody in the world and she tried to cut her wrist last night. My twin – my sister – and she could have died last night without me knowing she ever existed. She has nobody who cares whether she lives or dies. If we don't do something she'll try to kill herself again, and I won't let her!"

Shock number three. Sara vividly remembered the twitchy twin shrinking away as Sara approached her by mistake, and she understood why Tiara was reacting as she was. How long Tiara's reaction was likely to last may be debatable, knowing Tiara's track record, but that did not invalidate the sentiment.

Nor did it dispose of the problems. Sara had been coming back whenever she could since Tiara's expulsion from boarding school, but knew it had not been enough, and that Brett was struggling to control her. How the hell was he going to cope if they took on another troubled teen, probably even more troubled than Tiara? How to cope when they also had to cope with a stepmother and stepsister who were not only new but aliens. Would Modesty and her daughter help or hinder?

Yet Sara knew that she was already accepting that they could not pass by on the other side from the twitchy twin.

"You really do want us to leave you in Juvie?" Sara asked her sister directly. "Might not be so easy! First conviction for someone your age is not likely to lead to a custodial sentence unless it's a very serious charge."

"No problem, actually," Brett declared unexpectedly, and Sara wondered what the hell her brother was smiling about. "Brennan is up for re-election soon, so he'll jump at the chance to prove he can stand up to people like us by going after a custodial sentence – if only a token one - rather than just probation or community service."

"You seriously think you can get away with that?"

"Lying to the police is a serious charge – as is D.U.I. without a licence. If we offer to plead to all charges we could probably bargain a token month or two. Just don't tell anyone why you agreed. We'll have to pretend you're suffering from an attack of true penitence."

"That'll need a very gullible court," his twin input.

"We could start the ball rolling," Brett ignored the interruption, "by telling the court that we're still not applying for bail. We could say you've accepted that you're getting a custodial sentence, and would rather get it over and done. Problem would be matching the length to little Emily's. No idea what her sentence might be. I can't guarantee you can leave with her. In fact, if we overtly tried to arrange it someone would probably smell a rat."

"Doesn't matter," Tiara shrugged calmly, "as long as I don't leave before her and you take her home where she is safe."

"But that would mean you staying in Juvie," Sara pointed out. "She might be in for years! You got attacked on your first morning. What if you stay here for weeks? Or months?"

"I'll be fine. I can look after myself against those idiots. I've played the 'hate crime' scam so that should scare them off me, but no-one will protect Emily if I don't, and they've been tormenting her for ever – they drove her to suicide. Well, nobody is doing that again – not if I'm around. You've got to help me save her. Please! Please! Please! Please! Pretty please!"

Roger and Sara exchanged disbelieving stares. Unpredictable might be Tiara's middle name, but this was way beyond anything their adopted freak had done yet. On the other hand, Sara considered – and she was in no doubt that Brett was thinking the same way - Tiara was putting herself out to help someone else, which had to be a first, even if it was her identical twin. A development in their sister's character growth greatly to be desired.

But if Tiara was such a handful with all her advantages in life, what sort of termagant might this Emily be? The scared little girl image which she had presented earlier might overlay a drug-fuelled little sociopath who might lead Tiara down an even more self-destructive path.

"Two problems I can see," Brett began.

"Trust you to see the problems," Tiara eye-rolled elaborately.

"Can't see Dad and Modesty agreeing or even getting approved as foster parents," Brett ignored the interruption.

"You can fix it," Tiara asserted angrily. "Come on, Brett. You know you can."

"Maybe – maybe not," Sara interrupted. "But then there is the matter of Emily – could we cope with a girl like that – would she even want to come with us?"

"Nobody else in the world gives a damn whether she lives or dies. She has nowhere else to go. Of course, she'll want to live with us."

"Okay," Brett put a placating hand on Tiara's wrist. "We can certainly make enquiries - find out everything we can."

"I'll talk to Sylvia Godwin," Sara offered. "Catch up on old times, and pick her brains at the same time."

"Old times?" Brett queried. "You really did know her?"

"We were at school together, and she came to our eighteenth birthday party."

"You mean your birthday party. Everything was done the way you wanted it. I just turned up with a few of the guys."

"Yeah, I didn't have much choice. If I had left it to you we'd just have had a few friends round to watch movies and eat burgers. A real party is supposed to have music and dancing – which you really should have tried doing with a girl or two."

"Was Sylvia one of those girls?" Tiara cut in eagerly. "I mean who came hoping Brett would ask them to dance and spent the evening pining away when he didn't?"

"Yes, actually."

Tiara almost collapsed in a fit of the giggles.

"I don't remember her," Brett declared with a frown.

"No surprise. The only girls you ever remembered were the ones who pole-danced in front of you - Sylvia not that sort of girl."

Tiara dissolved back into another fit of hysteria.

"Sylvia seems to have got involved in Emily's case," Sara pushed on, "so she could be a great help. Then – sorry, Tiara – but we'll have to call Dad even on his honeymoon. Which planet is he orbiting at the moment? Saturn or Jupiter?"

"I've got another idea," Tiara suddenly chirped. "If I get released first we swap places so she gets released as me and you look after her while I pretend to be her until I-slash-she gets released when we swap back. How about that?"

———

Three years earlier

Emily had not been in such a panic for months.

Every five minutes she rushed out of the Burden apartment to the window on the stairway to stare down the street – hoping to see her foster mother returning home. Timmy was sounding awful. Emily had persuaded Sukie to go to bed, promising to watch over Sukie's little brother until their mother got home. Sandra normally came home about nine unless she stayed late for a drink or with a guy, which she had been doing more and more – to Emily's secret stress as she could never let herself go to sleep until she knew that Sandra was home.

Sandra had promised to leave promptly this time because Timmy had a bad cold. Emily did not remember feeling so tired, but panic trumped exhaustion and kept her running from window to bedside.

Where was Sandra? Emily knew how they needed the money with Sandra's alimony so unreliable and fostering payments not increasing in line with rent, utilities and everything else, so it was Emily's job to clear up and put away all dinner stuff, help Sukie and Timmy with any homework or games, then put the younger one to bed, and mercilessly clean the kitchen before doing her own homework and extra homework and advance reading and lesson preparation while Sukie put herself to bed.

Her teachers had rated Emily as so academically outstanding that they wanted her to skip a grade and advance to High School early. They had asked Sandra in to discuss it, but Sandra had only ever been called into school before when Sukie had got in trouble, so had jumped to the conclusion that Emily must be in trouble and bawled her foster daughter out before going in. Embarrassment at the thought of having to apologise for her mistake played the primary part in her telling the teachers that she was firmly against the idea because the extra work would put too much pressure on a girl who already got very tired in the evenings.

Sandra did not mention that Emily's tiredness was exacerbated by doing most of the household chores on top of schoolwork, or that Sandra was almost as dependent on Emily's housekeeping services as on the fostering payments which paid the rent and put food on the single parent table.

When Emily got home that day Sandra told her that the teachers were only concerned about Emily's lack of self-confidence and reluctance to speak up – a subject they had genuinely mentioned. Inevitably Emily interpreted the information as an indirect telling-off and it only served to further undermine her self-confidence, as did her disappointment that the teachers had apparently not mentioned graduating from school early, a concept that had really excited Emily from hints dropped by one of her teachers. As a poorly-dressed, socially inadequate, academic high-flier she had become the verbal equivalent of a soccer ball – a constant butt of jokes and mockery – so the more schoolwork she did and the less she mixed with other pupils suited Emily, and the suggestion of finishing school early and even getting a scholarship to college had begun to give her actual hope for her future.

That unspoken hope vanished, crushing the modicum of optimism that she had been starting to acquire, including her hopes that her teachers' encouraging words were more than just them doing their job, so she buried herself back into her comforting routine.

But that night Emily's comforting routine was devastated as she got more and more frantic with worry about Timmy. She kept trying to ring and text Sandra on her cellphone, and eventually tried ringing the number of the bar itself only to find it constantly engaged. She walked round and round in circles wondering if she dared ring the bar again, or even follow Sukie's suggestion of dialling 911 if Timmy got really bad. Only her love for the family gave her the courage to try ringing the bar again.

Emily felt more settled with the Burdens than with any family since the Galleys. She had found a better way of fitting in with foster siblings than trying to make them neat and tidy – namely taking over virtually all the housework. Sukie and Timmy and Sandra were more than content to let her, and Emily was content to do it, and so proud when a social worker visited and congratulated Sandra on providing such a spotless house for a lucky foster child to live in and how Emily should be very grateful to Sandra, and Emily had honestly assured the social worker that she was both grateful and happy – not mentioning how tired she got doing so much every night and getting breakfast in the morning when Sandra did not surface early enough to help.

Emily's bedroom was very small, but she had evolved a very tidy system of hangers from a curtain rail to supplement the cupboard where she stored her clothes with military precision and order while neatly arranging books and school stuff on top.

Food was good – Emily did most of the shopping and cooking incorporating nutritional guidance that she had studied at school. The Burdens lived close enough to school that Emily could get there in twenty minutes even after walking Timmy to his school first, and Sukie was very helpful at picking up Timmy on her own way home so that Emily could go to the school library to do assigned homework and read ahead on her studies and any other books she fancied then do the shopping on the way home.

Emily was very grateful to both Sandra and Sukie for their tolerance of her obsessions and tendency to panic, and for letting her use their computer when Timmy was not using it to play games - usually only meaning after Timmy was in bed. She was particularly grateful than nobody mocked her love of reading - she even dared to bring home library books. It helped her to endure the mockery of other girls at school.

But she was most comfortable at school when in the library with a tolerant school librarian, books, and other studious girls who were the closest Emily had to friends – though her friendship with them was limited by not being able to meet them in the evenings, or on Saturdays when Sandra took Timmy to soccer or Sukie shopping or both while Emily got the groceries and cleaned every inch of the apartment.

Sandra Burden had been living a stressed and unhappy life since the break-up of her marriage. Her waitressing helped pay for Timmy's toys and gadgets and Sukie's clothes and music and smartphone, supplementing foster payments and erratically paid maintenance from her children's father. Luckily Emily, though a year older, was inches smaller and slimmer than Sukie so could wear clothes that Sukie had outgrown or no longer wanted – so Emily did not need to be bought any, and never even asked for a cellphone. Emily never mentioned to Sandra that the passed on clothes were a bad fit and exposed her to frequent derision from other girls – as a foster kid Emily was long accustomed to being constantly picked on at school.

Sandra was also fortunate that Emily did not expect money spent on her beyond her pocket money, so was not upset at her birthday being forgotten or doing most of the work at Christmas while only getting a token present. Emily was just grateful for the safety and security of her home, and that gratitude finally gave her courage to ring the bar again. This time a man answered, but there was a terrific cacophony of noise and Emily could hardly hear him, while he could not hear her soft and timid little voice at all over the noise around him. After a couple of minutes being told to speak up Emily gave up in despair, and sunk to the floor in tears.

After a few minutes she rallied enough to realize that Sandra was due home in half an hour and Timmy did not seem any worse, and by the time she had finished tending to him it was ten to nine, so she began to feel better.

It was after quarter past nine that she really started to panic, rushing between window and patient. She thought of ringing the bar again but guessed Sandra could be on the way home so tried Sandra's cellphone again. Emily was not to know that Sandra had forgotten to charge up her cellphone, or that the Big Game which everybody had been raucously watching in the bar had been interrupted by a newsflash that a gigantic alien spacecraft had appeared in orbit closely tracking a NASA spacecraft as if preparing to attack it. Sandra had completely lost track of time and taken aboard more alcohol than usual before finally remembering her sick son and heading home – much more worried about alien spaceships than a son with a cold because Emily had not phoned as instructed in case of emergency.

It was ten before Sandra got home. Emily had twice picked up the phone to dial 911, but lost her nerve, terrified of getting into trouble by wasting adult time with an unnecessary 911 call, having recently read about people being prosecuted for making hoax calls, so when Sandra arrived Emily was barely coherent in her panic. Sandra blearily tried to make sense of Emily's babbling – wearily accustomed to Emily panicking over anything and nothing. Sandra went in and looked at her son, but Timmy had fallen asleep for a while and seemed peaceful, and Sandra was accustomed to dismissing her foster daughter's neurotic wolf-crying, so she told Emily to go to bed and said that she would take Timmy to hospital in the morning if he was no better.

Next morning Emily roused Sandra at six saying Timmy sounded dreadful. This time Sandra was alarmed enough to follow Sukie's advice and call an ambulance. Sandra went with Timmy but ordered the two worried girls to *go to school saying that the hospital would sort it out now and there was no need to worry.*

Timmy died in hospital four hours later. A social worker from the hospital asked about siblings, and a distraught Sandra remembered Sukie, so the social worker rang the school, who told Sukie that her brother had died and took her to join her mother.

Nobody remembered Emily, but she was worried enough to leave school as soon as it ended instead of going to the library.

When she did get home, an hysterical Sukie started throwing everything she could find at Emily, and shrieking that it was all Emily's fault that Timmy had died because she had not dialled 911 when Sukie had suggested it.

For the second time in her life Emily ran away from home in panic. Late that evening two concerned passers-by spotted her curled up foetally on a bench in a small park, and alerted a local police patrol, who took her to the police station when all they could get out of her was a whimper that she had 'killed Timmy'.

Three months later Sandra died after mixing alcohol with sleeping pills.

Three years later Sukie was in Juvenile Detention after being convicted for several burglaries with other members of a girl gang that she had joined. She still blamed Emily for the deaths of Timmy and Sandra.

So did Emily - in her silent darkness of her soul.

———

It was hours later that JassaVar was finally introduced to Brett's twin sister, Sara, and it had been the strangest few hours in JassaVar's life.

All her life JassaVar had served others, so it had been hard to comprehend when Mrs Henderson had explained that JassaVar need not do any chores as she was family - though it would be appreciated if she would keep her bedroom tidy. Living in a household without doing chores was an odd concept for any alien girl.

Mrs Henderson had offered to arrange lunch for JassaVar, and took her into a gigantic kitchen possessing unimaginable quantities and varieties of food and drink. JassaVar opted for salad and bread with fruit juice – all concepts familiar to aliens, although only the bread tasted like anything she knew.

JassaVar had expected to eat with Mrs Henderson and other staff - in alien households the housegirls always ate with family, but bizarrely even Mrs Henderson never ate with lesser staff. JassaVar had desired to befriend the other housegirls – or housemaids as humans called them – but they showed no desire to reciprocate, and talked to each other in a language not among the Earth languages that JassaVar had been trying to learn.

JassaVar comprehended that humans possessed a phenomenal variety of languages and dialects on top of cultural divergences and species variants which they called races. Many housegirls and stowaways had found lucrative employment learning an enormous variety of languages both to act as interpreters or as colonisation researchers or target-identifiers for the Hunters.

JassaVar had been rather attracted by the thought of becoming a target-identifier, though most jobs going were on *Freedom*. It was a challenging job, but only paid well if expert in languages other in English - which was why JassaVar had started studying a language commonly used by hostile tribes. The job entailed controlling observation systems tracking hostiles and potential hostiles using *Freedom*'s observation technologies.

It took patience to identify hostiles to a level acceptable for names and faces and location locks to be passed to Hunters for extermination – especially when wading through tedious cultish diatribes for declarations of hostility to aliens, and a girl had to be very careful not to classify calls for non-cooperation with alien activities as calls for obstruction of alien activity or even calls for violence against aliens. The former merited no response, the second qualified the human for closer scrutiny, and the latter earned the human automatic termination. For example, just because a human mentioned the term 'Holy War' did not automatically mean that he was advocating it and therefore a target for the Hunters. Get something like that wrong and a non-hostile human could be killed – problematic when even alien-friendly humans tended to dislike aliens slaughtering other humans.

Surprisingly she was allowed to take her meal on a tray to her bedroom, where she ate while trying to ensure that nothing fell on the very thick and soft carpet. When finished she took her tray back to the kitchen intending to clean it herself, only for it to be snatched unceremoniously from her hands by a maid who promptly turned her back on JassaVar, blatantly not interested in talking.

JassaVar possessed no response option to that, so walked away and found a door to the gardens. She walked out revelling in the novelty of toll-free doors into an immense garden – not totally devoted to food and oxygen production like a garden deck. There were wide spaces of remarkably flat grass – in some places with fences or netting in place. A couple of the places she vaguely remembered might be called tenor courts or tennis cots. She possessed no idea what the others could be.

A path beyond the tenor cots led her to a wide spread of grass surrounded by fences, and inhabited by gigantic animals. Horses, she remembered, supposedly herbivores and tame. JassaVar was unfamiliar with tame animals, especially large ones, so retreated nervously to her bedroom and into the massive dressing room. So much space for clothes? Enough for eight girls, at least. How could it all be for her?

She spent some time exploring all corners, all cupboards, and herself in the mirror – and the latter gave least pleasure. She loved pictures of beautiful and glamorous human girls in stylish dresses, and hated how unglamorous she looked even in her last quality dress. Yet Brett had called her beautiful! Maybe he was just being kind, but a girl could dream.

Brett did not repeat the word 'beautiful' when he finally returned, accompanied by a human girl who turned out not to be Tiara but his other sister, Sara.

A twin sister, JassaVar remembered, reminding herself again of the very strange Earth evolutionary variant by which babies could be born male instead of only becoming male at puberty. Their mother must have simultaneously borne both male and female daughters – how strange to not be born female!

Sara was Brett's age, but looked older by alien norms where alien girls aged much more slowly than alien men. She was taller than most regressions – alien males medically reverted back to female as punishment for crimes. Yet Sara remained very glamorous in JassaVar's eyes, and seemed quite suspicious of JassaVar until Brett suggested that Sara look at JassaVar's wardrobe and give her advice on what JassaVar needed, and Sara liked that idea. JassaVar herself was puzzled by it until she double-checked the translation of 'wardrobe' and discovered that it could mean a collection of clothing as well as a piece of furniture.

Two girls headed upstairs to JassaVar's bedroom – which apparently once belonged to some bitch called Astra. JassaVar checked that the huge room was all for her, and asked what other girls would share the storage space in the dressing room? Sara frowned oddly to both questions, but did not seem angered by them, then expressed astonishment at the limited quantity of JassaVar's dresses. JassaVar tried to apologize as Sara grabbed JassaVar's hand and dragged her along to what Sara announced to be Tiara's bedroom – and then into Tiara's dressing room.

To see one of the most astounding sights imaginable.

Tiara's dressing room was as big as JassaVar's, but it was full of more clothes of all sorts than JassaVar could imagine one girl finding time to wear out in an alien lifetime. And all so gorgeous! And all Tiara's!

Sara seemed to find JassaVar's reaction amusing, and promised that as soon as Sara could sort out her schedules and her rug-rat – whatever a rug-rat was, JassaVar did not like to ask and her translator gave a most confusing variety of translations – Sara was going to take JassaVar shopping.

JassaVar just had to ask if Sara was sure she did not mind, and Sara just laughed, and said that she always enjoyed shopping for clothes.

Just like an alien girl!

CHAPTER FIVE

Emily Lovelace walked stiffly back into the cell where she had tried to kill herself less than twenty-four hours earlier.

She was feeling shaky, and not because ribs and wrist ached. Emily had been sternly interrogated by warders pretending that they would protect her from further attacks. Her refusal to talk had provoked threats of penalties for non-cooperation, but as she already anticipated punishments for attempting suicide and getting beaten up she refrained from repeating the mistake of getting drawn into talking again.

She also avoided repeating the mistake of looking up at interrogators who were growing more and more frustrated until, instead of announcing the anticipated punishment, the woman in charge simply ordered a return to her cell. Only then did Emily venture to look up at the woman – but this woman was not looking at her and did not notice the foolish gesture, so Emily got away without further questions but still not knowing how she would be punished.

There was nothing she could do about it, anyway, and she had something in her cell that was much more important to her.

Something called Tiara Maitland.

———

Two years earlier

Tiara exited the Principal's office with carefully downcast eyes, just managing to hold it until the door was closed behind her when she allowed her smile to skip as she giggled with delight.

Expelled at last. Getting herself caught shoplifting a second time had achieved its purpose. The Academy was not prepared to tolerate that even from a daughter of Edward Maitland. She was going home at last, and was going to dance the dust off her feet as she left. She had been getting so sick of the place in the last year, and was in any case desperate to get closer to the real action now that Dad was regularly meeting real aliens – even visiting alien spaceships while other aliens were conducting combat operations that made America's former 'War on Terror' look more like a schoolyard scrap.

Tiara could not have been more pro-alien – nor more furious at what she deemed to be the teaching staff's anti-alien attitudes. Tiara could have happily been a cheerleader for the aliens, and had openly derided the pathetic weakness of most of her ex-friends who had flocked to parrot their teachers' prejudices. Cowards and bullies most of them – was Tiara's considered opinion - too gutless to support Tiara when she argued with the teachers.

She guessed that the Principal had been as keen to find a pretext to expel Tiara as she had been to supply one. She was going to really enjoy her leaving gesture to the school - changing into her own clothes and burning her school uniforms and books in the grounds. It was not as if they could expel her twice, and should convince even her family how much she hated the place. She had tried to tell her Dad last time he had made a flying visit to see her. He had barely listened.

Now he would have to listen.

———

Emily was listening to Tiara.

Impossible not to – Tiara seemed unable to stop talking in her excitement. Emily had spent years learning the hard way to fear everything and everybody, but Tiara seemed quite unfazed at being in Juvie with a gang who had already attacked her once and would be seeking revenge at the first opportunity. Tiara even declared her confidence that the warders would protect her, dismissing Emily's stumbling attempts to suggest that promises of official protection from bullying were probably as worthless in Juvie as in school.

Tiara merely reacted by asking what Emily meant about school authorities not protecting a girl from bullying.

Had Emily been speaking from experience?

———

Two years earlier

Emily had adapted to life at her next foster family, though not as well as at the Burdens. Her new foster parents were a laid back couple happy to let her do all the cleaning as long as she caused no trouble and did not expect luxuries like new clothes or books or any personal attention.

Emily no longer even dreamt of finding a foster family to love her, and after Timmy felt that she did not deserve one, but had finally grown up enough to imagine becoming an adult and escaping the loveless limbo of foster care – finishing school and getting a job and one day meeting a nice boy with a nice family who would take her into their hearts and become her family. That novel-inspired dream inspired her to start noticing boys at school, but she soon learnt that the ones she liked were not interested in her and boys that were interested did not meet her concept of nice. She had no more success in making female friends – her social awkwardness only serving to compound her heinous crime of academic excellence.

Her new foster parents were much more generous with pocket money than Sandra Burden, and Emily found a Saturday job waitressing to get some clothes that were cheap but at least fitted. Zero personal property had followed her from the Burdens. Clothes could be replaced, but not photos and childhood mementos, and she never dared ask what had become of them.

Her foster parents were pleasant enough, but not invested enough to even notice that she had no friends. Emily coped, but kept sinking into bouts of black despair when anything reminded her of Timmy and Sukie and Sandra. Fortunately Emily had found herself for a few crucial months being looked after by a social worker who cared enough to work hard at reassuring her that Timmy's death had not been her fault, and Emily had accepted that in her rational mind, but doubts constantly rumbled away in the silent darkness of her soul.

In the meantime she anticipated transferring to the well-regarded nearby high school, but two weeks before term was due to start her foster dad obtained a better paid job requiring a move to another city. Emily was, inevitably, surplus to requirements. She was moved to a new foster home, and found herself abruptly transferred to a different but very large High School with a tough reputation.

It did not take Emily a week in her new foster home to realize that her new foster mother started her drinking quite early in the day. Earnings from waitressing had enabled Emily to buy a second hand computer, and she arrived at her new High School determined to get great grades ready for her escape from the prisons of High School and foster care.

First day she was mocked for her cheap clothes, and she ignored it.

Third day it got around that she was a foster kid. Naturally the mockery got more vicious, but Emily still ignored it and tried to avoid her tormentors — hoping that her lack of reaction would bore them to silence.

It had worked before, but these tormentors had too much self-esteem. Their leadership righteously resented Emily's arrogance in failing to grovel abjectly enough. The resentment got even deeper when they realized that Emily was scoring top grades at everything. They had long practice at their previous school in 'teaching lessons' to upstarts like Emily, and started by mobbing her just before class, stealing away her thoroughly crafted essay just before the class when she was due to hand it in, while telling her that if she told anyone that they had taken it they would say that she had given it to them to copy and cheat. They also called her a 'stupid little alien' who needed to be taught that she was no better than other girls.

The class was asked to drop their essays on the teacher's desk as they left class. A panic-stricken Emily did not know what to do. She had never learnt to ask for help. She was terrified to claim that her work had been stolen, because she could not prove it and it would be her word against the other girls. In her previous school she might have dared to say something, but her new teachers did not know her, and the school had not got its tough reputation for nothing.

Had Emily been the only pupil without her essay, and dared to speak to the teacher quietly alone, she might still have got the benefit of the doubt, but she was not alone. Another girl and four boys were also essay-deficient. The girl and two of the boys reacted insolently to the teacher's demands for an explanation as to where their work was. The teacher got angry and ordered all six along to the Principal, who was imposing a deliberately strict disciplinary regime to try and turn a troubled 'tough' High School around. Zero tolerance was the *rule, and neither teacher nor Principal were in any mood to listen to excuses even if Emily had dared to give one.*

Emily was given detention for the first time in her life.

———

"First time," Tiara laughed helplessly. "You're kidding me, little Miss Goody-Goody. I've lost count of the number of times I've been in detention. Why didn't you just tell the teachers your essay was stolen? Are you scared of everything?"

Emily could only stare back at her sister, not comprehending how Tiara could shrug off an ordeal as soul-destroying as detention.

"I knew they'd never believe me," was all she could whisper. "Why should they? Just a foster kid. I'd just have been punished for lying if I told the truth."

"Hell," Tiara hissed. "You're serious. You really are used to being treated like crap by everyone, aren't you? And to just taking it?"

Emily had not got near to replying before Tiara's verbal flow resumed to fill what seemed to Tiara to be an inordinately long silence.

"Nobody dares treat me like crap," she declared quite happily. "If they try they regret it, and I know how to get away with telling lies. Not always or I'd not be here, but mostly. Best lies are when you say what the morons want to believe. People believe any crap if it's what they want to believe - why else do people still keep voting for politicians? A great trick when you have enemies is to tell teachers they called you 'an alien'. Whatever they do to you – if they use the wrong word anything can be spun as a 'hate crime' – that way you can panic teachers or whoever into going Thought Police the Next Generation - if you've got the nerve – and I do."

"But lying is wrong," Emily finally interrupted Tiara's exuberant gush of words. "It is better to be silent than to tell lies."

She then remembered with sickening shame that she had herself told one massive lie not so long ago – and in court. She was guilty of perjury!

"OMG," Tiara exclaimed. "You really believe that, don't you?"

"I do," Emily asserted weakly – expecting Tiara to despise her for it, but still knowing that she was right.

The Galleys had said it – many times – so it had to be right.

"Someone has really done a number on brainwashing you, haven't they? Adults, of course. Never listen to adults – they talk garbage all the time. You know they always talk garbage – they never understand anything, do they? You get that?"

Emily was sixteen. That point she totally did get.

"So what happened after you got detention?" Tiara abruptly bounced the subject back. "That hyena pack that was picking on you? You didn't take them down, so they just got nastier? That always happens when you cave in to bullies, when you try appeasing them – they just get nastier!"

————

Two years earlier

It was three days after her detention that the gang pounced on Emily again.

Until then they had been satisfied with merely taunting and threatening her – a campaign that frayed Emily's nerves close to panic at every sight of them.

This time the gang forced her into a corner, and tried to steal away more important course work – but this time Emily fought – inexpertly, frantically, panic-stricken – pulling hair and slapping.

Teachers soon broke it up and dragged Emily and three others along to the Principal. The other three all accused Emily of starting the fight by attacking them for no reason. The Principal did not believe them, but nor did he listen to anything Emily tried to say. Fighting was not tolerated in his school, whatever silly little argument had started it. The three got detention - as would Emily had she not been in foster care. The Principal knew that the other girls had parents who would complain and cause trouble if he suspended them, but he could make an example of a foster kid without fear of comeback, so he suspended her for three days and summoned her foster mother to collect her.

Emily had not expected sympathy, but was still devastated by her foster mother's reaction. The woman angrily dragged Emily home and spanked her – the only time during her entire life in foster care that any adult would ever hit Emily.

But what really hurt Emily was that the woman confiscated Emily's computer.

———

"My sister spanked me once," Tiara giggled. "She figured that I set up my tenth birthday party to become World War Three! My fault for laughing too much but she lost it and I swear she only hurt her fingers - and I got her good in Dad and Brett's presence by telling her she miscounted and I should only have got eleven swats for my tenth birthday spanking. I timed it so perfectly! Dad shouted at her and forced her to apologize to me – and did she look stupid!"

Emily was finding this deluge of words hard to listen to – for so many reasons. Not least that Tiara should treat upsetting her family as a laughing matter, nor getting a sister in trouble. Had Emily been more accustomed to challenging people, or even interrupting them, she might have spoken out and challenged Tiara, but hesitation inspired second thoughts, and it was as much her nature to run away from any challenge as it was Tiara's to hurl herself into it.

That spanking from her foster mother had hurt little but humiliated a lot – Emily had not resented it - remembering the Galley mantra about accepting punishment when it was deserved and blaming herself entirely for getting suspended.

But she did resent the confiscation of her computer. The foster mother made a big mistake by not clearly explaining that the confiscation was temporary, but the foster mother was not given to explaining what seemed obvious to her. Her own parents had disciplined their children many times by confiscating toys and only returning them when the child did something to earn it, so the foster mother simply assumed that everyone would understand that and to her it was just a toy, but to Emily it was her proudest possession and she assumed that it was gone for good.

That was why Emily stole it back.

———

Two years earlier

Emily had no idea how to get herself out of the mess.

She had her default plan: keep quiet and work hard at school and at home in hope of persuading teachers to respect her and foster parents to like her - she had given up all hope of being loved - and she had no Plan B. Instead of devising a new plan, all she could think of was trying harder to make the old plan work.

But now – less than three weeks into High School and four weeks at her new foster home – and she had irrevocably forfeited both the respect of her teachers and the acceptance of her foster family.

She returned to High School on the Monday after two sleepless nights feeling even more scared than usual. The teachers would be so harsh, she just knew. Those girls would be seeking revenge. Emily was literally shaking with fear as she walked in through the gates of the school.

And stopped.

The girls were all there – standing right outside the door of the school – looking straight at her – lined up like a firing squad.

Emily stood and stared back at them for fully two minutes.

The squad stood and stared back at her – barely blinking, smugly smiling.

'Loveless Lovelace –

Always gonna be loveless.'

Emily cracked completely.

For the third time in her life she turned and ran away in panic.

———

Emily presumed that Tiara had finally fallen asleep, because Miss Maitland had stopped describing her triumphs in causing chaos at home and school.

Emily had retreated into silence in utter bemusement at the way Tiara seemed to love everything that Emily most hated – nightmarish scenarios like getting in trouble or being noticed. Was DNA the only thing they had in common? While Tiara boasted about all her social and personal triumphs all Emily could remember were her failures and humiliations.

And crimes.

Two years earlier

Emily ran blindly at first, but her brain slowly began to function and realize her desperate position and limited options.

She dare not return to school, there was nobody she dared to ask for help, and she would get in terrible trouble for running away, but she had no fourth option - and she would only be in trouble if caught.

She was fourteen. Her only hope was to pretend to be eighteen. She had no really clear idea how to do that, but she was in no state of mind to think anything through. She could only think of getting as far away as possible.

Luckily she did know that there would be nobody at her foster home that morning. She headed there, walking as fast as she dared, constantly watching for police cars and getting paranoid about every adult that looked at her.

At the apartment she packed her few good clothes, picked up the two hundred dollars that she had saved from waitressing and hidden, packed as much as she could carry — found her precious computer in her foster parents' bedroom and packed it too, feeling like she was stealing it but stubbornly taking it anyway.

Then Emily ran away from a second foster home.

JassaVar was eating the most extraordinary meal of her life.

The quantity of food on offer was terrifying. They were even served huge slices of real meat — nothing like the meat-simulating protein bars that had been luxuries in JassaVar's diet all of her life. She wondered aloud how they could afford so much food, before remembering with embarrassment that they were a very wealthy family even by human standards, let alone alien.

"Welcome to the family, Humility," Brett answered kindly, triggering an odd look from Sara. "Down here the rule is that you eat as much as you like, and don't worry about it. You've got less on your plate right now than Tiara when she has a new dress for a major party. Help yourself."

JassaVar stared wide-eyed at all the food on the table.

"Is it our duty to eat all food?" she could not help asking – just to be absolutely sure. "Three alone? Or does another join us?"

The twins exchanged glances that JassaVar could not interpret successfully.

"Brett means," Sara chimed in, "that you eat as much or as little as you like."

"Do I comprehend correct?" JassaVar added, seeing that she had not offended them. "It is acceptable if food is left uneaten."

"Sure is," Brett sounded puzzled. "Would it matter on *Anarchy*?"

"My mother's rule is always eat all food she puts on table," JassaVar hastened to explain. "Even if ill we waste nothing because next meal might not be enough."

"Does that happen often?" Sara asked sharply. "There is not enough food for you at a meal?"

JassaVar hesitated over that.

"There were meals when I possessed appetite to eat more than we possessed, even when mother gave us all her food."

Very many such meals, she refrained from saying.

"Have you never seen this much food on a table for three?" Brett asked with a frown.

"I do not remember so much," JassaVar replied honestly. "But nor do I remember meal I did not assist to prepare. Do I assist to clear?"

"No need, Humility," Sara told her with a smile. "Dad employs servants to do that here."

"Housegirls?"

"We call them housemaids."

"My mother told me that I was to be housegirl," JassaVar dared to press on, "but she did not state duties. So ..."

"I suggest," Brett interrupted firmly, and JassaVar silenced herself quickly in deference, "that you await your mother's arrival before you start worrying about that. In the meantime just relax and enjoy. To us you're just a kid – a teenager, anyway. At your age you should be enjoying life – and having fun."

JassaVar did not know quite what to make of that.

She had never been commanded to 'enjoy' before.

———

Tiara Maitland had not liked being woken up so insanely early after her first night in Juvenile Detention, but she had even less liked being woken up at three in the morning by someone whimpering.

It took time to remember exactly where she was, and longer to realize that the whimpering was coming from Emily. There was just enough light to see her twin twisting and turning on her bunk.

A memory from that first evening - 'already has nightmares'. So this had to be a nightmare.

Tiara did not hesitate. She firmly shook her sister to wake her.

Emily squealed and pulled away against the wall as she woke up.

"Wow, sis," Tiara could not help but exclaiming. "What is so scary about me? That is twice I've scared you to death. Having a nightmare?"

"Sorry," Emily whispered. "I'm sorry. I'm sorry. I'm sorry. I'm sorry. I'm sorry. I'm sorry. I – I just …"

"Just what?"

"Just for a moment," a confession came out with a rush. "I thought it must be – doesn't matter?"

"Might be – what? Some guy? Did some bastard rape you?"

"Rape me!" Emily squeaked, shocked that Tiara should jump to that idea. "No. No. No. Never!"

"So you were never raped? Or sexually abused."

"No," Emily reassured her twin with a shudder. "Still a virgin. Never been raped."

Tiara paused for a few seconds before slumping to her knees and uttering words that shocked Emily to the core.

"I have," Tiara declared with deadly seriousness. "I've been raped."

CHAPTER SIX

Sylvia Godwin had last driven to the Maitland Mansion for a birthday party hoping to dance with Brett Maitland – an adolescent memory that she now looked back on with amusement.

Back then her mother had driven her. This time Sylvia Godwin drove herself at the slow pace recommended by security guards. The roads into the enclave were gated and had armed guards – but only two each and they only had handguns and seemed quite relaxed, while the borders of the enclave possessed nothing more obviously secure than fences and walls to deter intruders. Presumably there were alien drones somewhere overhead able to detect if she were carrying guns or explosives. While aliens might be safer in American enclaves than in enclaves in other countries, it had been in America that their first embassy had fallen victim to the suicide bombers who had provoked the aliens' massive retaliation - starting with multiple tactical nuclear strikes. And it was in D.C. that the aliens' original spokesgirl had been gunned down just outside her husband's church.

Sylvia knew that there were aliens resident in the enclave – reportedly around the power plant. Alien residence meant giant alien men, alien weapons, and lethal alien response options to any threat. Maybe the guards were just for show.

Last time that Sylvia had driven up to the Maitland Mansion, nobody had known of the aliens' existence, even though alien researchers had been visiting secretly for years and there had been a secret alien base on the dark side of the moon. Now the world was in the throes of the most dramatic changes in history – no surprise that there should be such terrible global conflict surrounding it. Christian churches of every denomination routinely incorporated special prayers for peace and reconciliation between aliens and humans.

Rather ironic considering that the alien enclave was a sort of symbol of conciliation between alien and human – especially so the Maitland Mansion because of Edward Maitland's marriage to an alien. Sylvia was not immune to human jealousy of alien girls for their long lives or good bodies. Countless young human men must have been slapped or shouted at by human girlfriends for staring at alien girls. Edward Maitland's alien wife was still on honeymoon, but his alien step-daughter had arrived at the mansion that morning. Sylvia felt excited to meet her first alien – or visitor as some authorities were insisting on calling them.

She wondered how teenage aliens differed from the human teenagers she dealt with on a daily basis. For a start, did they have the same problems of loneliness and social isolation? Did they get suicidal? Did they become delinquent?

Did they run away from home?

———

Two years earlier

Emily was completely drenched by the time that she stumbled into the dark Church porch to shelter from the thunderstorm.

She had been walking all day except for sitting down to rest in obscure corners of city parks, but it was not just walking that had exhausted her – her despair shared responsibility for that. Her first aim had only been to get as far as possible away from school and foster home. She was soon heading roughly west towards the area where the Galleys had lived.

The thought had struck her that she might go and see the Galleys and ask for their help. Maybe they would believe her, was her thought. She could not imagine anyone else doing so, but the closer she got less she believed even in them. Why would they care? They had sent her away, after all.

'Loveless Lovelace –

Always gonna be loveless.'

Then it started raining heavily. Thunder and lightning crackled overhead, and she was lost. It was getting really dark, and the spire of a church loomed ahead of her. She remembered going to church with the Galleys. It was not their church but it was a church. The door was locked, but there was some shelter in the porch, so it was easy to slump down in a corner to rest.

And fall asleep.

———

Sara came out to meet Sylvia in the hallway, and led the chaplain into an elegant reception room which Sylvia did not remember.

Brett she did remember – he was already in the room with a teenager who was wearing a simple dress with little make-up and no visible jewellery.

This was Humility - the first alien that Sylvia had ever met in the flesh.

———

Two years earlier

Emily did not realize that the porch belonged to a Catholic church.

Not that she would have cared - it was Christian - that was enough. A parishioner who lived nearby called the priest to tell him that there was someone lying in the porch of his church, and joined him to find the bedraggled and exhausted Emily. It was to the woman's nearby house that Emily allowed herself to be escorted and wrapped up warm and dried off and fed – and to the two of them that she attempted to explain why she had run away.

Attempted being the operative word. Emily lacked skills at asking for help, and found it hard to convey the sheer panic that had driven her to run away. She could also imagine how bad she must look to adults, and could not imagine why they would believe her. As a result her attempts to explain sounded defensive and stuttering and unconvincing in her own ears, yet the Catholics seemed quite credulous of her statements that she had been bullied at school and was afraid of her foster mother, and did not want to go back to either.

The social workers who came were openly sceptical, and Emily lost her last shreds of confidence and got even more defensive and unconvincing.

The social workers put her in the back of their car, declining the resident's offer of a bed for the night, and took Emily to Juvenile Detention instead. A social worker looked through her bag and found a computer and nearly two hundred dollars in cash, which was taken into custody while Emily was petrified to be locked in a cell. The social worker checked Emily's file, and rang her foster parents to let them know the girl was safe (assuming them to care), and asked if a computer and money belonging to the foster parents was missing (assuming that Emily had obtained them from the foster parents and hoping that she had not stolen them from elsewhere).

The foster mother was in a foul mood when she got the phone call. She had rowed with her husband and had downed plenty of gin before the call came through about the wretched little trouble-making brat. The foster mother had not even noticed that the computer was missing, so dropped the phone and scurried off to look for it the moment that it was mentioned.

Seeing that it was not there recalled the woman to the circumstances in which she had taken it off Emily, after spanking the little brat. The woman's alcohol-fuelled brain panicked at the thought that Emily might accuse her of abuse. That could have cost her the fostering payments which were keeping her family solvent or even have led to her facing charges, or so she thought in panic.

Panic and alcohol combined to offer a solution which she had neither the time nor the sobriety to think through. She went back to the phone and told the social worker that Emily had stolen the computer and the money from them – thinking as she did that the little bitch must have stolen the money from someone – never in her life having managed to save any money she genuinely could not imagine a foster girl being able to save so much money from a Saturday job.

In the cold light of morning sobriety the woman repented equally genuinely about accusing Emily of stealing the computer. In panic she confessed to her husband – who panicked in his turn but did not dare to admit it and struggled to find a way out of the mess.

In the same cold light of morning Emily faced not only a very stern interview from two social workers, but one from police officers to take a statement about the 'stolen' computer and money. Emily panicked, knowing what the police must be thinking, and not expecting to be believed when she claimed that the money was hers, and half-believing herself that taking the computer from her foster parents' bedroom really was theft. So guilty did she feel about how guilty she must look that she could not have sounded or looked guiltier to her interrogators.

The interviews ended with Emily being warned that if her foster parents decided to press charges she was in serious trouble.

Emily's foster father jumped on the opportunity when a police officer called to ask if they wanted to press charges on the thefts of cash and computer. Desperate to square their consciences without incriminating his wife, he stated *firmly that they did not want to press charges, and creatively added that they could not prove the money belonged to them, while trying to sound magnanimous in suggesting that possibly Emily had misunderstood about the computer. He thought of offering to let Emily keep both money and computer, but fear that such an offer might sound suspicious made him hesitate and lose his nerve.*

After three terrifying days in Juvie, Emily was told that she would not be charged providing she admitted the offences and accepted an official caution. By then she had accepted in her own mind that she had stolen the computer, and having hardly eaten or slept for three days she had neither the energy nor the courage to argue. Signing her confession earned her the promised release from custody though not until a new home was found for her.

She could only listen numbly when told that the 'stolen property' was being returned to its 'rightful owners' to whom she should be very grateful, and warned that she would be in serious trouble if there was any repeat of such delinquency.

It took two weeks to find a new foster home and release her from detention. Two weeks in which the resident predators had enormous fun with a new victim who dared not defend herself or complain to anyone whatever they stole from her or however they bullied her. Two weeks of sleeping little and eating less.

Two weeks of learning to suffer in silence.

———

"According to her file," Sylvia told the Maitland twins with precise restraint, "Emily had no previous convictions before her arrest three months ago. She was remanded in custody until the jurisdictional hearing when she pleaded guilty and was remanded back in custody for reports pending sentence."

"Remanded in custody just for car theft?"

"Her foster family refused to take her back, and it's not easy to find good foster families who will take girls straight out of Detention. Unfortunately there are foster parents who take kids like that purely for the money, which would be worse than useless for a very troubled girl who desperately needs a genuinely loving home or I fear we could lose her – one way or another.

On top of which the court were not sympathetic because the stolen car was involved in an accident and a child was seriously injured, and though Emily was not driving she refused to name the driver."

Sara and Brett exchanged unhappy glances.

"Convictions can only be the tip of an iceberg," Brett asserted firmly. "What is her school disciplinary record like?"

Sylvia considered that very carefully. She had warned them that she was not in a position to supply confidential information in any detail, but that did not mean that she was prohibited from saying anything. These were special circumstances.

"Mostly very good," she finally decided to say. "But you must understand why I can't go into detail."

"But not perfect?"

"No, not perfect, but very good – and her academic record is outstanding."

"Still sounds no worse than Tiara," Sara intervened. "Maybe we should worry more about Tiara corrupting Emily than Emily corrupting Tiara."

Sylvia was tempted to say that she thought exactly that herself, as Tiara was clearly the dominant character, but tactfully refrained.

"Or possibly corrupting each other," Brett said instead. "Rather than just double trouble, they could be trouble squared. Maybe it is just as well there is no chance of us being considered as a foster family. Definite about that?"

"I ran it by a couple of people in Child Services who know their business and don't think it would be a good idea. Maybe you could pull strings and fix that, but – to be honest I still don't think it would be a good idea. All depends on finding her good foster parents. She is an exceptionally bright girl, but in despair – clearly lonely, resentful, and embittered. I fear for her - but maybe finding Tiara might make her feel less isolated. Having a real sister to talk to – if only digitally – may literally be a life-saver – a life-line. For now, I'm ringing round all my church contacts within a hundred miles to find foster parents who will take parenting her seriously. That might be easier knowing that she has no real family – except Tiara."

"Real family is a problem, is it?"

"Real family can make life hell for foster parents."

"Promise we won't. Oh, here is the coffee. Thank you, Humility."

Sylvia could not hide her fascination as a girl who looked human approached with a tray and three steaming mugs. Sylvia would have guessed her to be a year or two younger than sixteen.

Though she had thought the same about Tiara and Emily.

"Thank you, Humility," she said as she took the coffee that Humility had volunteered to collect ten minutes earlier. "How are you settling in? If I may ask?"

"Desirable," the teenage alien replied with perfect ease. "This residence amazes. It is enormous, but strange."

"Strange how?" Sylvia asked, noticing that the twins were equally curious.

"Housegirls – maids – do not eat with family," the girl frowned endearingly. "You possess excess space and food, and I possess more clothes than I ever saw!"

That produced stifled laughs from both the Maitland twins. Some sort of in-joke was Sylvia's guess.

"Permit me to ask?" Humility ventured with a dip of her head.

"Anything," Sylvia hastened to reassure her.

"Your collar? A symbol of your cult – apologies, religion – do I comprehend correct?"

"You do," Sylvia just had to smile. "I'm a minister in – a Christian church. I believe GracefulGirl called us the Cult of Love?"

"Cult of Love? Your cult follows strange habit of monogamy – if I comprehend correct. AvernaVar – GracefulGirl - was killed when she visit one of your churches."

A glance sideways revealed that the last sentence had suppressed the smiles of the twins, as Sylvia acknowledged that Humility did, indeed, comprehend correctly. Sylvia then asked if Humility had known GracefulGirl.

"No," Humility laughed. "I was housegirl on *Anarchy*, but all girls admired AvernaVar. We listen to all her words, and many came aboard because of her reports about your planet and your men."

"What did you think about her marrying a human?"

"I envied her marriage, but still consider concept of monogamy strange."

"It does not seem strange to us," Sylvia went on to amplify. "We consider it to be the best way to live – morally and culturally."

"It interests, but is it not hard for girl to satisfy all sexual desires of man without another girl to share burden? Or do you train men to show extreme restraint?"

"They do, believe me," Brett cut in with a smile. "Human women are supreme experts at training their men to come to heel."

"To heel?" Humility frowned. "I do not comprehend. Apologies."

"My brother," Sara explained, failing to suppress her own smile, "is admitting that men behave best when trained like dogs to do what their women command. Dogs are trained to walk to heel."

"Do they? I can't imagine ever commanding a man unless I become mother to son – that is not likely. I know I never achieve Physician or Organizer. I may never rise above housegirl."

"You've already risen above housegirl," Sara told her firmly. "You're part of the family, now. Remember that."

"Mother said I will be housegirl."

"This is our father's home," Brett told her. "Your mother signed a pre-nup which I checked over. This house will stay his."

"But as his wife," Sara cut in, "she'll probably get to run this house her way as long as she keeps him happy."

"Doesn't mean she'll be able to tell Tiara what to do when Princess Brat gets out of Juvie."

"Do you know when Tiara will regain freedom?" Humility asked Sylvia. "I did comprehend correctly – your employment is at prison?"

"We don't know yet, and yes I am. You don't have prisons in your culture, do you?"

"No," Humility confirmed with a shudder of her shoulders. "To us deprivation of freedom is considered barbaric and uncivilised, but I comprehend that many of you consider killing and flogging to be barbaric and uncivilised. We possess many differences. I hope I do not offend by questions."

"We still do practice legal capital punishment in some states," Brett told her, placing a hand on Humility's elbow and clearly indicating that she sit on the settee beside him. "And corporal punishment – though only of children and that is heavily limited by various laws."

"I tried spanking Tiara once," Sara admitted with a shrug. "A few years ago. Kind of lost it for a moment, and I think I hurt my hand more than I hurt her."

"My mother punishes me when I do not please her," Humility stated without the slightest hint of embarrassment. "Would my mother be housewife or businesswife in this household?"

Three humans stared at each other.

"Do I ask bad question?" Humility asked anxiously into their silence.

"No, honey," Sara hastened to reassure her. "It is just that the concept of different types of wife is not one we use."

"I comprehend. It was stupid question."

"Not at all," Brett seemed set on reassuring the girl in a very protective masculine way, and it clicked with Sylvia that feigning vulnerability was allegedly one of the tricks which alien girls used for seducing human men.

But Sylvia observed nothing feigned nor manipulative about this girl's attitude. A shared glance with Sara convinced the chaplain that the two women were in accord in this assessment. Humility was for real, which was why Sara was not intervening to protect her brother.

"As wife to my father," Sara continued, "she could give orders in this household – within limits - as a housewife does in your culture, I understand."

"Accurate. A housewife command and discipline all daughters and housegirls in household where householder is man. Where householder is girl she herself would command and discipline. Does your housekeeper command and discipline in household?"

"Only maids and other employees," Sara chimed back in. "Mrs Henderson does not command daughters in this house – and you count as a daughter like Tiara. I don't know whether Dad would allow your mother to discipline Tiara. Maybe she'd do a better job than us, but probably anyone would – which is why it might not be wise to bring Emily here. A suicidal girl must need a lot more care and attention than we could possibly give."

"Tiara is going to spit blood when we tell her that," Brett remarked – then hastened to reassure an alarmed Humility that he was not speaking literally.

"I was hoping," Sylvia chose the opportune moment, "that you'd agree to them staying in contact. Digitally, at first, perhaps – but then meeting regularly – subject to agreement by the courts and Emily's new foster family – praying I find a good one."

"Sounds good to me. Doubt Tiara will agree."

———

One year earlier

Climbing out of the pit was hard.

To find herself labelled a thief and truant and troublemaker was demoralising, but it compensated that Emily was not forced back to that foster home or that school. Luckily her new foster home was over ten miles away. It almost made it worth the severe lectures from social workers and the principal of her new school. The prejudice she met from her new foster family and her new teachers was humiliating – they treated her every action and every word with overt suspicion.

She reverted to default response – working hard at school, being quiet and obsessively tidy at home, and avoiding trouble by keeping herself to herself. Slowly she began to hope that she was climbing out of the pit. By her second year of high school, it seemed to be working with her teachers, at least.

Her 'delinquent' label even proved helpful. Her new school principal was an enthusiast for rehabilitating troubled teens, and a delinquent as academically bright as Emily ticked all the boxes for a case study to exploit and boast about. Her teachers were pushed to advance her work until she was poised to skip a grade. The Principal was eager to boast that his school had turned one delinquent round so totally that she graduated a year early.

Her delinquent label proved more of a mixed blessing with other pupils. Rumours got about that she had been in Juvie, and since shame prevented her from either denying or explaining she acquired a 'reputation'. It meant that she became much less of a target for bullying, but it made it even harder for her to make friends with any girls of the type she wanted.

What went for female students went double for male students – just at the time when boys were first starting to notice her and she was first starting to dream about boys. That second year hormones conquered fears just enough to try two informal dates with two boys, but she cut both short after one boy offered her alcohol and the other seemed unable to comprehend the concept of keeping his hands to himself – and both sneered at 'a girl like her' objecting to what seemed to them like perfectly natural behaviour, driving Emily to the characteristic over-reaction of concluding that boys would only ever be interested in her for the wrong reasons, and her over-reaction twisted even her dreams about boys, helping to drive Emily even deeper into her solitary lifestyle. Her paranoia compounded itself when she began looking for the worst from boys who tried to talk to her – and purely because of her own prejudices interpreting everything they said as confirming her prejudices.

But while her social life floundered, life improved at her foster home. As the suspicions of her teachers eased, so did those of her foster parents, and Emily had acclimatised to them. She was basically just a lodger, but a well-treated lodger – given privacy, not over-worked, warm and well-fed, but then her foster parents discovered that they were expecting twins and needed her room, so Emily acquired a new foster mother early in that second year. At first, all seemed well. She had her own tiny bedroom and Donna, her new foster mother, was undemanding and pleasant most of the time – happy to leave Emily alone providing Emily caused no trouble. Once again just a lodger, but Emily was fine about that.

She was not fine about her new foster brother.

———

"They can do it, Emily," Tiara told her twin as they went to breakfast. "My father is Edward Maitland. He can fix it even if Brett can't, but I bet Brett can do it."

"No, Tiara," Emily hissed back. "No way will they want a girl like me in their home. Nobody will ever take a girl like me without a pay check attached, and your family don't need the money."

"There must be a way. I want you with me. Oh, crap – who let you lot out of the cattery?"

Emily stopped in shaking fear, and backed away towards the nearest wall. Sukie and two of her gang were right in front of Tiara – looking back at the twins with obvious hate in their eyes. Emily could not look them in the face.

Tiara could – without difficulty.

"You think you're something special, do you?" a girl Emily knew as Alice hissed from beside Sukie.

"No, I know I'm something special," Tiara smirked. "That is why I'm giving you a final warning. You leave my sister alone, or I drop you in so much crap you'll wish you were boys."

Emily could hardly believe her ears. Was Tiara completely mad? It was as if Emily's twin really believed that she could win against bullies, even that authorities might genuinely protect her from them. Maybe Tiara was so amazing that she could win such a battle, but Emily knew that Emily never could and Tiara could be released any day. Tiara had a family. Emily had nobody.

Even if Tiara's family were going to help Emily as Tiara had blithely promised it could be weeks or months before Emily was released. She could be stuck in Juvie after Tiara's discharge – stuck and once again at the gang's mercy.

A nasty thought came to Emily that she could ensure her release before Tiara by betraying Tiara, but Tiara had been unimaginably supportive and protective of Emily, despite having already been beaten up because of Emily, and it was not Tiara's fault that Emily was so pathetic. Tiara was the one and only person in the world to whom Emily mattered. She might be the one and only person in the world to whom Emily ever would matter. Scary though Tiara might be, Emily had to stand beside her. Tiara was doing everything possible to help Emily, and silence might be the only way Emily could ever repay that debt – so Emily was determined to do it, and be proud of it.

Emily stepped forward to stand behind Tiara's right shoulder.

CHAPTER SEVEN

Brett escorted Sylvia to her car and held the door open for her.

Such old-world courtesies from Brett always amused Sara, chiefly because they tended to delight girls and encourage them to hope that they were getting special treatment. It still amazed Sara that Brett could have grown up with a twin sister, a bitchy stepmother, and an incorrigible adopted half-sister, yet still be completely clueless about girls.

An observational blind spot inherited from their father. God alone knew how Edward Maitland had charmed his way into his first wife's heart at college – there had been times when Sara doubted whether her father could spell the word 'charm' – yet there had always been moments when Edward Maitland could prove unexpectedly observant – usually at the most inconvenient times for his daughter.

No secret as to how he had charmed his way into Astra's or Modesty's hearts. Wealth in a man's possession would always possess charms to captivate some female beasts - to Modesty's credit she had never pretended otherwise. The pre-nup that Modesty had signed and registered and accepted limited Modesty to set financial allowances during her marriage and recompense at its termination, with strict penalty clauses for breaches of marital behaviour on her part but not his. Sara would never have accepted such terms as Brett had negotiated and Modesty agreed, but she realized that aliens treated marriage as primarily a business arrangement. Modesty was prepared to cater to Edward Maitland's sexual fetishes, which Sara would rather not have known about, and double as Personal Assistant. Sara had reluctantly accepted Brett's contention that they could tolerate Modesty as a stepmother much more easily than Astra. After all, Sara herself lived in another city with husband and son, and Brett no longer lived at the Maitland Mansion.

Sara had worried a bit about Modesty's daughter Humility being wished into the household, but it was only one of Modesty's two daughters, and was by human terms still a teenager so it was natural that Humility should live with her mother, and Sara was convinced that the girl was not on any calculating mission - despite her eyes widening whenever she looked at Brett. Sylvia reacted the same way, for that matter, as did many other girls – nothing suspicious there.

Sara was as accustomed to girls reacting that way to her twin as to Brett failing to notice it.

———

One year earlier

Tiara was once again alone on her birthday, and even more annoyed about it at the age of fifteen.

Sara was away on her honeymoon. Her Dad was away on an alien spaceship, and in an angry moment she had told Brett to stuff his offer to take her out for an evening meal, and to leave her alone. Unfortunately, Brett had taken her at her word instead of coming anyway to show that he really cared. Why did he not have the simple common sense to try changing her very-ready-to-change mind?

Typical guy – insensitive idiot through and through.

Dad had promised to make it up to her by throwing her a party, but only if he or Brett supervised the planning personally, and Tiara had rejected that offer on the grounds that their leaden hands would have stifled all the fun - and banned the alcohol, though she did not mention that - making her a laughing stock among her friends.

Dad had instead promised to take her out somewhere special when he got back from his latest business trip – though she knew that he would only remember that promise if she pestered him repeatedly.

She had arranged to go out with friends from school that Saturday, but her actual birthday was mid-week during exams, so none of them were allowed out on the evening itself. Tiara never bothered much with revising for exams – her memory was so good that she could easily pass most exams without really trying. While over her birthday dinner tray in her bedroom she amused herself circumventing the family safety protocols on her computer to browse porn sites, but that could not amuse her for long, and was definitely not enough for her birthday. She did not want to be alone on her birthday, so she had accepted an invitation to the Garroway house at the other end of the enclave – almost the only place to which she could walk and find other teenagers and be welcomed. As both Garroway siblings were teenage boys hell would freeze before any teenage girl would be unwelcome in their house – especially when their parents were out.

The coolest bit about the Garroways was that they did not mind sharing their illicit stocks of alcohol – and Tiara did not mind repaying them by snogging both Ralph and Ed at the same time. At eighteen and seventeen years old they knew what they were doing better than boys her own age, and as they were neighbours she was confident that she could control them even when sexually teasing them.

Too confident to imagine them raping her.

———

Tiara was the most awesome human being that Emily had ever met.

Scarily so. Tiara was brilliant at picking the moments to provoke members of the gang with snide whispers or mere mocking stares. Moments when guards were in place to observe the other girls threatening Tiara or even lashing out at her. Even so it did not take the authorities long to work it out, and after four incidents Tiara and Emily were hauled into an office together and ordered to stop it or else.

"My apologies," Tiara responded cheerfully as Emily nearly dissolved in terror. "Sorry if I overstepped the mark but this is my twin sister who I was separated from at birth so naturally I want to protect her. All her life she has been bullied and nobody has ever done anything to protect her – that is why she was too scared to make a statement about being beaten up. Maybe if you can convince her that you really will protect her instead of punishing her then I'm sure she'll be willing to make a statement – won't you, Emily?"

_____

One year earlier

Tiara's memories of that evening would always be hazy, but not as hazy as the brothers had intended.

She remembered the movie – she liked horror movies, but this one was ultra-gruesome even for her taste and included several naked girls but no naked guys so Tiara did not enjoy it.

She did enjoy the unusually large box of her favourite chocolates, and willingly repaid both brothers with serious snogging.

She remembered the second beer they gave her, and thinking to herself that she had better not have any more.

She remembered losing all ability to make her limbs do what she wanted them to do. Remembered barely being able to focus her eyes on anything.

She remembered the brothers carrying her upstairs and into a bedroom, casually stripping clothes off her, laying her face forward over the edge of the bed.

Then her memories got really vague after a while until she remembered them helping her into her own dark and silent house – whispering to her to be quiet until somehow she managed to push them away and stagger upstairs on her own.

She woke next morning on the carpet in front of her bed.

_____

Emily realized that Tiara had set her up, but not only her.

Tiara had forced the adults to take her statement seriously while forcing Emily to speak up out of loyalty to Tiara – but Emily kept it simple and never hinted at previous assaults, and did not want to betray Sukie, so offered no explanation of why they had attacked her, but she made and signed her statement.

Emily left the room hand in hand with her sister. For the first time ever she had a protector who really cared for her. As they walked Emily pledged her soul that she would die rather than ever breathe a word that would harm Tiara in any way. At that moment Emily felt a perverse pride at her criminal record. Emily was determined to face her sentencing in silence.

To be worthy of Tiara.

———

One year earlier

As usual there had been nobody at home for Tiara to talk to or even to notice that she had come home late – as she had unwisely told the brothers.

She was too shaken – more distraught than at any time since Astra had departed spitting fury and spite at the little girl she was abandoning. Tiara had to research exactly what had happened to her, and it took a day to work out that there might be no evidence left in her bloodstream, and that it would be her word against theirs, and that she could prove nothing if she told anyone.

It would take a fortnight for her to be confident that she was not pregnant.

She also guessed that they could not have given her a big enough dose – a mistake for which she was going to make them pay.

———

Emily's spasm of happiness did not last long.

It had dissipated within the week, as the demoralising grind of detention began to get even under Tiara's skin. The only bonus about their assigned chores in the kitchen was that they were kept working together for the week – giving Emily time to explain the concept of chores to a twin who had never done any in her life. At first Emily tried to do Tiara's share, but then Tiara realized what Emily was doing and started asserting herself until doing just enough that their overseers made no comment – though it still seemed to Emily to be an abysmally low standard of work.

Then Emily received the news that her dispositional hearing was coming up on Monday. She had no clue what sentence she might get, and though determined to embrace her martyrdom for Tiara's sake she was still terrified of it. She had not seen her defence attorney since pleading guilty, and only twice before that - when he had spent their limited time together telling her to plea-bargain and ensuring that she had gone to trial taking conviction for granted and terrified at the hostility she would face if she tried to defend herself.

Despite her earlier determination not to lie all courage fled when surrounded by that terrifying clique of stern adults. She thought that pleading guilty would make them less angry at her. Thought wrongly. Her defence attorney was scathing about her pleading guilty after refusing to plea-bargain for probation in return for naming the driver of the car. Equally harsh were the detectives who subsequently asked her again to name the boy. Emily could only remain miserably silent. Pleading guilty had avoided the public humiliation of the trial, but not the humiliation of being returned to custody pending her dispositional hearing and warned that not naming her boyfriend would count seriously against her.

Yet the scorn of the adults had been nothing compared to the scorn being daily inflicted by Sukie's gang – increasingly augmented by physical assaults that ultimately turned into kickings. Only Tiara had given Emily a spark of hope for her future, but even Tiara's eternal optimism could only partially mitigate Emily's unrelenting pessimism. Emily dared not hope that Tiara's family would help her, and had no clue whether she could expect years in Juvie or immediate release. At least in Southside she had Tiara – but for how long? Whatever Tiara might promise about staying with her until she was discharged, Emily doubted that even Tiara could outwit the merciless suffocations of the legal system.

If Emily was released immediately, would they let her stay in contact with Tiara? Maybe one day even live with her.

That was Emily's only hope.

_____

One year earlier

Tiara's first move was to breeze casually back into the Garroway home early the next evening when she knew that the brothers' parents were home, and ask if she had left her purse there the previous evening.

The parents had never been told that Tiara had visited. The sons reacted guiltily at her turning up looking so calm and confident. When she went on to remark that she had no clear memory of when she had left them, because she had been unbelievably tired, the brothers relaxed visibly.

Until they noticed the suspicion on their parents' faces.

Tiara soon departed, pretending merely to be worried about the whereabouts of her stupid purse, but satisfied that the brothers would face some tough questioning while relaxing in the delusion that she had no memory of being raped.

'Revenge was a dish best served cold' was a line that Tiara had once heard. She now knew exactly what it meant.

———

Emily no longer found it hard to believe that Tiara had managed to get revenge on her rapists.

Tiara had refined her tactics against Sukie's gang. Again and again Tiara had pulled Emily beside her to stand in front of one of the gang when they met. Every time Tiara did not actually do or say a thing – just stood there, arms folded, head tilted, unblinkingly staring as her target squirmed.

Emily had heard that Sukie and two other members of the gang had broken ranks to admit assault but blame another girl for calling Tiara an alien – which the authorities were treating as massively more serious than the actual assault.

To Emily's overwhelming relief she would not have to give evidence in any trial – her imagination had run riot about the court not believing her and the gang being acquitted and Emily being convicted of perjury instead. Her imagination usually ran amok at any idea of stepping outside of her extremely limited comfort zones, and even Tiara's incurable optimism could not cure Emily's terminal pessimism.

Emily soon began to feel sorry for the gang. Especially for Sukie, whom she still could not look at without feeling waves of shame and guilt. It was because of that shame and guilt that Emily finally found the courage to plead with Tiara to call a halt on intimidating Sukie, at least. It took literal begging to persuade Tiara to reluctantly agree to let up.

But only on Sukie.

———

One year earlier

It was not hard to gather interesting scuttlebutt about the brothers and their previous girlfriends.

Though instinctively derisive of girls who tied themselves into emotional knots over boys, Tiara knew how to prise out all the gossip about other girls at her school and their complex webs of friendships and enmities and crushes and heartbreaks. It took only a couple of weeks to identify three girls who had been left pretty distraught, according to gossip, after spending time with one or other brother – or both.

And only another week to get enough from one of them to know for sure that Tiara had not been their first victim, and to blame herself for having trusted them.

But self-criticism had not weakened her plans for the two brothers whom she had been systematically lulling into a sense of false security.

———

The night before her sentencing Emily took ages getting to sleep, and woke in the small hours.

Not another nightmare, so fortunately she had not woken Tiara. It was incredible that a girl as useless as Emily could have a twin as amazing as Tiara, but depressing that they might not meet again for ages. Emily had been warned to pack all personal property – most of which Tiara had given her - as she might not be returning to the Detention Centre, and Tiara had cheerfully declared that her brother must have fixed things, but Emily was incapable of optimism. She was not even sure that she wanted to be released if that meant leaving Tiara behind.

However horrible yesterday might have been, if tomorrow was the same then Emily knew what to expect and could adjust to it, but if tomorrow was different it might be even more horrible. Just because her intended martyrdom was worth it did not mean it would not be agony. How many in history had endured horrific torture or death or both for worthwhile causes?

At least she would not have to make any choices or do anything clever.

She could surely manage to just take her punishment without messing up again.

———

One year earlier

Carl Goodenough's father was one of the lawyers at a local law firm used by Edward Maitland.

As such the Goodenough family had been invited to the Maitland Mansion for one of its garden parties, and a sixteen year old Carl Goodenough had lost his sulky distaste for the boring party when meeting a fourteen year old Tiara Maitland — fresh home in disgrace after being expelled from her boarding school.

Carl had been one of three teenage boys who had followed Tiara like sheep down to the stables to let out some horses and drive them into the garden where a huge party full of important guests was being held, and one of those who had taken the initial blame when Tiara was mysteriously back in the midst of the party while the horses began mingling happily with the cream of local society.

And therefore one who had later been thanked for it by her sitting on his knees and snogging him for several minutes, leaving him quite dizzy when she finished by giggling and hurrying away.

So when Tiara came to him a year later, and started chatting him up again, Carl was even readier to let himself be kissed into helping her take down the Garroway brothers — and did not mind her knowing that he knew where and how to obtain certain illegal drugs. He was very easily persuaded to obtain quantities of a certain drug with money she provided.

Tiara had no problem getting access to the Garroway house again. The brothers were easily lulled into carelessness by her coming back to them for alcohol and make-out sessions. Easy to pick a time when Tiara's father was home and when the boys' parents were due home, then pretend to have drunk too much and insist on dropping her dress just as their parents arrived home.

Timing it right made execution of the rest of the plan easy. Angry parents had called Edward Maitland to come and collect her — and it had been no problem taking advantage of their confusion to swig down a drink including the last of the drugs that Carl had obtained for her.

She timed it perfectly, going almost paralytic just as her father entered – barely remembering to mutter something about the boys putting something in her drink before losing the ability to talk.

Edward Maitland had responded as she had intended, rushing her to hospital and demanding a blood test when she insisted again that she had only drunk two glasses and it must have been something that 'the boys had put in her glass'. She worried that she might have overplayed her hand there, but she got away with it. When the blood test was reported to the police, a search warrant was obtained for the Garroway house, but the Garroway parents angrily forestalled the police by handing over the stuff that they had caught their sons trying to throw away. The police had searched the boys' rooms anyway, and found the stuff that Tiara had planted in the elder brother's room – a fortunate precaution as it turned out to be a different drug.

The jackpot came when a disgusted father infuriated his wife by angrily mentioning Tiara's casual statement about not remembering an evening spent with his sons, and two detectives asked Tiara about that evening as well.

She perfectly deadpanned them about not remembering a thing about that evening, but let slip the names of three other girls about whom she had heard rumours about the Garroway brothers doing something to upset them.

It was a week later that statements from the other three girls were followed by the younger brother breaking ranks and blaming everything on his elder brother – who promptly returned the compliment.

Tiara decided that revenge was quite delicious when served cold.

———

The alien shuttle landed right on the lawn of the Maitland mansion to deposit the owner of the mansion and his new bride.

JassaVar would have scurried forward to curtsey before her new householder had not Brett caught her hand and held her back. As a result, it was DinzaVar who stepped forward to curtsey before her new stepson and utter the standard alien girl ritual greeting 'I hope my body pleases you'.

"No need to say that to Brett, honey," Edward Maitland walking up behind them. "You're his stepmother now, not a housegirl – and this is little Humility?"

JassaVar stepped forward and curtsied low before giving the same traditional alien greeting.

"May I know if my daughter has been obedient and pleasant?" DinzaVar asked Brett with a sharp note to her voice that tensed up JassaVar's stomach.

JassaVar knew that if Brett's answer had been even slightly negative there would have been painful consequences, but Brett was amazingly generous in describing JassaVar's company as an absolute delight. That earned JassaVar a rare smile of approval from her mother, and one daughter breathed easier as her mother's new husband turned the subject to Brett's adopted sister with an angry demand to know what the 'stupid little brat' thought she was trying to do to the family that 'made the big mistake of giving her a home'.

"Maybe," Brett told his father firmly – sounding almost as annoyed, "our big mistake was not giving her a home but failing to provide any parenting."

JassaVar could have sworn that the response was a growl as she trailed obediently at her mother's heels towards the house.

"Maybe," Brett added loudly, "you should have brought her identical twin with her, instead of separating them at birth."

The older man stopped abruptly, causing DinzaVar to stop equally sharply, and JassaVar to catch her mother's heel with an advanced foot, causing DinzaVar to lose her shoe and nearly fall.

"Identical what?" Edward Maitland yelled at his son, as DinzaVar turned round and slapped her daughter's face so hard that JassaVar fell over and lay on the ground while being angrily scolded in English for her clumsiness.

DinzaVar then turned back to her horrified husband and stepson and apologized for her stupid daughter.

The stupid daughter was still lying on the ground in shock because her mother had never hit her like that before.

CHAPTER EIGHT

Going to court got more terrifying every time.

This was Emily's third such ordeal. She cringed forward in her chair, trying to make herself as small as possible while she peeked nervously around – quite unaware that she was making herself look furtive. Her appointed defence attorney was there - supposedly representing her, as was a social worker who had visited her once – whom she believed to despise her, though it would have taken Herculean efforts on his part to dissuade her from her presumption that he must despise her.

Sylvia the chaplain was there. Emily had been taken to talk to her twice in the last week, but Emily had been determined not to let the woman get under her skin again, and succeeded in avoiding too many embarrassing admissions. Luckily the woman had not probed sensitive areas, sticking mostly to safe subjects like Emily's academic record, but also covered had been her taste in books and music and hobbies and movies and sports. With the exception of books, courtesy of school libraries, Emily's ability to talk had been severely limited by rarely having the money or the time to acquire or indulge any such tastes. It was kind of scary to have an adult taking a personal interest in her - and baffling. Emily could imagine no other reason for a chaplain taking such an interest other than an attempt to evangelise her – yet the woman had only briefly mentioned religion when early on asking Emily if she had ever gone to church.

Emily had explained about the Galleys, but Sylvia Godwin had not pressed the issue, instead moving on to the dangerous ground of Emily's college plans. Emily had petulantly spat out that she would not go to college. Sylvia had looked at Emily long and silently – and Emily been forced to drop her eyes in shame, and feel ever so relieved when the chaplain changed the subject again.

Sylvia was not sitting alone in the court, Emily noticed. Beside her was a woman – taller, with spectacles hanging on cords and – was that blue-rinsed hair? Fifty plus was Emily's guess, and glaring at Emily like a School Principal.

Then Emily's heart started pounding and her hands shaking and she wanted the ground to open up and swallow her and so desperately wished that Tiara could have been there to give the useless twin the courage to endure her martyrdom. Except that Tiara being there would ruin everything. Only by sacrificing herself could Emily believe herself worthy to be Tiara's sister.

Emily heard her name called out as she came up for sentence.

———

Six months earlier

Emily could almost hear the theme music behind the whole scene – a haunting nightmare chant that had pursued her throughout her life - that dreaded rhyming taunt which had first tormented her soul so many years ago.

'Loveless Lovelace –

Always gonna be loveless.'

'Just having a bit of fun' was another echoing taunt. Emily had good reason for hating it as the excuse and the catch phrase of bullies since forever. 'Just having a bit of fun' covered everything from spiteful trolling to practical jokes that publicly humiliated a girl in front of hordes of laughing teenagers.

Emily knew that 'just having a bit of fun' pupils infested every school, which was why she liked to hide in school libraries after school until all the 'just having a bit of fun' jerks would be gone home before creeping nervously back to her foster home – wishing that she could be invisible all the way.

The biggest plus of foster homes was that she had felt safe in them, or safer at least. She had felt especially safe with the Burdens – accepted rather than loved but safe from bullying and abuse, which was why she told social workers that she was happy there. Feeling safe was the closest Emily knew to feeling happy, and she had felt safe at the Rabbett home during the six months since she had been sent there - except for when Dylan Rabbett came home from college.

She knew the name Dylan Rabbett even before becoming his mother's new foster daughter - a move which provided the bonus that she did not have to change schools. Dylan Rabbett had been on the school football team and won a football scholarship to college. It was obvious that Dylan's mother had taken Emily so that the foster money could help towards Dylan's college living expenses. Emily expected nothing else, so found more Saturday waitressing to pay for everything except basic food and lodging which Donna Rabbett provided.

Emily would have been quite content to live the last two years of her foster care in the Rabbett household, hopefully graduate before her eighteenth birthday, and then get away and get a job and get a life.

But then Dylan Rabbett had come home for Christmas, and began a campaign of what he imagined was the sort of friendly teasing that a girl would enjoy but Emily interpreted as 'just having a bit of fun' harassment, and when his mother was not present the 'friendly teasing' morphed clumsily into innuendo and suggestions that were anything but brotherly. As a football star, Dylan was accustomed to girls being flattered by his attention, so was unable to comprehend how threatening his clumsy advances would sound to a girl as paranoid as Emily. Dylan had only been home for a couple of weeks at Christmas, and out with friends most of the time, but then he came home for Easter, and what Emily interpreted as stalking – but Dylan imagined to be courting - then began in earnest. Tiara could easily have made Dylan eat out of her hands, but Emily could only try to avoid him as much as possible - literally barricading herself in her small box room whenever Donna was out, and hoping that he would get the message.

Unfortunately Dylan was as temperamentally incapable of noticing a subtle hint as Emily was of believing that a guy like him could show interest in a girl like her without malicious intent. She was in the kitchen preparing dinner before Sandra got home, when he crept up behind her and patted her bottom. Her panic reaction was to turn round and nearly put a sharp little fruit knife into his face as she called him a creep and told him to leave her alone.

Dylan Rabbett was not good at thinking generally, and still less at thinking things through, but he was good at doing the first thing that came into his head. His reaction to being threatened with a knife was a straight copy of something he had seen done on television – and had he been dealing with someone who knew how to use a knife and meant to use it Dylan could have got himself killed.

He simply grabbed her knife hand and twisted it up and round her back –
forcing her face forward into the wall.

———

"Have you anything to say, Miss Lovelace?"

The question from the Judge nearly gave Emily a seizure. Until then she had been listening almost with detachment, just wanting them to get it over with so she could get on with her martyrdom.

She did notice that all her public defender had done for her was point out that she had no previous convictions. If anything the prosecutor had been more helpful, pointing out Emily's academic record and surprisingly not demanding a custodial sentence. He even mentioned that Emily had been assaulted while in detention, and attempted suicide – both facts apparently a complete surprise to the public defender.

Emily had a feeling that the woman judge was not impressed by the ignorance of the defender, and could not decide whether that was a good sign or a bad sign. Then came that dreaded question aimed direct at Emily, and the terror of being asked to speak up. She had pleaded guilty specifically to dodge that torture, so just gave a simple negative to the question – but had to repeat it twice before she said it loud enough for the judge to hear.

"We are deciding your future, Miss Lovelace," the judge responded with a terrifying frostiness. "Do you really have nothing to say?"

Emily just shook her head and repeated her negative – hoping and praying that it would be enough.

It was not. The judge ordered her to approach the bench so that they could talk properly.

In abject terror, arms wrapped around her like a frightened child, Emily allowed her defender to escort up until she was nearly within arm's reach of the judge, and the prosecutor came to join them.

"Look at me, Miss Lovelace," came a firm order, and Emily found herself skewered by a gaze that she naturally assumed to be contemptuous.

"You seem to have been to a number of foster homes," were the judge's next words, "but none of them wanted to keep you. Why do you think that is?"

Emily would have loved to know why. She was sure that all families that she had lived with would have succumbed to Tiara's personality, but all she knew how to do was work hard. Scared though she was, Emily could not think of a thing to say.

She ended up just lowering her eyes and shrugging.

———

Six months earlier

"Let me go," Emily hissed in panic as Dylan firmly extracted the kitchen knife from her hand, and stared at it in disbelief. "Let me go or I'll tell the police about that stuff you're hiding in your room. I know what steroids do. I'm good at remembering names, and they're easy to look up."

Dylan had been intending to release her anyway, but she assumed that it was the threat which made him step away and stare back in shock as he declared that he did not know what she was talking about.

Emily's words tumbled over themselves as she hastened to enlighten him on what she had overheard him saying on the phone, the names of the people she had heard him saying it to – the man in a car that she had seen talking to Dylan and handing him a package in exchange for what looked like cash. Emily had a first class memory. She could quote his words back like a script, and give detailed descriptions of people, cars, and car numbers.

"Are you threatening me?" he asked incredulously.

"Too right I'm threatening you," she told him. "You stop stalking me or I start talking."

Dylan flinched at the word 'stalking' and stared at her for a terrifyingly long time as her heart pounded and her hands shook.

The sound of the front door opening broke the silence, and Dylan's mother's voice called out that she was home.

Dylan actually flinched. Just for a moment Emily thought he looked scared.

"You crazy bitch!" he spat at her. "Go around threatening guys with knives when they're just trying to be friendly, and you'll end up in Juvie. God's sake, what is the matter with you?"

Knife still in hand, he turned and walked out.

Emily scurried to her room, shut the door, sank down with her back against it, and spent many minutes trying to stop shaking. She knew that she had played her trump card. She also knew that it was a bluff. What were the odds that anyone would believe her word against a football star like him?

She dared not do what she threatened, she knew.

She just had to hope that he dared not risk it.

———

"I'm waiting for an answer, Emily."

The judge had not spoken to Emily for the agonizing eternity of a minute, and words that finally came could not have been scarier. Being pressurized to say something inevitably pushed Emily into panic mode.

"I know there is something wrong with me," she blurted out frantically. "I just don't know what it is. I've always tried to work as hard as I can – to make myself useful – but – I don't know what else to do but work. I know there is something very wrong with me but I don't know what it is. I don't know what it is."

"Okay, okay," the woman stopped the futile repetition. "I get the message. I acknowledge that your records confirm that you work hard at school – which is why I want you back there as soon as possible – I see you've already missed two weeks of term - but I think it appropriate to place some restrictions on your activities outside school. I regret that you suffered an assault in detention, but please understand that were it not for that I'd be returning you to detention now, despite your school grades. That is because I'm told you still refuse to name your boyfriend – out of seriously misplaced loyalty, I assume. Remember we are not just talking about car theft – there is a girl near your own age still in hospital as a result, so your failure to co-operate is not appreciated. Do you understand what I'm saying, Emily?"

The judge gave her a long and very stern look, as if expecting Emily to respond with a name, but Emily's backbone almost survived the stare in a brief spasm of pride at her martyrdom.

"Now," the judge finally broke her stare with a snort of what Emily guessed to be disgust. "I understand we have someone approved to act as foster parent?"

Emily stayed where she was as she heard people approaching from behind her right hand shoulder. As they arrived she sneaked a look, and was astonished to see the formidable figure of blue-rinse lady standing beside her.

"Mrs Redfern, I believe?" the judge asked the woman.

"Correct," Mrs Redfern announced in a voice that would have carried from the back of the court more clearly than Emily's voice had carried less than the six feet to the judge's ears. "My husband, Professor Redfern, and I are very ready to give Emily a home. From what Reverend Godwin has been telling me, I am sure we can help a girl like her back on the straight and narrow!"

———

Three months earlier

Carl Goodenough had hardly been able to believe his luck.

That a hottie like Tiara Maitland should date him was way beyond his expectations, which was why he was willing to spend every cent doing crazier and crazier things to keep her amused.

Unfortunately the regular routine of parties, concerts, movies, and high-speed drives had cost him severely in money, wear and tear on his old car, plus moving and parking violations. So when his licence disappeared and his car was towed and he was very grateful that she tolerated going out with him by taxi, and he could not find a taxi to take her home in the rain, and saw through a haze of alcohol that some idiot had stupidly left a car unlocked with keys in the ignition, borrowing it had seemed like a good idea at the time.

Tiara had been tipsy enough to agree and pile in with him, and Carl would appreciate the fact that she did not get too furious with him when he broadsided another car and skidded so fast round the next corner that he lost control and they ended up in a shop window. Had they been caught or injured – other than Tiara catching her hair in the car door - it might have been different, but they managed to escape, though Tiara had to clamber over the car roof to get back out of the window.

Fortunately for Carl's self-esteem, his date would declare that it had been her most exciting date ever. Tiara was worried enough the next day to ask Carl if anybody had been hurt. Carl reassured her that there was nothing to worry about – and Tiara missed the fact that he had not actually answered the question, so Carl could keep that little detail to himself without exactly lying to her.

But Carl did not realize that there was a security camera in the shop. The chance of its placing meant that only the back of Carl's head was visible in the video, but when Tiara clambered over the car roof, her face was fully and clearly visible.

The shop had been near the city centre, and well away from where they both lived and were known. Even so, Tiara would tell Carl that it had been a thrill wondering if the cops would ever catch them – such a thrill that Tiara was inspired to drive off in another car when provocation and intoxication coincided.

The police did not publicize the image of the girl in the video because a policeman happened to recognize her face. Purely by chance he had interviewed a girl who had run away a couple of years earlier after stealing a computer from her foster parents.

A girl whose DNA matched to hairs found in the stolen car.

––––––

Emily had been left huddled on a chair in a corridor for half an hour before she was taken to pick up her bags – two that her social worker had brought from the Rabbett home, and the bag that she had brought from the Detention Centre.

The latter bag contained what little she had acquired while in the detention centre – mostly make-up and underwear given to her by Tiara, which Emily loved just because it came from Tiara who had done a spectacular make-over of Emily's hair, eye-brows, nails, and face quite unlike anything anyone had ever done for Emily. Spectacular by Emily's standards, anyway. Tiara had apologized that it was just the best she could do in the circumstances, and she would do a much better job when they were both out until nobody would be able to tell them apart.

Emily wondered what Tiara was doing at that moment. How soon would Tiara find out that Emily was not returning? What would she do next?

Okay, that last question was unanswerable. Emily could not imagine anyone predicting what Tiara would do next. At least Emily was not going back to Southside – but she had never met a foster parent who unnerved her more than the woman in whose car she found herself ten minutes later.

"My name is Redfern, Joan Redfern," the woman announced majestically as she was driving them away from the court complex, "but you will call me Mrs Redfern. Are we quite clear about that?"

"Yes, Mrs Redfern," Emily responded immediately. She actually found the woman so intimidating that she would never have dared call the woman anything other than Mrs Redfern even if the woman had invited Emily to call her Joan.

"Good I think you need to know exactly where you stand. You'll live with me until the court decides otherwise – until they decide that you're fully rehabilitated or that I've failed to help you. Don't assume that will automatically be when you reach 18 – although it may well be. I know you were given a curfew of six in the evening but I had a discussion with the court about that."

Emily could not help but wonder how Mrs Redfern managed to make 'had a discussion with the court' sound like 'laid down the law to the court'.

"I pointed out that rehabilitating you into responsible juvenile society would be seriously inhibited if you're never allowed to go out in the evenings with appropriate friends or to events like school dances or social events at places like my church. They agreed that with my approval and your parole officer's agreement you will be permitted to attend such events subject to my knowing exactly where you are and who you are with at all times – and the proviso that any betrayal of trust in that respect may find that privilege withdrawn – so we can start by inviting your friends round to my house first. Any friends that you might want to go out with, anyway."

Too unnerved to be anything but direct, Emily simply replied that she had no friends.

No sooner said than regretted. Clearly Mrs Redfern did not like what she had heard. Emily steeled herself for some reproving response, and dipped her head even more than normal as she angrily scolded herself for opening her mouth again.

No response came – but that did not stop Emily worrying herself dizzy. Her biggest fear was that she might be prevented from seeing Tiara, but just knowing that Tiara was alive was enough for now, and she could be proud of herself for protecting Tiara from the law – though she could never tell Tiara or anyone else what she had done. But that did not matter. For the first time in her life she had done something for which she could feel really proud.

Her pride in her unheralded martyrdom buoyed her up as she headed towards an unknowable future.

———

Three months earlier

Emily had a regular Saturday job waitressing at a diner.

It was a job that she liked because she did it well and had avoided any serious humiliations while doing it. She had no problem remembering the most complex of orders for multiple clients, carrying them in her head, and efficiently supplying the services. She had no problem talking to customers, since the dialogue was settled and the relationship strictly defined. She also got on okay with the other staff. As all were adults Emily being quiet and hard-working made her liked instead of despised so she had been offered a full-time summer job, which had encouraged her to buy another computer, which was a delight – except for the suspicion that it immediately produced in her foster mother.

Life at the Rabbetts had remained uncomfortable ever since that incident with Dylan. Fortunately he had returned to college a week later, but in angry absentia he had still found a way to retaliate. His mother had found a hundred and eighty dollars missing from her kitchen cupboard the day after Dylan had left, and when she rang Dylan to know if he had taken it she was met not only with a fervent denial but the spiteful advice to search Emily's room – citing the fact that Donna had been warned about Emily stealing from previous foster parents.

That reminder destroyed any hope that she would be believed if she accused Dylan of anything – or so Emily assumed, already worrying that he might accuse her of threatening him with a knife. Donna Rabbett's search of her foster daughter's room had found over three hundred dollars hidden under her sanitary towels, and Emily was accused of theft for the second time in her life. *She desperately denied it, claiming that the cash was her savings from her Saturday job, but Donna had taken back 'her two hundred dollars', and warned Emily that in future all cash in the house would be marked and if any went missing the police would be called.*

And that Donna would insist on charges being brought.

Less than an hour later Emily had found a hundred and eighty dollars hidden in a sneaker, and worked out exactly what Dylan had done and intended. There seemed little prospect that Donna would now believe anything Emily said against Dylan, so she went ahead and put the money she had found towards buying another computer. From that day Donna remained very suspicious – constantly checking for possible thefts. It made the summer term very stressful for Emily.

Most of all, she dreaded Dylan coming home for the summer vacation.

———

The Redfern home was well out into the suburbs to the west – beyond where the Galleys lived – an area that Emily had never seen.

Some houses were really big, and when Mrs Redfern turned into a leafy avenue Emily wondered if the Redferns lived in one. She had not got the impression that the Redferns were rich, purely from the age of Mrs Redfern's car and the woman's clothes. Comfortably off but not rich – that was Emily's guess, and if her husband was a college professor that made sense.

Until they turned into the leafy avenue, Emily had not been paying much attention to the road because Mrs Redfern had spent most of the drive talking non-stop. Apart from a couple of early questions as to whether Emily had any other family apart from Tiara, the woman had mainly talked about her own family and her husband – a subject selection which totally suited Emily.

Professor Anthony "Tony" Redfern turned out to be a Professor of English Literature. His specialty was apparently nineteenth century Literature, which Emily found intriguing. Her explorations of school libraries had included entertaining discoveries of the Bronte Sisters, Twain, Alcott, and others. She could not help hoping that the Professor might have some good books to lend, but quickly scolded herself against that fantasy. It sounded as if fostering delinquents like Emily Lovelace was Mrs Redfern's pet project. The Professor would surely resent her bothering him. Better to avoid the humiliation of rejection.

It also turned out that the Redferns had only 'been blessed' with one child – a son now married and 'fled the coop' – a phrase that instantly led Emily to comparing Mrs Redfern to a mother hen, and feeling almost tempted to smile. Their son had recently married an Australian girl and settled down to live with her in Australia.

"I never thought of fostering until a friend died of cancer," Mrs Redfern added, "and left her fifteen year old son with nobody to look after him – his father had a new wife and family and no room for Peter, so Peter stayed with us, and became almost a second son. He still lives not far away. We usually see him at church, and he often comes for Sunday dinner – though he has a job in the enclave on the new alien power systems, and might still be up on *Freedom* right now. Anyway, when Peter left I had energy to burn and I always wanted a daughter, so I applied to foster. I told them I wanted a girl and a challenge – not signing up just to provide lodging. They said that teenagers with criminal records were the hardest to find good homes for so I asked for one. You're the third girl sent to me. I'm hoping you'll be the first to want to stay."

That did not sound too promising. Emily's imagination was soon rampaging around possible reasons for the first two girls not wanting to stay, while Mrs Redfern talked about her husband's love of books and golf and chess, and her own love of detective stories and Jane Austen and Angela Thirkell novels.

Mrs Redfern also listed an extraordinary range of voluntary work for her church and other charities, and Emily realized that she was just another charitable project about the time that Mrs Redfern pulled into a short driveway and announced that they were home. It was bigger than most houses that Emily had lived in, but not massively so.

"Time to get out, child," came a cheerful command. "And unpack your bags. Are you quite sure nothing is missing? Never known a teenage girl with so little luggage."

Emily had taken a quick look at the bags handed to her by her social worker as having been packed by Donna to await Emily's discharge. She was in no doubt that there was stuff missing. Most of her clothes were there but not much else and no sign of her computer. She could not help wondering if it had been Dylan rather than Donna who really packed her bags – maybe he had feared what she might have on her computer.

Whatever the case, she could not prove that anything was missing.

"No, Mrs Redfern," she replied very carefully. "I don't think there is anything else I'd expect to be there."

————

Three months earlier

Emily had turned sixteen in May, though Donna had failed to notice.

That had meant that the diner were happy to employ her for longer hours, and staying away from the house as long as possible had become a major plus for Emily. Emily felt more at home at the diner than at the Rabbett house, which was why the diner was the most humiliating possible place for the police to handcuff her and march her through the diner and into a squad car.

But that was nothing to the trauma of being shown a short video from a store security camera of an expensive car crashing in through a store window, and the male driver and female passenger clambering out of the car and disappearing. The girl had been forced to climb over the car to escape, and her face had appeared clearly and unmistakably on the screen.

The face was Emily's face.

Emily had almost disbelieved her own denials that she was the girl. Donna had gone out that evening leaving Emily alone in the house, so Emily had no alibi. Even her public defender had derided her protestations of innocence, and insisted that her only sane option was to agree a plea bargain.

But that was only an option if she named her boyfriend.

————

"Emily Lovelace has a new foster family," Brett announced as he came back into the room. "Sylvia Godwin called as promised. Mr and Mrs Redfern – actually Professor and Mrs Redfern. Sylvia found them through her church contacts, recommended them very strongly, even went to see them, and we both made some phone calls."

Edward Maitland guffawed loudly, startling his wife and stepdaughter.

"What that old battle-axe!" he kept on laughing. "Great! Sounds like just what the little crook deserves."

"Do you possess contact knowledge of Mrs Redfern?" Modesty asked the question for daughter and stepson.

"Met her and husband hen-peck at a couple of our garden parties. The sort who is always pestering for donations towards something or other. Always pushing everybody about in pursuit of her latest good cause. Maybe she'd take our own resident hellspawn off our hands. Maybe Tiara was bound to go bad on us because it was always in her genes. Hell, I mean we've given the brat everything."

"Except attention," Brett asserted forcefully, knowing that anything less would not be listened to when his father was in one of his 'Tiara' moods, as Sara had christened them on the grounds that only Tiara could make Dad that mad. "The one thing none of us ever found time to give her."

"She chooses to do time just to get our attention!"

"No she chose that to spend time with her twin. Maybe both twins ending up in Juvie is less to do with their DNA than with our failure to do a better parenting job than a string of foster parents."

"You can bet the Redfern battle-axe isn't doing it for money. Offering to let her have Tiara as well might not be such a bad idea – if we pay the costs. Reckon she'd make a good foster parent?"

———

JassaVar left her en-suite to find her mother waiting for her.

JassaVar had spent a long time enjoying a shower, so possessed no idea how long her mother had been waiting. Or searching - DinzaVar was leaving the dressing room as JassaVar exited the en suite.

"Where did all those clothes come from?" DinzaVar demanded.

Her tone would have sounded harshly accusatory to most human girls, but JassaVar simply answered that Brett and Sara had taken her shopping and bought all those wonderful clothes for her.

"Did Sara pay for them? I will not refund extravagance."

"Brett paid for them. He named it welcome-to-the-family gift. Sara selected most - she said all clothes I should possess. They were very generous."

DinzaVar looked seriously smug at that. JassaVar could not remember her mother smiling at her that warmly for a long time.

"Quality," DinzaVar purred. "I took chance bringing you down from *Anarchy* instead of LaskaVar. Brett must consider you possess attraction for him to spend money on you. Excellent. What advances were made? Compliments on your body?"

"He did call me beautiful when we first encounter," JassaVar was happy to be able to say. "No man call me beautiful before."

"Humans possess strange concepts of beauty," DinzaVar remarked thoughtfully – reminding JassaVar that her mother had never considered her as pretty as her sister. "Excellent. Take advantage. Wear revealing clothes when near him. Seek his company any opportunity. Always do anything he desires. If subject of duvay ever raised, submit to any desire and ask nothing."

Commands that could not be more explicit. JassaVar doubted her chances of success in such a mission, but perfectly comprehended her orders.

"Just duvay him once," DinzaVar placed an admonishing finger on JassaVar's forehead, "and you earn me great profit. If he marry you - we earn great profit! Now, did you encounter Tiara?"

"No, mother. She was in prison before I arrive."

"How barbaric! But that could be advantage. She could be greater problem than sister who already possess man and daughter and reside away. I will remark that alien housewife would eject girl who behaved that bad, but it would be hazard to do more. If she return you befriend her. Do anything to please her unless it would displease BrettYar - he must take priority. Then tell me all she says and does. I can select what to tell my husband that will damage her. The more he reject her, the greater chance for profit we possess."

JassaVar did not know how to respond. She did not desire to damage another girl or family.

But JassaVar knew better than to question any command given by her mother.

CHAPTER NINE

"This is your room," Mrs Redfern announced as she ushered Emily through the door opposite the top of the stairs. "All cupboards and drawers are yours. Put posters on the wall as you wish – anything reasonable – please avoid anything nauseating. The main bathroom is next door along – we have our own en suite in the master bedroom so you mostly have the bathroom to yourself except when we have visitors when they'll share with you. I suggest you make a habit of having a shower or a bath or at least a wash before coming down to dinner – which will be at six – our normal time unless we have some sort of engagement."

The room was not the largest bedroom that Emily had ever known, but it was the largest that she had slept in alone. Having a whole bathroom to herself – if only temporarily – was wonderful, and unprecedented, but then Mrs Redfern made Emily wonder if she was in Paradise by saying that it was Emily's responsibility to keep both bathroom and bedroom clean and tidy.

"Lunch first," Mrs Redfern continued as if inventing a new commandment. "Then you obviously need a proper bath or shower. I repeat that I will expect you to wash properly every day, and look and smell clean and tidy at all times. Then some clean clothes. Let us see if you have anything decent to wear. Are you quite sure those bags are everything you own?"

The woman hardly waited for Emily's nervously mumbled prevarication before opening the bags and checking every item of clothing. Emily was too intimidated to even resent the intrusion, and in any case too busy sniffing herself, and deciding with shame that she really stank. She had to make herself pay attention to exactly what Donna and Dylan had packed for her. Most of her clothes did seem to be there, but not the nice new

113

coat and dress and shoes to which she had recently treated herself with her earnings from waitressing. And definitely nothing of value.

"I don't know what your last foster mother can have been thinking," Mrs Redfern expostulated. "There is really nothing that I would call nice here, but it'll have to do. We are seeing the Principal of your new school at ten tomorrow – ready for you to start Monday. Clearly I'll need to take you shopping tomorrow for a decent wardrobe – and a hair-dryer. I always believe that a young lady is more likely to act like a young lady if she dresses like a young lady."

Emily was frankly doubting her own ears. The promise to buy her new clothes was generous, but she could not help worrying that she might end up wearing stuff that would make her even more of a laughing stock than usual.

"But I don't think you need any more jeans," the woman continued imperiously. "Some nice skirts and dresses to impress the boys. I wish my legs had been that good when I was your age!"

————

Tiara was finally visited by one very angry adoptive father.

She remembered a long-lost loving Daddy taking her on his knee to cuddle and play. Admittedly a workaholic Daddy who was rarely around, but when around a proper Daddy bringing a present every time he came home from wherever. Often a nice dress or a pair of shoes or a piece of jewellery or a beautiful doll – the only common factor being that it was expensive, as expensive as the present that he bought Mommy.

That had all ended when Mommy had gone. Tiara had not heard a word about Mommy since, let alone a word from her. Tiara had virtually lost Daddy, too. Never once had her Daddy cuddled her or played with her since that date. The presents had stopped except for birthday and Christmas presents – which had got much more expensive but much less imaginative.

Tiara had long accepted that the only way to make her Daddy pay attention to her was to cause trouble – when his reaction would range from amused exasperation to restrained anger. Wrecking her tenth birthday party might have annoyed Sara into spanking Tiara, but Daddy had been more amused than anything, and reserved his ferocious ire for Sara to a level that Tiara had never seen before – nor would again until Tiara got expelled from boarding school. Tiara was not surprised that her Daddy was livid when they met in Southside, but Daddy being angry did not scare Tiara. She was confident that he would get over it and go into overdrive to sort everything out, which was why she had planned to take this chance to beg him to let Emily live with them. Tiara was ready to accept any terms, to promise to behave and really mean it this time, so it was annoying that Emily had gone to court that morning, and might not be back.

Tiara was still totally confident that her Daddy could fix anything for her if he chose. It did not occur to her that her Daddy would no longer believe her promises. He barely restrained his impatience long enough to hear her out, willing his face to imitate the animation of a statue until her fanciful rambles ground to a halt – leaving just that cute face which he had once felt unable to resist.

"Forget it, Tiara," he told her – working at sounding cold rather than angry. "Your thieving sister is never setting foot in my house."

She reacted as if he had slapped her, and he lost it a bit as he leant aggressively forward to forestall her "But Daddy!" protest before it had left her mouth.

"If I had my way, nor would you," he snarled at her. "But I seem to be stuck with legal responsibility for you until your eighteenth birthday. I asked if it would be possible to keep you locked up until that great day arrives, but apparently not."

Tiara backtracked quickly. Dad was clearly seriously mad, but there were subtler ways of skinning a Daddy. She allowed her eyes to well with tears, and quickly adopted her best 'don't you love me?' face.

"Daddy," she whimpered with careful tremulousness. "Daddy, I said was sorry. I know I shouldn't have been drinking, but I am taking responsibility! I'm accepting my punishment. I didn't even ask to be bailed. I'm going to learn my lesson. I'm never getting in trouble like this again. I promise. Promise! Promise! Promise squared! Promise cubed!"

She would have gone on longer, confident of wearing down his anger to irritation level when he would do anything just to avoid a scene, but he forestalled by an angrily snapped "Enough!" Snapped more angrily than she had ever heard him, and that triggered a moment of hesitation as she reviewed tactics.

"Listen hard, Tiara," he declared tightly. "This may be the last time we ever talk together. If you do return to my house – and if I can prevent it I will – but if you do return it will only be until your eighteenth birthday when I wash my hands of you. You'll never see or hear from me again, and never receive a cent from me again – before or after I die. Credit the aliens - they really know how to treat delinquent daughters. Get used to being treated as you deserve."

"As I deserve!" Tiara lashed back – shocked into deploying the only weapon she had left. "What - you getting my stepmum to chain me up, dress in leather and whip me like she does you?"

———

"He is really going to do that," Sara's image on the screen asked incredulously. "Just throw Tiara out?"

"So he says," Brett told her from the driving seat of his parked car. "Apparently our new stepmother has filled him in on alien customs on dealing with disobedient daughters. It seems that corporal punishment or summary ejection from the family are the recognized alternatives, and you know how Dad likes alien ideas."

"You know Dad," Sara suggested. "Chances are he'll change his mind after he has cooled down, but refuse to admit it and pretend instead that it was all a bluff to scare Tiara into towing the line. Done it before."

"Before he married Modesty, yes."

The twins equated silences as they contemplated their latest Tiara Crisis.

"Not going to say it," Sara contributed from her distant home.

Both knew that the 'it' she was not going to say was 'I told you so'.

"Thanks," Brett conceded the point. "On the other hand, Modesty has no reason to care about Tiara and has her own daughter."

"A daughter now ensconced as the resident daughter in our household. Like a cuckoo pushing out the original fledgling."

"I don't think Humility is like that, Sara. You liked her. A lot, you said."

"I did and I do. No malice in her, but she is her mother's daughter – not meaning that she is like her mother but that she'll do what Mommy tells her. You do like Humility, don't you?"

"Sure. Nice kid."

"Remember she is just a kid. Also remember that alien girls see nothing wrong in having sex for money, and it is not only legal but can even be arranged by their mothers. You can bet Modesty wants Humility to profit from you."

"But Humility is just a kid. Okay, point taken. I should keep my distance."

"Better to get yourself another girlfriend. Even *you* should be over Tessa by now. Okay, okay – but you're my twin so it is my business, whatever you say. What the hell are we going to do about Tiara?"

"In hand. I've already booked a viewing on a place not far off where Tiara can live with me. Made sure I can move in quick, and vacate my city flat. Also not far from her twin's new foster home. Haven't told you about Emily, have I? Just got paroled to a foster family Sylvia found through her church contacts. I get the feeling that Sylvia really went above and beyond for our sake, and I don't mean by praying."

"For your sake," his twin corrected him. "Not ours. Trust me."

———

"Mommy told me," Tiara pressed on into his father's staring silence. "You think I don't know why she got ten million when you divorced her for screwing around. Let's face it – you wanted her to take me away – you never wanted to keep me."

She paused – suddenly shaken by the knowledge that she had just played her final card against her father and had nothing more up her short sleeve.

"I never wanted you in the first place, honey," Edward Maitland finally declared with calm satisfaction. "Just bought you as a toy for your lying bitch of a mother, and by the way that was one of the many lies Astra spread around to get back at me. If you're interested she told other people that I did it with animals or little boys – also lies. I took responsibility for you when Astra dumped you, and for the record I gave her ten million to

117

leave you behind, and I'll spend whatever it takes to look after you until your eighteenth birthday. If you're good until then I might be generous and give you a leaving present, but don't count on it."

Tiara returned her father's stare, and tried to hold it unblinking – tried not to show the turmoil inside her. She had played her last card – in a totally not planned way – and it had back-fired big time. She suddenly realized that she could not remember when Daddy had last hugged or kissed her or told her that he loved her.

"Good bye darling," Edward Maitland said instead. "We won't see each other again until you're released, and if I can help it not even then. Love you - not."

He got up and went without another word. Tiara watched him go and stayed staring at the door until a warder came in and ordered her out.

Tiara was shaking and crying as she stumbled back to her cell.

———

Emily could have enjoyed the most luxurious bath of her life, but her fear of keeping Mrs Redfern waiting made her bathe as if sharing the bathroom with three impatient siblings then rush to dry herself and dress as if late for school.

It sunk in as she used the hair-drier which Mrs Redfern had lent her that, apart from the faint noises of Mrs Redfern doing something in what Emily guessed was the kitchen, there was a peculiar absence of sound. She could not hear any traffic, and could not remember living without a busy road nearby. She knew that she was in a tree-filled suburb at the end of a cul-de-sac but had not expected it to be so quiet.

She sat on the bed and looked properly around the room. A simple bedroom – so nice that her instinct was to fear spoiling it. No way was she putting up any posters even if she had the money. Mrs Redfern had not mentioned pocket money yet, and Emily was almost incapable of asking for anything, so was already worrying how she could get a job with evening curfews and community service on Saturdays – even if she could find a job in walking distance of this house when she told prospective employers about her criminal record. So perversely proud had Emily become of her 'criminal record' that her imagination was exaggerating the trouble it would cause her as if it made her martyrdom nobler and her a worthier twin to Tiara.

A clatter from below reminded her that, if she was to avoid getting sent back to Juvie, she had to be on her best behaviour at all times. So Emily slipped on her best shoes, checked herself in the mirror, checked bedroom and bathroom and spent fifteen frantic minutes eliminating every speck of dirt she could see, then hurried down to await whatever orders her new foster mother chose to give her.

And wonder why Mrs Redfern was surprised to see her downstairs so soon.

———

Professor Tony Redfern had confessed to a colleague that he felt real trepidation at coming home to another new foster daughter that evening.

He had not lacked early doubts about Joan's latest obsession. Having just seen his energetic son and foster son move into their adult lives, he had been looking forward to a quieter life with retirement looming, and to maybe improving his golf handicap, but he recognized that his wife still had energy to burn and had always loved her 'force of nature' personality. She could exasperate at times with her enthusiasms, but he was proud of her dedication to helping others.

So he raised no objections to her scheme of fostering delinquent teenage girls, and declared his support when examined by social workers, but had still been nervous when the girls started arriving – even though unaware that social workers had rated their house as a place to dump hopeless cases.

Miranda he had started to like. She had seemed quiet at first, until throwing an epic tantrum and unleashing a volley of swearwords that he had not heard since his stint in the National Guard, but she had collapsed in tears afterwards and regained some sympathy.

He could understand the girl chafing against the restrictions that Joan had tried to impose on her. It had seemed rather risky to him for Joan to try playing the world's strictest parent on a modern teenager accustomed to coming and going – and getting into trouble – at all hours. Even so, it had seemed even to him that they were starting to make progress – Miranda was starting to calm down - even starting to talk sensibly during meals, but had gone to a school dance and never come home. Two days later Miranda had been arrested with a gun-carrying boyfriend in a stolen car, and headed straight back to Juvie.

That had upset Joan badly, he knew. More than it had upset him. Maybe she had been too quick to accept Shazza as a replacement, because the girl had been openly hostile from day one, and been gone in a week, stealing some of their money and Joan's family jewellery to fund her flight not only from them but from the law. As far as Tony was aware, Shazza had still not been apprehended, and they had been forced to change all locks and security codes and card numbers.

Now this Emily would be waiting for him. When the Reverend Sylvia had come all the way to personally beg them to give Emily a chance, his irrepressible wife had agreed without hesitation, but Tony had demanded to know more. He was not sure whether he had been persuaded by the literary potential of the twins' backstory, or the report that Emily loved books, but knew that he would have agreed anyway to whatever Joan wanted.

So that evening Tony headed home at his usual time to a rather dreaded introduction – anticipating any number of problems – not least the unknown boyfriend. According to Sylvia the police were unsure whether she was keeping his identity secret out of infatuation or fear or both – in any case keeping him away had to be a priority, but Tony still worried that the strict curfew imposed on the girl was overdoing it, and more likely to provoke rebellion than anything.

More worrying was the reported suicide attempt. Had the boyfriend abandoned her? Tony could only speculate about that, but it was a real fear that she might try again and succeed in their household because that would devastate Joan beyond anything imaginable. Yet Joan had committed herself, and thus him as well, and he would always support her - if only to preserve his own self-respect.

His first impressions of the girl genuinely surprised. Looking younger than sixteen to him - very neat and tidy, but plainly dressed and little make-up, and very quiet as they sat down to dinner, helping to take dishes to the table with no hesitations - no attitude at all. She never spoke unless spoken to, when she answered very quietly – even calling them 'sir' and 'ma'am' which Tony found unsettling. She did not even help herself to food until specifically invited, he noticed, and took very modest helpings. She waited with head dipped while Joan said Grace, waited for them to start eating then ate quickly with head still dipped and shoulders slightly hunched – almost as if cringing.

Seeing Emily clear her plate while the adults were barely half way through eating their own food, Joan urged the girl twice to have some more, and earned nothing more than 'no, thank you, Mrs Redfern' each time as the girl just sat silently - not moving except for nervously twisting her fingers.

Tony exchanged glances with his wife, and recognized that she was not sure what to say next – not usual for Joan, but not unprecedented. When they faced academic minds talking on academic subjects, there was an unspoken agreement that Tony should take up the conversational baton, and this girl was reportedly a good student.

So he asked her about her schoolwork, her subjects, and her grades.

She answered every question he asked, without hesitation on matters of fact, but never went on to volunteer anything beyond that, and minimised her replies to questions along the line of how she liked this subject or that subject down to unhelpful responses like 'okay' or 'never thought about it' or 'don't know'.

It was not until after Joan and he had finished eating, and Joan had collected the dishes - ordering Emily to stay where she was while Joan served up the dessert - that Tony managed to provoke a more forthcoming response.

He noticed that she had been surprised at being ordered to stay in her seat when she had seemingly been jumping up to help. Impatience prompted him to ask the big question.

"I'm told you have an identical twin," he pressed on, and that question finally jerked her head up. "That you were separated at birth, and didn't know she existed until a couple of weeks ago."

She swallowed visibly, and peered nervously up at him.

But all she said was "Yes, sir."

He had hoped for more.

"What is she like? I don't mean to look at."

"Amazing, sir. Tiara is amazing."

That was a surprise. Emily sounded adulatory. Every professorial instinct told him to challenge such a statement from a student, and make her justify it.

"How is she amazing?" he asked politely but firmly. "I understood you met in Juvenile Detention."

"Yes, but she didn't need to be there," came a stunning response. "She could have got bail, but she told her brother to refuse bail so she could stay and look after me - to protect me. I don't know how I'd have survived if she hadn't. Tiara does everything so well. She is amazing with people. I'm useless with people. She is the amazing twin. I'm the useless one."

Tony exchanged glances with Joan, who had just come back to the table at that moment, and saw from her face that she was equally surprised by that revelation.

But Joan reacted first.

"Nonsense, my girl," she asserted firmly. "If you're so useless how come you're such a good student that you were nearly skipping a grade?"

That was a very good question. Tony waited eagerly for an answer, and the girl seemed really nervous about answering it.

"Just schoolwork," she muttered. "It's not hard. You just do what work you're given. You don't have to be clever – not clever like Tiara. She can *talk* to people!"

It was with that statement that Tony Redfern would come to date his deep personal fascination with his new foster daughter. During his long career in academia genuinely original statements from students were few and far between, and always much appreciated – especially when they involved looking at a basic convention with a completely new perspective. But what a strange perspective to write off academic achievement as easy and imply that talking to people was hard? He remembered Sylvia describing Emily as suffering from depression and even showing symptoms of O.C.D., and wondered if anyone had assessed her for A.S.D.

"Don't run yourself down, girl," Joan commanded, and Emily dropped her eyes as if scolded. "I'd have given my eye-teeth for your grades. Ah – the pie is ready. Stay where you are. Back in two shakes."

Tony watched Emily as the girl watched his wife steam back into the kitchen to shut off the beeping oven timer. The girl was still observing from under a dipped forehead, and he realized that he had still not seen her smile.

"We were told you love reading?" he switched the subject deliberately.

Her still dipped gaze swung round to him.

"Yes, sir," she replied quite simply – still without smiling.

But she did smile after dinner, after almost eagerly helping Joan clear up. He escorted Emily into his study, showed her walls covered with books, and invited her to pick one. As she wandered wide-eyed around the shelves, possibly even forgetting that he was there for the moment, there was a genuine smile on her face.

The Professor fudged the reality by remarking that her reported love of books was what had decided him to agree to foster her. The last two girls they had tried to foster had not worked out – the girls had refused to put up with Joan's strict regime, so they had thought of having another boy.

When the girl showed no reaction to that he went further than intended by telling her that his wife's rules might seem rather strict at first, but that Joan was far from rigid and only wanted to help Emily.

"I know I'm a work of charity," she replied, and he did not know how to respond. She sounded neither sounded grateful nor offended – maybe a little despondent.

He opted to change the subject and return to something more congenial.

"Please feel free to borrow any book on the shelves. Many are literary criticism or biographies but you're free to read them as well. My only rule is that you read one book at a time. Joan has her own rules for her own books. Her tastes are mostly different – except that we both read Jane Austen. Have you read any Jane Austen?"

"I've read *Pride and Prejudice*, sir."

"No surprise. Enjoy it?"

"Yes, sir."

"Also no surprise." he picked out a volume from its place on the shelf. "You could try this one. That is *Mansfield Park* – her next publication – and as you see I've just a few among the thousands of books written about her work and her life and just about anything and everything even remotely connectable to her. Mine are mostly literary criticisms but Joan has some coffee table books – not my taste, but she is the JASNA member – Jane

Austen Society of North America – did a trip to England to see every place Jane Austen passed within a hundred miles of in a buggy, as far as I could gather. Full Metal Janeite."

She looked blank at the name 'Janeite' but was already opening the book - a hopeful sign - literary addiction was healthier than drug addiction. He hoped that she would read it and then talk about it.

It might be a great ice-breaker.

———

Tiara had relaxed her guard somewhat when she knew that she no longer had to protect Emily from the other girls in the Detention Centre.

She had also lost more than a little chutzpah after her traumatic interview with her father. She had riled him up intentionally, had known what she was doing, but not anticipated his reaction. It had backfired on her, and that night she felt real stirrings of fears for her future as if Emily had infected her.

Fears that made it really hard to fall asleep.

———

Emily also found it hard to fall asleep.

She was tempted to switch the light on and read more but did not dare in case Mrs Redfern would be angry.

Emily could not remember sleeping in such a comfortable bed, nor in such silence, but her brain was in a turmoil of anxiety about her future – and about Tiara alone back in the Detention Centre. Emily was incapable of not imagining the worst – exacerbated by how terribly she was missing Tiara. Emily was accustomed to feeling alone and unloved and unwanted. Had she not met her twin she would hardly have realized it, but after an amazing fortnight of not being alone, unloved, and unwanted, she now felt lonelier than ever.

The Redferns seemed very kind, and their home very nice, so it could be a good hiding place, but it could never be her home any more than the Redferns could ever be her family, and she still had to endure a new school as a convicted criminal, and some humiliating community service.

She could pride herself that she was enduring it for Tiara, but it would have been so much easier to endure if she had not been separated from Tiara.

———

JassaVar also found it hard to fall asleep after a disturbing day.

She had heard a truly shocking argument between Brett and his father about ejecting Tiara from the household. Nothing odd about ejecting a disobedient daughter or housegirl, but strange for a man to do it.

JassaVar knew that she was now old enough to be ejected just as brutally. The incredible luxuries could be snatched away in a second if she displeased her mother – and being homeless on an unfamiliar planet was a scary prospect.

It also worried that she might find it difficult to speak to her sister for some time. The other housegirls – called housemaids - clearly possessed no interest in befriending her. JassaVar had hoped to befriend Tiara, but DinzaVar did not want Tiara around. Brett possessed his own household, and after that row with his father might not even visit. There were no housegirls in nearby residences to befriend, and she lacked the social access media that she possessed aboard Freedom. Wonderful luxury she possessed, but also a real prospect of loneliness.

Had it been like that for Tiara?

CHAPTER TEN

The Principal of Emily's new High School did not look particularly severe, but that did not stop Emily being so scared that her hands shook when the Principal handed her an 'introduction to the school' folder - and afraid to look up as Mrs Redfern apologized for Emily's clothes, saying that they were the best that Emily had arrived with, and that she would take Emily shopping later to purchase more appropriate clothing for school.

Mrs Redfern made it sound like Emily was getting a school uniform, but the girls that Emily had seen had not been in uniform – some had even been in jeans, although possibly designer jeans. This was a school in a prosperous suburb with prosperous parents – making Emily even more of an outsider than usual even before everyone learnt that she was a delinquent from Juvie.

"I see, Emily," the Principal opened the attack – sounding authoritative rather than actually hostile. "I'm pleased to see from your transcripts that your disciplinary record has been pretty good, and your academic record is excellent. Keep it that way, and I'm sure you'll do fine here. We'll judge you by the future, not the past."

Easy platitude, Emily thought. Whatever the woman might say, Emily's record was sure to dominate everyone's judgements of her for the foreseeable future.

"I'll also sort out your academic program," the Principal continued. "Your excellent academic program. Rest assured that we make great efforts to encourage and reward academic excellence."

Another platitude. Emily was old enough and intelligent enough to understand that when public authorities use phrases like 'great efforts' the greatest effort involved was usually only frequent declarations of intent to use 'great efforts' while the reality was usually only box-ticking. Even if teachers made token great efforts to reward academic excellence, no doubt there would be plenty of students making genuinely great efforts to punish it.

Maybe she was being unfair – it was just possible that they might permit her to resume her bid to graduate a year early. It did a school credit if a pupil did that, so it might suit them, and if she graduated early she could quit school and get a job and save some money before she was eighteen and homeless.

Only time would tell if it was all just the usual stream of official platitudes.

"If anyone tries to bully you or harass you about being in foster care or juvenile detention or anything like that," came the next platitudes, "I expect you to tell a teacher, or me, or Mrs Redfern here, and not retaliate nor suffer in silence nor run away – am I quite clear about that, Emily?"

"Yes, Ma'am," Emily whispered quickly.

She meant that she understood the instruction. There was no way that she would ever dare to tell anyone – certainly no adult. She knew that whatever happened, her only option would be to suffer in silence, as both self-defence and running away had been proven by experience to be disastrous options.

She was accustomed to suffering in silence.

———

"School?" JassaVar frowned as she tried to grasp the bizarre concept.

"Yes, school," Edward Maitland told his alien stepdaughter firmly. "According to your immigration file you're sixteen, and sixteen year old girls in America go to school unless they're drop-outs or delinquents. Is your daughter either, darling?"

"There will be severe consequence if ever she misbehave," DinzaVar smiled intimidatingly at her daughter.

"Clearly you could not be expected to walk straight into a school," the householder continued so authoritatively that JassaVar would never have dared question a word even if her mother had not been there. "You will require some personal tutoring to adapt to American life. There is a very good school twenty miles away, St Edmunds, so you could attend daily.

I planned to send Tiara there but she screamed and threw things and insisted that she'd play permanent truant rather than wear – and I quote - 'pervy Catholic schoolgirl uniforms' so I inflicted the local High School on her – or perhaps I should say I inflicted the brat on the local High School, but rest assured that I'm not inflicting the local High School on you. I've booked an appointment with the Principal this afternoon to get an assessment of where you stand academically. Any questions, little lady?"

Even if she could have thought of any that quickly, JassaVar would not have dared to ask them.

———

Emily arrived back at the Redfern residence tired and confused.

She had never known a day like it. Mrs Redfern had been as generous as she had been talkative. The talking had been about a whole range of subjects – her son and foster-son, her friends, her church and other charitable activities, and a long peroration about her trip to England to do a Jane Austen tour – the latter because she knew that Emily was reading *Mansfield Park*, which apparently made Emily an apprentice Janeite in the woman's enthusiastic imagination.

In between the perorations Mrs Redfern had spent even more generously on clothes and other personal supplies than the Frasers – despite firmly informing Emily that she was not made of money and not to expect anything expensive. Emily hoped to score approval points by declaring that she always shopped for clothes in charity shops – actually true as she had never been able to afford anywhere more expensive.

They spent several hundred dollars in five shops, stopped for a snack, and then arrived at a hairdresser – then went to get Emily's nails and eyelashes professionally done for the first time ever. Looking in the mirror at the end, Emily decided that she looked almost as good as Tiara!

Why was Mrs Redfern being so generous? Emily was rapidly losing her initial fear of the woman, but felt bewildered by the fuss being made of her. She would have been amazed to learn that Joan Redfern and Sylvia Godwin had spent hours discussing how best to help the girl, and had agreed that making Emily feel more attractive would be a good confidence-booster. Another surprise came at dinner when her new foster father announced that he was taking her out Saturday morning to buy her a computer and a smartphone – or would one device do both? Nothing elaborate or expensive, he insisted, or would she like a separate e-reader?

Joan was just as surprised at her husband's offer. He had not put himself out like this for either Miranda or Shazza – he was even giving up his usual round of golf. She asked him why as they went to bed.

"Because," he replied simply, "hell will freeze over before that girl asks for help. I've seen students like her before, but mostly male. Has she yet spoken to you without you speaking to her first – other than to ask what you want her to do?"

Joan had to think hard about that. She could not really remember.

"Besides," her husband added, "you'd be free to go the Centre, after all."

"Right," his wife agreed. "I could talk to Lucy about another girl doing community service there. Sylvia Godwin did recommend to the court that helping other people would be more therapeutic than sweeping the streets."

"You think you could get the court to agree to that?"

"I'll do my level best."

"They won't have a chance, will they?"

"Now, now, dear – none of that."

"Sorry, love," the professor had to chuckle. "We're really going big on helping out this girl, aren't we?"

"Well, it is clearly long overdue time someone did," his wife asserted very firmly. "I consider it my Christian duty that it be me! I think God called me to do this. How else explain Sylvia coming to me at exactly the right moment! It just has to have been God's work."

———

Edward Maitland received the promised call from the Principal of St Edmunds at breakfast time that Saturday morning.

It was a pleasantly surprising call. Humility had seriously impressed the Principal with her abilities, particularly her astonishing capacity to remember large quantities of words and facts verbatim – which had made the Principal wonder if she had an eidetic memory? Modesty had been brutally dismissive of her daughter's academic ability, so Edward had to hastily re-evaluate his perspective when he heard his new stepdaughter's problem solving assessed as above average and her mental arithmetic skills as remarkable considering that visitor mathematics were based on an octal system rather than a decimal system. Her reading of English was also remarkably fluent considering that she had not, as the Principal had expected, been wearing one of the visitors' fancy translation devices attached to ears and eyelashes.

The Principal concluded that Humility was ignorant of many subjects that the other girls would already know, so would need special tutoring which would cost, but the school would be happy to accept the challenge of teaching their first visitor.

"First what?" Edward demanded irritably. Considering the amount that he had promised to pay their school he took it for granted that they would be happy to take the job on, and did not appreciate the implication that accepting his stepdaughter as a pupil was a concession. "I think you mean first 'alien', not first 'visitor'."

"We are advised that we should not be using the term 'alien' because it is deemed offensive and that we should be using the term 'visitor' instead."

"Well, don't do it in front of my wife. She gets furious when anyone refers to her as a 'visitor'. She quotes AvernaVar at them – 'alien' is the correct translation."

"I fear that 'alien' is also commonly used as a term of abuse, and therefore is officially deemed offensive."

"You can't offend an alien by calling her an alien. I work with many aliens and they all call themselves aliens, and they have nothing but contempt for what they call our 'primitive obsession' about not giving offence. Humility is here to stay – not a visitor but an alien. Are we quite clear about it?"

The Principal indicated that he was, then changed the subject by recommending that Humility be given a couple of weeks of personal one-to-one tutoring by a private tutor to assess exactly her strengths and weaknesses and devise an appropriate learning strategy. The Principal could recommend or even supply someone, if that was agreeable?

Edward Maitland grunted assent.

"May I ask, Mr Maitland?" the Principal added even more cautiously. "Would Humility be considered exceptionally bright for an 'alien' girl?"

"Not at all," he replied directly. "I know for a fact that she definitely did not rank in their top sixteen per cent. Her mother does not rate her intelligence highly."

"That is impressive," came a slow response. "In that case I'd really like to know what a top sixteen per cent 'alien' girl could do."

"You'll be impressed. I've met many aliens, including housegirls who are bottom of their social ladder, and never met one I'd call stupid – swear to God."

———

Tony was also thinking about God – in the sense of remembering his wife's reference to their fostering as 'God's work' - when he took his new foster daughter in for coffee and a sandwich at his favourite coffee shop that Saturday morning.

Somehow he did not think that this over-controlled girl was going to easily accept that she was 'God's work' or even one of God's children. He had looked in at her bedroom to collect her to go out that morning, but had not realized what was so odd about the sight until they were down in his car. A teenage girl had been living in that room for nearly two days, yet it still appeared at a glance to be uninhabited.

The bed had been remade so perfectly that it might never have been slept in. There were no clothes out anywhere, no posters on the walls, nothing on bedside table or vanity or even floor. Only the presence of one pretty teenager in a nice new coat and dress made the room seem occupied. Admittedly, it had been less than two days, but it had taken Miranda a day to give her room a lived-in look, and Shazza little longer to achieve so well-trashed a look that they had been forced to do some redecorating. He had not read that Emily had ever been in military school.

To cap that, they had spent half an hour in the car driving to the mall, another hour in the mall, and were now sitting in the coffee shop, and Emily hardly said anything to him except in answer to questions.

In a stereotypically monosyllabic teenage boy it might have been normal but not in a pretty teenage girl, and he was quite positive that she had not smiled once that morning. He did remember Sylvia and Joan mentioning Emily's resolute silence about the name of her boyfriend. How had a girl like her got so damaged? The brains were obviously there – quite apart from her academic record she had done the maths of calculating the gross bills at both store and coffee shop in her head without apparent effort and got both bills right to the cent.

So she should be very interesting to talk to if he could only get her to talk.

"So, Emily," he asked her quietly. "How exactly did you meet Tiara?"

It got her to look up from her normal eyes down posture that resembled a permanent cringe, and there was almost a smile on her face.

"She was shown into my cell, sir," she replied directly.

Not exactly full disclosure. Next second the gaze had dipped again and all hint of smile had disappeared as if it had never existed.

Nothing more coming evidently. Time for another prompt.

"How long did you share a cell?" he asked.

"Nearly two weeks, sir," she held back from sipping the coke that she had preferred to coffee as she peered up from under her fringe of hair.

"And she protected you while you were in there? From other girls, I presume. How did she protect you?"

Emily looked confused – clearly unsure what to say.

"We're not talking about fighting anyone, are we Emily?" he presumed, and got no indication that his supposition was wrong.

Finally inspiration seemed to strike her.

"Tiara knows how to talk to people," she burst out almost eagerly. "She can make them listen to her. Make them believe her. Persuade them to do things. She is amazing. I don't know how she does it."

Interesting. To put it mildly.

"You don't know how to make people believe you?" he probed cautiously.

"No, sir," her head really dipped low this time. "I can never make people believe me, or even like me. I don't know why. I just can't."

She choked up with the last words - clearly fighting for control. Not the ideal place to get behind the girl's defences, but at least he now knew it was achievable.

He also now knew that he had acquired a new obsession – his choice of an academic career had begun with his habit of becoming obsessively interested in understanding and explaining his subjects of interest. His first obsessions had tended to be literary characters or authors, but over decades of lecturing and tutoring he had added the understanding of living students to his list of obsessions. Not all students nor many students - just individuals that intrigued him, and this individual was intriguing enough to be a literary character.

"What was it, my dear?" he asked gently, accepting that he would not be satisfied until he had figured her out.

His phrasing alarmed her, so he changed tack quickly.

"I had another girl – a student," he fabricated smoothly, "once said she had trouble making people believe her. Turned out she meant about being raped and sexually abused. I hope …"

"I've never been raped, sir," she cut in sharply. "But Tiara …"

She cut herself off sharply, but what had she been going to say? Something about Tiara?

"Nor sexually abused?" he thought he had better ask while the iron was hot.

"No, sir."

To his astonishment she followed that terse negative up with a classic teenager eye-roll.

"Unless," she added with a welcome first hint of teenage petulance, "you count boys with wandering hands."

"I don't if you don't," he promised her, hoping to elicit a smile.

He failed, which disappointed, but did not surprise. At least some boys were paying attention - more important that she was talking.

"Are we talking ex-boyfriends?" he tried to sound casual.

"Never had a boyfriend," came back instantly, but not defensively.

If that were the case who had been driving that car?

"Dates?" he tried instead.

She paused, but then did answer.

"Couple. Didn't last long. I'm not the sort."

Abrupt stop, he thought. Had she been going to add something more?

"Not what sort?" he pressed on, remembering his wife's plan to build up the girl's self-esteem. "You're definitely the sort of girl a lot of boys will want to date."

"Not like Tiara," she responded. "I'm not the sort of girl boys want to take home to meet their parents."

That was unexpected. Why would a teenage girl prioritize meeting her boyfriend's family when selecting boyfriends? Maybe if the girl had no family of her own and wanted one? That would make sense.

"And I never will be," she added despondently.

———

"Must I go to this school?" JassaVar pleaded with her mother.

The more she thought about it the less she liked the idea. Aliens did not send daughters to school. All education was digital or personal. Surrounding a young girl with other young girls instead of adults was considered to be the very worst way to teach anything. A mother was supposed to control her daughter's education, and DinzaVar had force-fed her daughters with whatever learning packages she could afford at the time - with the emphasis on force.

"You must," came the unbending response. "Your householder decrees so you obey. It will educate you to exist with humans. You should possess no difficulty in surpassing most human daughters in study. You *will* excel at study."

The words 'or else' were not added, but when DinzaVar gave an order to a daughter they did not need to be.

"Any questions," DinzaVar demanded. "You possess hesitation."

"What about Brett, mother?" JassaVar ventured. "You desired me to entice."

"That remain relevant."

"But I will not see him when at school."

"Nor when he works, but comprehend that many human males find girls in school uniforms sexually attractive. Remember and use. If you seduce Brett into duvaying you in uniform he may possess guilt and pay more."

JassaVar could not but smile at that. Her mother had always been firm in telling her daughters that girls on lowest levels of housegirl hierarchy – like DinzaVar had been all her life, were wise to deploy all means to extract advantage from every man encountered, especially in duvay. JassaVar comprehended the sense, but could not suppress secret fantasies of enjoying a relationship with a man like those she had watched on intercepted transmissions of human television.

JassaVar and her sister had been united in being excited at the concept of monogamistic human romance, though doubting its practicality.

Such dreams were probably just that – dreams, she told herself firmly. She could never expect to be more than a casual duvay to a man like Brett. He probably only called her beautiful to be polite. Duvaying Brett sounded wise, but trying to inspire guilt felt wrong.

JassaVar did not risk mentioning that feeling to her mother as DinzaVar showed JassaVar a screen image of the school uniform. JassaVar doubted that a uniform revealing so little would attract men.

"Meanwhile," DinzaVar moved on, handing what looked like a primitive hand-held communication device to JassaVar. "This is prototype of device my husband will market worldwide in association with two companies in Freedom Consortium. It is composite memory system, communication system, visual and sonic recorder, and analysis machine. I believe they market it as 16G for some human reason. You do not deploy to assist with school studies unless I or teachers approve. You may use to communicate but all usage will be copied to my device to monitor. Any inappropriate usage will be severely punished. Comprehend?"

"Yes, mother."

"Good. Maybe I was wise to bring you to Earth."

———

It had been two days since Emily had entered the Redfern household, and the surprises were continuing.

Her two new foster parents had spent a terrifying amount of money on her, but Emily knew that they were just being charitable to a troubled delinquent. They did not know her. They spent because they were good and generous people – not because they knew and liked her. Why would they? Nobody else ever had.

She feared that she had said too much again in that coffee shop - nearly betraying Tiara, which would have been unforgiveable.

Emily had a new dream for the future. Finding a loving family was long abandoned. Finding a nice boy with a nice family had followed into the dustbin of lost causes. Her dream now was to live with Tiara. With Tiara to inspire her, maybe Emily could become less of a disaster.

If she could just keep her head down while living with the Redferns, maybe they would let her stay until she could live with Tiara. Tiara had promised that they would live together one day. That was a dream for which it would be worth enduring anything. In the meantime, she needed to not offend the Redferns in any way. The Redferns had told her that they went to church every Sunday morning, but that Emily had the choice of whether to come with them or stay at home.

Her first instinct was to stay at home and read, but memories of life with the Galleys made her hesitate. She had uneasily wondered if God was punishing her by getting her arrested, and then started wondering if it was God's doing that she had met Tiara. Going to church would please the Redferns, but Emily was always scared of meeting new people even though she desperately wanted to please the Redferns - which was why she had dishonestly prevaricated when Professor Redfern had enquired what she would like to do in college – saying that she had not thought about it yet when in truth she had long abandoned all thought of college.

She tried to soothe her confusion by checking that both bathroom and bedroom were spotlessly tidy before going down to see if there was anything they wanted her to do before she got back to reading.

It turned out that there was something they had to tell her.

Sylvia Godwin had called Mrs Redfern about arranging for Emily and Tiara to meet after Tiara's release from Juvie.

———

Tiara was very relieved when Brett came to visit her.

She had lost her grip since seeing her father, and knew it. She was no longer terrorizing the other girls. With no Emily to protect she was losing motivation.

Bravura was a lot easier to display in public than sustain in solitude, and Tiara and solitude too easily mixed into despondency. Despite everything her father, and his money, had always been the rock on which her whole edifice of self-worth was built. To have it kicked from under her shook her even more than being raped.

So it worried that the gang were beginning to congregate. Tiara considered deliberately provoking them to attack her again. If they put her in hospital it might persuade Dad to relent, maybe get her bailed or lessen her sentence – maybe even guarantee a non-custodial sentence. Problem was: getting beaten up might cause permanent damage. Solution: alien Physicians could heal all injuries short of death – if she could guarantee that alien Physicians would be called in, but that would depend on someone very rich paying a massive medical bill.

Certain billionaires had struck deals to pay Physicians to run clinics at various locations around the world where serious injuries, disabilities, deformities – from genetic disorders to amputations to rabies – were brought to be healed, but such clinics, as charities, screened their patients – only the most deserving and serious cases were seen. Many missing limbs were growing again, many people were seeing and hearing for the first time in years, and new drugs were being considered for trial that were expected to cure cancers and many other diseases.

If Tiara could have been certain that her father would pull strings and pay a Physician? But Tiara could no longer feel confident about that. Tiara did not fear a few injuries, unless they involved her being permanently crippled or scarred.

So she had never been happier in her life to see Brett come to visit her, and very much comforted, at first, by what he had come to tell her.

First good news: he hoped to have fixed for her hearing to come up in a couple of weeks, and there was every chance that she would be released immediately – probably probation and community service loomed, but she could live with that.

Best news of all, her father had relented and agreed that she could come back to live with him – but was to regard herself as strictly on probation with him, too.

"You talked him round?" Tiara suggested. "Just you – or was it you and Sara."

"And Modesty. I suspect she might have been the hidden persuader."

That did surprise.

"I base that on the terms of your probation – and guessing that if Modesty is coming to your aid, her motives are not entirely altruistic – maybe not at all altruistic."

"So there is a price?" Tiara felt relieved to be told that. She would have found it uncomfortably hard to believe her Dad caving in too easily.

"Call it part of your probation – Dad's probation, not court probation."

"It had better not be that I don't see Emily any more. Is that it? Is that really it? No way!"

"No, not that. I've spoken to Emily's new foster parents – Sylvia kindly arranged it – I spoke to them this afternoon, and they agreed that you can keep in contact and meet once a week for now, but if you don't keep to the conditions, or if you misbehave – either of you – contact may be suspended either by Dad or the Redferns – Emily's foster parents. Suspension of privileges punishment you might say. For the record, that was my suggestion – trying to convince Dad that we did have a sanction to keep you in line. Reckon it would work?"

Tiara did not answer. She wanted to yell at him that it was not right, that it was unfair to not let her live with her sister, but having her foundations pulled from under her by her father had really cut back her confidence so profoundly that she even forgot to give her brother an eye-roll.

"Don't you want to know the conditions?" Brett continued without smiling.

Tiara swallowed. Somehow she suspected that they were not going to be particularly palatable.

"You seem to like protecting vulnerable sisters," were Brett's next words.

"What?"

"You have another sister awaiting you at home now," Brett continued. "Stepsister, that is – Modesty's daughter Humility."

"What about her?"

"Dad wants to assimilate her to American life, and they have officially classified her as sixteen, so he is sending her to St Edmunds."

"Seriously!"

"Seriously. Not sure I'd have tried it. Never been to school before – you know all aliens are home-schooled. Rather scared at the prospect, and God knows what she'll think of the religious stuff. Actually it'll be very interesting to know."

"Oh, crap." This time Tiara did roll her eyes.

"You got it. You go with her, look after her, and wear the – and I quote - 'pervy uniforms', and all that. You stay out of trouble, Emily stays out of trouble, and you keep Humility out of trouble, and you get to live at home – court permitting."

"You're enjoying this, aren't you?" Tiara retorted – trying to salvage the tattered remnants of her pride – and failing humiliatingly.

———

Brett was very pleased when he got back into his car outside the Detention Centre, and rang his father straight away.

"Like a charm, Dad," he reported. "Just as you planned. You threatening to kick her out convinced her to grab the lifeline. She agreed to St Edmunds - swallowed hook, line, and sinker. You really had her going, you know. But you had me going too, you could have told me sooner!"

CHAPTER ELEVEN

The thunderstorm started as Emily was going to bed that Saturday evening.

She had asked the Redferns several times if there was anything else they wanted her to do, but they steadily insisted that there was not and instead asked what she wanted to watch on television. She had no idea what was on, and was long accustomed to watching whatever her foster family wanted and having no say in the matter, so she immediately decided to take the easy option of never asking to see anything in case they wanted something else. Professor Redfern offered to set up her computer that evening so she could watch on it in her bedroom, but she had refused - not wanting to bother them – not understanding the concept of parents actively wanting to make a daughter happy.

The computer and smartphone were still in their unopened boxes packed tidily away at the bottom of her wardrobe, and Emily had not even contemplated unpacking them. Instead she devoted herself to the only chores she was allowed to do – making both bedroom and bathroom the epitome of tidiness before getting ready for bed, and only then managing to relax enough to read for a while.

Then it began to rain heavily against the window. Thunder soon followed, bringing memories flooding back of that church porch where she had sheltered from Nature's *son et lumière*. On impulse she went to the window, sat on the wide sill, and gazed into the storm.

There were more trees illuminated in the flashes than she remembered.

She was huddled into the corner of the window when the Redferns came in to check that all windows were safely closed. She reassured them that she was not afraid, then stupidly added that she felt very safe looking out at the storm, but that the storm reminded her of – she stopped there.

"Reminds you of what, Emily," Joan Redfern asked kindly.

Being asked for an explanation, however kindly, merely panicked Emily even more. She was desperately afraid of giving away too much, but equally desperate not to seem ungrateful.

"We're not just here to feed and clothe you, Emily," Professor Redfern stepped forward. "Nor just as agents of the court or the social services. We're here to act as your parents – and that means to help you with any problems – worries – bad memories."

"Yes," his wife joined in eagerly. "If you want to talk to us about anything, or ask our advice about anything, just do it. Trust me, we don't shock easily."

The Redferns were attempting to help her, she realized, and she had no idea how to respond. She desperately did not want to approach any of the real nightmares of her memory - not with anyone but Tiara.

Panic supplied inspiration, but inspiration is not always wisdom.

"Nothing to shock," she hastened to placate. "It is just – I mean – I once got caught out in a thunderstorm and took shelter in a church porch. I wondered – can I come with you to church tomorrow?"

It seemed to deflect their curiosity, and certainly pleased Mrs Redfern at least, which pleased Emily – but then she had to try to sleep while worrying how she would cope with going to church? Would she be unwelcome, or would they want to save her soul or something like that?

Either way it was odds on that she would screw up again.

She eventually dropped off, but three hours later she woke up whimpering – remembering Timmy and Sandra and Sukie – knowing she could have saved them all if she had only dialled 911.

She spent some time wallowing in futile guilt and listening to the rain - grateful that her nightmare had not woken the Redferns. Emily's default plan for surviving to adulthood was kicking back in. The fact that it had not worked before in making foster parents love her or keep her just had to mean that she had not tried hard enough.

She was determined to try even harder with the Redferns.

———

The Redferns were Episcopalian.

All Emily knew about Episcopalians was that they were Christians. The Church was not as big as she expected, but it was much more beautiful. She expected it to be full of people like the Redferns – middle-aged or older, well-dressed people. She soon saw that she was wrong – there were several teenagers, and younger children were escorted in at the end.

A good-looking young man in his twenties arrived a couple of minutes after the service had started, and sat right behind her. Joan Redfern picked the first opportunity to whisper an introduction to their foster-son, Peter.

Emily found no problems with the service. She quite liked the hymns, and did not have to do anything that risked getting noticed, just stand up and sit down when everyone else did, and speak with everyone else or stay silent with everyone else. When the Redferns went up for Communion she declined the option of going up for a blessing, and though they looked disappointed they did not press her. Other than that so little was demanded of Emily that she decided to come to church every Sunday to please the Redferns.

What happened after the service gave her second thoughts. Everyone gathered round the back of the church for coffee and chat. Emily had not anticipated that. She accepted an offered coffee from her foster mother, who was among a group of women organizing the refreshments. Then Emily stayed close to her foster father, hoping that nobody would speak to her, and furious with herself for not offering to help with the coffee. Peter had moved off immediately the service was over to speak to friends, so Emily knew no reason why anyone else might want to speak to her.

Except – inevitably – that the minister approached to speak to the Professor, and be introduced to Emily – a prospect that triggered Emily immediately into panic mode. Especially when the man revealed that he must already have known who she was by speaking directly to her after merely asking the Professor how he was.

"You must be their new foster-daughter?" he asked with a kindly smile. "How are you settling in?"

But Emily did not even hear the second question. She was too busy defaulting to script.

"Yes, sir," she rushed out. "Just released from Southside. I'm sorry, sir."

In rehearsing that line over the past days Emily had imagined uttering it with a touch of pride and defiance – like the martyr she craved to be – but spoken aloud the words just sounded abject – and she ducked her head in shame.

"Sorry for what?" the minister responded gently.

Emily still did not look up, unaware that she appeared to be almost cringing away from the question.

"You have a right to know who has entered your Church," she muttered. "In case – in case – in case ..."

Her voice trailed off, and she flicked a glance up at the Professor, suddenly convinced that she must have made him angry. The professor was looking at her with a frown of worry which she prejudicially interpreted as annoyance.

"I'm sorry," Emily whispered - convinced that she had screwed up yet again.

"I thank you for your honesty," the minister finally responded to Emily in a very gentle voice. "Be assured that you'll always be welcome here - as long as you want to come. Everyone is welcome in a Christian church."

Emily peered up at him from under a dipped forehead. She had never realized that her habit of peering was often interpreted as acting furtive by uncharitable observers. Fortunately her current observers were charitable.

"Even a convicted criminal?" Emily felt compelled to ask, but dipped her eyes back down out of fear of his response.

"Everyone is welcome there," came a very gentle statement. "Have you been to church before?"

"Sunday School, sir – until I was nine."

"What denomination?"

Emily blanked. She could not remember the Galleys calling it anything other than church.

"Christian, sir," she said – ashamed of sounding so stupid.

"No need to call me 'sir', Emily," he responded, and she flicked a glance up at him. "Most people here just call me 'Steve'."

He did not sound angry, to Emily's relief, and he was not smiling so he was probably not laughing at her unless he was just being kind. She could not imagine daring to call him Steve, but fortunately he had not specifically ordered her to call him Steve, so it seemed safer to say nothing and avoid getting it wrong again.

"And you can call me Julia," came from the deaconess who had just appeared beside the minister. "I'm a friend of Sylvia. Delighted to meet you."

Emily digested that with abject shame. They had clearly known about her all along. She should have kept her stupid mouth shut.

"If you like," the deaconess declared brightly, "I can introduce you around the group. We have several youngsters who I'm sure would be happy to meet you."

"Good idea," Joan Redfern declared firmly, as she came up that moment to hand Steve and Julia cups of coffee. "Go and make friends. We've things to discuss with Steve. We'll come to you when we're ready to leave."

Emily froze mentally. That had sounded like an order, and she desperately wanted to please her foster parents, but going to the dentist scared her less than trying to make friends. She numbly allowed the deaconess to lead her over to a group of two teenage boys and two teenage girls. Emily recognized the two girls and the older boy as being in the choir.

A glance back showed the Redferns talking with the minister and watching her, and she desperately wished that she could lip-read what they were saying about her.

In fact, they were discussing her disturbing lack of self-esteem. The Professor was listing Emily's obsessive tidiness, her reluctance to talk unless spoken to, her declared total lack of friends, her conviction that nobody would ever believe her – based on bitter experience was Tony Redfern's guess - and her declaration that she was not the sort of girl that boys wanted to take home to meet their parents.

And her total adoration of a twin sister who was not exactly an ideal role model.

The immediate agreement was that the girl needed help, and especially to make the right sort of friends. They all looked across to where Emily was virtually surrounded by four other teenagers – but still with dipped head and shoulders in a stance that looked like cringing – and it was their turn to wonder what was being said, but they had the advantage of Emily in that Julia came across and told them that Emily had responded to the introduction by the straight announcement that she had come from Southside.

"How did they react?" Joan asked before the men could.

"Taken aback at first," Julia answered, "and not sure what to say, but you know Bobby – he soon found something to say."

Bobby had, in fact, kindly made no comment on Emily's confession, but set about matching her introduction by telling her that he had just graduated from High School and was doing a year of voluntary social work as preparation for going to theological college with a view to becoming a minister. He started to wax enthusiastic about his calling before Sasha, a dark blonde who looked about Emily's age, chimed in and took over - revealing that she was a sophomore at the school where Emily would be starting on Monday.

So Emily felt duty bound to warn her that she would be at the same school. To her dismay Sasha immediately offered to introduce her to everyone.

Emily nearly panicked.

"I'll be junior year," she rushed out. "I'll manage. Used to new schools."

"No problem," Veronica, the black girl, just waved an airy hand. "My idiot brother here is a junior."

"But ..." Emily blurted out. "I mean – trust me you don't want to be associated with a girl like me."

"I do," Lawrie, the alleged idiot brother, chipped in cheerfully. "It'll do my rep a ton of good being seen with a hottie like you!"

A what! Emily did not realize that when Sasha and Veronica both giggled it was at her expression. Her default assumption was that Lawrie had made a joke at Emily's expense which they were giggling at. Another boy interested in her because she was a bad girl – she assumed – refusing to admit the possibility that he might purely be interested because he thought she was pretty.

Then a second fear intruded – had he been joking to put her at her ease? She was being treated very kindly as an act of Christian charity by the Redferns, she had already deduced, and clearly they had spread the word to the minister and the deaconess – had it been spread to these four to do the same?

"First rule, Emily," Veronica told her with a laugh. "My brother deludes himself that he is funny and cool when he is really just stupid – but you'll find him pretty harmless – for a boy."

The last phrase was spoken with disdain, Emily thought.

"First rule, Emily," Lawrie matched his sister's intonation very well, and pretended to be matching the pitch of her voice. "Never try to play it cool when your sister is there. No guy is a hero to his sister."

Emily would have felt horrible if her sister had derided her like that – even though she considered herself an idiot compared to Tiara - but Lawrie had reacted by laughing it off. Did he really not mind his sibling mocking him?

Bobby then cut in to say that he was hosting a small party at his house the next Friday to celebrate his acceptance at college and Emily was welcome to come.

Emily nearly panicked.

"I can't," she began nervously, then remembered her wonderful escape clause. "I'm under curfew. Court curfew. I can't leave the house after six."

The four looked really surprised at that, and Veronica said that she was sure that there must be some way round that, which panicked Emily more as she remembered that her escape clause was not exactly true, or not exactly the whole truth, and she did not want to tell lies – especially not in church.

"I'd have to get special permission," she improvised. "It would have to be something really special."

"No party Bobby would put on," Lawrie went for the joke, "is ever going to be that special. I mean, we're guaranteed to all leave sober!"

Emily wondered how the court could imagine that giving her a curfew was a punishment.

––––––––

On the way home later, the Redferns asked if Emily had liked the service, and how she had got on with 'the other kids'.

Emily was seriously stymied for an answer. She just ended up mumbling 'okay'.

"Any time you want to go anywhere with any of *them*," Mrs Redfern told her firmly. "I can promise you that it will be fine. You do need our permission, but unless the day is inconvenient it will be no problem."

She had no idea how guilty that made her foster daughter feel. Emily had rejected an invitation on the false pretext that she could not get permission, so she had basically told a lie, and sooner or later everyone would surely realize and think even worse of her than they already did. She thought of speaking up straight away and confessing, but how could she do that and still avoid going to that party?

Crippled by doubt, Emily defaulted to ducking the decision and saying nothing, but trying extra hard to please her foster parents – beginning with helping Joan to get dinner ready - for four, as Peter would be joining them. She got so frantic in her efforts that her hands started shaking and Joan told her to stop and calm down – an injunction that was anything but calming but did make her try to appear calm.

But she even failed at that. The stove was higher than she was used to, and when reaching over for a saucepan of baked beans her arm strayed too low over a hot ring and she scalded herself and dropped the saucepan.

The Professor hurried into the kitchen and held her shaking hand under cold water while his wife fetched ice out of the ice-box to cover the scald, and then went to the first aid box for anti-burn spray.

They brought up a tall stool and made her sit on it and the professor kept his arm reassuringly around her shoulder while the couple worked on her scalded hand. Emily was too embarrassed to do anything but co-operate silently, and not look up at either of their faces as they nursed her like a baby. She did not understand why they were not angry at her stupidity, but did not dare ask.

All she could do was whisper that she was sorry.

"No need to be sorry, Emily," Joan told her gently. "Just try to be more careful in future, and try to calm down. Lucky you never quite touched the ring."

They were still there when Peter arrived and got roped in to filling a bucket of cold water and placing it on a low stool next to Emily's chair with a towel beside it, so that Emily could dip her arm as often as she wanted during dinner.

She was surprised when they went ahead with dinner as if no disaster had happened, Peter and Mrs Redfern serving everything while the Professor sat beside Emily and checked that she was managing with her hand – encouraging her to keep it cool whenever she felt discomfort, and even cutting up her food for her.

What Peter thought of her she shuddered to think – he had to be thinking her really stupid.

Peter was thinking nothing of the sort. For men of his age other thoughts took priority when meeting pretty girls, but he could see that she was upset, so he was cautious about talking to her, preferring to talk to his foster parents about his latest trip up to *Freedom*. As an electrical engineer he had been lucky enough to get employment with the power consortium that was deploying alien energy around America. They calculated that within five years they could be supplying all electrical needs of North America much cheaper than any competition, and Peter was in on the ground floor of an exciting new industry – a powerhouse of an industry in every sense of the word. He was happy to talk about it, and happier to see a pretty girl listening with actual interest – which encouraged him to go into considerable detail about everything he had seen aboard *Freedom*, and in his encounters with aliens.

The Redferns had heard most of it before, but conspired in pretending to find the stories as fascinating as Emily, who was so fascinated that she forgot about her hand, and did not object when Joan Redfern dished extra sprouts and carrots and meat onto her plate, then extra pudding. Emily ate it all, but still asked no questions. The Redferns did all the questioning, and Emily continued not saying a word unless directly questioned, until offering to help clear up and having to be ordered to stay away from the kitchen and talk to Peter while he was there.

"Take the chance to sit down while it's offered, Emily," Peter told her, as she nervously sat back down and dipped her hand in the bucket. "Got to warn you that Joan usually does tea and coffee at church functions, and all sorts of other charity gigs – you might get roped into helping her if you're not careful."

"Only if she volunteers," Joan Redfern called from the kitchen.

"Or is volunteered?" Peter raised his voice to be clearly audible in the kitchen.

"I'd love to volunteer," Emily declared nervously – forgetting herself so much as to speak spontaneously. "I'm good at waitressing – I've waitressed a lot."

"Really? For money?"

"Of course," Emily declared with obvious pride. "I bought my computer with it."

"You've had your own computer before?" Professor Redfern asked with surprise. "What happened to it?"

Emily blanked for a moment. Terrible choice of subject, but after her dishonesty in church, and their constant kindness, she almost wanted to tell them – just in case they might be the first people, apart from Tiara, to believe her.

"I don't know – exactly," she still prevaricated for a moment.

"What do you know?" the Professor asked firmly, and came back and sat down beside her, looking her directly in the face. "No need to be exact."

Emily was not aware that Professor Redfern prided himself on his firmness in challenging answers out of his students in tutorials, still less did she guess how intrigued by her he was – to the extent that he was determined to exploit any opportunity of getting past her defences.

She just could not return his gaze. She stared down at the table feeling pure shame blended with panic as she struggled to think what to say. They deserved an answer, and they deserved the truth.

But not necessarily all of it – and thank God she had only mentioned a single computer, when she could have mentioned two. She need not mention both of them, but which one. Both had been humiliating, but if she mentioned the second one which she guessed that Dylan might have purloined she risked them trying to do something about it – and Dylan could accuse her of threatening him with a knife.

If she mentioned the first – why would they believe her version of events? The police had not, nor anyone else.

"I mean," she prevaricated weakly, "that when you move foster homes you don't expect to take anything valuable with you."

A silence greeted that, as Emily decided that had not been exactly what she meant to say, but was not exactly sure what she had meant to say. She did not dare raise her gaze to find out how they had reacted.

"So what happened to your computer, Emily?" the Professor asked gently, and silence followed, and Emily knew she had to answer, and part of her just ached for them to believe her.

"I couldn't prove it," she whispered, nearly shaking. "I couldn't prove that I had bought it for myself, so they didn't believe me when I said it was mine, so …"

For the moment, she did not dare finish, but she could see her hands trembling on the table in front of her eyes.

"So?" the Professor prompted gently.

"We promise to believe you," his wife added firmly, and Emily finally caved in.

"So they accused me of stealing it," she whispered. "I had to sign a confession and accept a caution so they wouldn't prosecute me. That was why I knew they'd never believe me about – anything else."

"That is outrageous," came a real hiss from Joan Redfern.

"We are willing to believe you," the Professor said, taking her hand and lifting her head to look up at him. "So you can safely tell us what really happened."

———

"Okay," Peter commented as his foster mother came back down the stairs to join the two men in the living room an hour later. "Nearly done, and I thought that my exploits in space would provide all the drama this weekend."

The 'nearly done' remark referred to the desktop computer and the smartphone that he was expertly setting up – complete with family filters and security software – for Emily to be given when she woke up.

"I've tucked her up in bed," Joan ignored his attempt at humour, "and told her to sleep as long as she likes. She might already be asleep. I don't think she is as much physically tired as mentally exhausted. Tony, I don't care what you think, I am absolutely convinced that it was the Will of God which brought her to us."

"Not ready to argue, darling," her husband responded. "But what about her meeting her identical twin in the same cell at Juvie just a couple of weeks ago?"

"Well, that just had to be God's Will, too. I'm not sure what that means we should do about the twin. I wonder what sort of help she needs right now."

Had Tiara been asked if there was any way that the Redferns could help her, she would have told them to mind their own business.

That Sunday afternoon her spirits were getting low, and she was getting irritable. Since she had lost Emily's company the restrictions and humiliations were beginning to really bite – and making her think. Getting in trouble to annoy her family might still be fun, but not if it landed her in this hellhole.

She even felt less able to dominate the gang now she was no longer motivated by her mission to protect Emily. Not that she expected retaliation any day soon, but she was smugly unaware that she had overplayed her hand. Too many mentions of the word 'alien' had diluted the authorities' panic reactions to what they were now interpreting as her wolf-crying. Worse for Tiara, they had come to share Tiara's false image of herself as tough – unlike her twin. There was longer a special watch on her – which Tiara did not even notice in her growing boredom.

Sheer boredom prompted her to attend a service conducted by Sylvia Godwin, and the chaplain had somehow slipped in a reference to alcohol misuse which struck home, so on a whim Tiara resolved to quit drinking – though possessing enough self-knowledge to doubt her ability to keep that resolution, and refusing alcohol when it was practically the staple diet at most teen parties would be challenging.

Before that challenge could be faced she still had to survive Juvie, where she had not tried to make friends but had made enemies who were not as easily intimidated as enemies in High School.

Enemies like Sukie Burden, who had just been told that her father had refused to take her back under any circumstances. His new wife did not want Sukie messing up her home or harming her new babies, so there was no escape from foster care even if she got released from Juvie. She was in as much despair about the destruction of her life and desolation of her future as Emily had been – a level of despair that Tiara was not capable of imagining.

Sukie's despair did not turn her thoughts to suicide, but to revenge. The one she blamed for the destruction of her life was Emily, and Emily had escaped, but a proxy was available. It took time to find a solid weapon, and to hide it until her chance came that Sunday evening when she caught Tiara alone in her own cell. As Sukie walked in the cell, Tiara turned and looked at Sukie for the moment, and opened with her patented superior sneer, which turned to sudden panic as she saw the weapon raised above Sukie's head.

Both expressions could have been deliberately selected to provoke Sukie's frustrated rage and despair to fever pitch, and she completely lost all control, after her first blow caught Tiara across the forehead and actually hit an eye.

By the time warders had dragged the screaming Sukie away and subdued her, Tiara had two fractures of her skull, plus a fractured cheekbone, broken nose, several broken fingers, and severe damage to one eye and one ear. Tiara was taken to hospital where she lapsed into a coma with suspected brain damage.

Sukie faced serious assault charges, but she had learnt her lesson and never mentioned the A-word when claiming that she only did it because she hated Tiara for being a vicious bitch, so her attack did not get classified as a hate crime, making the potential penalties far less severe.

It helped that the rest of the gang had managed to intimidate and blackmail their weakest and stupidest member, a girl named Amber, into taking the blame for the really serious offence of saying that word, and the rest had ended up admitting only the comparatively trivial offence of assault. The authorities were happy to collude with this as they could present the dreaded hate crime as an aberration of a single individual rather than a gang. As a result Sukie was hopeful that she would get not much longer a sentence than Amber - unless Tiara were actually to die.

Sukie felt so much happier now that she had finally got her hatred of Emily out of her system.

CHAPTER TWELVE

Emily was so worried that she struggled to fall asleep.

The Redferns had claimed to believe her, but Emily suspected that they had only pretended to believe her out of Christian kindness or whatever.

But what if they had really believed her? And tried to do something to help her? Any attempt to talk to the police about her case could involve more police learning about her twin, and if that reached one of the cops on her case they might guess that the girl in the security video might be Tiara.

Priority one had to be protecting Tiara - if necessary by telling more lies. Emily had already committed perjury by pleading guilty so telling the truth would not get her out of trouble and it was partly her fault that Timmy and Sandra were dead and Sukie's life destroyed – and all her fault if she had really killed someone in that car crash.

It had been stupid to mention computers. At least she had limited her disclosures, and luckily they had not pressed her, instead focussing on ensuring that Emily was ready for school – even showing her the bus stops. Mrs Redfern insisted on driving Emily in early first day, spelt out that she must go first to the Principal's office for her schedule, checked that she had the plan of the school, had selected what to wear, knew lunchtimes and break times - and knew to be home by five latest unless she had permission in advance to be late - then promised a healthy packed lunch and asked if there were any foods which she could not eat. Other teenagers might have resented having their day bossily planned for them, but Emily welcomed the obsessiveness of a kindred spirit making her feel less fear of the day to come.

It also convinced her that the Redferns must really care - if only out of charity rather than for herself. Emily could not imagine anyone loving her for herself, even Tiara, and would have been stunned to know how late the

Redferns stayed up talking about their new foster daughter. So late that Joan Redfern felt as though she had barely dropped off when she woke to hear Emily sobbing from a nightmare.

Next morning Joan told her husband that her main problem had been calming the girl's frantic apologies for waking her. She had only stayed until Emily was calm enough to promise that she was okay and would go back to sleep.

Joan had taken some time to get back to sleep, unable to stop thinking about Emily, and unable to stop reliving memories that she generally tried to silence by activity and commitment. Memories of her miscarriages, and of a stillborn girl who would have been only a couple of years older than Emily had she lived.

The outsider looking in – that was Emily. In court, in school, in church, even at the shops - always apart, out of it, isolated – the epitome of lonely - reminding Joan of a girl from her own schooldays – a girl called Rachel, from a poor family, always untidy, possibly abused, certainly neglected, always without money – always hungry enough to jump at the food which Joan would offer her from her own invariably over-stuffed lunchbox – initially overstuffed because Joan's mother had no truck with modern dietary fads and believed that kids should have healthy appetites, but later overstuffed at Joan's request so that she could share it with Rachel.

Joan was not unused to being laughed at herself for her ungainly ways, and had learnt to shrug it off, but Rachel was laughed at even more than Joan. And laughed at more cruelly because Joan had a loving family to go home to and Rachel never even talked about her family.

Joan would never forget the day when a dozen girls united to mock Rachel while Joan could only look on helplessly. Joan could not even remember what about, but did remember Rachel running off crying and disappearing from school, and never returning – Joan had heard one rumour of suicide and another of Juvie. Forty years later and Joan was still haunted by the feeling that had she only found the courage to stand up and defend Rachel that day then maybe Rachel might never have run.

It was to cope with her guilt over Rachel that Joan had finally learnt to pray and mean it and believe it instead of just going through the motions, and why she had tried going into social work herself – not very successfully in the view of her bosses because Joan had not been very good at keeping her boxes ticked or mouthing the fashionable mantras of social care, so when leaving to have a baby she had not been encouraged to return to work and had wound up beginning her long and much more emotionally satisfying career of voluntary work instead.

There had been times when a nonsensical wisp of a thought had intruded that her failure to give birth to the baby daughter Joan had always wanted was some sort of punishment for not standing up to the girls who were taunting Rachel that last day. Nonsense – she would always tell herself. God did not work that way.

Maybe Emily could be Joan's chance to make amends for Rachel? Maybe, maybe not – but whatever the case Joan desperately wanted to help this girl as she had failed to help Rachel. She had done much in the way of charity work and church work in her life, but never anything quite this personal.

It took some time, but she fell asleep eventually, and in the morning was woken by her husband's alarm clock – an unusual experience for her, as she was normally up and busy before he woke. That morning he was able to tease her that interrupted nights came with the territory for a new mother.

Joan nevertheless enjoyed the rest of the morning, fussing over Emily through breakfast, driving the girl to school, watching as Emily nervously joined the precursors of the throng entering through the school gates.

Meanwhile Joan had a fund-raising coffee morning to help run, but even though kept busy until lunchtime, she could not help feeling happy that she had taken a daughter to school, nor worrying how that daughter would be coping.

———

Emily worried more.

She collected her schedule in good time, and found the first two classrooms without difficulty. The teachers welcomed her without verbal comment, though she prejudicially assumed that they must be judging her negatively, but they said nothing to her except to issue her catch-up assignments so she was able to just listen, take notes, and keep silent - exactly as she liked it. Between classes she hung back to check her school plan, then hurried to her next class, avoiding talking to anyone, and kept this up at morning break by finding her way to the library.

Next class was advanced history, and the class had a test on their work of the last two weeks. The teacher told Emily that she might as well take it but that he would just use it to assess her knowledge on the subject. Emily found that she knew most of the answers anyway, and hoped that he would not mind if her guesses about the rest were incorrect.

Lunch left her in a quandary. In previous schools she had headed straight for the library rather than the canteen, but this time she had chicken salad sandwiches made by her foster mother and felt obliged to eat them, and rules said that packed lunches had to be eaten in the canteen.

She tried to find an empty corner table so that she could eat as fast as possible before anyone tried to speak to her. She was worried how other students would react. Wearing decent clothes meant that girls were less likely to sneer at her, but on the downside more boys might want to talk to her.

Then someone sat beside her, and she was surprised to see Lawrie had come over to ask how she was settling in, and apologize for not finding her earlier.

"Never realized you'd be in so many advanced classes," he remarked as he dumped his cooked meal on the table so firmly that some bits of food spilled off it. "Mind if I sit here? Why did the Redferns give you sandwiches?"

Emily did not answer. She was too busy restraining herself from clearing up the mess. She had no idea that Sylvia had told Joan that previous schools had recorded Emily as spending entire lunch breaks in the school library instead of eating lunch, and that Emily had frequently been observed avoiding meals in the Detention Centre. Emily would have been shocked to learn that anyone cared enough to even notice anything like that, and dumbfounded that Sylvia and Joan had agreed that Emily was more likely to eat if given sandwiches and ordered to eat them.

As to minding if he sat there - she naturally preferred to be left alone, but would never have dared to risk offending him by saying so.

"You must be really smart," he was saying as she dithered with a sandwich in her hand. "What do you want to read in college?"

"I won't be going to college," Emily replied without thinking, and Lawrie stopped in the act of sticking his fork into something resembling meat. "I'm not smart. Smart girls ..."

She stopped. She had been about to say that smart girls did not end up in Juvie, but just in time she remembered that Tiara was there.

"Clearly smarter than me," Lawrie replied with his mouth full, "if you're in advanced classes."

"That is just schoolwork," Emily defaulted, as she noticed Sasha and Veronica entering the canteen. "I just learn what they tell me to learn. Don't need to be smart – I mean it's not hard."

She took a bite of her sandwich, noticed a grin on his face, and wondered what she had said wrong. She looked away in embarrassment, and saw that Sasha and Veronica were at a table with what presumably were friends. Emily wondered if they had told everyone yet that Emily was out of Juvie.

"Okay," Lawrie laughed. "I know we're different races, but are you sure that we're not different species? For us ordinary mortals school work is hard most of the time and boring the rest of the time. If you find it that easy you've just got to go to college. Why wouldn't you want to go to college?"

Emily tried to eat her sandwiches faster. The sooner she could eat them the sooner she could get away on her own. Unfortunately she was not used to eating so much, or particularly hungry, so saw no way to politely avoiding answering.

"Foster kid," she finally went for it. "Criminal record. No college would want me even if I could afford to go. When I escape foster care I'll need a full time job or be on the streets. Stupid to want what you can never have."

Lawrie Johnson stopped eating in shock. For almost a minute all he could do was stare, but then he asked straight out if she was always so pessimistic.

A quotation came to her memory.

"Pessimists are what optimists call realists," she reacted immediately.

"Good one," Lawrie laughed. "So what do you hope to do in the future?"

"I try not to think about my future," she answered without thinking, worrying if she had got something wrong about the quotation. "It makes me want to kill myself."

Lawrie thought for a moment that she was joking again, then realized that she was not joking. Then he flinched in reaction as she flinched.

As two large male figures loomed over their table.

———

Five minutes later Emily walked away from the canteen in a confused mixture of jubilation and terror.

She had executed Tiara's plan for warning off unwanted attentions even better than she had imagined. Two senior jocks had sat down to 'make the new hottie welcome' and offer to make the 'altar-boy' leave her alone – classic 'just having a bit of fun' jerks of the sort that infested every school was Emily's prejudiced assessment, though the jocks genuinely thought they were just chatting up the pretty new girl and expected her to be flattered by their attentions. Instead they inspired Emily to channel Tiara and ask why they did not expect a 'hottie' to already have a serious boyfriend.

The jocks looked at Lawrie, and started to giggle.

"Not Lawrie," Emily had pushed on quickly. "I only just met him – no one would consider him a threat. I'm in foster care on parole from Juvie. I was sent to Juvie for not naming my boyfriend. If a girl is so scared of her boyfriend that she goes to Juvie rather than betray him – what do you think a guy that scary would do to guys who were bothering his girlfriend?"

She had phrased it with great care, rejoicing so much in the rehearsed precision of the dialogue that she missed Lawrie's reaction to her dismissive comment about him while relishing the visible deflation of her two swaggering targets.

When she then politely asked them to leave them alone, they had nervously done so, and Emily had returned to eating her sandwich feeling seriously proud of herself – and offering silent thanks to her genius sister for the brilliant idea.

But Lawrie had brought her pride crashing down by asking if she wanted him to sit somewhere else as well. For a dreadful moment, she nearly said 'yes', but then she realized that would be unkind and unfair, so hastily assured him that she had never had a boyfriend – and pointed out that she never said she had.

"I thought you said they sent you to Juvie for not naming him."

"They did. I couldn't name him because he didn't exist but the police refused to believe me – nobody believes you if you're a foster kid – or maybe nobody believes me because I'm me. I never told those two jerks I had a boyfriend. I just gave them a 'what if' scenario. They just assumed I must have a boyfriend."

"You were bluffing?"

"I just offered a hypothetical situation, and relied on their stupidity."

"Those two probably couldn't even spell hypothetical! Awesome! You are scary, girl."

Scary! Really?

"You do know that'll be all round school," Lawrie continued in a low voice. "Everyone will think you have a dangerous boyfriend."

"Works for me if it makes guys like that leave me alone."

"I get that. Trouble is it might not be just them who leave you alone. What if it gets to the teachers? Or back to the Redferns?"

That was why Emily was in turmoil as she headed for the library, as the transient jubilation of success was slowly dissolved by a rising fear of the consequences.

By the time she was sitting in the library, trying to concentrate on her catch-up assignments, she was convinced that she had made a disastrous mistake. What if it did get back to the teachers? The Redferns? Social Services? The Police? Would she get re-arrested by the police and taken in for questioning?

As the afternoon wore on, she worried more and more that she had got herself into even worse trouble.

———

JassaVar saw Brett's arrival from a window and rushed to meet him, after checking that her dress was revealing enough to comply with her mother's orders.

It was not only her desire to obey orders that sent her scurrying to meet Brett. She was feeling lonely. Even when living alone in her room on *Anarchy* there were other housegirls in neighbouring apartments whom she could meet every day, and she could receive calls from LaskaVar.

Now she had no way to call her sister other than by the 16G that her mother had given her, but her mother could monitor everything she did on the 16G and had forbidden her calling her sister in orbit without explicit maternal sanction – officially on expense grounds, but JassaVar knew that there must be another reason. Back on *Anarchy* JassaVar had been able to call LaskaVar from the systems of friendly neighbours – usually in return for help with chores, though not allowed to call direct without permission as the caller paid the cost of calls.

Not being able to talk to LaskaVar for a period was miserable, but worse was not being able to talk to the resident housegirls – or housekeeper and housemaids as the humans called them. True that Mrs Henderson was always perfectly polite to JassaVar, and willing to answer any questions, but the older woman had made it plain that she possessed no interest in making friends. Meanwhile the housemaids, though much closer to JassaVar's age, were barely even polite to her.

Brett was not hostile, and smiled kindly and asked if she had any problems, but quickly made it clear that he did not possess time to talk when informing her that his sister Tiara was in a coma after being attacked in Juvie.

"In a coma!" JassaVar gasped, only realizing later that she had spoken in Earth Primary Language without having to think about it - for the very first time.

In retrospect she would be pleased that her deliberate policy of reading and speaking English regularly was paying off, no doubt helped by her seriously trying to stick to the recommended linguistic technique of trying to translate every thought into English when she was alone. At the time she was more pleased by Brett stopping to reassure her that his father and JassaVar's mother were seeking an alien Physician to treat Tiara.

DinzaVar had apparently known a Physician's Assistant and made direct contact, and Edward Maitland had offered a large payment and was seeking court approval for Tiara to be flown directly to *Freedom* for treatment.

Brett himself had come to collect some clothes for Tiara to wear while recovering – trusting that there would be a recovery. JassaVar was resigning herself to a lonely evening when Brett stopped on the stairs, and came back down.

"I'll need some clothes for Tiara while she recuperates on *Freedom*," he explained. "Your mother said that was likely after a head injury. Perhaps you could help me sort out clothes suitable for an alien spaceship?"

———

Emily had retreated to the school library after the bell rang to end normal school hours.

She had been told that this school allowed more latitude than most schools to stay after hours in the school library, but Emily only needed long enough to avoid meeting other students on the way home. In some previous foster homes she would have needed to get on with homework assignments, but the Redferns had made it obvious that she would not need to do that while with them, so she decided that half an hour should suffice – but she had been there less than ten minutes when she was startled by the approach of her foster mother.

"I thought you might be here, my dear," Joan Redfern remarked as Emily jumped up – instinctively fearing that she must be in trouble. "I was in the car anyway, so I decided to pick you up and see how your first day went. Did you tell everybody? As you did yesterday?"

"Not everybody, Mrs Redfern," Emily replied without thinking. "But I told – I expect ..."

"That it'll spread like wildfire," the woman finished for her. "Yes, I'm sure it will soon get around to everybody. Well, I respect your honesty, Emily, but I'm not sure it was necessary. However, what is done is done, and we must live with it. I assume that you came to the library – oh, hello, Diana – this is my new foster daughter, Emily – has she introduced herself?"

Diana turned out to be the school librarian, Mrs Travers. The two women promptly spent the next ten minutes catching up on each other's families and charitable activities with the familiarity of old friends, while Emily stood and waited for them to finish, not daring to interrupt.

Eventually both women recollected their other business, and Joan turned to Emily asking her to pick up everything she needed and they would go straight home.

Emily obeyed silently, and they were half way out to the car before Joan Redfern noticed how much Emily was carrying, and thought to ask if she had needed to go to her locker first.

Emily finally dared to admit that she did, really.

"You could have just said so, my dear," her foster mother sighed. "You don't need to wait for permission to speak. Go ahead and I'll wait at the gate. Hurry up."

Emily scurried to obey. There were still a few students and staff around, but thankfully none paid her any attention. She was nearly out the door again when she realized that she could not remember packing a book that she needed. She frantically searched through her bag and failed to find it, scurried even more hurriedly back to her locker to search for it, panicked when she could not find it in there, started towards the library even as she searched her bag again – and just before going through the door of the library found it at the bottom of her bag.

Worried about how long she had already taken, Emily started to run back outside, but was stopped by a teacher who told her off for running in an empty corridor – reducing her to literally shaking with fear before letting her go.

By the time Emily reached the gate she was in a near-panic, but Joan Redfern simply shrugged off her apologies and set a brisk pace towards her car.

"You're fine, Emily," she continued as they got in the car. "You worry far too much. I'm not your slave-driver, I'm your foster mother – and I mean mother not landlady. It is not just my job to feed and house you but to care for you. Now, I know I'm an old fusspot, but I think you need fussing over. I may overdo it, but I'll never neglect you. You've been neglected far too long. Do you understand me?"

The last few sentences were delivered firmly and fully face to face. As if she really meant it, Emily thought. Maybe she did. Had she not said that she had only had a son and always wanted a daughter? Emily had never been fussed over like this in her life. She was starting to like it.

Except that it was not really her Mrs Redfern was fussing over – it was the idea of her. They did not care about her because they knew her - just because they were good people. Maybe because they were Christians? Were they good people because they were Christians? Or were they Christians because they were good people? Once they got to know her they might stop caring - everyone else had - when they found out what was wrong with her they might get rid of her.

What would they do if a rumour got back to them that she had a violent boyfriend? Emily stewed over that worry as Joan Redfern drove her home.

But she was not given long to stew.

"So, my dear," Joan Redfern plunged in. "Who exactly did you tell that you were in Juvenile Detention? And what did you tell them?"

As they were stopped at traffic lights Joan was able to look directly at Emily, and detect what she now recognized as Emily starting to panic again. Hands nervously twisting - slightly cringing posture – and the eyes. How did a girl get to be so scared so easily? Joan suspected that she would not enjoy finding out, but that made her all the more determined to find out.

"There is nothing to be afraid of, Emily," she tried to sound girl reassuring. "Whatever you tell me I won't get angry. I promise."

The lights chose that inconvenient moment to change, and Joan wondered if it would be better continuing this at home, but patience had never been one of her virtues.

"So who did you tell?" she repeated – trying not to sound insistent. The girl always answered questions, but could need coaxing to go beyond simple answers.

"Just a couple of guys." The words finally stumbled out. "They wanted to – I had to put them off me – make them go away."

"Why did you have to make them go away?"

"Because ..." Emily began, then hesitated.

"Emily, whether you love it or not boys will want to talk to you. You're going to have to learn to talk to them, and there is no reason why you shouldn't let nice boys talk to you."

"They weren't nice boys. Why would they want to speak to me if they were?"

Exactly the negative attitude that Sylvia had warned about. Joan Redfern's instincts always veered towards bluntness.

"They're young men," she told her daughter firmly. "Only natural they should pay attention to a girl as pretty as you."

The car turned up the long avenue leading to their own road. A straight road, and clear of traffic ahead. Joan felt able to take a glance at her foster daughter. Still clearly in panic mode. As Sylvia had warned, Emily panicked very easily.

"No but," came the words which sounded as panic-laden as Emily's face appeared. "No but – they were jerks. They made fun of Lawrie, and Tiara had suggested how I could use my criminal record to hint at having a violent boyfriend and make jerks like that leave me alone."

Tiara again – maybe Emily had good reason for gratitude towards her twin, but this sounded more like worship than gratitude.

"Inventive of her," Joan declared as she spotted the turn into her own road, "but being inventive is not the same as being clever."

"No – it was me that wasn't clever. Tiara's idea was brilliant. They always are. I just screwed up again. Whenever I tried to defend myself, to stand up for myself, I always make everything worse. I'm sorry. I just don't know what to do."

Joan made the turn with relief. They really needed a serious talk without interruption. Sylvia had said that getting Emily to start talking could be difficult, but the girl could get quite forthcoming once started, and they needed to get her talking as much as possible.

"I think, my dear," she told her foster daughter firmly, "that you need to explain to me exactly how you made everything worse so that we can make it better again. Soon as we're home I'll get us something to drink and we can sit down and talk properly. Okay!"

She risked a glance sideways as the road was clear, and saw Emily quite apprehensive.

"Okay?" Joan repeated.

"Okay, Mrs Redfern," a very small voice replied.

"I'm glad Lawrie talked to you," Joan changed the subject slightly after gaining her point. "I understand they're all going to Bobby's party on Friday, and wanted to invite you. You have permission to go – you really should start going to parties like that. I spoke to your probation officer – he'll want to see you soon, by the way - it'll be a few weeks before your community service is sorted so you need not be up early on Saturday so there is no reason in the world why you shouldn't go out on Friday."

As she was talking Joan had driven into her driveway and parked in front of her house, so she was able to switch off her engine and look Emily squarely in the eye, and realize that the girl was looking positively terrified – making even Joan Redfern wonder if she was pushing too hard.

Emily was, in fact, desperately wishing that the court had not left that loophole in her curfew, but she realized that Mrs Redfern had only negotiated it with the best of intentions, and only had the best intentions right now in pushing her to go to this party – so how the hell was Emily to get out of it?

"But I don't belong at a party like that," she blurted out.

"Of course you do," came the blunt response. "You're a smart and pretty teenage girl. You need new friends, and you'll be perfectly safe at Bobby's parties – he'll make sure you'll face no alcohol or anything inappropriate there – it is exactly the sort of event you should be going to – I'll repeat it as often as it takes to get through to you – you need to start making friends."

"But why would they want to make friends with me?" Emily abruptly blurted out. "I guess everybody knows about me by now."

"Far from it, I'm sure, but so what if they do know you've been in Juvie? Do you think that would make them shun you? That is not how we treat people."

"You mean because they're Christians?"

"No, I mean because they won't condemn you as a lost cause just because of one mistake."

"But it would just be because they're Christians," Emily suddenly burst into tears. "The only reason you're helping me is because you think it is the Christian thing to do – isn't it? You don't know me yet. You just see me as some sort of – I don't know what – lost lamb – prodigal daughter. You don't know what I am. You don't know what I've done. I'm not a good person."

The last line was a plaintive wail that could have come from a ten year old, but Joan Redfern would later remember it as the moment that she really lost her heart to the teenager, and on impulse she caught hold of the girl's hand.

"Yes you are, my dear," Joan asserted. "I've lived over fifty years, and visited many countries, and I was a social worker before I married, and met thousands of people, and I promise that it is usually only good people who think that they're not good people. Bad people usually think they're good, but it is only evil people who sincerely believe that they're models of righteousness. If you think yourself flawed that merely proves you have a conscience and are basically a good person."

That seemed to silence the teen, but did not stop her tears, so Joan bustled her indoors and steered her to the settee.

"You're partly right, my dear," she conceded as she sat down. "When I first decided to take in foster girls it was an impulse to help girls who needed help in general. Of course I didn't know you personally, but now I do and I care. And so does Tony. He didn't offer to take either of the other girls to buy all that stuff, but he took you – because he said that hell would freeze over before you'd ask for help however much you needed it – and you've already told us more than enough to know there have been times in your life when you've desperately needed help and never got it. But those days are over, Emily, I promise you. From now on you're going to get all the help you need and deserve."

Emily heard the words, and appreciated the kindness behind the intent, but doubted how much actual help the woman could provide. Maybe she could intervene to shield Emily from her new teachers, but no way could Emily imagine the Redferns helping her against the police or the legal system, which maybe that was just as well because any attempt to help Emily might damage Tiara.

Emily would rather die than harm Tiara in any way.

CHAPTER THIRTEEN

JassaVar watched with Brett as her mother and stepfather followed the survival capsule while it hovered into the small alien shuttle, shepherded by LactoVar the maggicondovar – alien title for physician's assistant so probably a trainee Physician.

Physician FrageaVar had not come. Physicians were busy and expensive. FrageaVar, LactoVar's Physician, was only a junior Physician so less expensive but even busier so LactoVar had come instead.

Soon the shuttle had lifted silently off for its sixteen minute trip into orbit – leaving JassaVar alone with a very anxious Brett Maitland. The man really cared about his sister, JassaVar observed with pleasure, even though Tiara was not genetically related nor a potential duvay partner. The awesome AvernaVar had told all vars that human yars could be much more sensitive than alien yars, and JassaVar was of the strand of var thought that liked it – though she never told her mother so as DinzaVar was not of that strand of var thought.

As the shuttle vanished from view Brett turned to JassaVar and asked if she was ready to go home, as he had to be elsewhere.

JassaVar considered saying that she would prefer to go anywhere with Brett rather than return to the loneliness of the Maitland Mansion, but did not dare – besides which she had dressed revealingly and was feeling chilly after living so long in the sultry warmth of *Anarchy*, so she let him drive her back to the Maitland Mansion.

To find Sylvia Godwin parked outside the front door.

———

"So," Joan Redfern struggled not to sound amused as she reviewed what a very penitent-looking foster daughter had just confessed. "So, you gave those two young men the impression that you had a violent boyfriend who'd be jealous if they bothered you. Yes, I can see how that might convince them to leave you alone."

"But I didn't think it through," Emily whined disconsolately. "They're sure to tell everyone else, and if it gets back to the teachers it might get back to the police, and maybe back to the courts, and I don't know how much trouble it might cause you. The more I think about it the stupider I feel. Whatever I do I screw it up."

"You worry too much, my dear. I assure you it won't cause me any trouble that I can't handle – now I know – and you did the right thing by telling me. I don't see why you need to do anything more than not repeat it. We all make mistakes, and we never stop making them. The thing to do with mistakes, my dear, is learn by them. You made the best possible start by acknowledging your mistake – so many people compound their mistakes by refusing to admit them but you confessed your mistake to me, so I can sort it out – as I can very easily. I won't say don't worry, because I doubt you're capable of not worrying, but don't worry too much. Your past and its mistakes are there to be learned from – your future and its choices are there to be enjoyed. You need to start thinking more about your future than your past – that is my advice."

She left Emily mulling over that while they both got their coats off and used their respective bathrooms, then Emily came down to ask what needed to be done.

"Don't you have any homework?" Joan asked firmly.

"Yes, Mrs Redfern, but if you need help it can wait."

"No, it can't. Homework assignments always takes priority. Always get them done before offering to help around the house. House rule. You're not a housemaid, Emily. Assignments always come first – get them done."

Joan sounded scarily strict to Emily who scurried to obey, and got seriously stuck into her maths, which she found very simple, and then into her English essay with obsessive focus until she heard the Professor arriving home and hurried to finish – she could review and revise later. Then she rushed to the bathroom, treble-checked that every inch was spotless and frantically rushed to tidy her room to perfection with only homework on view before rushing down to help.

She found her foster parents in the kitchen, but instead of being given any chores was instead firmly asked if her homework was finished.

Between trying to be honest and trying to tell them that she could help out with any chores, Emily managed to tie herself into a verbal knot that the Professor had to forensically unpick to decipher her embarrassed confession that she had sort of finished her English essay but was not entirely satisfied and wanted to revise it.

"Good practise for homework," he declared with an approval that completely shocked Emily, who had been expecting him to tell her off for not getting it perfect first time. "Very good learning method – to write once, take a short break, then read it through and do it better. Can't do it in an examination, of course, but for practising essay writing skills it is a very praiseworthy attitude. Too common a mistake of students to just dash off an essay and then leave me to tell them what is wrong with it when they could read it over and work out for themselves how to do it better."

"Okay," his wife responded automatically. "Emily, I really don't need your help today. Why don't you finish that essay, then watch television or surf the web or read your book or something."

"Very few essays," the Professor waxed on lyrically. "Or literary compositions, for that matter, are not better for being rewritten. The really good novelists often do extensive rewriting before publication. Have you finished *Mansfield Park*?"

"Yes, sir."

"Would you like to exchange it for another book?"

Emily hesitated, nearly dissolving into panic again.

"Do you need it back straight away, sir," she flustered out. "I'll go and get it."

She would have rushed off had he not caught her by the shoulder.

"No, Emily," he told her very firmly. "I don't need it back yet – not if you'd like to re-read it."

"Would you mind, sir?" Emily asked – amazed to be asked what she would like.

"Of course not. It is the defining hallmark of the quality novel and the intelligent reader that the more times the one reads the other the more the reader gets out of it. Just reading a novel to know what happens next is the essence of unintelligent reading, and a story that is only interesting to read in order to know what happens next does not deserve the title of novel. So what did you think on first reading? Did you like or dislike Fanny Price? Opinions have always been divided on her."

With that he led her to the sofa, sat her down beside him, and coaxed her into talking about the novel until his wife commanded them to get ready for dinner.

———

DinzaVar could hardly believe her ears when LactoVar whispered the results of Tiara's genetic scans.

They had arrived on *Freedom* less than an hour earlier, and Tiara had been in the Body Repair Capsule long enough that full scans were completed. FrageaVar was briefing DinzaVar's husband about the results as father and Physician stood over the teenager's capsule.

"JuntaVar resigned employment at correct time," LactoVar whispered as DinzaVar's mind raced feverishly through the options for turning this extraordinary development to her advantage. "The match was exact. There is no doubt."

"Will the girl recover?" DinzaVar whispered back as interesting options began to percolate through her brain.

"Physically," came the whispered reply. "FrageaVar did not predict problem except brain damage – we assess when conscious. Brain cells can be regenerated, but personality and memory may reboot with variance."

DinzaVar absorbed that and reviewed her options and opportunities. Her eyes strayed down the corridor to her husband hanging on FrageaVar's every word.

"I desire private speak to FrageaVar," DinzaVar whispered to LactoVar. "Will you arrange?"

"Possible," came a cautious response. "For what payment?"

———

It was during dinner that Joan Redfern finally mentioned the dreaded subject of Friday evening, and reduced a teenager to cringing with fear at the prospect of going to a party.

Emily tried to prevaricate, saying that she needed to settle in at school and catch up on homework before she considered anything like that. It did not sound very convincing even to her, and Joan Redfern demolished the argument with three words.

"On a Friday?" she asked.

Three words that made Emily feel even stupider than normal, and shocked her foster parents by making her start crying.

The Professor asked the teenager what was wrong, but Emily was barely capable of understanding what was wrong let alone articulating it. A wave of despair had engulfed her. It was all that she could do to choke back her tears. She was nearly hyper-ventilating.

As she struggled to contain her panic attack, both adults moved their chairs to sit beside her and try to calm her. Emily could not face them for shame, and buried her face in her hands, and leant forward until her face was almost on her knees as she lost all control of her tears.

———

Sylvia Godwin arrived at the Redfern home in Brett Maitland's car.

She could not resist accepting a ride in his expensive car, and it made sense to go together – she could secretly imagine being eighteen again and going out with the biggest crush of her teenage years.

Tony Redfern met them at the door, expressed surprise when Sylvia introduced Brett, but invited them in to meet Joan, who had been clearing away after dinner. When explaining that they wanted to talk to Emily they were told that Emily was very fragile that evening, and was it important?

Emily was surprised when the Professor came to her five minutes later. She had just been to the bathroom, spending five minutes using it and fifteen minutes cleaning it, and then returned to her bedroom to make it perfectly tidy before revising her essay. The carpet was not totally speck-free when he walked in, making her worry that he might notice.

In fact he was more worried that the room looked too neat and tidy, since the schoolwork on the table was the only sign of occupancy apart from Emily herself.

He asked if she had revised it yet. She frantically assured him that she had been just about to start – sounding for all the world as if she were afraid that he would scold her for not having finished it already – so he offered to look it over and offer comments before she started, then told her that two people downstairs wanted to speak to her.

She instantly asked if they were police. He had to gently reassure her that it was only Sylvia Godwin and Brett Maitland – which made her eager to hurry downstairs hoping for news of her sister. Tony followed anxiously, knowing what she was about to hear.

Somewhat to his surprise, Emily took the news that her twin was in a coma without breaking down.

"She is getting the best possible treatment," Brett reassured gently. "Up on *Freedom* by an alien Physician. I spoke to Dad just now. He was told that we can expect Tiara to make a full physical recovery. The only thing the Physician could not say for definite was whether there was any significant brain damage. Apparently aliens can physically regenerate brain cells, but not restore - 'lost data', they call it - so she may not remember everything, or may have to relearn some things. We won't know that for a few days – but I promise that as soon as I know anything, I'll come and see you again. Okay, Emily?"

Four adults waited with baited breath, half-expecting another teenage meltdown, but Emily simply sat there, head and shoulders slightly cringed forward, eyes looking down at twitching fingers. Was she taking the news in her stride?

Then she whispered a response that only one of the listeners understood.

"Was it Sukie?" Words so faint that the Redferns could not make out the name.

Sylvia Godwin immediately took up the baton agreed with Brett in the car.

"It was," she declared directly. "But that does not make it your fault, Emily. You were only twelve. It was not your responsibility to look after a sick little boy – it was his mother's responsibility."

Even Brett was surprised by the nature of the intervention, and the Redferns stared at each other in complete incomprehension.

"It wasn't your fault!" Sylvia asserted again. "You were only twelve. It wasn't your fault your foster mother left you all alone while she went out. It wasn't your fault she forgot to charge her cellphone. It wasn't your fault she came home late. It wasn't your fault she didn't dial 911 when she got home. Sukie had no right to say it was your fault. Sukie was only eight months younger than you, and it was her brother. She could have dialled 911 herself instead of going to bed and leaving it up to you. Sukie just blamed you because she needed someone to blame, but you were not to blame. Do you hear me, Emily? You were not to blame."

Emily had heard others before Sylvia telling her the same thing. She accepted that Timmy's death had not been all her fault, but she still could have saved him and his mother had she not been too afraid to dial 911. She was still culpable to that extent, and the guilt for her cowardice would always burden her soul.

But she owed them better than to tell them that – Miss Godwin and the Redferns. Emily knew that she had to let them all think that they had convinced her.

"I know," she said simply - grateful that her earlier emotional meltdown had left her too drained to dissolve again. "Please let me know when you hear anything."

"Of course."

"Will you be able to do anything to help Sukie?" Emily added quickly. "She was very good to me – I mean, before. She is only lashing out because she is in pain – you've only got to look at her to see how much pain. I think of Timmy and Sandra every day, and it makes me want to die sometimes, so I can't bear to think what she must feel like. Can you do anything to help her?"

That produced a silence around the room that Emily could not quite read. Sylvia Godwin took her time before a very careful reply.

"If I can," she said. "If she'll let me. Will you let us all help you?"

Trapped, Emily thought. She could hardly say no – not after all that.

———

"That," Brett declared as Sylvia got into his car, "is a genuinely good kid."

"She is," the chaplain responded thoughtfully. "Possibly better than we know."

Even as she spoke, Sylvia wondered whether she ought to pass on her suspicions to Brett. She had decided that it ought to be down to Emily, but she could not help doubting her decision.

"Is that why you're going out of your way to help her?" Brett asked, obliviously.

"Partly," she replied carefully, feeling guilty that she would never have got so involved but for Tiara and Brett. "And partly because she has no family anywhere – except Tiara."

"How the hell did she end up so alone?"

"Long story. Also confidential, I'm afraid."

"Do you think you convinced her not to blame herself for that foster sister going psycho?"

"Not a chance," Sylvia admitted. "She'll blame herself. Always. I can pray for her to come to terms with it and get on with her life, despite it, but I don't think she'll ever stop blaming herself. If only she would. She will always think that. It will always be there. I don't think anyone realized how traumatized she was – and still is."

The two of them sat in the car for a while, contemplating that, before Brett decided to grab at his fortuitous opportunity.

"Have you eaten?" he asked.

She looked at him in surprise.

"Because if not, neither have I. I was going to drop in at a bar I know that does some really good food – nothing exotic, just good. On me?"

He was rather surprised when his passenger burst out laughing.

"Okay," he tried to take her reaction on the chin. "Must admit you're the first girl to laugh when I offered to buy her dinner."

"Sorry," Sylvia got herself quickly back under control. "I just remembered that I would once have done almost anything just to spend five minutes with you. I bet you never knew that you were my big high school crush."

He grimaced with engaging embarrassment.

"My sisters both love telling me how unobservant I am," he disparaged himself frankly. "Apparently I need highlighted subtitles on a mega-screen before I notice anything where girls are concerned. But Sara said you were one of the girls who turned up at my eighteenth birthday hoping I'd dance with you."

"Remind me to throttle her next time we meet. Okay, I confess that I wore my best little black dress to your eighteenth birthday party and you never even noticed me – maybe because all the other girls were wearing even less."

"I did notice all the girls who kept trying to talk to me seemed to be wearing very short skirts. I was eighteen so that is probably why I never noticed their faces. If you wanted me to notice you might have done better to wear a crinoline."

"I'll remember that next time I'm eighteen."

"Sara tells me I only showed real interest in older women – told me I was born cougar bait destined to be a toy boy. Got to say I found all girls completely baffling back then – don't know what that makes me."

"I think the technical term for suffering that cognitive handicap is being male."

"Guess that would explain it. Is that an official disability nowadays?"

"In certain circles."

"Good to hear. I'll look into what disability benefits I can claim. But to return to the point – may I buy you dinner?"

"Are you asking me out or do you just want to talk about Tiara and Emily?"

"Are the two mutually exclusive?"

"No, but I'd like to know where I stand."

"Well, I certainly don't want to spend a whole meal talking about them – so I am asking you out – okay?"

———

"Maggivar FrageaVar," DinzaVar began with a formal deference to the young Physician. "I apologize if I sound assertive, but I draw your attention to reality that girl named Tiara will face incarceration in prison if returned

175

to Earth after treatment. I desire her not to suffer such barbarity. Especially not if – if …"

"Did you inform her?" FrageaVar snapped aggressively at LactoVar, and the assistant shrunk visibly back and dipped her forehead and hunched her shoulders submissively. "Did I grant permission to disclose?"

"No, Maggivar," LactoVar hurried to explain. "But DinzaVar is alien, and the patient and her father are mere humans. I considered that DinzaVar did …"

"You considered incorrect," FrageaVar snarled at her assistant. "Go to your room and wait for me. Go!"

LactoVar retreated with a speed that alarmed DinzaVar. It seemed that LactoVar had not been exaggerating about her superior's strictness. DinzaVar had to steel herself not to flinch when she dipped her head submissively as FrageaVar's attention turned on her.

"Did you inform your husband?" the Physician snapped a direct question.

"No, Maggivar," DinzaVar hastened to defend herself.

"Do not without my permission."

"No, Maggivar."

"Correct to inform about barbarity if returned to planet. You possess my gratitude for that. Do not forfeit."

"My gratitude, Maggivar. You can trust me. May I ask?"

"Ask what?"

"Will you inform Tiara?"

"Of course. As soon as I judge her to possess adequate level of recovery, I will explain that her mother was an alien."

BOOK TWO

ADAPTING AND ADOPTING

'If I go forward, he is not there;
or backward, I cannot perceive him;
on the left he hides, and I cannot behold him;
I turn to the right, but I cannot see him.
But he knows the way that I take;
when he has tested me, I shall come out like gold.
Job 23

"I certainly have not the talent which some people possess," said Darcy, *"of conversing easily with those I have never seen before. I cannot catch their tone of conversation, or appear interested in their concerns, as I often see done."*
From Pride and Prejudice, by Jane Austen

CHAPTER FOURTEEN

Tiara Maitland – alias TarraVar or PrettyGirl - was ejected from her residence in the early hours of Christmas Day.

Early hours by American time, that was. Alien time aboard the alien spaceship *Freedom* was a very relative concept compared to Earth's globally agreed time zones. As Tiara understood it, every household could use whatever time they chose providing that they adjusted to the time of whoever ran whatever section of the ship they were traversing. The Freedom Consortium used a central ship time for all interactions whether in space or on Earth, and most households followed Consortium time while most of the rest maintained a fixed correlation to Consortium time. Households that did otherwise were few and far between but one had leased the next corridor which was the most direct route to the nearest staircase.

When the arrangements had been first explained to her, Tiara had joked about getting jet lag from walking down the corridor. Nobody had laughed, and reactions had been scathing when she had suggested that it would be better to make everybody aboard the ship use the same time zone. LactoVar had accused her of talking like a tyrant, and Tiara had retaliated by calling LactoVar a bossy bitch – a retort for which LactoVar had made Tiara pay ever since.

At least living in a household running on Consortium time had made it easy for Tiara to figure that it was on Christmas morning, by American time, that she was ejected. Not that she was missing any celebration. It was an alien household – leased by Physician FrageaVar – and aliens possessed no Christian heritage, so did not celebrate Christmas in any way. It was not even a holiday. Aliens did not possess any equivalent to national holidays – not even week-ends. Every day was an ordinary working day, and the corridor was an ordinary corridor, so even on Christmas Day there should be aliens using the corridor. Hopefully soon, because until then Tiara was trapped.

She picked up the four bags that LactoVar had dumped on the floor, and checked their contents. At least it was all there - nothing compared to the amount of luggage that she routinely carried back on Earth, but still a lot to carry, and she had neglected to purchase any self-powered alien suitcases which followed their owners like pet dogs. LactoVar had smugly refused to lend her one, forcing Tiara to girlhandle them down long and dark alien corridors – almost wishing that she had not spent so much on alien dresses that felt so fantastic on her skin, or cleansers and creams that made the same skin feel incredible. The only reason that she was not completely laden was lack of money. The allowance that Brett had sent her via LaskaVar's contacts had sounded plenty considering that food and rent were covered, but the rate of exchange proved very adverse and everything proved terribly expensive so she was constantly overspending, but very reluctant to admit defeat and beg Brett for more.

Big mistake, but not as big as failing to realize earlier that LactoVar hated her. That hate had ruined everything. Without LactoVar, Tiara was sure she could have won FrageaVar over and passed the tests, and would now be looking forward to becoming a Physician.

Instead of being homeless and destitute on an alien spaceship.

———

Fourteen weeks earlier

Tiara understood that she had been in a coma, and that she might have suffered some memory loss, but she wondered if she had gone nuts.

It was three days after Tiara had recovered consciousness, and she was feeling recovered enough to read more than a page or two at a time and go to the bathroom and back without needing help. Daddy and Brett had both been to see her, and left only an hour before Innocence, the Physician – alias FrageaVar - had come and asked a few questions to test Tiara's mental alertness.

Then declared it satisfactory and casually announced that Tiara's biological mother had been an alien.

———

Emily woke early on Christmas Day.

Early and worried. She dressed quickly, and sneaked into the bathroom to use it before the guests awoke, then deployed some of her private stockpile of cleaning materials - secretly bought with her own allowance - to make it spotless again.

Joan Redfern had just thought that she was trying to instil some responsibility into a teen by asking her to keep the bathroom and bedroom tidy. It had never been her intent that Emily should go postal on every speck of dust or dirt in sight, as Joan had tried to explain to Emily - provoking Emily to resort to extreme subterfuge. That morning she used a flashlight in case the light got noticed by the Redfern's son Thomas, who had brought his Australian wife Cathy for Christmas, and was in his old room next to the bathroom.

Twenty minutes careful checking and cleaning, and she scurried silently back to her bedroom to worry herself sick about the day ahead.

———

Fourteen weeks earlier

Emily escaped having to go to Bobby's party that Friday.

The Redferns did not press the matter. She assumed that this was because she was so obviously worried about her sister still recovering from a brain injury, but in fact the Redferns had concluded – after her meltdown earlier in the week – that it was no time to put pressure on an obviously traumatised girl.

They had also realized that Emily was much more in need of encouragement than restraint. Less than a week into the placement they saw Emily panic at dropping some crumbs on the carpet and rush to clear them up with her fingers as though her life depended on it.

More upsetting to Joan had been the lack of posters on the walls, and lack of pictures and toys and personal mementos around the room. Most upsetting of all had been Emily's admission that she owned no childhood pictures whatsoever, no favourite toys, no keepsakes – lost during her many moves. That had reduced Joan to tears, even though Emily kept secret the fate of her last and favourite soft toys given by her mother, the Galleys, and the Frasers. In Southside Sukie had taken an early opportunity to gloat that Emily's pictures had gone in a shredder and her toys down a sewer. That had upset Emily too much even to tell Tiara, let alone the Redferns, who could only hope that Emily would relax more in time. The girl had clearly been worried about her sister, but seemed reassured by bulletins kindly passed on by Brett Maitland.

Joan had used her friendships with teachers and principal at the High School to assure Emily that her 'violent boyfriend' scam would not cause her any problems. That had really impressed the teenager, who had been persuaded to talk rather more at mealtimes – albeit mostly about books and schoolwork with her foster father, though Joan had joined in enthusiastically when Mansfield Park *had been mentioned, and been thrilled that Emily had been impressed by it – so thrilled that Tony had later cautioned Joan not to rush to enrol Emily in JASNA.*

Thursday night had seen a relapse, with Emily having another nightmare that had woken Joan. That Friday at dinner, Emily had shrugged off the nightmare, but the Redferns had been warned about them, so Tony had suggested seeing a therapist – provoking the first hint of attitude out of Emily.

She had rejected the idea point blank, saying that she hated counsellors.

"I take it," Tony pressed immediately, "that you had a bad experience with one?"

She did not answer at first, but he motioned Joan to remain silent while maintaining his tried and trusted the-tutor-is-waiting-with-diminishing-patience-for-the-student-to-answer gaze at the girl - quickly guilt-tripping Emily into admitting that she had been sent to a counsellor once before Juvie.

"All she did," Emily added bitterly, "was try to make me say that Daddy did stuff to me, but I knew it was wrong to tell lies. I knew it was better to say nothing than to tell lies."

Joan repeated that last line to Sylvia Godwin over the phone that evening, and they shared a prayer of thanks that Emily had been brought to them.

Emily was just as thankful that the nightmare prospect of going out to meet other teenagers at a party that Friday evening was replaced by the safe prospect of staying in her bedroom to think about Tiara and read a book.

———

Property rights on alien spaceships were complicated.

Each spaceship was the property of either a consortium, like the Freedom Consortium, or a shared-ownership business, like the Choice

Corporation, or a looser alliance of independent businesses, like the Anarchy Cartel, and none of them actually managed most of their own spaceships. Every corridor and residence was leased by some business or individual – responsible for maintaining functionality and safety, but charging for all use of their property including transit.

That meant that everybody had to pay tolls to pass through every airtight hatch separating every section of corridor, and to pay tolls you needed alien digital money.

Tiara had drained herself dry of funds again, and would need food sooner or later, and drink and bathroom facilities even sooner, so did not want to pay corridor tolls. Fortunately she had learnt during forays to the alien equivalents of clubs and bars that there was an accepted alien version of hitch-hiking. She just had to wait beside each hatch until someone came along kind enough to let her go through with them. Luckily most aliens willingly let young housegirls through. She just had to wait. The only problem was that it could be a long wait.

Giving too much time to dwell on how she had got herself into this mess.

––––––––

Thirteen weeks earlier

The fact that it had taken FrageaVar several days to get back to Tiara confirmed that it was a most original request, and every bit the surprise that Tiara had hoped.

She loved doing the unexpected – it was so empowering. Meeting her demoralised doppelganger had only motivated her more to get everyone dancing to her tunes, and nobody called the tunes with more authority than an alien Physician – or Maggivar, as the aliens called them, so Tiara was delighted when two Maggivars came and she could stand and greet them without difficulty, and all the more delighted when FrageaVar introduced the second Physician as KristaVar - the senior alien Physician aboard Freedom. *KristaVar – her name translated into English as DesireGirl - was the mother of the late and famous AvernaVar or GracefulGirl.*

AvernaVar had been first spokesgirl for the Freedom Consortium – so famous that conspiracy theories proliferated around her murder by a lone psycho — theories ranging from an assassination by the CIA on secret Presidential orders to a total fake allowing AvernaVar to leave the planet without appearing to have abandoned her human husband and hybrid baby daughter.

KristaVar had come in person to see Tiara! Score one for Tiara really getting herself noticed. Then it got so much better.

"I possess confirmation from Physician network," KristaVar told Tiara with majestic authority, "that you may take tests if you possess desire. Assessment same as any alien girl. Please comprehend that no allowance will be made for human inferiority, but time permitted for preparation."

Tiara did not waste time on expressing gratitude, but went straight to the point.

"Does that mean," she demanded, "I could qualify to be a Physician like you?"

That provoked slight smiles on the faces of both Physicians.

"Do you consider you to possess superiority over most you encounter?" KristaVar asked — with no sign of hostility to Tiara's question.

"I'm smarter than most of the idiots I know," Tiara cut back quickly.

"Intelligence is not sole requirement for Physician. A Physician must possess ability to control or manage stupid inferiors."

Direct and to the point, Tiara thought, and went for the dare.

"I've lived among humans all my life," she asserted. "Human family, children, teachers, cops, and parents — I'm very experienced at managing stupid inferiors."

The Physicians fell silent. KristaVar stared fixedly at Tiara, while FrageaVar switched her gaze uncertainly between Tiara and KristaVar. Tiara did her best to match the senior Physician stare for stare, and almost succeeded, but not quite.

It was an enormous relief when KristaVar finally broke the silence.

"You are half-human," she declared neutrally. "It is most unlikely that you possess intellect to meet that grade, even without brain damage."

"You've tested other half-humans before, have you? If not, how do you know a half-human wouldn't make the grade?"

"Your point possess validity. We do not know."

"Only one way to find out," Tiara asserted the point forcefully. "You're a Physician - a scientist. You must believe in experiments. In learning by experiments."

She made it a statement, not a question, but still awaited the answer eagerly.

"Agreed," came an answer which nearly provoked Tiara into a squeal of glee. "You are permitted opportunity to test. But you suffered brain injury. By custom it would not be wise to submit you to major test until brain regeneration complete. That would normally include replacing data loss so rational to include data never downloaded into your brain due to being bred among primitives. You must study language, customs, and history before test. Interim you become housegirl and earn bodykeep – if someone agree to employ you. FrageaVar?"

"I possess room in my household for training period," FrageaVar agreed with neither enthusiasm nor reluctance. "LactoVar will supervise."

KristaVar barely glanced at the Junior Physician before turning back to Tiara.

"First you recover," the Senior Physician ordered. "When Fragea confirms full body recovery you begin preparation. Sixty four days to learn language, customs, philosophies, and histories - and prepare for tests – if you assess high I decide if you train as Physician. Until assessed you earn bodykeep as housegirl, but all necessary information will be available for your study at my expense in memory of your mother. Do you possess knowledge of your mother's name and family?"

Earning a living as a housegirl sounded rather exciting – was Tiara's first thought, strictly provided that it was only temporary. If only because it should give her opportunities to meet some big, black, alien men.

"JuntaVar was your mother," KristaVar continued. "She was early researcher based on moonbase."

Tiara remembered that the aliens had been visiting Earth secretly for decades before the gigantic spaceship Freedom *had arrived, and done so from a small base hidden on the dark side of the moon, so that news was no surprise.*

"She encountered a human male," KristaVar added, still not surprising Tiara, "and exercised Freedom of Departure from employment to marry him."

"But they both got killed," Tiara pushed on, "while Mommy was nearly ready to drop, so they kept her corpse on life support until they could rip us out, and then tossed us to adoption – guess what – no known relatives! Have I got some relatives now? Can you trace them?"

The Senior Physician was frowning, and Tiara savoured the delicious smell of adult disapproval.

"Or would that be too difficult for you?" she teased with what she hoped was her best innocent face.

The majestic one was clearly not amused, but answered – and in a way that shocked Tiara to the core.

"We possess a common motherline," KristaVar told her clinically. "Lines of fourteen and twenty-seven."

"What!" Tiara reacted. "Do you mean that we are …?"

"KristaVar means," FrageaVar intervened snottily, "that you possess common motherline ancestor – fourteen mothers line her but twenty-seven mothers you."

"So we're distant relatives?"

"You and I possess common motherline," FrageaVar added. "Lines of seventeen and sixteen."

"So we're more slash less distantly related. Cool. Is that why you're giving me a go? Can I call you my aunties?"

Two adult faces now radiated disapproval, which cheered Tiara up immensely. If stuffy adults were getting pompous she had to be getting something right.

"Please comprehend," KristaVar asserted firmly, "that you can be ejected or rejected any time if you fail to achieve required standards."

"I don't fail," Tiara asserted equally firmly. "Not if I put my mind to it."

FrageaVar still radiated disapproval, but KristaVar smiled slightly, and Tiara just knew that KristaVar liked Tiara's attitude - a bonus to bank for future exploitation.

"You will possess Freedom of Departure at any time," KristaVar continued as if Tiara had not spoken. "But please comprehend you depart by self-resource. If ejected it be from household not spaceship. I comprehend that you would be victim of primitive barbarity if you return to Earth, so we will never eject you to Earth. You return there only by self-choice."

Tiara started to reassess her sense that her brain was working properly, because it took her an annoying forever of several seconds for her to realize that 'primitive barbarity' was alien-speak for 'Juvenile Detention'. KristaVar's own daughter had spelt out at the very first press conference outside the White House that aliens never sent anyone, not even dangerous criminals, to prison, because they considered imprisonment to be barbaric, and Tiara had no problem empathizing with that sentiment. Then she recalled what punishments the aliens did consider to be civilized – corporal and capital punishment, with lethal private revenge an accepted option, and forced gender change an alternative to execution for some male crimes.

"So if I stay up here," she assumed aloud, "I'll need never fear imprisonment."

"You comprehend with accuracy."

"I just need to fear being flogged or executed?"

"You comprehend with low accuracy. A girl would never be flogged or executed unless for act of extreme violence."

"So I would just have to fear being spanked?" Tiara triumphed, without even trying to sound afraid.

"During your sixty-four days you will live as housegirl subject to normal command and discipline," KristaVar nearly smiled again. "You possess Freedom of Departure from household any time. If you exercise Freedom you forfeit chance to become Physician. Ability to live by strict discipline is essential to Physician."

Tiara accepted that without a blink. She scented power and success and achievement. She was determined to do whatever it took to become a Physician.

That would show them all.

———

At last Emily heard the sounds that she had been straining to hear.

Joan was going downstairs to make preparations for Christmas dinner. Emily crept out of her room, holding her house shoes in her hand to walk barefoot down the stairs. At the bottom she slipped the shoes on her feet and followed Joan quickly into the kitchen, quite startling her foster mother by asking what she could do to help.

Joan was accustomed to Emily offering to help many times every day. On occasion Joan had found it difficult not to get irritated at the pestering, but had quickly learnt that any sign of annoyance would cause the girl to cringe away as if slapped. Patience was not one of Joan's natural virtues, but she had learnt fast – and thanked God every day that Emily had come to live with them. She had never been more committed to any of the many consuming enthusiasms that had characterised her entire life, but was still duly grateful that it was not a solo mission.

Tony was almost as committed as his wife, and revelled in encouraging Emily academically – possibly because neither Tom nor Peter had shared Tony's own academic mentality. Emily had received more close personal attention from the Redferns than from all previous parents in her entire life. Many teenagers would have rebelled at being so closely supervised, but Emily relished it, especially the extent to which the Redferns had pro-actively involved themselves in every aspect of her school curriculum, almost hothousing her academically. Where Emily was afraid to approach teachers to ask for advice or help, the Redferns were not, and had taken Emily with them. With the help of Tony's academic advice and guidance and Joan's good contacts with what seemed to be almost every teacher at the school, Emily was going back in January as officially in Twelfth Grade and due to graduate from High School a year early. The Redferns were gently persisting in encouraging her to think about college, and she was almost wanting to take the idea seriously.

Joan and Sylvia were still chatting about Emily regularly, and the chaplain had gone above and beyond in using her experience and training as both qualified counsellor and chaplain. They had agreed that Joan should never brush off Emily's offers to help – unless to tell her to do her homework first - but carefully try to minimize what she did ask Emily to do. This time Joan just asked Emily to help get the goose and sprouts ready, and gave her the responsibility to set the timer – watching her and not forgetting to praise her on doing it right, remembering how distraught Emily had been the time she had got it wrong - before insisting that Emily have breakfast and then relax for a while before getting ready for church, and asking if Emily was sure that she wanted to go to church that morning.

Joan asked that question every time, and Emily always insisted that she wanted to come. It had become a ritual, as had Joan suggesting that Emily should go up for a blessing and Emily declining the suggestion. If nothing else it served to accustom Emily to saying 'no' to her foster parents, though Joan always hoped that one day Emily would say 'yes'.

Emily ate her usual breakfast of cereal and toast while trying to ignore the large pile of presents around the Christmas tree. She had secretly checked the pile and seen a frighteningly large number addressed to her, despite her persistent refusal to name anything that she wanted for Christmas, literally pleading with the Redferns not to bother with anything big after all that they had already spent on her.

Emily was in despair that she had neither the time nor the money to match the Redferns' generosity. She still remembered failing the Frasers the same way – no wonder they had sent her away – so she was desperate not to fail the Redferns the same way when they were doing so incredibly much for her. She had already spent most of her savings on presents for the Redferns and Peter before discovering at the last minute that Tom and Cathy were coming after all – wonderful for the Redferns but horrifying Emily into scrambling to find presents for them in case they had bought her presents – they might not have but she was embarrassed to ask the Redferns so had bought boxes of chocolates anyway.

But there was nothing more that she could do about it, so she meticulously cleaned up tablecloth and dishes after her breakfast, then slipped off her shoes to go back to her room as quietly as possible, and spend an hour worrying how much the Redferns had spent on her presents.

———

Thirteen weeks earlier

Joan Redfern did not realize that Emily was not taking the smartphone with her to school until the Friday when Emily was late home to meet her parole officer.

The man had booked to arrive at the time that Emily usually arrived home from school, but Emily missed her usual bus when her English teacher had buttonholed her in the library to compliment her on her work, and ask if she had considered reading English at college. Emily was too frantic to catch the bus to remember if her answers made any sense whatsoever but did not dare to interrupt a teacher.

She missed the bus and the next one was due in twenty minutes. She dithered for five minutes over whether to walk or to wait. It was a forty to forty five minute walk, so quicker to wait for the bus – providing it came on time, or at all - so after five minutes dithering she tried walking as fast as she could for home, sometimes breaking into a run, while all the time trying to look over her shoulder to see if the bus was coming so she could catch it anyway.

Unfortunately it came when she was nearly midway between two stops, and she ran herself breathless towards the next stop. If it had stopped at the stop she could have caught it, but there happened to be nobody waiting and nobody wanting to get off so the bus just kept going – leaving Emily staring after it in despair.

When she finally stumbled in, breathless from running most of the way home, the parole officer was demoralisingly curt with her, but far worse was that Joan had sounded annoyed with her when asking why she had not rung to tell them that she was going to be late.

Emily had been forced to confess that she had never taken her phone to school because she was too afraid of losing it. Confessed in a flood of tears that shocked the parole officer. While waiting, he had been listening as unimpressed by the new foster parent as he had been by the psychiatric assessment supplied by Southside. He had never met Joan Redfern before, and seriously doubted that the woman was up to dealing with a juvenile delinquent – especially when she tried to tell him that the girl was seriously traumatised and emotionally unstable.

He had naturally assumed that the old woman was being taken for a ride, but when he saw a teenage girl having a panic attack over her fear of losing a cellphone he decided to take that psychiatric assessment seriously.

It took several minutes for Joan to calm Emily down enough for the parole officer to tell her where his office was and promise early details about her community service - probably involving helping out at a day centre for the elderly. Joan did not mention that she hoped it would be at the centre for which she helped with fund-raising.

When the officer had departed, Joan resumed reassuring Emily that she was not in trouble for not taking the phone to school, and more importantly that she would not be in any trouble were she unlucky enough to lose it. Further questioning elicited the facts that Emily had not even switched it on since being first shown it working, nor had she switched on the computer but that she would be switching it on soon because she would need it for a homework assignment.

Joan and Tony spent some time that evening trying to convince Emily that they had not bought her a computer just for homework but also for pleasure, and her phone was intended for calling friends. They were only successful in *getting Emily to pretend to accept their point and promise to take the phone with her when she went out.*

They failed to realize that they had not extracted a promise to switch it on.

———

JassaVar woke on the first Christmas morning of her life, and wondered if she would finally comprehend the festival, or share the excitement of her school friends.

Those friends had offered extensive explanations about the strange human tradition of giving Christmas and birthday presents, and Mr Maitland had promised her a very special joint Christmas and birthday present. Joint because the policy when guesstimating the age of aliens in America was to assign a standard birthday of the first of January to all, so JassaVar would officially become seventeen in a week.

It was strange to get unearned gifts, but might verify her mother's assessments of how much profit could be obtained from pleasing Maitland men – and Brett had bought her all those clothes without requiring duvay. It was a pity that Brett would not be joining them for Christmas. JassaVar only saw him occasionally – and all JassaVar's fault, according to her mother.

Brett was briefly dropping round Christmas morning before going on to collect his girlfriend from work to spend the day with her family. JassaVar had not exactly been happy about Brett spending so much time with Sylvia, but had accepted it, and felt uncomfortable when her mother was overtly hostile to Sylvia. JassaVar vividly remembered overhearing DinzaVar making what even JassaVar knew to be an error by telling her husband that Sylvia was only interested in Brett's money. Edward Maitland's response had been immediate and decisive.

"The lady is a prison chaplain," he had retorted icily. "Nobody takes a hellish job like that if making money is important to them, and anybody who does deserves our respect. Since you only married me because I'm rich you'd better drop the subject if you want to see any more of my money."

JassaVar had enjoyed hearing that scolding so much that she had not moved away fast enough. DinzaVar had walked away from her husband in a foul temper, found JassaVar and realized that she had been listening - and dealt with that impertinence so severely that JassaVar's squeals had drawn Edward Maitland into the room to drag DinzaVar away and stop the punishment. Despite that the bruises had still been an issue two days later at school. Her best friends Josette and Vicky had even noticed her discomfiture, and been shocked by her explanation.

Friends made school fun – to JassaVar's surprise and delight. Human girls were not as hostile to alien girls as rumoured, and 'boys' – as JassaVar had learnt to call young men – were anything but hostile. The only hint of unpleasantness from her early days had been when two smirking 'boys' asked in front of others if she was an alien and how much they would have to pay her for duvay.

She had simply and openly given them her mother's contact number to negotiate a price, saying that would be her mother's decision, but warning them that her mother would desire a large price.

She had been perfectly serious, although trusting that her mother would never consider anything that they could afford to offer, but quickly realized that her friends and everyone else had assumed it was a joke at the boys' expense, and the 'funny' story had rapidly spread round the school to her great credit. By some mysterious alchemy that incident had, according to Josette and Vicky, established her as 'cool'. JassaVar still did not comprehend what that meant.

She then made herself even more popular by insisting publicly and openly to teachers and pupils alike that alien was an accurate term, and quoting her mother as saying that only stupid primitives would try to suppress a word just because some equally stupid primitives used it as a term of offence. In consequence there had been no overt hostility to JassaVar, and many efforts to make friends, especially from Josette and Vicky who had already been best friends with each other and may have bonded with JassaVar over their shared lack of height – and shared wealthy families.

The height of humans had required some adjustment – JassaVar was inches smaller than most girls in the school, yet as tall as one or two of the 'boys'! Human men were so very small compared to alien men, and strangely few boys possessed dark skin while there were even dark-skinned girls like Josette.meaat

Hardest to adjust to was the concept of school. The work was no challenge except when she was expected to present projects, but the sheer number of students was astonishing. JassaVar had briefly resided in one very large household with five adult housegirls, two wives, and eleven pre-choice daughters, but in this school there were hundreds within a few years of JassaVar's age – and half of them boys of which astonishingly many showed a willingness to pay her attention.

She completely understood why AvernaVar had liked human men. JassaVar had quickly learnt to enjoy their company, and loved the sensuous human custom of dancing and the even more sensuous custom that her new friends called 'making out'.

They had dances at the school and locally, and both stepfather and mother had encouraged JassaVar to attend them, and were in any case away on business three days out of four, so JassaVar had attended as many as she could, and had gone to cinemas and clubs with Josette and Vicky and other friends both male and female and loved every minute, and learnt to really love dancing. Almost as enjoyable was young men asking her out on dates where they really spent money so she had not felt underpaid when 'making out' afterwards.

JassaVar had established herself as one of the most popular girls in the school, and one of the most fashionable thanks to her shopping trip with Brett and Sara, Josette and Vicky's local fashion tips, but above all thanks to her alien dresses, cosmetics, and cleansers. She had repaid Josette and Vicky for their friendship by importing supplies of alien soaps and beauty treatments that had soon got not only Josette and Vicky but several other girls at the school drooling with delight, then with her mother's help had opened a line to supply schoolfriends with expensive alien dresses, including the ultimate luxury of imagewear – earning serious financial profits for DinzaVar and popularity profits for JassaVar, who had become one of the acknowledged 'hotties' of her year – a strange but enjoyable concept for any alien but especially one lacking a distinguished motherline.

Not only boys but also teachers found her alien 'eccentricities' cute rather than offensive – even her open declaration that she was not monogamous offended few, and least of all the boys. JassaVar loved the undisciplined lifestyle of American teenagers – especially parties, dances, and dating - and all this without needing to duvay anyone. In accordance with maternal commands JassaVar was not planning to go that far unless serious profit beckoned.

Her biggest initial problem with the regimentation of school life was its obsession with times – times school started and finished, lessons started and finished – exacerbated by human hours being shorter than alien hours and numbering twenty four instead of sixteen per day. It had taken major adjustment, but fortunately the staff were very tolerant in her first week about her issues with timekeeping, and particularly considerate of her linguistic oddities – possibly because her mother-drilled manners were always very respectful to authority figures, if only to their faces.

JassaVar was learning English fast, and by Christmas the school complimented her on her ability to learn and to catch up – praise that earned a smile of approval from her mother, and the reward of a gorgeous little black dress – accompanied by an order to wear it when Brett came for Christmas.

And a private order to make it count this time – or else – so that was the dress which JassaVar obediently donned for Brett's arrival that Christmas morning when she waited downstairs to greet him. Her mother came to join them followed closely by her stepfather, and it was a pleasant family gathering - if only for half an hour.

The climax for both DinzaVar and JassaVar came when Brett handed over presents, insisting on opening his presents for JassaVar and DinzaVar on the spot - two small packages that proved to contain beautiful diamond necklaces.

Even DinzaVar was happy to let Brett drape one around her neck, while JassaVar could not help giggling as Brett gently draped her present round her neck while she held her hair up. It felt amazing and looked gorgeous in the mirror, and JassaVar knew that diamonds were valuable and there was some human proverb about them being a girl's best friend – which she presumed was a reference to their financial value, extrapolating that from her experiences of boys spending copiously on her in return for her company. Humans disapproved of girls accepting money in return for company or duvay, but not of them accepting meals or drinks or even jewellery. There was allegedly some moral distinction which JassaVar still did not comprehend.

Within minutes Brett had departed, and JassaVar was only more disappointed than her mother because DinzaVar was furious rather than disappointed – and JassaVar knew that it was JassaVar with whom DinzaVar was furious.

But then Brett's father cheered DinzaVar up by taking mother and daughter round to the garage complex to show them their Christmas presents from him in the form of two expensive cars – the latest models just rolling off the production line, powered by alien batteries instead of gasoline and with alien enhanced control and safety designs and materials. Then JassaVar was told that a specialist professional driving instructor would be coming to explain how this car differed from the one that she was being taught to drive at school.

Then, JassaVar thought but did not say aloud, she could go out without her mother knowing where she was going. JassaVar had learnt a lot from her new schoolfriends about disrespect for adult stupidity, and rebellion against parental authority – not that her mother had expressed any disapproval of JassaVar's long list of male admirers at school as she and her friends practised what JassaVar had learnt from her friends to call 'playing the field'.

That was definitely what humans called fun!

CHAPTER FIFTEEN

Tiara did not have to wait long before two weapon-carrying alien giants came striding along – either trying to look macho or in a hurry or both.

Neither demurred at a pretty girl accompanying them along several corridors, although Tiara had a problem keeping up with their long legs, getting increasingly out of breath scurrying to match their strides even though they carried her bags for her despite already being laden with combat gear ready for a fun day out down on Earth exterminating humans.

She did get from one of them a declaration that he would be interested in duvaying her if she were available when he got back, and a promise of generosity if he enjoyed himself. He told her the location of the social area that he usually frequented in search of duvay after a safari, and she filed the details in her memory.

Just in case she was desperate for money again.

———

Ten weeks earlier

It was a new experience for Emily to like visitors.

Most visitors in her life had been social workers or cops, but Brett and Sylvia had first come to break the news of Tiara's injuries, and Brett had called back a few days' later to reassure Emily that Tiara was recovering – then again a week later to explain that Tiara had accepted an invitation to live on Freedom *– which had infuriated Edward Maitland into once again vowing never to have anything to do with Tiara again.*

Emily could not understand why Tiara was staying on the spaceship.

"That I'll try to find out," Brett had replied. "Dad insists she is staying of her own free will, and I can't imagine aliens forcibly detaining her, but I aim to go up myself in a few days – if I can find her – the place is vast and Dad and Modesty are refusing to co-operate. Modesty has even forbidden Humility from helping."

It could not fail to occur to Emily that Tiara staying on Freedom *might make Emily's dream of eventually living with Tiara more remote, but it was still for Tiara's safety that she worried more until Brett returned, with not only Sylvia but also Tiara's alien stepsister Humility, to say that alien tests had revealed that Tiara's mother had been an alien researcher living secretly on Earth – that Tiara was half-alien.*

Therefore so was Emily.

————

Emily liked attending church with the Redferns.

Churchgoers were much less judgmental than teenagers, so Emily felt safe from humiliation and could go without that threat constantly haunting her.

Apart from church Emily left the house as little as she could. There was school which she could never enjoy but knew how to survive. Her academic year-skipping progress had earned her no friends, but her loner habits were her real problem. So fixated was she on the theory that only the wrong sort of boys would like her that she literally flinched away from all approaches, and was scarcely more responsive to attempts at friendliness from girls – earning herself the sarcastic nickname of 'Smiler'. But she had known much nastier nicknames, and could cope with the snide jibes that sometimes accompanied it.

On the plus side, Lawrie often sat beside her while she bolted down her lunch before hiding in the library, and she had relaxed enough to talk to him unless others joined them. She was even coping with the school counsellor to whom her parole officer insisted that she talk for an hour every week. All the counsellor had done was ask about her week, with occasional mild enquires as to why she did things that way, and even Emily realized how obsessive her answers to the latter often sounded. Meanwhile Emily had never had teachers who were so friendly and encouraging, though primarily because of the Redferns, who had in the last few weeks come in to school several times to meet individual teachers with Emily to discuss her work and future. Emily was amazed how many teachers Joan Redfern knew personally.

Emily had also adapted to the day centre. She almost liked dirty jobs that involved cleaning stuff up, and genuinely relished the allegedly punitive work of cleaning up after frail elderly people when they dropped food and other things, though she came home even more exhausted than after a day at school and often fell asleep early – with the problematic side effect of waking up in the small hours and not falling asleep again until it was nearly time to get up, so Joan Redfern sometimes had to rouse Emily when she slept through all three of her alarms.

The centre staff had hosted previous community service cases, but never one quite like Emily. Initially her supervisors kept a wary eye on her in case she skimped on her work, but soon discovered that they had to restrain her from frenetically over-tidying until the clients had gone, then unleash her like an attack dog on cleaning up. The staff appreciated her total lack of attitude and her willingness to work hard and late on dirty jobs – and often had to actively insist that Emily could not get the rooms any cleaner and should go home.

By Christmas Emily had considered offering to continue volunteering there after her community service hours were complete, but she knew that the Redferns wanted her to stop so that they could take her out to places like museums and theatres and concerts, and Emily had concluded that she needed to devote Saturdays to earning money before the terrifyingly imminent future when she was out of foster care and homeless and struggling to find work with a criminal record.

But that fear was relegated to the back of Emily's mind as she stood in church worrying whether the service would go without a hitch, how she could keep the bathroom clean - and all points beyond. There was nothing she could do if anything did go wrong during church services, but that did not stop her stressing out if someone missed a word during readings, or was slow taking the collection plate around. The Redferns knew that their foster-daughter was a compulsive worrier, but were just happy that Emily willingly went to church, and hopeful that she would eventually make proper friends there. Bobby and Lawrie usually made a point of talking to her, and Peter when work permitted him to attend, but Emily showed disappointingly no sign of even trying to make close friends with any girls. The Redferns had still not figured out that Emily hated being asked questions about herself so never asked other girls about themselves – so naturally appeared to other girls to be unfriendly or even arrogant.

Emily remained unwilling to attend any social events without the Redferns, and resolutely avoided all school events – despite her court-imposed curfew having been lifted after three months. The Redferns were unwilling to put any pressure on her despite their distress at her continuing lack of friends, so Emily was spared worrying about the Redferns pushing her to talk to anyone.

Emily had more than enough to worry herself frantic about with the Christmas meal and present-opening to survive, the bathroom-cleaning challenge to overcome, and guests to face, but her biggest worry was hearing nothing from Tiara for so long.

The only part of her life that worried her less than it did the Redferns was the fact that she was part alien.

———

Ten weeks earlier

JassaVar was relieved to get into the back seat of Brett's car after leaving the Redferns.

It was not that she minded meeting the half-breed, but Emily did seem quite odd. JassaVar exchanged contact details, and agreed to talk about alien history and customs whenever Emily wanted, but the girl evidenced no interest in making friends – which suited JassaVar who did not want her mother discovering her efforts to help Brett contact both Tiara and Emily.

"Thank you so much for coming, Humility," Sylvia spoke over her shoulder while getting into the front passenger seat. "I'm sure Emily will be reassured knowing Tiara is safe."

JassaVar acknowledged the gratitude, but refrained from mentioning her doubts about Tiara coping with alien lifestyle disciplines.

"Time to get you home," Brett said as he started the car. "I owe you and Patience more than ever, and I promise never to tell Dad or Modesty."

JassaVar was duly grateful, though still seriously puzzled that Edward Maitland should decree that Tiara was no longer part of the family and refuse to even help Brett speak to 'the little bitch'. JassaVar then heard him shouting the same thing down the phone to Sara. Tiara perfectly comprehended ejecting a disobedient daughter or housegirl from a household – that happened with alien households, but it was almost always the mother or housewife who took the decision. Men rarely got involved in disciplining daughters or housegirls, but humans were different. Or maybe it was really DinzaVar behind it.

DinzaVar had explicitly banned JassaVar from helping Tiara, but not forbidden talking to Brett about it, and had previously ordered JassaVar to do anything Brett asked. When Brett asked for JassaVar's help to locate Tiara, JassaVar considered using that order as an excuse – but her mother never tolerated excuses.

As a bonus for helping Tiara, Brett bought JassaVar another 16G so that she could call her sister LaskaVar without their mother knowing, and arrange firstly for LaskaVar to identify where on Freedom *Tiara was living, and then meet Brett when he got passage into space, and escort him to the household of Physician FrageaVar.*

Now JassaVar would be able to talk to LaskaVar whenever she wanted – if she could hide her private 16G from her mother.

———

The best part about staircases on *Freedom* was that you could usually get from top deck to bottom deck on the same staircase.

The worst part was that they had toll hatches every four levels, and most decks had to be entered through another toll hatch. Tiara had to ask a passing alien which deck covered the garden deck that she wanted to find, and that woman was unfortunately heading in the opposite direction. It then took three separate helpful passers-by to hitch her up to the relevant deck and the desired garden deck hatch.

Fortunately she did not have to wait for the garden deck hatch to be opened. It was a business so was open to customers to buy food fresh off the trees or out of the soil. She was nevertheless able to identify and afford to buy a pear-like fruit that she did recognize, and the girl called RollaVar who came to serve her was friendly enough to a customer to let her use a nearby deck bathroom.

But, when Tiara asked for LaskaVar, RollaVar explained that LaskaVar no longer worked or lodged there, having departed three days earlier following a visit from her mother.

———

Seven weeks earlier

Tiara had been getting desperate when LactoVar made the offer.

Twenty days into her sixty-four day acclimatisation period, Tiara was very short of money. Alien digital money, to be precise. The keep that she had been promised in return for what seemed to her sensitivities like positive skivvying – though Emily would have thought nothing of so few chores – was no better than boarding school food, and LactoVar the most crotchety and parsimonious of taskmasters.

Tiara had got accustomed to supplementing her diet by buying food during what passed for nights out on an alien spaceship.

In fairness, it could have been worse. The other housegirls whom Tiara had met seemed friendly enough, and some sort of wine-like alcoholic drink was purchasable without any age restrictions. Unfortunately it was not cheap. Tiara had rationed herself to one drink a night, and few housegirls could afford even that. Not that Tiara did not enjoy going out with other housegirls, especially when joining in the first passion that aliens had learnt from humans – namely dancing, which apparently had never been an alien pastime until young alien girls had seen humans dancing on screens and taken it up with enthusiasm - to the bemusement of their elders.

Tiara was happy enough to join in, though the current dancing rage among alien girls derived from Bollywood rather than Hollywood, but Tiara had managed to sneak in a few of her own moves and get other girls to imitate her. The downside of alien dancing was the fact that only girls danced. Not only did no men join the dancing, but they rarely even turned up, and when they did all dancing stopped as girls competed for male attention. Tiara had tried to gain male attention by more exotic dancing, but it had gone down badly with both girls and men so she had not tried it twice.

Alien men might look awesome, but socially they were hard work. Sense of humour was a rarity — sense of fun an endangered species. Men rarely stayed around long enough to do more than pick a couple of girls, and none had yet picked Tiara — not that she wanted a threesome with a guy she did not know. Tiara craved an alien to dance with and to pay for the expensive but legal alcohol, but too many of the testosterone vehicles had turned out to be residing in alien enclaves or doing business down on Earth or exploring Mars or hunting humans. If a girl was not ready to duvay they showed little interest, and Tiara had confirmed that no direct alien translation existed for 'chatting-up'. Being deprived of male admiration made Tiara even more querulous about other petty irritations, and she got serious satisfaction from delivering regular critical commentaries on the quality of food, and the general dreariness of bedroom, apartment, and neighbourhood - relieving her feelings but irritating LactoVar.

Tiara's real problem with life in FrageaVar's HouseHold was being subject to command and discipline by FrageaVar's assistant and trainee physician LactoVar.

LactoVar literally meant CandourGirl, but Tiara had soon learnt to secretly call her FaviCheriVar - which Tiara translated as ViciousBitchGirl. Tiara was convinced that FaviCheriVar was determined to make Tiara's life difficult purely out of spite, piling on tedious chores just to humiliate the half-breed.

Tiara was partly right. LactoVar had made a mistake by telling DinzaVar about Tiara without FrageaVar's permission, and been humiliatingly punished for what FrageaVar judged a serious breach of civility. As a result, LactoVar had started out resentful enough to be determined to make it as hard for Tiara as it had been for LactoVar herself, but it had been Tiara's own attitude which had turned LactoVar's initial resentment into bitter hostility.

Emily could have won the older alien over quickly by doing all chores without protest, showing respect for her teacher, and not finding fault with food or facilities. Tiara had never done chores, did not like doing them, and did not do them well — and could not easily abandon ingrained habits of disrespecting adults at every opportunity. To Tiara LactoVar's punishments were just the spite of a humourless bitch. They hurt, but only briefly, and Tiara soon learnt to shrug punishments off - determined not to be so easily deterred from her new mission in life. Unfortunately it was a mission for which childhood had ill-equipped her. Her memory meant that schoolwork had always come very easily to her, but nobody had ever taken enough interest to push her to achieve her academic potential, and her lifestyle offered so many other distractions that she had never developed the necessary work ethic. LactoVar could have supplied the push, but was instead determined to sabotage Tiara's mission.

Unaware of this, Tiara's main worry was that she had permanently burnt her boats by telling her father that she wanted to stay on Freedom *despite his threat to cut off all support and contact. She had not anticipated him being so brutal, despite that time in Juvie. Even when storming out, telling her that he would never see or speak to her again, she had been confident that he would soon relent.*

So confident had she been that when Brett found her a week later she had defiantly boasted to her brother that she was fine, and blithely agreed the amount of the allowance that he had offered to arrange to send her from his own resources without bothering to check alien prices or rates of exchange - being at the time more interested in asking him to tell Emily the truth about their mother.

Brett had been so dumbfounded that he had not gone ahead with offering to double the allowance as he would had she pushed, but he had given her contact details for LaskaVar – Humility's sister. LaskaVar could pass on any messages, and if Tiara needed to be rescued and returned to Earth, Brett promised to come and get her. Tiara had thanked him, but proudly boasted that she could look after herself, so it would have meant swallowing a lot of pride to ask for a greater allowance when the problems began to strike home over the next few weeks.

Not only was alien alcohol expensive, so was walking the corridors because of all the toll doors, and if she phoned LaskaVar or any other friend on Freedom *she had to pay per call – making her moan about super-advanced aliens not being advanced enough to have call plans!*

Meanwhile the cost of either verbal or visual calls to anyone on Earth made even alien alcohol seem dirt cheap, and though they possessed an equivalent to e-mail it was paid by the digit like stupid prehistoric telegrams, and Tiara needed all the credit she could scrape together to buy clothes and accessories and cosmetics and similar life essentials. Alien clothes were fantastic but expensive, so Tiara struggled to keep to her allowance, finding herself managing for two weeks with the incredibly demeaning total of only four top quality alien outfits which she had to wear in rotation, and because of the cost of cleaning sometimes stooping to putting on her clothes sent up from Earth! She was desperate to get more, but determined not to admit her mistake by calling Brett to beg for more money. He might have offered to send up more clothes from her dressing room down on Earth and all that Earth stuff was so last-species and lacked the exquisite feel of alien dresses.

Then she found two of her alien dresses somehow ripped when she was also running low on make-up and the glorious alien body cleansers that, once experienced, no girl could possibly live without. Even so she was about to admit defeat and send Brett a begging message when LactoVar showed a most unexpected hint of sympathy with Tiara's moaning about her clothing problem. On impulse Tiara threw pride to the winds and let off a few 'pleases' and 'pretty pleases' and pretended to be all apologetic if she had been difficult at times but she really did respect LactoVar and trusted her to give a poor little hybrid good advice.

Her impulse paid off as LactoVar begrudgingly offered to suggest ways for Tiara to earn money, and Tiara was too pleased with herself to even suspect that the show of reluctance was just cover, or that LactoVar was counting on Tiara's partial comprehension of alien culture making her easy prey for LactoVar's trap.

Tiara knew that alien girls who achieved high enough intelligence scores at puberty could choose to be 'ascended' by medical treatments that re-wrote the DNA in every cell in their bodies and turned them into men. Tiara knew that the 'newly-ascended' then underwent a long and rigorous regime of physical and mental training to prepare them for the traditional duties of alien men. Tiara did not envy the men those duties, which seemed to include all the dangerous jobs and all the fighting.

LactoVar explained with complete truthfulness that housegirls were entitled to earn money however they chose while doing housegirl duties in exchange for bed and board. She neglected to mention, though Tiara worked it out easily enough, that Tiara's rigorous education program left her no time for money-earning activity without working evenings which massively exceeded the tolerance levels of her work ethic, so when Tiara sought advice LactoVar calmly opened the trap for Tiara by truthfully explaining that families of the newly-ascended commonly arranged for them to learn skills in duvay by paying girls for practice sessions. LactoVar neglected to truthfully add that girls *recruited to train young men were supposed to be significantly older and more experienced than Tiara in order to supply the training required.*

Tiara was convinced that she could handle any boys her own age, and found the thought of playing hooker rather exciting – just the once – up here where nobody would ever know and there was no risk – and the men were so big! She knew which of her dresses would be just right to wear when meeting such a client, and it would avoid the humiliation of sending a begging message to Brett. She would be proving to herself as well as Brett that she could look after herself – and her family need never know, need they?

If LactoVar had acted helpful and friendly in making the offer Tiara would have instantly smelt a rat, but LactoVar simply outsmarted the half-human younger girl by taunting the offer with a sneer that Tiara would never be experienced enough to cope with the job. In all but words she dared Tiara.

Emily would have run a mile from the very idea, but Tiara was a hardened veteran of a dare-taking teenage sub-culture.

––––––

Emily was completely stressed out throughout Christmas dinner.

The others laughed and joked and relished food and company - and the stories that Cathy told of Australian Christmases, but Emily was constantly worrying about everything being ready on time and done just right. It even took a conscious effort not to scurry for a cloth to clean up every tiny spill of gravy, and she struggled to pay attention to the stories, and never spoke unless spoken to - assuming that the guests would not be interested in anything she might say.

The Redferns knew better than to press Emily to talk in unfamiliar company, not wanting to give her a panic attack on Christmas Day. They had deliberately seated Peter next to her, and he quietly asked her about her plans for the holidays, to which she only answered that she had volunteered to do extra days at the day centre.

No point in suggesting that she should go out with friends - knowing how that idea would scare her. He briefly considered asking her to go out somewhere with him, but he was twenty four and she was only sixteen and he dare not suggest anything that anyone could suspect of being a date.

Then Cathy innocently asked if Emily had a boyfriend, and Peter and the Redferns froze. They should have said something to forestall this, they knew, but hesitated as Emily calmly replied that she had never had a boyfriend.

"Never!" Cathy exclaimed. "What is wrong with guys around here, Tom?"

"Nothing," Emily responded so calmly that the Redferns hesitated still further in interrupting. "It's me that's all wrong."

Joan jumped in where Tony feared to tread.

"The only thing wrong with you, my dear," she defaulted to a line that she had been long planning to use at the first good opportunity, "is that you think there is something wrong with you. You must try to dig yourself out of your Slough of Despond and go out and start making friends again – and you see why I never joined the Samaritans! You've made friends before, haven't you?"

Had anyone else said all that Emily might have got upset, but her face almost showed a hint of a smile until she noticed Cathy and Tom looking at her with a confusion which Emily inevitably misinterpreted.

"Yes," she exaggerated, convinced that they suspected her of being guilty of something and desperate to change the subject. "But I never stayed anywhere long enough to keep them. I don't know how long I'll be here. Slough of Despond is from Pilgrim's Progress, isn't it?"

"Yes. You've read it?"

"No."

"I've got a copy if you're interested in reading it?"

"Yes," Tony chimed in. "Believe it or not Joan actually does have some books that are not by or about Jane Austen."

That produced a laugh right around the table, including Joan herself, but not including Emily, who was rightly convinced that she was making a bad impression on Tom and Cathy, but had no idea how to make a good impression.

"Does she ever laugh?" Tom whispered to his father as Joan and Emily were clattering dishes out in the kitchen some twenty minutes later. "What is she afraid of? What is she hiding?"

"She smiled more than once during dinner," Peter assured his foster brother. "Though you might have blinked and missed it. Gotta give your Mum credit – Slough of Despond really fits her."

"I've never heard her laugh yet," Tony declared sadly. "The day we can get her to laugh I'll start worrying a lot less."

"Does she never relax?" Cathy joined in the whispering. "I've never seen anyone so tense around any dinner table – let alone at Christmas. You'd think she was expecting to be arrested any minute!"

"Trust me. She is much more relaxed than she was. Shush!"

As Emily sped in with the dessert plates - like a waitress with a dozen impatient customers and her job on the line – he firmly changed the subject.

———

Six weeks earlier

It was not exactly as if Tiara had been a virgin.

Quite apart from the brothers who had raped her, she had two other notches on her bedpost even before Carl. She could hardly claim that any notch had been earth-moving, but nor had any been traumatising - so Tiara was confident that she could manage a young male her own age providing that he did not use drugs or force.

Her self-confidence made her much more gullible than her paranoid twin.

Declaring to LactoVar that she was not a virgin did not faze Tiara, since aliens invested virginity with zero moral or social status, and Tiara had agreed the contract – feeling like she was playing truth and dare and taking the dare but getting paid for it.

Once committed, there was no going back – whatever the consequences.

LactoVar told Tiara that the payment was for duvaying the young male to exhaustion – an interesting concept of itself – but also for providing feedback on how he was doing - letting him know what worked for her and what did not.

"You must work the whole night if he desires," LactoVar told Tiara, and it did not occur to Tiara to doubt her word – blindly trusting LactoVar's advice and not even questioning LactoVar's explanation that LactoVar received eight per cent of the fee for negotiating the deal. It did not even click that the alien octal system of counting meant that instead of the maximum percentage being

a hundred per cent it was sixty-four per cent, so the eight per cent amounted
to one eighth of the fee.

Nor did Tiara doubt LactoVar's assertion that the pill which LactoVar
had supplied would stop her getting pregnant. The fact that it had been given
her as a present instead of sold her for profit should have tipped Tiara off that
LactoVar had some ulterior motive.

Tiara forgot that aliens possessed no traditions of giving presents nor free
medicine, so never suspected that LactoVar had neglected to mention that alien
birth control pills were not all contraceptive.

———

JassaVar was still in awe about her presents when all three of them were
around the dinner table and her stepfather surprised both aliens by asking
JassaVar if she had spoken to her sister that day.

"What was her name?" he continued as JassaVar observed her mother's
surprise at the question. "I remember. Patience. At our wedding. Pretty
girl."

"Yes, Edward," his wife replied cautiously, and her daughter saw
the irritation beneath the smile. "You remember she still resides aboard
Freedom."

"Yes, of course. But it really is time that your sister came here to visit,
Humility, and preferably to stay. Wouldn't that be a good idea, darling?
You'd love to have both your daughters here? Wouldn't you?"

JassaVar translated her mother's smile – all mask and no sincerity.

"Of course, darling," DinzaVar replied with perfectly faked happiness
at the idea. "But you know – Patience is adult. She possess own career now.
She may not desire to reside with mother again."

"Was that what Patience said last week? I know you visited her while
we were on *Freedom*. No need to keep that secret from me, darling. I'm
happy for you to see your daughter any time."

The show smile remained on DinzaVar's voice, and JassaVar wondered
uneasily why DinzaVar had gone to see LaskaVar. Was that why LaskaVar
had not responded the last two times that JassaVar had tried to call her?

"I'm sure she'd like to visit anyway," her husband breezed on, and
JassaVar remembered her last meeting with Sara – a week ago at Brett's

home. Sara had declared that once Edward Maitland had finally been persuaded to a course of action he would steamroller all opposition. "All daughters like to visit their loving mother regularly. I totally understand. Don't worry about me. I'd love to see her."

JassaVar had needed to decipher the contextual relevance of 'steamroller'. She remembered Sara smiling and telling JassaVar not to get in front of the steamroller when it started rolling, but to jump on the cab and go with it. Then Sara and Brett had laughed conspiratorially, and left JassaVar wondering what they were talking about.

Was this the steamroller beginning to roll? Her mother was still smiling, but now it was her suspicious smile.

"Why don't you call her, Humility?" Edward Maitland rolled on. "I'm sure your sister would love to see you and meet your friends. She could go dancing with you and your friends – I bet she'd like that."

JassaVar looked at her mother in confusion, and trepidation. Was her mother now going to reverse her orders? Surely not – from the annoyance-disguising smile on her face. Whenever DinzaVar was unhappy about anything she got extra strict. The last three times DinzaVar had taken her temper out on JassaVar when Edward Maitland was in earshot and had intervened. Each time JassaVar had been a witness to angry exchanges between them. Each time DinzaVar had asserted that disciplining JassaVar was her responsibility and duty as defined by their marriage contract, but each time she had deferred to him and curtailed the punishment.

JassaVar had never understood why her mother was doing it. She could just as easily have delayed JassaVar's punishments until mother and daughter were alone – especially considering her mother's often repeated mantra that it was vital to please and appease men like the Maitlands in every possible way.

"I doubt," DinzaVar eventually dismissed. "If Patience declines to visit mother, I doubt she will be willing to visit her stupid sister."

"Her school report," came a quick response, "indicates that Humility is anything but stupid. She is adapting well, has an exceptional memory, and a good attitude."

"By human standards no doubt she appear intelligent. By alien standards I define she is stupid. You spend little time with her, or you would consider her company tedious. You would not waste money buying her presents if you comprehend her."

Husband stared at wife very thoughtfully while his wife resumed eating as if she had not a care in the world, but JassaVar knew her mother well enough to know that DinzaVar was very tense – almost excited – about something. Edward Maitland appeared to be annoyed again – which really worried his stepdaughter.

Being dismissed as tedious and stupid by her mother did not bother JassaVar, but her stepfather's annoyance did. Outright arguments between husband and wife were happening with increasing frequency. There was nothing new about DinzaVar denigrating her daughters, nor alluding to the stupidity of the human species in comparison to aliens. In the first weeks of marriage Edward Maitland had acted amused by his bride's barbs against idiotic humans and their funny little ideas and habits. But he had stopped laughing some weeks ago, and now it seemed as though he was getting more annoyed every time.

JassaVar had even begun to wonder if DinzaVar was deliberately trying to provoke Edward Maitland, but remembered that her mother had a long history of annoying housewives enough to get them all ejected from households.

"Okay, *darling*," Edward Maitland resumed – and JassaVar had never heard that endearment uttered with such a strange intonation. "I get the point – you're the opposite of a proud and doting mother – I get that – but you're still a mother – our species are not that different. You must still want to see her sometimes?"

DinzaVar hesitated, but JassaVar recognized her venomous smile etching into her face, and JassaVar could not help wondering how Edward Maitland would react if DinzaVar provoked him too far. He could eject his wife from his household at any time, JassaVar knew, according to something called a pre-nup and subject to some sort of financial arrangements, and if her mother was ejected JassaVar was sure to be ejected with her, and JassaVar did not want to leave this incredibly luxurious lifestyle.

"So that is settled," Edward Maitland steamrollered on. "Why not try later today, Humility? That 16G should work providing you only know where to call. Don't worry about the cost. Tell your sister that I'll pay all transport costs – no problem."

JassaVar looked at her mother anxiously. DinzaVar had been very specific about orders not to contact her sister – and JassaVar was worried enough about how much she had been breaking those orders already – but now she had received orders from her householder that conflicted with those of her mother.

By alien custom daughter obeyed mother above all others in a household – but mother almost invariably commanded daughter to obey householder. JassaVar dared not openly disobey her mother, so what would her mother say now?

"JassaVar," her mother declared with a glacial smile. "Always remember to obey your orders. Do as you are told."

"Thank you, darling," Edward Maitland responded. "You heard, Humility. I know you're a good daughter and obey your mother, don't you?"

"Yes, sir," JassaVar replied automatically, and then winced internally, and did not want to take another mouthful.

Her mother had just told JassaVar to obey orders.

But she had not specified which orders.

CHAPTER SIXTEEN

Tiara nearly panicked when told that LaskaVar no longer lived on the garden deck.

LaskaVar had openly enjoyed Tiara talking about life in America, and declared a desire to live there, but they had not spoken for over a week while Tiara was busy studying for and taking all her tests. It had never occurred to Tiara that LaskaVar might not be there for her when Tiara needed her.

RollaVar hesitated, then sidled close to her.

"Is your name Tiara?" she whispered – and it took Tiara several seconds to realize that RollaVar had spoken in English instead of alien.

"In English – I mean human," she acknowledged. "I'm Tiara – or TarraVar. Did LaskaVar tell you about me?"

"Yes. LaskaVar is friend. She ask I take you to her if you come, but only you."

"Why only me?"

"Because she hide from her mother."

———

Six weeks earlier

Tiara had learnt enough from LaskaVar and other girls to expect the newly ascended to be clumsy and quick and only think to ask how it felt for her afterwards.

Tiara did her best to tell him, but her own experience was limited, and she found an unexpected language barrier as the youth knew little English and Tiara's study of Alien had achieved good everyday functionality without

212

acquiring the fluency needed for this purpose. As a result it never got much better for her. When he fell asleep she was relieved until his weight lying on top made her feel increasingly crushed. Fortunately he soon rolled sideways in sleep and she could struggle out from under. Tiara was glad that he did not wake until morning after they both overslept – then had to hurry off to training without time to do more than promise payment that day.

At least she had coped, and done what she had to do to avoid having to beg for help from Brett or Dad. The credit came as promised, and she stocked up her wardrobe with some alien dresses that were an absolute dream to wear. Too dreamy - she overspent and left herself nearly out of alien money again. And, gorgeous as they were, the dresses also supplied a constant reminder of how she had earned them.

It took weeks for her to start worrying that she might be pregnant, and she spent another week insisting to herself that she must be crazy. LactoVar had given her a pill, after all, and Tiara knew that alien medicine was infinitely superior to human medicine, and that LactoVar was a Physician's Assistant – a sort of cross between nurse, medical student, and personal assistant. Tiara had automatically trusted LactoVar – bitchy martinet though she might be – to possess normal medical ethics.

She had forgotten that until coming to Earth the aliens had never heard of any medical profession possessing anything remotely resembling a Hippocratic Oath.

———

The opening of the presents had been as shaming as Emily had feared.

The Redferns had been even more heartbreakingly generous than she had imagined. Had they just given her two boxes of chocolates instead of one she would have been content, but getting a veritable deluge of books, clothes, and accessories completely overwhelmed her – and made her feel desperately guilty at the hopelessly inadequacy of the return presents over which she had agonized for weeks and spent every cent she dared – even saving on bus fares by walking home from school.

She meticulously thanked every present giver for every present, but was so obsessed about getting that right that she totally forgot to smile or look happy even once. The Redferns observed this with distress. They

213

had considered themselves very restrained in the quantity of presents they had bought for Emily, and were dismayed by how much she had bought them and the thought that she had clearly put in to choosing them. They made no attempt to restrain their pleasure and gratitude at the gifts, but were at a loss to know how else to make Christmas a happy day for their foster daughter. It had gone even worse than when they had asked her to decorate the Christmas tree - Emily had soon been bombarding them with questions as to what they wanted as if she was doing it all to please them instead of herself, and ultimately resorted to sticking every available decoration up as if trying to balance them out all around the tree so as to avoid toppling it over. Then she had offered to do it all again if they did not like it, and they had almost had to restrain her from doing it anyway.

The Redferns had so desperately wanted to see Emily opening her presents with delight and enjoying a happy Christmas like a child should, but it was miserably obvious from Emily's face that she was anything but enjoying herself.

Obvious not only to them. Their son and daughter-in-law noticed it as well.

––––––

Six weeks earlier

Emily had long been convinced that there was something not normal about her.

Being told that she was half-alien did not, therefore, horrify her as the Redferns had feared. Her only worry was that the Redferns might be repulsed, but realizing that they were merely intrigued by the discovery had helped them bond in trying to find out more about alien culture. The mutual interest had helped them to get Emily to talk more about herself under the guise of wondering how her alien genetic heritage affected her – though strictly following Brett's advice to tell nobody who did not need to know, and reassured by his offer to arrange alien medical treatment for Emily should it ever be necessary.

The Redferns were right to hope that their foster daughter was a bit less anxious about life by then. But only a bit. The more she came to know the Redferns the more she liked living with them, but the more she feared ruining it all again. When Peter let slip one Sunday that the Redferns had dropped a plan to go to Australia for Christmas, she immediately assumed that they had done so for her sake, and suffered a quiet meltdown of guilt that night before redoubling her efforts to do everything she could think of doing about the house, and working harder at school than ever before.

But she feared that she was only covering up the problems that she was causing them.

And that parent-teacher night would expose her.

————

LaskaVar had moved to the household where RollaVar resided, so Tiara only had to wait two long alien hours for RollaVar to end her shift and go home.

It transpired that RollaVar's mother was housewife in the household to a householder nearer to RollaVar's age – though the 'housewife' still looked the younger, and made Tiara hope again that her alien genes dominated her human ones in that respect. Alien women aged much slower than alien men – and normally lived well over two hundred Earth years – up to twice as long as alien men - and could normally still have children when they were a hundred years old.

Alien men lived much shorter lives, and were much fewer in number, and barely one man for every eight women. Alien mating habits reminded Tiara irresistibly of racehorse breeding with the men as stud stallions, so Tiara quite understood why so many alien girls were interested in human partners, and Tiara's own mother had been the very first to succeed in that quest – a definitive trailblazer. Tiara was proud of that, and keen to emulate her mother and blaze her own trails – given half a chance.

But for her to get that chance she would need LaskaVar's help.

————

Six weeks earlier

Parent-teacher night seriously stressed Emily out.

To begin with, her foster parents actually went - a scarily unfamiliar experience. Emily miserably anticipated being criticized for not speaking up because she had long experience of teachers lacerating her threadbare self-esteem by delivering what they intended to be encouraging pep talks to have more self-confidence and speak up more – unaware that Emily was incapable of interpreting any behavioural advice as anything other than scolding or reacting any other way than negatively. To her all teachers and most adults were just people who told her what to do or told her off.

This time she feared that the teachers might be even more critical, even though they had been almost uniformly gentle with her. Emily was so perversely proud of martyring herself for Tiara that she was still exaggerating the negative consequences for her and assuming that all the teachers must believe her to be a delinquent, and it upset her to imagine what the Redferns might be hearing about her. She felt very guilty about lying to them, even to protect Tiara. They deserved so much better, and Emily could not think how to adequately show her gratitude.

She tried to calm her nerves by an orgy of cleaning while the Redferns were out, including cleaning out a kitchen cupboard nobody else could believe to need cleaning. To avoid betraying her efforts, she meticulously mapped out where all the cups and plates were standing before starting, and carefully put them back where they came from - just in time before her foster parents got home. As she looked out the front window, she saw their car and dashed upstairs to the bathroom. While in there she heard them coming back into the house, and as soon as the cleanliness of the bathroom allowed she came hurrying down to help her foster mother get dinner.

The Redferns could not help noticing her trepidation, and hastened to assure her that her teachers were very pleased with her hard work and academic progress, and supportive of allowing her to skip a grade and graduate a year early – but several had expressed concern about her lack of confidence when speaking up in class. No surprise – Emily felt relief that her teachers had not been much harsher.

What the Redferns did not mention at first was that several teachers had asked Emily to start thinking about college and talk to her foster parents, but she had said nothing to them at all, so over dinner they raised the subject – trying to be tactful about it – meaning that Joan left it to Tony. Joan was glad to leave it to him, having noticed unhappily that passing on the praise of Emily's teachers had produced no slightest sign of pleasure in their foster daughter.

It had been an integral part of Joan's dream of fostering a troubled teenager that she should establish a strong maternal bond with her charge. She had been fully prepared to deal with stubbornness and resentment and temper tantrums and outright rebelliousness – had been confident that by mixing firmness with love and generosity she could build a good relationship and make a real difference. She had never imagined that, far from an out of control teen needing restraint, she would be faced with a girl who restrained herself to the point of obsession and could be devastated by any criticism. They had emphasized this to all the teachers, and in several cases persuaded teachers to agree personal meetings with Emily and the Redferns to discuss Emily's school curriculum and her future.

Tony and Joan had spent the car journey home discussing tactics, so it was as they were finishing the main course that Tony bit the bullet and mentioned the word 'college'. Joan half-expected Emily to go into meltdown, but she just went silent and looked down at her hands.

"We are your parents, Emily," Tony told her gently. "We're here to help you."

Emily twitched sharply, but did not look up.

"I don't," she whispered, but then twitched again and shrank back into silence.

"Don't what?" Joan finally lost patience. "Don't need help? Of course you do. Please, Emily. We all need help sometimes, and we all deserve to be helped when we need it – maybe some more than others. I'm sure there have been times when you both needed and deserved help that you never got, so don't refuse it now."

Joan wondered if she had overdone it, but Emily did not run to her room again – so maybe not. Emily's plate was empty in front of her, as she always ate fast and often scraped the plate so clean that it looked almost unused. Joan and Tony had not cleared their plates, but neither cared at that moment.

"Joan is right, Emily," Tony supported gently. "It is our job to help you as long as we're your parents."

"But you're not really my parents," came Emily's first words, and Joan was shocked how much it hurt to hear her say that.

"As long as you're with us," Tony repeated gently by firmly, "we are your parents. Parents de facto, if not de jure."

"But ..." Emily began, but stopped.

"No buts, my dear," Joan could not hold back. "For the present we are your parents. That is what we want to be, and I believe God meant us to be. All you need to do is to let us be - please let us in."

"I wish I could," Emily suddenly almost shouted, raising her head to look at them – and show that she had tears in her eyes.

"So do," Joan replied immediately. "Just let yourself."

"It's not that simple. It's not that possible. It's not possible."

"Why not?"

"Because you're not my parents. You're not my family. You're just my foster parents and this is just a foster home – a temporary refuge, and I'll have to leave within two years. I can't let myself – it will hurt too much – it scares me to think how soon I'll have to leave."

"Not that soon, Emily," Tony told her firmly. "One day you'll want to leave. Every child does – it is called growing up."

"Yes, you'll want to forge yourself a life," Joan added enthusiastically. "A career to enjoy, a husband and children to love. We'll be sorry to see you go and happy to see you go – you know what I mean. Before that you'll go to college. With stellar grades like yours you can get into a first class college – though your teachers did say it would help if you could participate in more extra-curricular school activities. But you do need to start thinking about it. It is not just about what you do at college. It is about the rest of your life."

Emily stared back at her foster mother for a moment, before coming back with an answer almost in staccato.

"I just want to finish school," she said. "If I survive that – I start worrying what I do next."

The Redferns exchanged unhappy glances, but could not leave it there.

"But you're doing really well at school," Tony Redfern took the baton up. "You're a really special girl. Why can't you let yourself believe it?"

———

"What are you on?"

The question came from the open door of Emily's bedroom - where she had retreated to tidy away all her Christmas presents and render the room spotless.

It was Tom standing and staring at her. Emily interpreted his expression as one of contempt - like any anti-prejudice campaigner she could interpret anything as prejudice whether it genuinely was or not. How could he not view her as a criminal delinquent exploiting his parents' generosity? It must look like that to any son who wanted to protect his parents. Emily was flooded with guilt at the thought that she must look guilty – so inevitably she did look guilty.

"You could at least have tried to look happy at everything they gave you," came the next words – which made no immediate sense to Emily. "All they wanted was to see you happy so they're heart-broken down there. They think they've failed you. Either you're on something or you need therapy."

Heart-broken? Heart-broken! Those words got through to Emily, though the exact meaning of Tom's whole speech did not.

"I'm sorry!" she cried out desperately. "I got them the best presents I could. I just couldn't afford anything better. I begged them not to spend so much on me. I didn't know what else to do. I'm sorry!"

Tom just stared at her. Emily was convinced that she had made him angry. She had long experience of unintentionally annoying foster siblings.

"I vote therapy," Cathy interrupted, slipping lithely round Tom into Emily's bedroom. "Are you sure this is your bedroom? It looks unoccupied."

Tom looked around the room as if he had never seen it before.

"I keep it tidy," was the best response Emily dared give to the awesomely confident young woman now standing over her. "Mrs Redfern told me the day I arrived that it was my job to keep it tidy, and I do my best."

"I'm sure she didn't mean this tidy. Anybody who chooses to keep their bedroom looking like this clearly needs therapy."

Cathy calmly sat down on the bed right beside Emily, not so close as to make Emily stand up in panic but close enough to make her cringe away.

"Don't you even have any pictures?" the young woman asked. "None of when you were a kid? None of your friends? None of your parents? Do you remember your parents? How old were you when you lost them?"

Emily swallowed. She hated talking about herself, but dare not refuse to answer.

"I was six," she whispered, peering up at Cathy from under her dipped forehead.

"That must have been tough. How much do you remember of them?"

That hit hard and cut Emily's defences off at the knees. Unconsciously she pulled her actual knees up onto the bed and wrapped her arms around them.

"How much?" Cathy whispered into Emily's silence, so quietly that Emily made her usual stupid mistake of answering without thinking.

"I just remember watching Daddy strangling Mummy," she whispered, then buried her face between her knees in shame.

She should not have said that. Not ever! Why had she been so stupid as to open her mouth?

"They were just your adoptive parents, weren't they?" Peter's voice floated into the room from behind the direction of the doorway.

Emily could not look at him, or anyone, at that moment. She was too ashamed to respond.

"Your identical twin sister was adopted at birth by another family," Tom intervened. "Until you met – in Juvie."

Cause for even greater shame to darken Emily's soul, and silence her tongue.

"Car theft, wasn't it?" Tom remembered aloud. "Both of you – separately."

Emily could smell contempt in his voice – though it only existed in her imagination. She knew that she could do nothing to exonerate herself, and was glad of it – because she had to protect Tiara if they were ever to be together.

But it still all meant that she could never belong in this family.

"All ancient history now," Peter began – but Cathy cut in instead.

"Have you heard from your sister this Christmas?" she asked.

That question dragged Emily's thoughts from the family to which she could never belong to the family to which she might one day belong, and she acknowledged that she had received a message via Humility's sister only a week ago.

"Tiara is doing her tests this week," Emily added hopefully. "Then she'll know whether they'll let her train to become a Physician!"

———

Six weeks earlier

Clearing up after dinner could wait, Joan Redfern decreed, and Emily dared not question such a decree, though the thought of dinner not being tidied away asap nearly gave Emily a panic attack.

Instead the Redferns sat her down between them on the sofa, and earnestly assured her that they had no intention of throwing her out of their house when she was eighteen or when she graduated from High School – that they wanted her to stay with them until she wanted to leave, and that did not just mean between college semesters but even after college until she had found a better place to live.

The words 'better place' buoyed Emily's heart for a moment – it made her think of Tiara and living with her amazing sister one day.

Then she reminded herself that the Redferns would be getting payments for fostering her which would end when she was eighteen. Were she to stay after them it would be at their expense unless she paid rent, and it would be wrong to stay at their expense, and how could she afford to pay rent if she was going to college?

"This is your home for as long as you want it to be, Emily," Joan Redfern told her firmly. "I promise you. Please believe that we love you."

'No, you don't', Emily thought stubbornly, but did not say aloud. 'You can't love me. You don't really know me – you just think you do. You mean well, but it is only because you're good people trying to save the bad girl. You're trying to love the sinner you think I am, not the freak I really am.'

Saying any of it would hurt them, she knew, and it was better to say nothing than to lie – even if that was giving them false hope, but maybe their false hope was better than her no hope.

So Emily said nothing, and found it very hard to sleep that night.

———

"Found her!" LaskaVar declared triumphantly. "Only two decks away. It is surprise she not reside in wealthy deck. Her residence will be small."

"Thank you," Tiara hugged her gratefully. "I can find that – no problem."

"You should eat first," RollaVar offered. "As our guest, please, we desire you to eat."

Tiara was too hungry to reject such an offer, but she had resided long enough on an alien spaceship not to just sit back and be served as she would have done at home. She helped the family with preparing and serving the meal, and even remembered to politely offer payment when she possessed money, but that offer was just as politely declined, and Tiara just as politely did not insist.

She was learning alien social etiquette, she decided with pride.

"Are you positive?" LaskaVar asked during the meal. "Do you not desire me to message my sister to message your brother to come?"

"Absolute positive," Tiara responded – even more proud that she was conversing so fluently in the alien language. "Decided to fend for myself. I can succeed minus their help. I possess courage."

She saw that all the girls around the table were impressed and admiring at her attitude. She was scoring on her mission to understand aliens and live among them.

And manage stupid inferiors.

———

"You really don't get it, do you?" Cathy told the teenager gently. "Tom's Mum and Dad just care about you and want to see you happy. They don't care what presents you give them or what chores you do. They just want to see you happy."

Emily peered nervously back up at the attractive and confident young woman – trying to make sense of the words, and only really absorbing that she had got it wrong again. She had been worrying about the presents that she had bought not being good enough, about every imaginable thing going wrong with the dinner or the church service. It had never occurred to her that they might just want to see her look happy.

She covered her face in shame. Guess what – she had screwed up again.

But how did she pretend to be happy? Smile and laugh? The mere thought of that sent her imagination dizzy with scenarios of how she could get it wrong.

It was not as if she could remember what being happy felt like.

———

Tiara had to wait for almost two hours outside another apartment door, after hitching her way from LaskaVar's residence.

Humanity and Humility

She refused to contemplate the possibility that it might be the wrong apartment, or that the householder might not return for days. Come hell or high water she was going to make this work, but she knew this was her riskiest gamble yet. Manipulating stupid inferiors was not the gamble – she had to manipulate a brilliant superior.

Finally – after what she seriously over-estimated to be hours – a brilliant superior hove into view down the corridor – walking briskly back to her apartment, and barely pausing at the sight of Tiara standing up to meet her.

The most brilliant of all superiors, according to everything Tiara had heard.

The senior alien Physician aboard *Freedom*.

KristaVar. In English, DesireGirl.

CHAPTER SEVENTEEN

KristaVar was known to most of her human acquaintances – she only possessed human acquaintances, not human friends – as Desire, because her name KristaVar literally translated into English as DesireGirl.

KristaVar was the senior alien Physician aboard the three alien colony ships that had arrived to exploit the exceptional potential of this system. After thousands of years of swarming across the galaxy, terraforming and colonising planet after planet, the aliens did not get easily excited about new systems or new planets – not even semi-civilised species like humans on Earth. Aliens had encountered many such species during thousands of years of space colonisation. Some they had tamed, some they had nurtured, some they had subjugated, some they had caused to go extinct, and some they had deliberately made extinct – but never before had they encountered a species that not only looked so alike but were so genetically close that mutual sexual attraction was natural and interbreeding possible without medical assistance.

The fascination of finding a lookalike species in the same Galaxy had drawn many aliens to study them, but few had displayed more enthusiasm than AvernaVar, youngest of KristaVar's sixteen daughters. AvernaVar had long been a favourite daughter – because of rather than in spite of AvernaVar rejecting the career of Physician even though possessing the proven ability. KristaVar had spent a hundred years acquiring habits of command – especially over junior physicians and daughters, including four who had chosen to become sons - but AvernaVar's enthusiasm had made it impossible to resist the challenge of a colony planet of lookalike primitives with serious potential for eugenic exploitation.

KristaVar had come, and watched with pride as AvernaVar conceived the entire First Contact scenario, sold it to the Freedom Consortium, and executed it with great success until one of AvernaVar's own daughters had been killed by a violent attack from adherents to a tyrannical sect of one of the planet's major cults.

KristaVar had taken what she considered appropriate revenge. The gender-changing virus that she had implanted into a surviving enemy was spreading through his genetic kin and culture - causing increasing terror among primitives infected or fearing infection – a result which gave KristaVar great satisfaction.

Then a mentally ill human acquired an irrational fear that he could be infected despite possessing a completely different genetic inheritance that should have kept him safe for many generations. The psychotic had deluded himself that AvernaVar was the source of infection and shot her shortly after AvernaVar had given birth to a daughter by her human partner – the first hybrid in KristaVar's personal motherline – a joy to KristaVar both personally and professionally.

There had been other hybrids born both before and since, so KristaVar and her fellow Physicians were already beginning to acquire significant invaluable data on the genetic consequences of interbreeding – both plusses and minuses. KristaVar was of the strand of thought to welcome such a massive addition of eugenically exploitable variations to the gene pool, but also interested to investigate the psychological capabilities and limitations of hybrids to better prepare her for assisting her daughter-daughter with any problems.

Hybrids like the one waiting outside her door as she returned home that day.

———

Emily knew that she had to go back downstairs and dreaded it.

She had promised Tom and Cathy that she would come down and try to look happy, and Emily really wanted to look happy but the longer she hesitated the more afraid she got. She delayed by going to the bathroom and spending too long cleaning up. Back in the bedroom she checked herself in the mirror, grabbed brush and make-up out of a drawer to repair face and hair, put everything meticulously away out of sight, hesitated, dithered, and worried that she had forgotten something.

Finally she resuscitated enough detachment to admit that she was just making excuses, and forced herself to slowly head downstairs and walk quietly into the television lounge, where everybody was watching some comedy movie and laughing cheerfully between munching on candy or cookies.

Had they made a fuss of her arrival she might have had a panic attack, but they did not – having consulted and agreed to downplay everything as much as possible purely for her sake. The only empty seat was beside her foster mother, and she sat nervously down, blinked in confusion at the offered choice of chocolate or cookies, wondered how they could all still be eating after their massive Christmas feast, and then selected a cookie to nibble.

Emily forced herself to lean her head back against a cushion and try to relax and find the comedy funny enough to laugh at as the family talked and laughed around her - and Emily tried to be part of them, but never dared to speak up except when asked a direct question.

She was surrounded by good people, she knew. They were all being so kind and it was entirely her fault that she was not fitting in – just as it had always been entirely her own fault that she had never fitted in anywhere.

All around her now was another family – the sort of family that she had always dreamt of finding.

But she did not belong among them.

———

JassaVar stared at her 16G, and wondered if she dared to use it.

She had received direct instructions to call LaskaVar, but from her householder not her mother, and JassaVar feared her mother much more. Custom was that daughter obeyed mother above all, but normally mother instructed daughter to obey householder. In this case daughter desired to obey householder, but if she used the 16G that her mother had given her it would automatically copy in her mother - a problem if either JassaVar or LaskaVar said the wrong thing, like referencing recent conversations which DinzaVar had forbidden.

If she used her secret 16G she could not tell anyone for fear of her mother, entirely defeating the purpose of calling LaskaVar - unless she secretly called LaskaVar first to agree what they would and would not say on her official device.

That seemed the best option, but meant delay because JassaVar dare not use her secret device where her mother might appear. Possibly she could walk around the grounds of the Maitland Mansion and find a quiet spot? She would have to time it very carefully for a period when LaskaVar would not be working and so would be available to properly talk. She would also need to know her mother's location in order to minimize the risk of maternal interruption. JassaVar retreated to indulge in a shower while considering options for achieving that solitude, and returned to her bedroom with a germ of a plan in her brain.

To find her mother sitting in a chair waiting for her.

————

Pictures on the wall, but not paintings.

Moving pictures, but not movies.

There were pictures on the wall – but on screens not in frames – the alien equivalent of gifs showing girls moving and smiling and laughing silently. Pretty girls all of them. Aliens no doubt, but only one that Tiara instantly recognized.

One of them was AvernaVar, KristaVar's daughter - the first alien face and voice to be plastered over Earth's media. A legend among alien girls, or so Tiara had been told by every alien girl who mentioned the name since Tiara had arrived on *Freedom*. AvernaVar was one of the first alien researchers to arrive at and study Earth and the human race from the secret alien base on the far side of the moon – arriving long before the aliens had revealed themselves and initiated colonisation.

AvernaVar made herself legendary down on Earth as well, but much more controversially. She began as exposition girl for explaining alien philosophies and values to humanity and being less than complimentary about most comparable Earth philosophies and values – especially Earth concepts of law and government, but also human belief systems. She had persistently referred to even Earth's major religions as 'cults' – calmly asserting that a belief system existing a paltry two thousand years and possessing as few as two billion followers hardly merited the title of religion.

Yet AvernaVar had still married a human and attended church with him – though possibly only out of personal loyalty to her husband.

Then AvernaVar had been gunned down by a deranged psychiatric patient while leaving church one Sunday, and that was not even the first bereavement that KristaVar had suffered on Earth - AvernaVar's own daughter had been killed in the first terrorist attack on the alien embassy near Washington, so KristaVar had lost both daughter and granddaughter in quick succession.

No doubt one of the pictures was of the granddaughter, but Tiara could not remember which. KristaVar did not look grief-stricken - just very professional and focussed on the screen in front of her.

Tiara had never been very good at waiting patiently and in silence when told to do so, but the formidable presence of KristaVar studying Tiara's medical data was quelling enough to still even Tiara's hyperactive tongue.

"Do you confirm you devoured pill sixteen hours before duvay contract?" KristaVar asked like an army officer questioning a subordinate during a battle.

Tiara hastened to confirm, adjusting herself automatically to alien timings, which only loosely resembled human time measurements. What were translated as hours, minutes, and seconds did not match their Earth equivalents at all closely. Alien seconds were perceptibly longer than human seconds. There were sixty four alien seconds in an alien minute, sixty four alien minutes in an alien hour, and sixteen alien hours in a day. It all served to exacerbate the 'getting-jet-lag-walking-down-a-corridor' problem that Tiara had joked about.

But she was not in any hurry to make jokes in KristaVar's presence, though her vocal chords soon protested at their lack of exercise. With LactoVar and FrageaVar Tiara had rarely managed such herculean restraint, despite neither owning anything remotely resembling Tiara's idea of a sense of humour. Their lack of humour genes had, if anything, only spurred Tiara on to give her sarcasm genes freer rein – and even when provoking painful reprisals she had never been more than temporarily quelled. Her punishment experiences had served to enhance her expertise at the arts of brinkmanship – aiming always to irritate them just not quite enough for them to retaliate. It had been all amusing trial and occasional painful error, but before her final eviction Tiara flattered herself that she had got the two bitches figured.

Tiara could only hope that she had got the alien woman in front of her similarly figured. From the start she had been convinced that KristaVar had been more amused than annoyed by Tiara sticking to her proudly developed sarcastic teen persona. Standing up to and arguing with both LactoVar and FrageaVar had been a risky exercise. Neither had responded well, and Tiara had on occasion even considered pretending to show deference, but thankfully had never quite sunk that low.

It had cost her, she conceded, but whether it had been worth it depended heavily on KristaVar. During three previous encounters the woman had shown no annoyance at Tiara's attitude, but Tiara realized the risks in coming to see KristaVar so boldly. It was possible that the only reason for KristaVar not penalising Tiara earlier had been that a senior Physician delegated such chores to menials.

Tiara's instincts were always optimistic, but as she waited for KristaVar's reaction even Tiara could not help but feel trepidation. The alien's next words could be make or break for Tiara – her whole life could depend on them.

"Unusual timing," KristaVar remarked clinically. "Function of hormonal prompt that early could be to render conception probable, not impossible."

Tiara let out the breath that she had unconsciously been holding, then worked it out, and momentarily forgot all else for sheer indignation.

"So she meant me to get pregnant?" Tiara demanded to know.

"Or made improbable basic medical error," KristaVar replied. "Did you annoy her extensive?"

Tiara did not even consider pretending innocence.

"Probably," she declared with a smile. "I certainly hope so. She never missed an opportunity to annoy me."

"You fail to predict that she would perform reprisal for annoying her?"

"Guess not," Tiara conceded. "That is one mistake I won't make a second time."

"Do not. If you annoy me while you reside here expect painful reprisal."

Tiara took several seconds to register the reference to residence in that threat.

———

"Okay – that kid really needs help. Major help."

Tony and Joan Redfern appreciated their daughter-in-law going straight to the point for them – because they were both seriously worried about what their son might say after a Christmas Day exposed to Emily round the clock.

Their foster daughter had retreated upstairs - looking very tired and planning to leave early in the morning to spend the day volunteering at the centre. Peter had gone back to his own apartment, so just four of them remained in front of the television.

"I mean," Cathy continued. "That bedroom alone! No teenage girl keeps their bedroom that tidy. No teenage girl would be capable of keeping their bedroom that tidy unless they're seriously O.C.D. or something. Has she been diagnosed?"

"She sees the school counsellor regularly," Joan told her daughter-in-law. "From what Lizzie tells me, nobody has made such a diagnosis, but they have said that Emily is very insecure and suffers from severe low self-esteem."

"We could have diagnosed that ourselves," Tony put in. "I swear I never met anyone with so little self-confidence."

"We could have diagnosed that ourselves," Cathy agreed, "from just having met her yesterday. Is that scar on her wrist from where she tried to kill herself?"

"Not very efficiently for a girl that is supposed to be so smart!" her husband finally spoke up, looking as grim as his parents ever remembered seeing him. "I find it hard to believe that a modern teenager could be that uptight. Are you both quite sure that she isn't playing you?"

"No, love," Cathy spoke before her in-laws could respond. "Not faking anything. Trust me on that. Just really damaged."

"Okay, but she clearly needs professional help, and you should not be having to take on a burden like her at your age – either of you. Dad, you're due to retire in a few years. Mum, I know you always wanted a daughter, but you deserve one that can love you and look after you if you need it – not one that may need looking after for the rest of her life. Kids who are that damaged stay damaged – they don't suddenly become all loving and loyal just because you're kind to them. Emily may never be anything but a burden."

He did not know that Emily was listening from the stairs. Though she knew that it was wrong to eavesdrop, and she had never heard good news when she did, she had not been able to resist.

History repeated itself. What she overheard was so horrible because she knew in the darkness of her soul that it was all true.

She was irreparably damaged and nothing but a burden.

She fled to her bedroom, not stopping to hear the Redferns valiantly try to persuade their son that Emily was not irreparably damaged, and was not just a burden.

Burying her head under her pillow to keep herself from hearing anything more, Emily could only wish that her eighteenth birthday could come sooner, or that Tiara could by some miracle come to rescue her.

———

"How have you been talking to Patience?"

The question hissed viciously out of DinzaVar's lips, and made JassaVar literally buckle at the knees. Kneeling down in front of her mother and looking up at her mother's coldly furious face, JassaVar knew real fear.

But also real resentment. Had she not come to Earth and been infected by human values from her schoolfriends, DinzaVar would just have remained her mother, but JassaVar had met other mothers since then, and been told a lot about them – especially by Josette and Vicky, who were forever telling JassaVar that her mother was a total bitch – even calling her mother abusive.

Even so, JassaVar dared not openly defy her mother. Quite apart from the ever-present threat of physical punishment, JassaVar counted by Earth values as a juvenile and her mother as her 'legal guardian' so repressive Earth laws could forcibly prevent her exercising her Freedom of Departure from her mother's household. Or worse, allow her mother to take JassaVar away from her luxurious new life.

Not answering the question earned a stinging slap to her left side of JassaVar's face – a slap so hard that it made JassaVar fall over, and lie there feeling dizzy and confused. Why the face? JassaVar had no idea why her mother had taken to hitting her face. DinzaVar had punished JassaVar many times but never slapped her face before coming to Earth. Was it an Earth custom? Slapping a daughter in the face?

"Don't answer," DinzaVar by placed one foot on her daughter's stomach to keep her on the floor. "I met Patience last visit on *Freedom*. I forced confession that she contact you and Tiara. I verified that her employer would earn no contract to supply anyone on Earth while she employ and house disobedient daughter like Patience, so you will possess problem speaking to Patience in future."

Was that why she had lost contact with LaskaVar? JassaVar wondered how much this punishment would hurt, and if Edward Maitland was anywhere near.

"Brett asked me to help him contact Tiara," she whispered more to delay than avoid punishment. "You told me to co-operate with him in any way."

"You knew what I meant, brat," hissed the retort.

Very Earth word – brat. JassaVar still did not comprehend why DinzaVar always berated JassaVar using English - still less why she was calling LaskaVar by the translated name of Patience when only talking to JassaVar. It would surely raise the odds of DinzaVar's husband overhearing and intervening.

As he did that precise moment.

"Get your foot off her!" came a furious yell from the doorway.

Edward Maitland had come to JassaVar's rescue once again.

———

"Do you desire to return to Earth?" KristaVar asked with what sounded to Tiara very much like disdain.

"Negative," Tiara reacted instinctively. "I was hoping for advice – even help – to remain – on *Freedom*, I mean. Not expecting you to give me a home."

"I give nothing. I invest. I expect return for investment."

Tiara boldly returned the majestic gaze of the senior alien Physician. Emily would have disintegrated in panic under such scrutiny, but Tiara merely felt a thrill run up and down her spine - a thrill of fear and excitement that made Tiara all the more determined to play Truth or Dare.

Tiara Maitland always chose Dare.

"I bet you want me to do more than become your housegirl," she challenged the Physician. "If being your housegirl were all you were offering? To put it bluntly – I'm not interested in just skivvying. I'm not stupid, and I know I'm worth more than that."

The alien merely looked puzzled, which served to puzzle Tiara.

"Skivvying?" the alien repeated. "That word is absent from my translator."

"Dogsbody?" Tiara suggested instead – wishing she had worked harder in learning to speak alien. "Gofer? Drudge? Lackey? Minion? Underling? Or try servant – I know you can translate that word."

"Certainty. Your language possess excess of words."

"Your language possess severe lack of words."

"Yet your fluency in our language is not at standard of highest quality, or we would be talking in my language instead of yours."

Now that was a definite telling off, Tiara knew, but she also had no intention of doing anything less than standing up for herself.

"Does me fine for nights out with other housegirls," she asserted, then reviewed and revised her approach. "Trouble is they all want to learn English to go to Earth and score human husbands or boyfriends. Does that mean they're stupid or desperate?"

"It mean they are vars. If you reside here you must learn to speak alien all time when not translating."

"Or when making suggestions to improve your colloquial English? Sorry to tell you, but your English is still distinctly odd at times. Maybe we could tutor each other?"

Tiara paused at that, wondering if she had gone too far. She had sent up LactoVar's flawed English on more occasions than were wise, but was still determined to stand up to this alien and earn her respect. If KristaVar offered Tiara a place to stay, it would not be out of kindness.

KristaVar only smiled. LactoVar, or even FrageaVar, would have been furious with Tiara for speaking to them like that – but KristaVar only smiled, and Tiara just knew that she was winning.

"So," Tiara pushed on, determined to go for it while she was still not being slapped down. "So what must I do to earn my residence here? Why would you offer me a home? Not out of charity – I know that."

For a moment Tiara thought that the alien was not going to answer.

"You are first hybrid of human and alien," KristaVar finally declared. "I desire to study you – genetics and abilities – and your daughter in additive – when born. She also will be first of her kind."

Tiara had not expected that, but immediately decided that she should have.

"The study won't include dissection, I trust," she quickly retorted.

"Was that intended to be joke?" came a cutely pompous response that made Tiara really warm to the centenarian.

"Obviously not a good one," Tiara reacted immediately. "Losing my touch at jokes that annoy my elders and betters. Don't know why. I thought I'd mastered the art of annoying LactoVar, but clearly I've still got a lot to learn."

"I do not annoy at your desire."

"I'll have to work harder at it."

"You must work hard at many things."

"At just being a test subject? Doesn't sound like work."

"You would also possess value by performing as intermediary and guide to human customs. You could possess great value to me – if you desire."

Tiara liked the sound of that. She also liked the thought that KristaVar seemed to really mean it, but another thought occurred to her.

"I have an identical twin, you know," she reminded the alien. "Have you forgotten her? Could she be equally valuable?"

"I do not forget, but I do not consider her now of additional value. I possess detail reports on her."

"How? No, let me guess. Hacking? Aren't you supposed to be able to hack into any computer on Earth?"

"We possess specialists. I contract one to research your sister. It is evident that her mind possesses damage. She does not possess your potential. I will monitor her. Her mind may heal and create value. Your daughter may be of extra value. Subject to your continued suitability in performance and attitude, you may give birth to your daughter in my residence."

That was an authentic downer, but not a door closer.

"Can I call Emily direct?" she demanded. "FrageaVar and LactoVar refused to let me call her direct unless I paid a fortune, but …"

"One call every day," a peremptory command cut her off sharply. "Maximum time 16 minutes for each call. Any excess you pay."

"Alien minutes?"

"Correct."

Tiara nearly let out a 'wow' at that. Alien minutes were longer than human minutes, so that made a reasonable call plan.

"Thank you," she almost forgot to say. "That is very generous."

"You will keep me informed of her progress – that will cost less than paying company to make enquiries."

Dismissively said, but Tiara refused to believe that KristaVar had made her offer just as an economy measure.

"I still say thank you," she repeated – really meaning it. "But what else? If I didn't qualify to become a Trainee Physician, what else can I be, because I'm definitely not going to just be a housegirl, so I really wanted to know whether that was final? I definitely did not qualify – there is no option to retake the exam?"

"Irrelevant," KristaVar declared decisively. "I do not assess you correct for Physician. My daughter AvernaVar did not consider herself correct for Physician, but she achieved great success in career path she selected. You possess potential. You are first hybrid, and your daughter will be first daughter of hybrid. In that alone you possess historic importance. You also clearly possess brains and courage – you lack discipline, but you will learn if you desire to achieve while you reside here."

Learn discipline, Tiara groaned inwardly, but accepted without comment.

———

"Patience does not reside in this house while I do," DinzaVar shouted at her husband as they entered his bedroom. "She is a disobedient daughter!"

Edward Maitland did not get violent when angry. He had never punched anyone even as a boy, and never considered hitting a woman. He had never even banged tables – but had there been a table to hand at that moment he might have broken it. Instead he channelled his anger into decisive action – as he had done many times in the past.

"No problem," he retorted, not caring that he was committing himself. "You're leaving this house and this marriage – immediately. I'm filing for divorce and firing you - because I've had enough of you. The way you treat your daughters – both of them – is sickening, and your advice about Tiara …"

"Nowhere," DinzaVar smiled disdainfully. "Nowhere in pre-nup did you mention how I treat my daughters! How do I break marriage contract?"

Straight to the marriage contract? Okay, if that was how she wanted it.

"I'm sure I'd find something if I wanted," he asserted, "but I'll offer you a deal."

"I obey contract to the letter," she still smiled. "But what deal?"

"We divorce without arguments, and you get every cent promised of your settlement, but you leave your daughters alone from now on. That means that you grant me legal custody of Humility until she is an adult by American law, and she stays living here with me as my stepdaughter, and you cause no problems to Patience if she accepts my offer to come and live here as well."

She still looked amused!

"Do you plan to employ her in my place in your bed?" she even dared to ask.

"Of course not!" Edward shouted. "I would no more want that from her than I would from Humility. Or from Tiara. We have moral standards on Earth about that sort of thing."

"Do so." Her smile suddenly became aggressive. "They may be stupid and useless, but they are my daughters."

"If you had ever treated them with a spark of maternal decency I would not be offering them a home!"

"You possess strange concept of motherhood on this planet." That annoyingly superior smile had returned, making him wonder why in the name of God he had ever found her smiles so alluring. "First duty of mother to daughter is to nurture, but second duty is to discipline – both are essential to wise motherhood. But you are welcome to employ them if they consent to reside – they possess free choice."

"Do we have a deal?" he demanded.

"If that is your desire. We possess a deal."

"No pretending you ever loved me?" he asked, then wished he had not shown such a weakness.

"I never pretended to love you," came the direct reply. "I merely pretended to lust you."

Modesty was so brazen! Edward could not help it. He just had to laugh.

"Every now and then you can still remind me why I married you," he conceded. "Go pack, and be off tomorrow. I'll transfer a year's salary to your account in lieu of notice, and you take your car and all your possessions and be gone by noon."

"So be it. Choice is yours. Responsibility is yours. Consequences are yours."

"I'd not have it any other way."

"I won't require long to pack," the woman smiled completely calmly – and so differently from the abusive histrionics that Astra had unleashed when he had given that cuckolding bitch her marching orders. "I will depart in morning."

So just like that wife number three turned to leave. In that moment Edward Maitland was struck by the thought that he would never find another partner and would live alone for the rest of his life.

So be it. He could cope.

"As you would say," came the lethal response of wife number three. "It has been pleasure doing business with you. I regret business has been only pleasure."

CHAPTER EIGHTEEN

Emily was up early next morning.

Joan was surprised to go downstairs – late for her but it was December 26th - and find that Emily had already eaten breakfast and tidied meticulously up after herself and was nearly ready to go to work. The older woman barely managed to express her surprise before Emily was scurrying to get breakfast for Joan and had to be calmed down and told not to bother and asked if she really needed to go this early.

"If I walk I should be there when Mrs Steele arrives to open up," Emily spoke as if making an apology. "No bus yet. I mustn't be late."

Joan could hear the defensiveness curdling almost every word – as if Emily had only just come to live with them. Every time they seemed to be making progress in getting Emily to relax more a relapse had followed. It recalled the terrible fear that Tom had vocalized only the previous night – was Emily too damaged to be helped? Joan remembered spending half an hour asserting otherwise, but knew that the fear would not disappear that easily.

"It could rain," Joan tried again, scolding herself for doubting. "There could even be snow overnight. Give me twenty minutes and I'll drive you."

"No, please, Mrs Redfern," Emily reacted as if the offer were a threat of punishment. "I can walk. It is only a couple of miles, and you can't keep driving me everywhere. I must learn to cope on my own."

"No hurry for that, my dear," Joan asserted firmly. "We're lucky not to have snow already. Maybe we should get you a bike."

"Please don't," came a begging response. "I never learnt to ride a bike."

Joan barely managed to avoid groaning at yet another in the list of experiences that Emily had never known or been given or enjoyed – none of them exotic or special, just ordinary childhood experiences for most children. Emily may never have gone hungry or been physically or sexually abused, but the girl was living proof of the damage that simply being unloved could do to a child.

"Emily, please don't be like that," Joan tried not to sound scolding. "It is no problem to drive you to work."

"But I don't want to be any more of a burden to you!" came a pleading protest sounding oddly like a teenage tantrum.

"None of that," Joan asserted with all the maternal authority at her command. "You are not and never will be a burden. Be ready in fifteen minutes and I'll drive you. I only had one glass of wine last night so I'll be perfectly safe, and someone will collect you from work at the usual time. Are we quite clear about that, Emily?"

Joan had not wanted to sound that forceful, but at least it got Emily's submission – albeit at the price of making the girl look thoroughly scolded.

———

JassaVar also got out of bed early, but did not leave her room for a long time.

Her hesitation was not laziness but trepidation. Separation from mother was a major life event for any daughter – whether by free choice or punitive ejection.

When she had arrived on Earth she had been landing on a new planet to live among an alien species – but this was a much scarier prospect. After her mother and her householder had walked away last night they had not returned for hours – until JassaVar had been getting ready for bed.

Only a brief appearance but it had still turned JassaVar's universe inside out. They had informed JassaVar that terms had been agreed and DinzaVar would be leaving the house permanently the next day – but JassaVar equally permanently staying on, and that legal custody for JassaVar until she was eighteen would become that of Edward Maitland not of DinzaVar.

JassaVar had found sleep elusive in her turmoil over whether to be terrified or exhilarated. Staying on sounded exciting if it meant keeping the incredible luxuries of the Maitland lifestyle and not having to face her mother's orders or punishments any longer. What was not to love about that prospect?

But it also meant no longer living with her mother - nothing if not scary for any daughter. What would her new duties entail? Normally daughter obeyed mother first as long as they resided together, and any commands or punishments from householder would be agreed by mother, but now there would be neither mother nor housewife and JassaVar would be directly subject to householder and in his 'legal custody' - an Earth phrase carrying terrifying connotations of the barbaric human tradition of imprisonment. If she was in Edward Maitland's 'legal custody', did she no longer possess Freedom of Departure from his household?

A tap on her door signalled Edward Maitland requesting entry to JassaVar's bedroom. In alien tradition no man ever entered a girl's bedroom without that girl's express permission, but Earth traditions were very different from alien traditions. What exactly would Edward Maitland expect of her living in his household like a housegirl?

What exactly did 'legal custody' imply?

She remembered odd remarks from her mother about what she had to submit to during duvay as part of their marriage contract.

————

Tiara overslept.

Yesterday had been exhausting, she was pregnant, and a teenager – all good excuses for oversleeping, but sleeping late had never been permitted by LactoVar. Tiara would have been forcibly woken up and made to get up quick or else, so the mere fact that she had been allowed to sleep boded well, but Tiara still got up quickly just in case.

She found KristaVar in the main room of the apartment - apart from two bedrooms and one bathroom there were no other rooms. This main room was basically a combined kitchen diner, reception room, and study furnished more for function than style. Despite KristaVar being a Senior Physician, her apartment was smaller than FrageaVar's apartment.

KristaVar was already finishing alien breakfast – quick preparation food from what Tiara could see. More astonishingly, a place at the table and food were already put out for Tiara. No way had Tiara ever expected that, even less being politely asked if she had slept well and felt healthy.

"Very, thank you," Tiara responded in her best alien. "Do I possess correct in assuming that food is out for me to eat?"

KristaVar spared her an amused glance – possibly amused at Tiara's bad alien accent – or possibly her worse alien grammar.

"Correct," she replied in alien. "I depart for employment immediate. You will clear up – you comprehend how?"

That chore Tiara had been forced to perform many times, but she had never before felt happy to do it.

"You comprehend how to call Earth from communicator?" came the next question.

That was a skillset which Tiara had learnt as a priority.

"You are permitted sixteen minutes today to call any number on Earth and other sixteen minutes to call any number on *Freedom*. System instructed to permit no more. You can call me direct any time – in addition. Comprehend?"

Sixteen minutes – alien minutes. Not much compared to the amount of time that Tiara could easily spend on the phone, but - after months being unable to call anyone without special permission and a witness listening to every word - it sounded like an eternity, and she wondered at KristaVar's generosity.

But not for long. Emily would have been paranoid with suspicion, but Tiara saw nothing odd about people liking her and treating her generously. Before her previous experiences in FrageaVar's household she would have taken it for granted.

It would not even have occurred to her to feel genuine gratitude towards her new landlady.

———

Edward Maitland was sitting in the same chair that DinzaVar had used to interrogate, lecture, or berate one increasingly resentful daughter.

JassaVar was listening nervously to what turned out to be a mixture of interrogation and lecture. Her stepfather was trying to be gentle and reassuring, if she interpreted human mannerisms correctly, but could not help sounding pompous.

"According to what your sister, Patience, told Brett," he pressed stiffly on, "your mother has been very harsh on you two girls, but you've always remained loyal to her despite everything. You're very young – just a kid – so I'll understand if you still want to live with your mother. She is quite willing to abandon you and give me legal custody if I pay her enough, but I'm not buying you. You're not property. You're a beautiful girl and a daughter any father would be proud to have – and any mother!"

He called her beautiful, JassaVar prioritized, immediately remembering when Brett had called her beautiful. Common housegirl talk that human men really liked alien girls, and many boys had validated the talk, but it remained wonderful that a man should call her beautiful when not seeking duvay.

"What I mean, Humility," Edward Maitland continued. "I want you to stay. And if you do I promise I'll never hit you and I'll provide for you as if you were my daughter. I'd love you to stay and be my daughter, but it is your choice. Do you understand me?"

"Yes, sir," JassaVar replied obediently, but really liking that phrase about treating her as his daughter. He was an incredibly rich man even by human standards. DinzaVar had always stressed the potential for profit in pleasing human men, but had suggested that JassaVar's best prospects lay with Brett Maitland. JassaVar had got nowhere with that project, and possessed no such desire. Would becoming a daughter to Edward Maitland be more profitable? Delicious prospect.

She did not exactly like Edward Maitland, but she did respect him – and DinzaVar always said that men cared more about being respected than being liked.

But there was one question she needed to ask.

"If I stay, sir," she began cautiously. "If I stay, could my mother come later and use your law to take me away."

"I'll make certain she can't," he asserted. "Your mother really knows how to strike a hard bargain - born businesswoman – always liked that about her, but it'll be part of the divorce agreement that I get full legal custody until you're eighteen – only one year - then you become legally adult and can live where you want, though I hope you'll stay around to continue brightening up my life."

Brightening up his life? Had she really done that? Simply being told that she had brightened up his life was a big incentive to stay even had she not most definitely desired to retain her wonderful new home and lifestyle. She liked wealth.

––––––

It took a while, but Tiara finally managed to reach Brett and eagerly boast that she had changed address after failing to qualify to train as an alien Physician.

Brett had risen later than usual that morning, having really enjoyed himself the previous day, so was not at his most mentally alert and slow to realize that Tiara was cheerfully admitting failing to achieve what she had not so long ago declared to be her mission in life. But when he wondered how she could be so cheerful about not achieving her ultimate dream, she immediately dismissed it as just a passing phase.

"I'm going to live with KristaVar!" she announced eagerly. "Grace's mother! Desire! The KristaVar! I'll live with her, and work for her, and learn from her. And maybe I could still be a Physician but there are so many options!"

"Does that mean that you'll be staying permanently in space? Never coming back to face court again?"

"Not the worst plan," Tiara shrugged – exasperating as ever, in Brett's frustrated opinion, and short-sighted as ever.

"So are you happy?" he tried to make her see reason. "Happy never to be able to come back to America without getting arrested?"

Brett's adopted sister merely giggled back at him at first, but then visibly hesitated as Brett could see the implications finally beginning to sink in, so he pressed on before she got away with shrugging potential problems off yet again.

"If you come back soon," he suggested, "I'm sure we can fix it that you don't go back to Juvie - you'll probably just get probation. But that could change – the court could get really annoyed."

For just a moment he thought that got to her. Fat chance.

"So what?" she giggled again. "KristaVar, remember. Not just employing me. She has taken me under her wing. The KristaVar who has

243

already unleashed one pandemic virus on Earth and doesn't care who knows. Can you seriously imagine even the White House daring to say no to anything she asks?"

"No, but I can seriously imagine our D.A.s office saying no to anything anyone asks at any time just for the hell of it."

"If any of them get mad you can always ask them if they fancy getting infected with a sex-changing virus!"

"One of these days, Tiara," he tried again. "Maybe one of these days you'll find out that not everything is inevitably going to turn out for the best in the best of all your possible futures. Actions can have consequences – like getting sent to Juvie and having your head bashed in. Or worse."

The eyes rolled again – just like old times – and she started tunelessly singing '*Always look on the bright side of life*'.

"If you're not going to be a Physician," he tried a different tack, "what are these so-called options of yours?"

Another eye roll shrugged off his fears for her future.

"There are lots of careers," she told him firmly. "KristaVar has promised to help me study for them. Organizer maybe. Interpreter. Analyst. Whatever. Besides KristaVar says that being a mother is a greater responsibility even than being a Physician. Oh – did I forget to mention that I'm pregnant?"

———

JassaVar had been feeling happier as her conversation with her stepfather had continued, but she had one confession that she still felt rather nervous about making.

Then he asked her if she had been in contact with her sister yet?

"Not today, sir," she replied anxiously, "but I … I mean, my mother …"

"Has been ordering you not to call her?"

"Yes, sir," JassaVar replied.

"No longer relevant," Edward Maitland steamrollered on. "From now on the only person in this household who can tell you what to do will be me. But I'm not going to order you to contact your sister - only ask you. Please invite her to visit, and maybe live here permanently. I'd like to meet her again. A man can't have too many pretty stepdaughters in his life, and I know your mother forced her out of her job so I'll pay all expenses. It'll give me a chance to thank her for helping you contact Tiara in defiance of not only your mother's explicit orders but also my own."

"You knew?" JassaVar whispered aghast, wondering why he was not as angry about her disobedience as her mother.

Or maybe he was, but not showing it for some strange human reason.

"I've known for weeks, my girl, and let slip to your mother a few days ago, which was why she took the chance of a visit to *Freedom* to be nasty to your sister. That was what convinced me to divorce your mother but to offer you a permanent home when she leaves. I will be eternally grateful that you disobeyed my orders."

Had he really just praised JassaVar for disobeying him?

Humans really were weird.

———

Emily would not have got in trouble had the centre not closed an hour early due to a forecast of severe weather.

Emily was not even allowed to enjoy her usual therapeutic orgy of cleaning before being literally pushed out of the door and ordered home. She was offered a lift but declined on automatic reflex before remembering that there was no bus and that her foster parents were not due to collect her for over an hour.

She had her phone, so could have phoned them, but she calculated that she could easily walk home in an hour, so not forcing them to come out unnecessarily. It was getting very cold and dark early, as rain threatened, but she had a lovely coat that the Redferns had given her as a Christmas present.

So Emily set out to walk as briskly as she could.

Ten minutes later it started to rain. Within another five minutes she was facing directly into driving rain, so she looked for shelter, could not find it, and tried to run for it until five drenching minutes later she found shelter in a shop doorway that looked unfamiliar, but it took her out of the deluge and gave her time to work out how much further she had to go.

It took a whole minute for it to sink in that she did not even recognize the street.

For ten minutes, as the rain kept pouring down, Emily tried to work out where she was. Had she taken a wrong turning at the last intersection? What if she was wrong? If she was not home soon the Redferns would set out to collect her, and it would be nightmarish if they drove all the way and she was not there. They ought to be furious, but would probably just be worried. Emily would have preferred furious rather than worried.

She thought of phoning them. Maybe if she phoned them and confessed that she had started to walk home but then it had started raining and she had taken shelter. Maybe they would not be upset if she said that. In a way she would be telling the truth, but it would still feel like lying, like taking advantage of their good nature. She was just being a burden to them, like Tom had said. Was that all she could ever be?

If she did phone them, how could she tell them where she was if she did not know herself? She had to retrace her steps until she found somewhere familiar – however soaked she might get – however she might be ruining the beautiful new coat. She had selected the coat to show her gratitude to the Redferns without considering that it was designed more to keep her warm than dry. Another unforgivably stupid mistake.

She finally decided to run for it. At least she was now running with her back to the wind and the rain, and she could see where she was going.

A hundred yards along, and she saw a set of traffic lights that looked familiar. At the junction she was sure that this was the right road, and managed to work out that she must have angled off one junction early. On the right road, and she could not be more than ten minutes from home.

She could try and find some shelter to phone the Redferns, or resume heading home. She checked her watch – it was still fifteen minutes before she should have been collected from the centre. She dithered in the downpour over which to do, then chanced to look up as the sound of a car caught her ear – an oddly familiar sound - and saw a very familiar car driving through the junction. That was Joan Redfern's car. Emily would have known it anywhere - driving to the centre early.

All Emily could think of was how upset Joan Redfern would be to get to the centre and not find her. Emily raced into the road, running desperately right across the junction towards her foster mother's car, waving her hands and screaming, but Joan was busy concentrating on the road in the atrocious driving conditions. Emily was in any case approaching from

Joan's blind spot, and Joan could not hear Emily's small screams in that downpour. The car accelerated anyway – going slowly for a car, but much faster than Emily could run.

A hundred yards down the road, Emily stopped in despair as the car disappeared into the waterlogged distance, then realized that she was in the middle of a main road, and frantically dashed for the sidewalk. A squealing of brakes panicked her even more, but she reached the sidewalk before tripping and falling onto ground covered with a flowing film of water.

For a moment she lay there in soaked despair, remembering causing another accident, but struggling to tell herself first that it could not have been Mrs Redfern, and then that she had not heard any crunch following the squeal of brakes. Somehow she found the strength to stand up and look around.

A gust of rain-drenched wind nearly knocked her over as she turned, but she saw no sign of any crash through the blinding rain.

But she saw something even more terrifying - a police car pulling up.

Emily was incapable of even imagining that the police officers inside might just be stopping to see if she was all right. In her distraught and bedraggled state she was only capable of reacting in one way to the sight of police officers coming towards her.

She panicked and ran.

CHAPTER NINETEEN

"Was anyone killed?"

The small voice startled both police officers, and set them on full alert.

"Killed?" Officer Debbie Thompson asked cautiously.

"In the accident," whispered the girl curled up on the back seat.

"What accident?"

No answer.

"What accident?" Officer Bob White repeated his partner's question as he drove the patrol car back to the precinct.

"I wasn't looking. I heard the brakes. I heard the crash. I'm sorry."

"There was no accident, honey," Debbie Thompson told her.

"There wasn't?"

The drenched girl in the back of the patrol car sounded really surprised, and peered up at the policewomen beside her.

"Nearly was," Bob told her. "I nearly skidded into you. What crash did you hear?"

"What crash? Was there a crash?"

"You said you heard the crash?" Debbie told her firmly, wondering if the girl was right in the head.

"Did I? Oh! That was last time. Sorry. Just heard brakes. Sorry."

"Last time?" Debbie asked.

The girl curled her arms even tighter round her dripping legs and looked even colder, but did not answer.

"When was last time?" Bob asked firmly.

"When I was six," came a small reply. "What is the charge this time?"

The officers exchanged glances before Bob made the final turn into the shelter of the precinct building. Words had not needed to be spoken. A record – maybe a long one – maybe a psychiatric one. Odds on they

248

would not just be calling parents to collect their daughter. Safe bet there would be more to it than that.

"What is your name?" Debbie asked.

"Emily Loveless," came back rather faintly, so Debbie asked her to repeat it, but instead of repeating the name, the girl just dropped into a sort of quiet sing-song.

"*Loveless, loveless, always gonna be loveless.*"

The partners exchanged meaningful glances again.

———

LaskaVar was surprised that the apartment of the most senior Maggivar on *Freedom* was so small.

KristaVar was very senior and respected so it was surprising that she had even come to Earth – even though KristaVar's youngest daughter AvernaVar was famously the principal brain behind the Freedom Consortium's business plan for infiltrating Earth to soften it up for colonisation with minimum resistance.

Rumours existed that KristaVar had faced competition back in her previous system, but it was still remarkable that a Maggivar qualified to perform Full Species Genetic Modifications on her own initiative should have ventured so far beyond previously explored sectors of the Galaxy. Most who had come were, like LaskaVar's family, from less prosperous colonies or families and seeking better living conditions.

When DinzaVar and her two daughters had stowed away on *Anarchy*, they lacked the credit to buy more clothes than they already carried, and had barely enough to buy food. It had been an enormous gamble, but DinzaVar had made it pay off. LaskaVar was very excited about her mother's success and the opportunity it had opened to LaskaVar herself, but still worried about TarraVar's reaction - which was why she had come to visit the hybrid before seeking transport down to Earth. TarraVar could cause difficulties to LaskaVar and JassaVar if she resented their moving into the Maitland residence and used her family contacts to oppose it, so LaskaVar was hoping to smooth away any resentments that the girl might feel.

TarraVar was happy to reassure LaskaVar - happy at everything, as far as LaskaVar could tell. Happy to be pregnant, though exceptionally young by alien custom to be having her first baby. Happy to be living with KristaVar — understandably - it was an incredible privilege for any housegirl!

TarraVar was even happy not to be returning to Earth, which worried LaskaVar a little. If life in the Maitland household was so wonderful, why was TarraVar happy to abandon it? Why leave behind the incredible wealth and luxury that JassaVar had described? Why be separated so young from such a family?

That concern would nag away at LaskaVar as TarraVar eagerly encouraged LaskaVar to live in TarraVar's family home. LaskaVar did not ask the hybrid to explain - initially because the girl could not stop enthusing about her new life in flawed alien lapsing quite frequently into English, then because LaskaVar was worrying that she might not want to know the answers, and then because KristaVar came home.

And proved unexpectedly friendly - even inviting LaskaVar to stay for a meal!

———

"Why did you run?"

Officer Debbie Thompson was not trying to conduct a formal interview with the bedraggled teenager who was curled foetally on the chair in the interview room. Debbie was just trying to provoke some sort of response from a girl who had gone very silent since arriving at the precinct building.

They could not, in any case, conduct a formal interview until a parental figure was present but the girl had stopped responding – not even reacting to an offer to take off her coat. Debbie was not sure what the girl had done, other than run into the road without looking, and run away when they stopped to talk to her – run up a side alley that was a dead end so giving them no trouble catching her.

Debbie and her partner Bob White had been glad of the excuse to come inside in such weather, and this girl clearly needed careful handling. They had barely got a name out of her – Emily Loveless - which drew a blank on the file until she handed them a very wet card giving her probation officer's contact details.

Bob had called Debbie to the interview room door to let her know that they had got the correct name from the probation officer, that it was Love*lace* not Love*less*, and that the girl had been convicted of stealing a car that had caused a serious accident while being driven by a boyfriend who she had refused to name. Bob had rung the foster parents who were on their way with dry clothes but claimed that the girl had been returning home from voluntary work at a day centre.

Meanwhile both probation officer and foster parents had warned that the girl had psychological problems and was prone to panic attacks, which was why Debbie ventured the question – making it a casual remark to pass the time rather than an interrogative challenge. Likely enough that the girl had simply reacted in panic, but the girl had been in a panic even before she saw the police car.

Had she been running from someone? Like a dangerous boyfriend whom she had not dared to name earlier? Debbie quite liked that theory, all the more because Bob had quite liked it when she had mentioned it. He had gone to speak to one of the original investigating officers, leaving Debbie alone with Lovelace.

It was unusual to have a teenage girl so unresponsive in an interview room. All Debbie's instincts cried out to get the girl talking in the sense of getting a dialogue going, and getting her out of those wet clothes. She hoped that the foster parents would be there soon, and not angry at the girl or Debbie's instinct was that they might only make things worse.

"Okay," Debbie spoke up when the girl entirely failed to react to that question. "No need to answer, but you really should get out of those wet clothes. We got a towel and blanket here, and your foster parents are coming with dry clothes. It would help if you could get dry now – give them less trouble."

Debbie was talking to pass the time more than anything, and not expecting much response until the foster parents arrived, but Emily reacted to the word 'trouble' as though to a starting gun. She jumped up so fast that her chair fell over, grabbed the towel, and started pulling her coat off as if it were on fire instead of soaking wet.

Or as if she was terrified of her foster parents?

251

———

A frantic Joan Redfern had been home for over half an hour before the local police finally rang to say that they had Emily in custody.

Tony drove them to the station, feeling as worried as she was. It was hard to imagine Emily doing anything criminal, and easy to imagine her running from a police car, but explaining that to hard-headed police officers was a daunting prospect, so he spent most of the journey mentally rehearsing a strategy for tackling police officers as if conducting a tutorial with students – more appropriate than going lecture mode, he decided, as the aim would be to manipulate his audience into drawing desired conclusions rather than just asserting them.

They had been in this particular building earlier because of their experiences with both previous foster daughters, and the officer on the desk even recognized them. Tony found that rather amusing, and reflected that it gave him a story to tell at the golf club, but then shrugged that thought aside and focussed on the priority of reuniting his wife and his foster daughter. Fortunately the police led them straight to an interview room in the unusually quiet station – quiet due to the date and the appalling weather, Tony assumed. Joan bustled in as if it were the doors of a department store on the first day of a major sale, and rushed up to Emily.

The girl was wrapped in a blanket, and jumped to her feet looking terrified as she tried to say something about being 'sorry, sorry, sorry' but got no further before Joan had enveloped the petite teenager in the tightest of hugs, actually lifting Emily off her feet. For a minute Emily just let herself be hugged, but then her own arms stretched around Joan's shoulders almost as tightly, and the blanket started slipping.

Tony quickly shoved the bag into the hands of the policewoman, said "dry clothes", and stepped backwards. The policewoman quickly shut the door on him.

"Professor Redfern," a voice from behind turned Tony's head to find two men standing behind him - one in uniform.

The one in uniform introduced himself as Officer White, and the man beside him as Detective Rosetti.

Rosetti asked Tony if they could have a word about his foster daughter.

———

All Joan wanted to do was hug Emily and keep hugging her.

The shock of reaching the centre and finding it closed and no sign of Emily had nearly sent Joan into Emily-level panic mode. It took all Joan's self-control to drive carefully home without crashing the car because she was peering through the downpour to see if Emily was somewhere on the road.

She even neglected to lock her car before hurrying into the house – not even waiting for Tony to emerge with the umbrella.

Joan launched the first attack on the phones, while Tony and Tom tried to reassure her that Emily had probably just taken shelter from the rain. It had taken three calls before Joan found someone from the Centre who said that they had closed early and that Emily had left an hour ago, and who unhelpfully suggested that Emily had probably just gone to meet a boyfriend and not to worry.

It had been many years since Joan had felt so terrified – not since her last miscarriage. She still deeply and painfully remembered that time, and the aftermath when she had been advised not to try for another child, and decided to be happy with Tom and all the voluntary work into which she had obsessively thrown every spare minute and every spare emotion.

Husband and son had come to her support - son calming her down while husband phoned the police and was promised a call back – which took what seemed an eternity to Joan.

Tony absolutely insisted on driving this time, saying that he should have insisted on going to collect Emily in the first place, sounding really annoyed with himself, and Joan was happy for him to take charge while she spent the journey frantically checking and treble-checking the clothes that she had brought for Emily.

So frantic was Joan that she rushed into the room, grabbed the girl into her arms and held her crushingly tight and burst into tears, while Emily was whimpering "I'm sorry! I'm sorry! I'm sorry!" over and over again.

———

"We stopped to check because she nearly got herself killed," the uniformed police officer explained. "She saw us and just ran. Plus from a distance she looked only about twelve. Then when we got to her she was not making much sense, so we brought her in. It seemed safest."

"Thank you for that," Tony aimed to sound as authoritative as he could. "I would agree that you took a sensible precaution. So I take it that she has committed no offence? We can take her straight home?"

That should make them get to the point, Tony hoped.

"There is the fact that she ran at the mere sight of a police car," the detective took over. "And made some odd statements when apprehended. Do you consider it possible that she might be taking something?"

———

Debbie Thompson was beginning to wonder if foster mother and foster daughter would ever let go of each other.

At least it bespoke a good relationship between them, though not explaining why the girl had seemed so afraid of her foster parents' arrival. Eventually Debbie pushed forward and suggested that the girl get her dry clothes on, and the older woman snapped into mother hen mode, bustling and fussing as she made sure that Emily was dry and helping the girl to dress as though she were six instead of sixteen.

Remarkably the girl did not seem to mind – Debbie could not imagine either of her own two teenage daughters letting her treat them like that – but the thought brought Debbie's mind back to Emily as a six year old.

And that remark about a fatal accident.

———

"One word," Tony declared, aiming to sound like he was answering a question posed by a class of students. "Panic. Emily panics very easily."

"Simply at the sight of a police car?" the detective replied more forcefully than Tony liked to hear. "Forgive me, Professor, but when anyone runs at the mere sight of a police car I always ask why."

Tony knew that he needed to assert himself hard, and provide concrete examples to justify his thesis. Fortunately concrete examples were easy to remember.

"We're talking about a girl who I've seen panic at dropping crumbs on the carpet. I've taught thousands of students in my life, gentlemen, and never met one half so insecure or with such low self-esteem. And no, I'm quite sure that she isn't taking drugs, and has no boyfriend. She literally only leaves our house for school or work or when we take her. As far as I can tell she won't even use her cellphone to call friends nor her computer to access social media. We're talking about a seriously traumatised girl here."

The detective seemed to be about to speak, but the uniformed officer cut in first – slightly to his colleague's annoyance, Tony suspected.

"One reason why we brought her in," the uniformed officer contributed, "was that she asked us if someone was killed in the accident."

"What accident?" Tony asked cautiously.

"She seemed a bit confused about that. She mentioned causing an accident when she was six. Has she mentioned any such accident to you, Professor?"

"No," Tony replied, racking his brains. "Nor has anyone else. Wait a minute – you said when she was six?"

"Is that significant?" the detective asked.

"We do know," Tony took the chance to say something that he hoped would earn some sympathy even from a couple of hard-nosed police officers. "We do know that she was six years old when her father murdered her mother, and from what Emily has said I believe that Emily witnessed it."

———

"The only thing that matters, my dear, is that you're okay. Nothing else matters."

The girl was finally dressed, and looking a little calmer, but still clinging on to her foster mother as the latter finally turned her attention to the waiting policewoman.

"Is there any reason," she demanded fiercely, "why I can't take my daughter straight home?"

———

"Are you aware about a very recent accident?" the detective took up the baton again. "Where the car driven by your girl's boyfriend crippled a young girl."

Battle joined, Tony concluded, and braced himself to defend 'his girl' with everything he had.

"Yes, I'm aware of the incident – and I have to say that – knowing Emily - I find it incredibly hard to believe. Not least the existence of a boyfriend."

"Believe it, Professor. She definitely had a boyfriend. He was definitely driving. She stubbornly refused to name him even after pleading guilty – which she did after stubbornly denying everything during all interviews and despite all the evidence. Your insecure low self-esteem girl, Professor, was one of the most stubborn little Madams I've ever interviewed - which is why I'm asking if you can tell us anything which might help us trace that boyfriend."

Years of debating practice with argumentative and assertive academics kept Tony solid against the man's certainty. Most unfortunate that one of the policemen who had investigated the case should be on duty and clearly be invested in the case – no doubt because of the crippled kid.

"You're quite certain it was Emily?" he could not help asking. "As I said, it all sounds totally out of character."

"She pleaded guilty, Professor. No getting past that."

"Proves nothing," Tony instinctively debated the point just because it was debatable. "I can easily imagine Emily pleading guilty just because she got too scared to fight."

"We have a clear picture of her on a surveillance camera, and found hairs in the car with her DNA."

The detective spoke with the triumph of a man scoring an unstoppable winner.

It took several seconds for the exact implications of that statement to register with Tony Redfern.

"Did you find her fingerprints?" he asked eagerly.

"No, but we found her DNA." Still triumphant.

"Did you find any fingerprints that you could not identify?"

That gave the man pause, and he turned to the computer beside him.

"Let me see," the detective pondered. "Yeah – quite a few. Checked at the time – no matches found."

"Have you checked them since?" Tony pressed on excitedly

So excitedly that the detective gave him a very strange look before checking the screen again.

"Let me see. No record of that as far as I can see."

"If the couple had been arrested for another crime since – like in another precinct – they'd now be in the system, right?" Tony pressed on eagerly. "Maybe you should check them again. You can do that just by pressing buttons now, I believe?"

The two officers exchanged glances that bespoke irritation.

"We can do that, sir," the detective agreed heavily. "Would have sooner or later, but that won't help your girl, Professor. We have her DNA and her picture and her guilty plea. No way round that."

"But she might have pleaded guilty out of despair," Tony rushed on enthusiastically. "And an identical twin would look the same and have the same DNA but not the same fingerprints."

"True, sir, but she does not have an identical twin." Getting really exasperated.

"Wrong," Tony declared triumphantly. "Emily does have an identical twin."

"What?" That made both officers jump, and the detective checked the computer file again. "There is no record of that. Or of her mentioning it."

"She didn't know then," Tony triumphed. "She didn't know Tiara Maitland – her identical twin - existed until they met in Southside, when Tiara and her boyfriend were arrested about three months after Emily – also for car theft, though not I believe in your precinct. Tiara's *boyfriend* – you should note."

The two officers stared back at him, and then at each other.

"Maybe you should run those prints again," Tony tried to make it just a polite suggestion. "And in the meantime let us take Emily home. We're talking about a scared and lonely kid who attempted suicide in Southside and who – if I'm right about what you find when you run those prints – was wrongly accused of a crime and was massively traumatised by the experience, exacerbated I'm sure by having nothing resembling a family to support her for years. Until now."

———

Emily was trying to calm herself down and focus.

She had made an unforgiveable mess of everything, yet all Mrs Redfern had done was come and hug her, when the Redferns would have had every right to be furious at their damaged burden of a foster daughter.

Now Mrs Redfern was asserting firmly that Emily should be released and taken straight home. Emily could not remember anyone standing up for her and defending her against the police before. An adult was actually fighting her corner. That was almost scary. Could Mrs Redfern get *herself* in trouble for defending Emily?

Emily was so scared of the police that she found it hard to believe that even the Redferns could stand up to them. She was even more afraid that she would let her foster parents down and make her usual total mess of explaining things when the police demanded it. She knew that she would sound incredibly stupid. She knew that the police would never believe a word.

If only she could avoid sounding quite so stupid. She tried to make herself calm down, but that was not helped when they were joined by the male police officer.

Fortunately Joan Redfern covered Emily's surge of panic by asking where her husband was.

"Talking with a colleague, Ma'am," the policeman replied – sounding almost defensive. "They should be joining us soon."

"Then I trust we'll be able to take Emily home," Mrs Redfern declared. "She needs to be home, warm, and fed before she catches her death, and I don't see why you need to keep her any longer."

"Not much longer, I hope, Ma'am," the policeman replied even more defensively, "but we'd like to clarify one or two points first."

"Then we can take her home?"

"I hope so, Ma'am."

"It had better be so," Joan Redfern asserted.

Emily could not believe her ears. They were just going to let her go?

No way could it be that simple!

———

Tony Redfern followed the detective into the interview room aware that he had to get this right first time or do Emily real damage, emotionally as well as legally.

But he had spent a career learning to perform in front of audiences of very smart students. Getting their attention and respect while giving lectures or tutorials was an essential job-skill for any college professor. Even more challenging was arguing his corner against other academics in faculty meetings. Appearing and sounding completely confident and in control was essential, even when all an act.

But this time a very special girl's whole future could be at stake.

———

The very special girl who could not have felt less special visibly cringed as her foster father walked in with a detective who had always terrified her.

Detective Rosetti had not scared Emily by threatening her, just by not believing her – by making it obvious that he thought she was lying. She possessed no defences against such disbelief, either intellectuality or emotionally. Intellectually because she could understand why her denials had not made sense: emotionally because she could empathise with anybody who disliked her. As long as she could remember she had been disliked or worse and at best ignored by so many that she expected nothing else. Even her resentment at nobody believing her had dissipated now that she knew what had happened and no longer even sought exoneration.

But though she no longer resented police hostility she still dreaded it. It had been bad enough before the detective and the professor had entered. The two police officers had merely asked her to clarify how Emily had got herself in the middle of a road junction in the pouring rain, and Emily had struggled out a humiliating explanation of how she had taken the wrong turning and reached the junction just in time to see her foster mother's car driving by – and ran into the road trying to wave her down.

Emily was aware how stupid she sounded, and not surprised that Mrs Redfern had gently scolded her for not phoning them to come for her instead of trying to walk home. She was surprised that the police officers did not immediately accuse her of lying, but horrified when Detective Rosetti came in with her foster father.

And confused when it was Professor Redfern who did the talking, taking a chair to sit beside her, take her hands in his, and made her look at him.

"Listen to me, Emily," he went Professorial - like when discussing books - she adored those discussions.

"Listen to me," he repeated. "I intend that we go home soon, but first I need you to answer a few questions, and I need you to tell me the truth and nothing but the truth – though not the whole truth as we don't want to be here all night. I'm asking you to trust me. Can you trust me, Emily?"

Emily felt as helpless as she had when pleading guilty. She knew that she was incapable of disobeying – however much it might hurt. He was waiting for an answer, and she managed a nod – dreading what the police officers must be thinking.

"A few months ago," Tony gently but firmly, "you were convicted of stealing a car. The evidence against you was basically security camera footage and DNA from hairs found in the car – both of which would have fitted the identical twin that neither you nor the police knew existed – not at the time."

Meaning they did know now that it could have been Tiara on the security footage. Meaning that Emily had betrayed her sister by getting herself arrested for the stupidest imaginable reason. She would deserve whatever charges the police chose to throw at her. How could she ever face Tiara again?

"I'm not asking who was in the car," Professor Redfern continued. "I'm asking a simple question to which you will answer yes or no, and I trust you to be honest. Was it you in the car?"

Emily's last shreds of hope collapsed. She was caught and she knew it.

"No, sir," she whispered, hanging her head in guilty shame.

What had she just done to Tiara?

"So why did you plead guilty?"

The question came from Rosetti, but it was the Professor whose eyes met hers when she peered up, and she knew that she would have to answer him.

Shame made her drop her eyes and close them, and struggle for the words.

"I knew that nobody would believe me," she whispered. "I just couldn't face – any more questions. I'm sorry, sir."

"Does your sister know," the Professor asked, "that you were convicted for something she did?"

"No!" Emily protested urgently, desperate to take the opening to defend Tiara as best she could. "I couldn't tell her that! She would have insisted on confessing to protect me, and she had already done everything for me – to protect me – to save my life – more than anyone - ever – so I never mentioned it – she obviously didn't know – it was all I could do for her – and now I've failed her – betrayed her!"

"Yes," Tony Redfern told his foster daughter fiercely – catching hold of her shoulders and making her look at him. "You did betray her – but not tonight. You should have told her the truth when you first met her – then she could have done the right thing and come forward to exonerate you – as I'm sure she would have - as I'm sure she will now, and would have helped herself very much had she done so earlier – had you given her the choice - because the police found fingerprints in the car, so sooner or later they would have run those prints again and caught her anyway. Nothing to do with you."

Emily absorbed that, and felt even worse. The Professor was saying that she had got it all wrong, and it was Emily's nature to immediately believe anyone who told her that she had got anything wrong.

She had betrayed Tiara from the start. Tiara had gone out of her way to protect Emily, and all Emily had done was betray Tiara.

CHAPTER TWENTY

JassaVar was very excited to see LaskaVar step down from the alien shuttle that had landed in the enclave.

Two sisters rushed to hug each other before LaskaVar checked that all her cases were hovering behind her, then followed JassaVar over to Edward Maitland who was walking round in impatient circles talking at his 16G. JassaVar whispered as they approached that he did that a lot, and two sisters waited patiently until he shut off his device and smiled and welcomed LaskaVar to Earth.

LaskaVar duly did deference and said that she hoped her body pleased him.

"Everything about you pleases me, Patience," Edward Maitland responded. "Your loyalty to your sister in defiance of your mother will always merit my respect, and the friendship you showed to my son and daughter will always merit my gratitude. I was very annoyed when Brett told me that your mother had forced you out of your job. I don't understand how a mother could do that to such a beautiful daughter."

JassaVar did not understand either. Her mother had always been strict, but why had she become so much harsher since coming to Earth?

"Our mother always follows her duty as mother," LaskaVar replied with perfect calm. "She follows orthodox traditions of motherhood."

Edward Maitland looked confused by that statement – understandably. JassaVar had never heard the phrase 'orthodox traditions' herself.

"A mother controls and disciplines daughter," LaskaVar explained helpfully. "She does so until mother decides daughter is in household or employment where daughter ceases to require mother's control."

"I see," the human replied – obviously being polite rather than honest. "I appreciate your loyalty to your mother. It does you more credit than it does her, in my humble human opinion. Now let me take you home. My home, but it can be your home and your sister's home - if you wish. This way, girls."

LaskaVar smiled slyly at JassaVar, again worrying the younger sister, before they both followed their new householder while JassaVar wondered what she had missed. It was not just LaskaVar's puzzling reference to 'orthodox traditions'.

There had to be more to it.

———

Emily was shocked when she saw her three alarm clocks on her bedside table.

It was nearly half past eleven, and she had barely woken up. Was something wrong? Why had the Redferns not woken her? Had she really slept through all three alarms again? Even the new very loud one?

She checked, and all were turned off – something Emily never did. Surely she could not have switched them off while half-asleep? She had gone to bed twelve straight hours ago, but woken at two in the morning and was sure that she remembered still being awake about four – awake and worrying about the day ahead.

What was going to happen to Tiara? Would Emily be charged with perjury? Emily naturally assumed the worst. She remembered being utterly exhausted when her foster parents had half-carried her into the house, and Joan Redfern had fussed over her until Emily was in bed without even bothering to have a shower or bath. She remembered Tom and Cathy looking at her with what she assumed must be contempt, but did not remember them saying anything. She remembered Joan Redfern offering to get her anything she wanted to eat and drink, and being too tired to do either.

But now she felt thirsty, and a covered glass of her favourite chocolate flavoured milk was on her bedside table, plus a plate of chocolate biscuits. Gratitude mixed with shame at the kindness of the Redferns despite all the trouble that she had caused - the mere memory of which made her want to run away and hide – except that she had to try to make amends – somehow.

God alone knew how. She actually found herself uttering a prayer for help – her first ever spontaneous prayer – but did not think that she really meant it.

She gulped down the milk - barely noticing how delicious it was as she demolished the chocolate biscuits almost as fast, leaning close and low over the plate to ensure that not a single crumb dropped on either floor or bed. Then she rushed to get washed and dressed, thankful that she was alone upstairs and could clean the bathroom properly before going back to finish getting dressed.

She heard movement and talking downstairs, and headed down as soon as her bedroom was perfectly tidy. Headed down slowly, carrying the tray, feeling more nervous than she had on Christmas Day.

As her first priority, she headed into the kitchen to clean up her cup and plate. The noise got her noticed, and the Redfern parents came out to see her, and Joan Redfern came right up and hugged her close and tight.

Nobody had hugged Emily like that for years. In fact, she could not remember anybody ever hugging her like that.

Except – she dimly remembered – Mummy.

————

LaskaVar was as stunned by the size of the bedroom suite allocated to her as JassaVar had been a few months earlier, but rendered a little wary by the fact that Mr Maitland led her into it.

DinzaVar had assured LaskaVar that Mr Maitland would not expect LaskaVar to duvay him, but LaskaVar knew that human males did not possess the same codes of honour as alien males. Despite all she had read and studied about humans, and DinzaVar's reassurances, LaskaVar could not help but tense up when Mr Maitland walked into her bedroom without her express permission.

But it was not really her bedroom until he told her that it was, so she dismissed that moment of nervousness firmly – annoyed with herself for even feeling it, then telling herself that it was only natural to be nervous when landing on a new planet or entering a new household with a new householder.

It still reassured when he left it to JassaVar to show her around, and said that he would give her a few days to acclimatize before discussing her future.

"Oh, and one last thing," he said before leaving the sisters to it. "You will need a decent wardrobe if you're anything like your sister – or a human girl."

LaskaVar looked around the room. Wardrobe was a cupboard for storing clothes, if she remembered her translations correctly, but there was so much furniture in the massive room already, and JassaVar had already pointed out the huge dressing room to store clothes. Or was she translating wrong?

"Tomorrow," Mr Maitland pressed on authoritatively, "I'll give you a card and Humility can take you shopping. I'm sure you can handle that, Humility. Ramirez will drive you wherever you want to go, and you can spend up to the limit on the card. Fine? See you at dinner."

He turned and left the two sisters alone for the first time in ages.

LaskaVar asked JassaVar why they would need to buy a large item of furniture called a wardrobe.

———

"Tiara already knows?" Emily asked – feeling horrible at how betrayed Tiara must feel but relieved at not having to personally confess to Tiara.

She was sitting on the main settee in the Redfern's main reception room, with foster parents either side, and not even wanting to escape Joan's firm grip.

"Probably," Joan declared. "Or very soon will. I phoned Sylvia last night and she rang back this morning after she and Brett talked it over, and said Brett would take it further. As I told you, Tiara has found a new home where she is free to call you or Brett regularly, and she tried to call you here yesterday, but she couldn't get you so called Brett instead, and he called us just before I set out to collect you."

Tiara free to call her regularly! Emily had wanted that for so long, but now Tiara would probably hate her too much to ever talk to her again.

"If you'd only switch on that phone sometimes," Joan scolded with a firm shake of one tightly gripped hand. "If you'd used it, like you once promised, you could have spoken to her yesterday – and you could have called us to collect you – so if you go to the Centre again we'll drive you there and back and you will call us when you're ready to come home and wait for us to collect you and no argument, young lady. This time you do as you're told. Do you hear?"

Another scolding, and Emily knew that she deserved it, just as she had deserved the scolding that Tony Redfern had given her in the police station. The Professor had been right and Emily wrong, and what were the consequences to be? Surely they could only be bad.

Remembering that police station brought back into focus one of the fears that had tormented her in the small hours of the night.

"When am I going to be charged?" she whispered, looking anxiously from one foster parent to another, and was surprised by their surprise.

"Charged with what?" her foster father asked.

Their bafflement baffled Emily.

"There must be something," she struggled out. "Perjury? I pleaded guilty to something I didn't do. Isn't that perjury?"

Joan gripped Emily's hand tighter. Tony frowned harder.

"I'm not a legal expert," he responded carefully, "but I don't see how it can be called perjury. I'm almost – say 99% certain that they won't charge you with anything else."

———

"If you steal anything while in residence here," KristaVar declared while helping herself to a second plate of cambarra soup, "expect painful punishment."

Tiara allowed herself to breathe again. Her new landlady had not responded with anger at Tiara's confession following Tiara's very startling conversation with Brett. Better still, KristaVar had not even hinted at ejection, and strongly implied that she expected 'TarraVar' to continue her residence in this refuge.

"Please comprehend," KristaVar declared after swallowing a mouthful. "I never permit you to endure primitive barbarities of human imprisonment unless your choice. Human gangs do not terrify me. I terrify them."

'Gangs' was alien for governments, Tiara knew, and had to force herself to quell an upsurge of sheer glee. She had come under the protection of what had to be the ultimate protector. KristaVar was the alien Physician who had personally unleashed a genetically modified and targeted, DNA-rewriting, pandemic genovirus on humans who had harmed her family. Everybody, but everybody – human and alien – feared a woman who could literally turn them into chimpanzees.

That made KristaVar an even more powerful protector than Edward Maitland, and one who was already taking close personal interest in Tiara.

Tiara loved the idea of being important, and not only was Tiara one of the two first human/alien hybrids ever born, but her daughter would be the first ever baby to be three quarters alien and one quarter human. That made both Tiara and her baby very special – not just to Tiara but also to KristaVar.

But there was still one problem that Tiara could not dismiss. Emily had taken the fall for Tiara, and tried to protect Tiara from the consequences.

That could not be allowed to continue.

———

"I rang my friend Greg," Tony Redfern told his foster daughter, taking her other hand in his. "I play golf with him. He recommended a woman in his law firm who specializes in juvenile law. We can go see her - early in the New Year - about getting your conviction overturned."

"But you can't!" Emily exclaimed in panic. "Lawyers cost a fortune. You can't spend money like that on me!"

"We can spend whatever we want to spend on you, young lady," Joan Redfern asserted. "We are your parents. We love you. We want to look after you. Are you quite clear about that?"

The words 'we love you' hit hard, and where it hurt.

"But you're not my parents," she whimpered.

———

"Send statement to your brother," was KristaVar's proposal, although it sounded more like a command. "You were not pilot so blame belongs to stupid man who was pilot. Fortunate such deficient breeding stock is not father of your child."

Tiara had to concede that. Why had she wasted so much time on such a loser?

"Confirm that girl injured in accident is classified as permanently injured by primitive human medicine?" KristaVar asked.

"So Brett said. Something about her spine and never being able to walk again. I didn't realize. Carl assured me that nobody had been killed and not to worry, that we had gotten away with it, and I was so relieved I never thought to ask more. Oh, God! He said we'd gotten away with it. He must have known Emily had been arrested. Probably didn't know she was my sister, but he must have known someone had been arrested. Bastard! He probably knew the girl was crippled."

"Irrelevant. Injured girl is of interest. Inform your brother I will treat her personally. Human spines are easy to repair. Inform him I charge no fee if he arrange relevant access. Inform him you will pay for my services personally."

———

"But you're not my parents," Emily whimpered. "I wish you were. But you're not."

She tried to stand up – to run away and hide, but Joan Redfern put an arm round her shoulders and firmly held her down on the settee. Then Tony Redfern moved closer on the other side and added his arm round her shoulders.

"But we can be," Joan asserted firmly.

"That is what we wanted to talk to you about," Tony added even more firmly. "So please calm down and listen."

Professorial voice - always silenced Emily.

"We planned to consult a lawyer anyway," he almost lectured her. "But we needed Tom's agreement first, so we had to wait for him, and to convince him that we knew what we were doing."

"Which we did," Joan chimed in. "He slept on it and talked it over with Cathy and gave us his blessing yesterday morning."

Emily could only look from one to the other in bewilderment.

"So all we require now," Tony Redfern affirmed, "is your agreement."

"We want to adopt you!" Joan burst out with sudden excitement, as if she had been desperate to get the words out for hours. "We love you, and we want to adopt you legally as our daughter!"

———

"I will not expect repayment in credit," KristaVar explained firmly.

Not reassuring. If KristaVar had just wanted money Tiara could have wheedled a Maitland into paying, but if she wanted something else – what?

"Your existence is valuable genetic research opportunity," KristaVar explained calmly. "Humans and aliens are genetically compatible but not genetically identical. Human genome possess many chromosomes aliens do not possess. As first hybrid you possess entirely new and unique combination of genes - most fascinating to study your physical nature, and your mental abilities in detail and continued monitoring. Also those of daughter – and sister – and any children of both. Your reactions to alien culture and understanding of human culture would also possess value."

"So," Tiara asked with fascination. "So, am I right? You let me live here, and make that girl walk again – all in return for studying me and my daughter."

"You comprehend accurate. You are unique. I wish to take maximum advantage. Comprehend I require you to submit to detailed physical and mental tests and examinations very regularly and for extended period. Every day to begin, and continue throughout pregnancy and for long period to come. At least four years."

Tiara decided that she could live with that – she liked being the centre of attention, and four years was not so very long – no longer than a college course.

Tiara loved the thought of being so unique that KristaVar wanted to know everything there was to know about her.

———

"Do you really not mind?"

The figure at the doorway of what Tom still thought of as the spare room of his parents' house could not have looked more anxious.

Too anxious for his taste. The previous day had given him second thoughts, which had talked over with Cathy while out that day introducing his wife to his best old friends and favourite old haunts. Emily was a mess, and Tom still felt wary at the prospect of the girl joining the family.

Not to mention – which he had reluctantly admitted only to Cathy – the prospect of her taking some of his inheritance when his parents died.

"He doesn't," Cathy spoke for him as she slipped past him and headed for their bedroom. "Tell her, Tommy."

Not the first time that Cathy had spoken for him without asking, but Tom had long accepted Cathy doing that - often very usefully in tricky social situations.

"I promise I'll try to be good to them," Emily pressed on almost feverishly. "I know I messed up totally yesterday, but I promise I'll try not to mess up again."

Try too hard, Tom guessed, and probably mess up by trying too hard, but at least the girl meant well and was not just trying to take advantage – as Cathy had assured him, and he trusted Cathy's judgement about other girls, if not other men.

"We all mess up sometimes," he declared magnanimously. "Just try to learn from your mistakes, and promise to look after Mum and Dad."

"I promise. On my life."

"I'm trusting you," he could not stop himself smiling at her childlike eagerness. "I'll be living in Australia so it'll be great to know somebody is here to look after them."

"I will," she nodded frantically. "I promise I'll look after them as long as I live!"

———

JassaVar was having the most enormous fun buying clothes for her sister.

The clothes might lack the material quality of alien dresses, but there was much more variety easily available and it was fun trying so much on with nobody expecting them to buy everything.

Life on Earth was good – especially in America with no mother to curtail their extravagance. They cut loose with the card that Edward Maitland had given them, and three hours later were heading out of the latest store heavily laden with bags that unfortunately were not self-propelling. They were just enjoying being together, well-fed, warm, and with a comfortable home on a planet where there were no carnivores hunting them and the air was free to breathe.

And no mother around to dampen JassaVar's spirits.

Until DinzaVar suddenly appeared in front of them as they turned a corner, and LaskaVar dropped her bags to run forward into her mother's arms.

EPILOGUE

Put not your trust in princes,
nor in any human power,
for there is no help in them.
When their breath goes forth, they return to the earth;
on that day all their thoughts perish.

Psalm 146

"You did not trust me," JassaVar could not help but mutter – unsure how to feel.

She covered up her uncertainty by taking a bite out of the delicious brownie that her mother had just bought her, as mother and daughters shared coffee and cakes amidst shopping bags in a diner.

"Necessity was that you image real distress when I strike you," her mother told her bluntly. "I provoke his male instinct to protect young females, and cause him to desire to release me and retain you. He react as I intend. A wise girl lets a man believe he is in command when she is in control."

"You knew all along?" JassaVar asked her sister. "She trusted you?"

"Not enough to bring me to Earth," LaskaVar responded. "But I did comprehend concept, and I trust her judgement that I could not deceive Edward Maitland."

"But I was confident," their mother cut in, "that she could deceive Tiara."

"Not difficult," LaskaVar agreed. "She is more clever than she pretends but less clever than she imagines. Weakness is she expects to be liked so trusts anyone who pretends to like her."

"But you spoke to Brett and his father more than once?" JassaVar asked.

"Only to assist them – not live with them."

"Mother knew all along that we were in contact?"

"Every detail," DinzaVar interrupted again. "I was impressed by your capacity to deceive, JassaVar. You exceed expectations."

"Did you always desire to end marriage?"

"I married for money, and never pretend other. The marriage contract specified any disloyalty in business or finance or duvay could earn ejection from marriage with little money, but contract neglected mention of treatment of my daughters. By being what his primitive culture consider as abusive to you I provoke his desire to end marriage without breaching contract, so he eject me with large payment and offer you permanent residence. Opportunity to employ LaskaVar to contact his daughter was fortunate. It permitted LaskaVar to earn his gratitude, and pretence to force her out of employment tricked him into offering her residence. Now you both possess opportunity to exploit his wealth. I pledge on *Anarchy* I would find you residence where you never go hungry again. Now it is time to feast!"

On delicious chocolate, JassaVar bit greedily. Now she comprehended why her mother had been so harsh these last months. Suddenly everything made sense.

"Meanwhile," DinzaVar continued smugly. "I enjoy his wealth without duty to endure his duvay. Nor will you as his culture inhibits him from duvaying daughters. My plan is total success. We possess great cause for celebration."

"Very definite," LaskaVar agreed smugly. "Do you see how many dresses he already bought me?"

"I possess many more at home," JassaVar boasted more smugly, "but Brett bought most of them."

"Make point of being very nice to Brett, LaskaVar," their mother commanded. "But do not push. I offered JassaVar as bait to him but she proved not to his taste – possibly too young. You may be more to his taste."

"Brett possesses a girlfriend," JassaVar surprised herself by daring to challenge her mother. "As human he is monogamous."

Her bet was that her mother would not this time respond with anger, and she won her bet.

"He possessed previous girlfriends, I comprehend," DinzaVar replied quite calmly. "They did not remain. This one may not. Be available, LaskaVar. The option might arrive. He would be profitable, and does possess rich friends who may show interest if he does not."

"Jassa informs me," LaskaVar remarked, "that young human yars can be persuaded to pay very generously for a var's company without necessity for duvay."

"Humans possess so few vars and so many yars," JassaVar hastened to explain. "It presents good profit opportunity."

"All yars with money present good profit opportunity," their mother declared with a smile. "I possess many opportunities to exploit when marriage officially cancelled. Most vars came to this planet to seek profit, but few succeed to our level. My duty as your mother was to provide you with opportunity and purpose and discipline, and that I achieve. Now you must exploit. You exploit well so far, JassaVar – in excess of my expectation. Edward Maitland is great opportunity for profit if you please as daughters. If you fail, locate me, but this I bred you to do. Do not waste opportunity I create for you."

JassaVar promised that she would not. Edward Maitland possessed enormous amounts of money to spend on daughters, and she remembered Josette and Vicky's tips on wheedling spending out of rich parents – and maybe JassaVar could outdo them in that respect, with LaskaVar's help. She would enjoy going into business with LaskaVar - and RollaVar if LaskaVar succeeded in persuading Edward Maitland to let LaskaVar's best friend come to 'visit'.

Between them they should be able to make their mother proud of them.

———

The small gathering of alien Physicians was a planned conference to review progress on genetically modifying Earth micro-life into targetable bio-weapons.

Never before had FrageaVar been admitted to such an important discussion. There was excessive presence of not only Physicians but Senior Physicians among the aliens colonising Earth – far more than profitable provision of medical services would have justified – and all because of the enormous genetic potential of a planet so profuse with life.

That was why Junior Physicians like FrageaVar spent as much time running clinics treating humans as supporting alien soldiers on missions. They were not just looking after their men or making profits, they were gathering and passing on every scrap of medical and genetic data they could obtain – all forwarding to one or other of this select grouping of Senior Physicians.

For a Junior Physician to be allowed in among such Senior Physicians was a great privilege, and to be singled out afterwards for the gratitude of the most Senior Physician of all was special honour. FrageaVar had been particularly excited to learn about the ideas for developing new biological weapons to more rapidly cull hostile tribes on the planet below – she would relish deploying them against tribes that justified barbaric misogynies by quoting archaic texts of primitive cults. She was revolted by some of the barbarities and repressions that human men in such tribes inflicted on human girls.

KristaVar walked up to FrageaVar as they were leaving the meeting, and formally expressed due gratitude for assistance with their little experiment.

"Pleasure," FrageaVar declared, always extremely happy to please a Senior Physician. "Success?"

"Total. Far above expectation because she breached human laws and required assistance, so accepted residence with maximum compliance to my experimental requirements. I can now monitor both first hybrid and first hybrid's first daughter in total detail, and she is eager to co-operate. She even accepted separation from twin – though I did not disclose separation was experimental control requirement. Nor did I disclose that getting her pregnant was experimental control requirement. Nor did I disclose the reason why her mother was murdered, but I may disclose later. For now TarraVar agreed to maintain contact with identical twin, and encourage her to procreate by human father. I assess that twin does not possess mental readiness to procreate yet, so it would not be wise to seek to force it as we did with TarraVar."

"Is twibat risk as was mother?"

...known to... For now she is secret and safe. For now ...ter will assist my study which human genes would ...t and expand our gene pool and which are best deleted. She is eager ... submit to all tests. Being a subject for detailed medical study feeds her desire to feel important."

"Eugenic exploitation of human gene pool was your primary interest in coming to planet, I comprehend. May I be permitted to assist in research?"

"You may," KristaVar conceded graciously. "I possess gratitude for your assistance in conditioning subject for study."

"It was pleasure," FrageaVar responded with equal grace. "Interesting strategy. How did you devise?"

"Amazing it is Earth stratagem which AvernaVar explained. They call it 'good cop, bad cop'. Concept is 'bad cop' seeks to impose obedience on victim by treatment unpleasant or cruel, then 'good cop' arrives and protects victim from 'bad cop' and pretends kindness until victim co-operates in gratitude by doing what both 'cops' desired. TarraVar does not suspect me as if I invite her to live with me first and I trick her into getting pregnant. She is happy to co-operate. LactoVar did as commanded. Ensure she keeps silent. How do you assess she perform duties in strategy?"

"She enjoyed herself," FrageaVar defined carefully.

"To excess?"

"Greatly to excess."

"Regrettable," KristaVar dismissed coldly. "Ensure she keeps silent about first hybrids. Repeat and assert that if she fails in silence she will not become Physician."

———

"Look after them. Look after them. Look after them."

Emily walked round and round in her bedroom with those words buzzing obsessively around her brain, even whispering them over and over in the mind-blowing confusion of the moment.

Barely had Tom left her room than Joan Redfern had come up from speaking to Sylvia Godwin. The chaplain had accessed Emily's social services file and found a reference to the accident when Emily was six years'

old. Just a single line, but it had said that Emily had caused a raccident in
which two people had received minor injuries. caused a raccident in
scolded her, Emily could have asked at almost any time and had gently
have told her that she had not caused anyone's death in that acc

All those nightmares she had suffered because she had been
cowardly to ask simple questions. She owed Joan and Tony Redfer
much. How could she ever repay them, except by looking after them
Tom had asked?

It was the least she could do. They insisted that they loved her. Emily
could not understand how anyone could love her, but she desperately
wanted to love them back. She was not quite sure what love meant, but
if she devoted the rest of her life to looking after the Redferns, through
whatever old age or illness might throw at them, that would make her
deserve their love – maybe. She could act as if she loved them – would
that count as love?

She stared around her room. Her room, her own room, in her own
home, in her own family's house. Had that not been her dream – once
upon an ancient time?

A more recent dream had been going to live with Tiara, but Tiara had
blown that dream away when talking to Emily only minutes before Tom
and Cathy had returned to the house from their day out. Tiara had started
with a fierce and deserved scolding of Emily for not telling sooner, but had
still told Emily that she was forgiven - so amazingly generous. Emily could
not believe how she could have such a wonderful sister – and felt all the
more ashamed of herself for not trusting Tiara right from the start. The
useless twin had screwed up again.

Tiara had already confessed all to her brother, and arranged for him to
pass on a statement to the police so that Carl would be arrested and Emily
exonerated. So typical of Tiara's awesome ability to get other people to do
things for her – and Tiara had even added that she was staying on *Freedom*
under the protection of a senior alien Physician who had offered to cure
the injured girl for free just because Tiara had asked! Tiara was the most
incredible person that Emily had ever met!

On the negative side the sisters could not live together in the foreseeable
future – Tiara would have her own daughter and family and life to forge,
and Emily could never be more than peripherally part of it. Emily would

have to create her own life without Tiara, but maybe that was best. How could Emily live at Tiara's level? At least they could now speak regularly - though Tiara would have so many other friends and Emily did not deserve to monopolise her sister's time, and Emily needed to devote herself to the Redferns. Emily's old fantasy of finding a nice boy with a nice family had been much more about a desire to find a nice family than a nice boy, but now she had found a nice family without the mission impossible of finding a nice boy.

Making her new family happy about their daughter could be a challenge. She had ruined their Christmas so stupidly. It had simply never occurred to her that all they wanted was to see her happy. But how did she pretend to be happy when she had no idea what being happy felt like?

She would have to start doing stuff that they would want their daughter to do, such as go to college. If she could go to the same college where Professor Redfern taught she could still live with them – that was not too scary – and the college work would surely be interesting. Mixing with other students might be difficult, but hopefully the college students would not know her or her background so she might be able to make a fresh start. It was a scary prospect, but she needed to try for Tiara's sake and for the Redfern's sake – even try to make real friends like other girls mysteriously managed – maybe even a boyfriend. Maybe she could try to become a real Christian – the Redferns would like that, too.

Above all the Redferns wanted to see her happy. To make them happy she had to convince them that she was happy. Anything to please the Redferns.

Emily had discovered an exciting new obsession.

THE END

Lightning Source UK Ltd.
Milton Keynes UK
UKHW01f2008080918
328553UK00001B/83/P